THE SETBACK

B. E. BAKER

Purple
Puppy
Publishing

For Eugenia Stuckey
You were an amazing grandmother, and you
taught me so much. But mostly I remember that
you loved me and you were proud of me, and
that's the important part.

AUTHOR'S NOTE

A lot of you preordered The Setback right after The Reboot... It helps authors so much when you preorder, so thank you!!

But.

I decided to write a *bonus* book that wasn't planned. It's called The Surprise. It became book 6, and this one moved back to book 7. It's NECESSARY to read The Surprise before you read this book, The Setback. So if you haven't read The Surprise yet, DO NOT start reading this one. Go back and get The Surprise first!

PROLOGUE: ABIGAIL

From the moment we're born, human beings are governed by fear. You can practically see the terror in a baby's eyes when you yank the bottle away too soon. When a parent walks away, even from a toddler, they'll often cling to your leg and sob.

You'd think that as adults who can walk, talk, and feed ourselves, that ever-present fear would abate, but the more we're capable of doing, the more our fear grows. With increased knowledge and capability comes an increased understanding of just how many things can go wrong and just how bad things can really get.

In fact, as a lawyer, almost my entire job is to mitigate risk. . .which means dealing with plans to try and limit people's fear of the future. Over the years, I've seen a lot of things go sideways. I'm called in after the fact too, to deal with the fallout.

Divorce. Death. A lawsuit. A will that doesn't say what you expect.

But if I've learned one thing in my forty years of life, it's that humans don't—can't—find joy while living in a state of fear. It's a natural state, and yet, we somehow need to find a way to overcome it.

The world is scary.

Terrifying, really.

Bad things happen at least as often as good things.

The sky, sadly, really is falling most of the time. Chicken Little had that part right. But we can't huddle in a bunker or wear crash helmets and football pads all the time. It's not a good way to live.

We have to square our shoulders, hold our heads high, and march into the unknown as bravely as we can, secure in the knowledge that while setbacks will happen, if we keep moving forward, we can conquer that fear that seeks to ruin everything that matters.

HELEN

Forty-seven people, including my parents, turned me down after I made my initial business plan and started looking for investors. Banks. Individuals. Mentors. Friends. You'd think the rejection by my mom and dad would have hurt the most.

But actually, the one that stung the worst was my boyfriend.

His parents owned one of the biggest regional banks in the entire state, and I knew that he could convince them to take a chance on me. Except, he didn't even try. Clearly, he didn't think it was a good enough proposal.

Finding a path forward after all the doors closed may have been the most important lesson I learned in business. There's always more than one way to accomplish something, especially if it's essential. I'm unfailingly surprised by how creative people can get when something really matters to them. Starting that first company mattered more to me than anything ever had.

When my parents wouldn't loan me the money, I

borrowed it from myself. I leveraged my own trust fund, which Dad and Mom didn't know I knew about, and I went all in.

It was the best gamble I ever made.

"I'm telling you, the numbers aren't there." Mandy folds her arms. "Gold Strike was always supposed to be a healing retreat. It's for women only, and women don't care about dude ranches."

I cringe. "Please stop calling it that."

"Why?" She arches one crotchety eyebrow. "They call ranches that for a reason. *Dudes* like them."

I roll my eyes. "I'm not at all sure that's why it's called a dude ranch, but I don't even care. Women are empowered now. If you really want a retreat that can compete with David Park's, we need to offer comparable amenities."

"You want to copy him," Mandy says, her tone flat and her eyes flinty. "You can't beat someone by copying them."

"Actually, you can. You just have to do what they're doing better than they are," I say. "But in this instance, I'm not suggesting that we copy. This area has very little to offer other than the majesty of its unique scenery. Sure, it's remote, but that just means there are ninety million other places just like it all across America."

"David won't budge," Amanda says. "I already asked him. Remember?"

I hate the smug look on her face, like if *she* asked him and he said no, that's the end of it. Does she really think that the power his childish crush on her gave us is the greatest strength we have?

"If I can convince him to sell us the Ellingson ranch and find something closer to his location?" I lift both eyebrows.

Mandy throws her arms up in the air. "Yes, girl, when pigs fly, you can have your dude ranch for our women's retreat."

That's all I needed to hear. It grates that I have to get approval from them—I really hate working *with* people, but since Mandy owns the land for the retreat, I'm stuck. I stand up.

"Where are you going?"

I arch one eyebrow. "I'm going to look into buying some wings."

It takes me a day to prepare, but the next morning, I march into David Park's resort with a slim brown briefcase.

"Where's Mr. Park?" I spear the very young, very green-looking concierge with a pointed gaze.

He splutters.

I look around, noting the check-in counter's location, the placement of the elevator bays, the spa and the gym layout, as well as the dining options. I close my eyes and think back on what I saw of the layout on their website a few days ago. "I bet the offices are that direction." I point.

His eyes widen, and he shakes his head. "You can't go back there without an appointment."

I laugh as I breeze past him.

The poor kid's totally horrified by my actions, of course, but he's not brave enough to stop me. In life, most problems can be solved by ignoring the idiots and doing what needs to be done. I can't help wondering how long it'll be before security shows up. I have more than enough time to turn the corner, head up the two flights of stairs—elevators aren't a good bet when you're uninvited—and duck into the main administrative office suite.

David Park's office isn't at the back of the suite as I

3

expected. He is in a corner, but the entire workspace is open. There aren't interior walls or even cubicles. There are several desks intelligently placed, each of them with a person hard at work, staring diligently at screens or talking earnestly on the phone.

A dark-haired man's smiling in the large corner office area as he chats on the phone. I always forget how slap-you-in-the-face handsome David Park is. His hair's thick and he's due for a cut, I imagine, but even so, it looks like something out of a print ad. The shaggy ends of it fall across his forehead almost artfully.

His jawbones are nearly a work of art, especially against the curve of his jaw. And if he didn't smile so often, his mouth would be devastating. As it is, he looks far too approachable. Easy-going and fun bosses can't get things done. He was annoying in business school, and he's been even worse of a nuisance ever since I came here.

That all ends today. Once this is done, I'll be able to breathe easier.

"David." I don't bother checking in with the secretary at the front.

Every head in the room snaps up, and the smile slides off David's face. An almost impressive frown replaces it.

"I'll call you back," he murmurs into the phone as I walk up.

"We need to talk." I don't sit down. We can't do it here, in the middle of this stupid fishbowl. Hippies like to run offices this way, as though somehow egalitarianism has a place in the office. It's an irksome new fad, and I'm not at all surprised this idiot has bought into it. He probably wants his employees to think of him as a friend, too.

4

David leans back in his chair and looks up at me, seemingly unconcerned that in this position, I tower over him. "Then talk."

I glance left, and then slowly, I glance right. "Here?"

He shrugs.

I shake my head tightly. "This is a private conversation."

He leans forward, bracing his arms on the desk surface. His cuffs are rolled up, and I can't help noticing that he has a surprising amount of muscle in his forearms for a Harvard alum. "Is it, now?" His sideways grin irritates me even more than it usually does.

"It's business." I drop the briefcase on the edge of his desk. "But I'd rather not make it public business."

His sideways smile spreads into a full-blown grin, for some reason. "Alright, alright. Where did you want to talk, then?"

"Do you have some place with walls?" I arch an eyebrow. "Or do those block the feng shui of your workplace?"

He stands up and starts walking.

If he thinks I'm going to follow him like a baby duck, he's lost his mind. But then, if I stand here like an idiot, or worse yet, outright ask where he's going, I look equally idiotic. I ball my fingers into a tight fist, my carefully manicured nails digging into my palms. Before he's gotten very far ahead of me, I stalk after him, hating the act of following him without a clear understanding of where we're going.

It's not really a surprise. I've always hated David Park.

He acts like he either doesn't sense the social and business rules in a given situation, or even when he does, he intentionally ignores them. Luckily, we haven't gone very far when he hangs a right and gestures to a door with a placard in front of it: conference room.

Would it have killed him to say we were going to the conference room? I shove past him and into the room, taking the seat at the head of the table.

David freezes, as if he's mildly annoyed at my usurpation of his seat, but he lets it go. Again, he has the air of a magnanimous king or something.

I can't help my nostril flare, even though I despise giving signs of how annoyed I am. "This won't take long."

He leans back in his chair. "Good to know, since you didn't have an appointment."

I slide the brown briefcase toward him. "I'm buying the Ellingson ranch."

He smirks in the most irritating way possible. "I believe I told you that it's not for sale."

I roll my eyes. "Everything is for sale. This is double what you paid, in cash. You can use it for anything you want, and it's just your incentive to sell to me. I'll also pay you exactly what you paid on paper." I lean toward him. "And I'd be happy to buy this resort from you as well."

David isn't smiling now. He's frowning. He's even hotter when he's frowning. I've so seldom seen it that I didn't realize how much more handsome he is when he's angry until right now. "Why on earth would you do that?"

"Do what?"

"Above all else, you've always been a very sharp business woman. If you spend three times its market value buying the Ellingson ranch, you can't possibly make this business deal revenue positive." Somehow, as he spoke, his frustration turned into curiosity.

6

I lean toward him. "Not all business deals make sense on paper. Didn't you learn that at Harvard?"

He tilts his head. "I mean, if you have the right paper, they do."

I laugh. "Yes, if I'm taking a loss here, there must be a reason." I sigh and glance at the ceiling. It would be better if he were a complete dolt. He's just smart enough to be a pain. "David, you don't want to fight with me. Just leave."

"How do you know?" His eyes are flashing now.

"How do I know what?"

He sucks air through his perfect teeth. "Maybe I do want to fight with you."

I can't help my laugh, but it's not fluffy and charming. It's bitter and hard, like the bark of a seal. "You wouldn't make it a single round. Trust me, David. Take the briefcase and go home. You have no reason to stick around anymore."

His eyebrows shoot up. "No? Last I checked, I have a resort here that just opened, and—"

My voice is low and way cooler than I expect it to be when I say, "She's getting married, David."

He freezes. "She's *engaged*," he says. "There's a difference."

"I know that English isn't your first language." It's not really a fair statement for me to make. His English is flawless. "But for you, it means the same thing."

"No one self destructs like an alcoholic rock star," he says, "and weddings are stressful."

I bang my hand on the table. "You can't be that pathetic."

"No?" He doesn't look pathetic when he leans back again, stretching slightly. "You don't really know anything about me, Helen."

I love how it sounds when he says my name, which

7

makes me *furious*. "I know enough. Take the cash wind-fall and leave me alone."

"Why do you want me gone so badly?"

"The Flaming Gorge area is quite small. You're not even a billionaire," I say. "But you're still rich enough to be obnoxious."

"So it's your sandbox, is that it?" I hate how impassive his expression is. He leans toward me, sliding the briefcase away. "The thing is, I was playing here first."

I want to slap him. "My sister's living here. She's pregnant. Her friends and kids are all here."

"Did anyone ever tell you that money can't buy everything?"

"People who say ignorant things like that are positively moronic."

"You want to be here because your family's here," David says. "That's not a monetary reason, which is why you're doing something that's patently unintelligent on paper." He smiles. "This may be the best thing I've seen since business school. I doubt any of our classmates would even believe me if I told them Helen Fisher was trying to *buy* me out of her teensy family town so she could reign supreme."

"I could buy and sell your entire family." I glare. "Just take the money, David, or things will get ugly. Very, very ugly."

"And I can't even go one round, right?" He smirks, and then he shakes his shoulders a little, like a boxer warming up before climbing into the ring. "You know, for some reason, the more you say things like that, the more I want to find out for myself."

"Are you really sticking around here for Amanda Brooks?" I can hardly believe I'm asking him that. I don't really care why he's sticking around, except that clearly I haven't yet found his price. That's probably

8

why I'm asking. You can't beat your opponent until you understand their motivations. "She's so mid."

"Amanda Brooks dazzles," David says. "She's vulnerable in a way you never will be."

"Vulnerable? If that's what you want, I can find you a whole host of cute women whom you could save while still making a lot of money." I stand up.

David stands up, too, his eyes flashing again. "Thanks for the offer, but I'd rather die than date someone you chose for me."

"I suppose the white knight needs to pick his damsel-in-distress for himself." I roll my eyes.

"Why are you really still here?" David asks. "It can't be easy for you to run your conglomerate chop shop from the middle of nowhere."

Chop shop? I should be pissed off, but instead it makes me laugh. "I'm bored with that."

As I say the words, I realize it's true.

It's boring to dice and slice companies that are struggling until they're profitable, and then to sell the pieces that didn't fit to other dupes who think they can use them. Admitting that hurts, because it means that I'm really, really good at something that I don't even like doing anymore.

"You're bored with seeing the patterns in the piles of unintelligible accounting documents and making billions in ways no one else I've ever met can?" David's not frowning or smirking now. He looks. . .intrigued. "I didn't expect you to say that."

"I'm kidding," I say. "Of course it's hard to rule the world from here, but my sister needs me right now."

"I heard she was sick," he says. "But I thought I also heard that now she's fine."

Mention of Abigail being sick makes me feel. .

9

.strange. My knees weaken, and my heart races, and I want to slap him. "She's fine. Everything's great."

"I'm glad."

"Why are you really sticking around, David?" He's standing two feet away from me. Surely he can be honest about his reason. "Amanda Brooks is marrying someone else, and you have zero ties to anyone here. Your company's headquarters are in California. As hard as it may be for me, my people do whatever I say, and I answer to no one. Your family must be livid that you're still here."

His lips compress, and he nods slowly. "Helen, I'll tell you this. The more you push me to go, the less likely I am to leave." His grin's irritatingly boyish. "My sister would tell you it's my most annoying trait."

His sister. I can't contain my grin. "Will she, I wonder?"

David's face falls.

"Will she say that, I mean?"

He shakes his head. "Do not call her, Helen. I mean it. Tattling to my family is below the belt."

Ah, he's sticking with the boxing analogy. He's even cuter than I previously realized. I lean in closer and whisper slowly. "But I'm not really a boxer, David, and I don't follow any rules but the SEC's. 'Below the belt' is actually my sweet spot." I glance down toward his belt for good measure.

When his face flushes, my grin widens. The briefcase full of incentive money almost always works, but even when it doesn't, it helps me flush out the real chink in my opponent's armor every time.

"Nice chatting with you today," I say. "I'm sure you'll be in touch soon." I wink at him before leaving, and his fury just makes me happier.

Eddy told me his parents were miserable, but I didn't realize what that meant. My parents are a disaster and always have been, but they do love each other. I think. In their own selfish ways.

Eddy's parents seem to detest everything about each other.

It's difficult to decide what frosting and cake flavors you want for your wedding cake when the people who come with you to taste it don't let you get a word in edgewise. They're too busy arguing to let Eddy or me say a single word.

"This is supposed to be chocolate frosting?" Eddy's mother asks. She curls her lip. "Really?"

"It's chocolate mocha," Eddy says.

"I think it's delicious," his dad says. "It goes great with that darker cake."

"The fudge," I offer.

"The one with the texture of rubber?" his mother sighs. "You have no taste at all. You'd eat glue if it was chocolate flavored."

Eddy's eyes widen and his head tilts. He's pretty

clear with his nonverbal communication. *I told you we shouldn't have brought them.*

But I had insisted. I figured they'd make an effort to get along with other people around. Boy, was I wrong. "Okay, well, I thought it tasted rich and delicious," I say.

"Surely you don't want a chocolate wedding cake," Eddy's mother says.

"Not everyone has to do whatever you say," Eddy's dad says. "Stop harassing her and let her choose what *she* likes."

"She asked us to come with her." Eddy's mom folds her arms. "She *wanted* my opinion."

"We're picking two cake flavors," Eddy reminds them. "One for the wedding cake, and one for the groom's cake."

"Wait, does that mean we gotta pay for it?" his dad asks, peering at the price list.

"No one has to pay for it," the baker's assistant reminds us. "We're offering the cakes free of charge, because Mrs. Brooks is going to document the wedding plans on her Insta."

Eddy's dad pulls on his right earlobe. He does it every time something confuses him, and lately, I've been worried that he'll pull it right off.

"Remember?" I say. "Most of the wedding expenses are comped because I'm doing posts about the wedding. It's my job, or at least, it used to be my full-time job."

"I just don't really understand why," Eddy's dad says. "It's not like people can buy their cake on Instagram."

"Look, Dad, you said you had to get back by one o'clock, right?" Eddy's hating this. Maybe next time I won't try to involve his parents by letting them know when these things are.

His dad and mom give us their last-minute thoughts —his dad calling the chocolate mint cake 'that green one,' and the coconut guava 'the piña colada cake'— and blessedly leave.

Eddy doesn't say a word. He doesn't have to.

"You were right." I sigh.

"I'm telling Mom you cancelled the dress shopping trip."

"But Abigail can't come, and without your mom—"

"Maybe your mother could go with you instead."

"I would rather die." I could invite Mandy, but I'm still angry at her at odd intervals, and so far, every time I've thought about having her pick out my wedding dress, I've wanted to throw a glass of champagne at her face. I know she was kind of the reason I got over myself and I'm getting married at all, but I'm still mad at how she got me past my hangups.

If I don't find someone to help me go shopping soon, I'll be stuck with Helen. That might be worse than my mom.

Luckily, once his parents are gone, Eddy and I have an easy time picking the cake flavors. "For the wedding cake, I was thinking the strawberry—"

"Champagne." Eddy's smile is broad. "I knew it."

"What does that mean?"

He takes another bite of that one with his fork and closes his eyes, speaking around the mouthful of sugar. "It screamed Amanda from start to finish. Delicious, but light and understated flavor. Flecks of real strawberries with a lovely beige color." He shrugs. "And that strawberry garnish with the sparkly gel stuff?"

Champagne is my signature item—it's in my Insta name, after all. I scrawl the flavor down on the paper they gave me for the wedding cake. "And for the groom's cake?"

"I was thinking the blackberry elderflower," Eddy says.

I burst out laughing immediately. "Sure you were."

He chuckles. "You caught me. Not really my style."

"The black forest? Or the fudge with mousse frosting and strawberries?"

"Am I really that predictable?" He scowls.

"People love chocolate."

"I do like to give the people what they want," he says.

"That you do." It's actually one of the things I love about him. He knows me well enough to guess that I want fancy and light and froofy, but he wants his pick to be something everyone else will like. Eddy's beautiful and simple and crowd-pleasing, which makes him a really good foil for me.

Plus, he appreciates strawberry champagne for what it is.

I write *Black Forest* on the 'groom's cake' line with a flourish.

"Do you prefer cherries to strawberry?"

"It felt like too many strawberries otherwise." Eddy spears a strawberry with his fork. "They're nice enough, but what if someone's allergic or just doesn't like them? Now they have options."

"What if they don't like fruit at all?"

"They can scrape it off," Eddy says. "I can't solve the world's problems."

On our way home, the private investigator I hired calls. He's proven to be pretty useless so far, and today's no different. He found a few more citations and a misdemeanor by my dad that's three years old now.

"Still nothing?" Eddy's driving, but I can still sense his judgment.

"I should have taken Helen up on her offer to loan

me her guy. I think this one's not very competent. Or maybe he's too legit."

"Isn't Helen's guy the one who finds dirt, and if he can't, he fabricates it?"

"You did look like you were holding a drink, and the photos of you and that woman weren't fake."

"They were just part of the tour publicity." Eddy's jaw muscles work.

"But anyone who can't find actual dirt on my family is not doing his job."

"He found parking tickets, speeding tickets, library fines, and that crime."

"It was over a year ago, and it was petty shoplifting. They'd never run all the way to me for something like that." I shake my head. "No, none of that explains why they're here now."

"Amanda."

"No." I grip the armrests on Eddy's truck. "No."

"Amanda."

"Don't say it again, Eddy. Do not."

"They *could* be here because they love you and they heard you were getting married. They could be telling the truth."

I can't help my very unladylike snort. "Right."

"My parents' fighting is almost unbearable, but they came to ruin my cake tasting because they *love me*."

"Yes, your parents are annoying," I say. "But they've always been the same. They've fought like that for years, and they've always shown up to ruin all your important activities in the same exact way. Mine, on the other hand, only come when they need something. You can certainly understand why I can't just sit and wait to find out what it is. I need to know now why they're here."

"But it's already been almost two weeks, and so far,

other than paying for their hotel and food, they haven't asked for a thing from us."

"That's exactly what makes me nervous," I say. "If they aren't asking for something yet, it means what they want is really big. Believe me. They're so shameless that if it wasn't staggering, they'd already have asked."

"Except you always tell them no," Eddy says. "Maybe they're still too afraid to ask."

"Right, that's why I need to figure it out myself. The longer they wait to tell me the truth, the worse the truth must be."

"I think it's probably time, then," Eddy says.

"Time for what?"

"To cut them off." I pick up my phone and dial Mandy.

"Yello?"

For some reason, she thinks answering her phone with *yello* is hip and cool or something. I sigh and force myself to ignore it. "Hey, it's me."

"Yes, this magical thing on my phone called saving numbers allowed me to know that even before you helpfully said, 'it's *me*.'"

"I want you to call and cancel my family's hotel rooms."

"Are you sure?" Eddy and Mandy ask the exact same thing at the exact same time.

"I am."

"But we've been paying for weeks," Mandy says. "Why are you cancelling their rooms now?"

"I was worried they'd come stay with us," I admit.

"You're not worried about that now?" Mandy asks. I can tell from her tone that she's as uninterested in that prospect as I am.

"Oh, I am. But we're at an impasse. They won't

leave, and I can't figure out why yet. So if we cut them off, one of two things will happen."

"Our dear friend, Mrs. Earl, will never speak to us again because she's not even being paid for the rooms they're destroying?"

"Wait, are they destroying them?" Now I'm even more embarrassed.

Mandy hisses into the phone. "Just tell me what you think will happen."

"They'll either leave, which would be great, or they'll come stay with us."

"Isn't that what you don't want?" Eddy asks. "You said—"

"It's not ideal," I say, "but it may be the only way for us to trip them up and figure out what's really going on."

Mandy grunts. "Are you sure they're not just here—"

"If you say 'because they love you' or 'to get to know you' I will paint your toenails green while you sleep."

Mandy hates green toenails. She thinks it looks like fungus. Her cackle is one of my favorite things about her. "Fine. I won't even suggest it. I'll cancel their hotel reservation, and then we can start our full-blown investigation into the villainy of your parents and brothers together."

"Yes," I say. "Sadly, that's our next step."

"They could come stay with me," Eddy says. "I have room."

"Not a chance," I say. "That would be worse than the hotel. They'd be spying on you, and I'd still learn nothing. Plus, my fiancé would be miserable."

He shrugs. "Alright, well, just remember this was your idea."

I've just started the process of shoving Emery's stuff into a bag so she can vacate her room when my phone rings again. I expect my mom. I expect my dad. I wouldn't be shocked if it was one of my brothers.

I'm happy to see it's one of Abigail's old friends calling me back instead. He used to be a detective and has all kinds of contacts, so I was hoping he might be a good resource. "Hey. Thanks for calling me back."

"Hello, Amanda. As you know, normally I don't do this sort of thing, but Abby says these people are your parents and they're trying to ruin your wedding."

I laugh. "Abby's not wrong. That's all true."

"I should hope not. She could be disbarred for lying."

Oh, man. That's intense. "Okay, and what did you find?"

"Well, you were right that they have a problem, but there aren't any active criminal charges pending, or at least, not according to anything I could find based on the names and known aliases you had. However, they are late on their mortgage and the bank has filed to begin foreclosure on their—" He clears his throat. "Their mobile home."

"You mean the bank's going to repossess their trailer?"

"It appears that it will, yes."

They wouldn't have driven this far over that, either. They'd just buy a new one in someone else's name or from someone else they managed to convince they were trustworthy. "There's really nothing else?"

"Not that I could find. None of the local police had any ideas, either."

I swear under my breath. "Alright, well, thanks."

"Don't forget about the purse. My wife is all kinds of excited."

Abigail told him that in return for the favor, I could send his wife one of the exclusive Chanel clutches that aren't even out yet. They're too small for anything but a dinner party, and I never go to any of those anymore, so good riddance. "Just text me your address. Thanks again for the help."

It takes my family hours to gather up the courage to show up on our porch—or maybe that's how long it takes before Renita or someone else in downtown Manila admits where we live—either way, they show up at Mandy's place around nine o'clock. Maren and Emery are almost ready to go to bed.

"Why are you here?" I ask, as if I have no idea.

"That hotel says we don't got rooms now," Dad says.

"Oh?" I feign innocence. "Were they booked up?"

"No," Mom says. "But I guess your boss isn't paying any more?" She lowers her voice. "Did we make her mad?"

"Mom," I say. "You've been here for two weeks. How long did you really expect someone you don't even know to pay for your hotel rooms and food orders?"

She blinks like I'm making no sense. "Well, you said you didn't have room for us here."

"You're adults, all five of you," I say as gently as I can manage. Which isn't very gently as it turns out. "It's not our responsibility to provide you somewhere to stay."

Mom straightens up, all of the righteous indignance swelling inside of her and spilling over. "Well, I certainly provided you with a place to stay for almost eighteen years."

"Really, Mom?"

"Well, we can hardly just climb in our car and drive away tonight." She glances over her shoulder at the

19

beat-up old station wagon they brought. "And the man at the repair shop says our car needs a new transmission and new brakes."

Of course it does.

"How about this?" I ask. "I'll pay for one more night, or maybe two, and I'll cover for the car repairs."

"That would be really nice." Mom smiles, her brownish teeth gleaming in the porch lights. She shivers, clearly still not dressed properly for a Northern Utah winter.

"But the second your car is ready, you and Dad, and Roy, Peter, and Xavier will load up and leave."

"But what about your wedding?"

"My wedding that's still almost two months away?" I grimace.

"I mean, the holidays are around the corner. We thought it'd be nice to spend 'em together for once." Dad bobs his head.

My three adult brothers are still in the station wagon, thankfully, but they're wiping at the fog on the windows and peering out at me expectantly.

"So is that a no to my offer?" I start to close the door.

"Alright." Mom's voice is small, her expression full of sorrow. "If it's really what you want, we'll head on home as soon as our car's fixed."

Maybe Mom's bluffing. She's an expert at conning people, which I know better than most, but she seems pretty sincere. For maybe the first time since I was very, very young, I actually feel almost *bad* for how I've treated her.

Then the most dangerous feeling of all starts to well up inside of me, a feeling I haven't encountered in conjunction with my family in at least three decades. A feeling I'd given up on ever feeling about them again.

I almost can't admit it, even to myself.

Hope.

I'm *hoping* that they're here because they care about me. I know it's stupid. I know it's going to make me feel worse later, like the very second they stop lying about why they're here. I mean, sure, they've held it together for a while, but it can't last. I know that better than anyone.

And yet, I can't help it.

I'm wondering whether it's possible that Mom actually saw the YouTube video, tracked me down, and drove everyone out here, just because she missed me. Does she actually love me? Could she regret ignoring me my entire life?

Could she actually be proud of me?

I mean, I have done a lot of pretty neat things. I have a famous blog. I'm getting my wedding—a dream wedding—for free. All I have to do is post a few photos of each of the big-ticket items, and they're mine. On top of that, I have friends and family here, and a smoking hot, generous, smart, kind fiancé. *And* I'm developing a new resort.

Why is it so hard for me to believe that they're proud of me?

Maybe it's not Mom's damage that's getting in the way this time.

Maybe it's mine.

"Look, I'll call the hotel right now. Once your car's ready, we can reevaluate whether you should stay or go. Okay?"

Mom and Dad both smile then, broadly, and it makes me happy.

I *really* hope I'm not turning into a complete chump.

❧ 3 ❧

DONNA

In movies and television shows, when they show someone sitting at the doctor's office, you know it's bad news. But in real life, most of the time spent in a doctor's office is boring. Waiting, waiting, and more waiting. In fact, sitting here isn't even the stressful part. No, that was yesterday.

Since I'm working for my boyfriend's mom, it's a little harder to get time off to actually drive over to sit at the doctor's office. It's not like Manila's large enough to have a really nice OB, so I'm stuck driving into Green River. That makes it an even bigger ask.

Although Mrs. Earl is the nicest boss anyone has ever had, she's a little chatty, and chatty easily starts to feel like nosy. So when I told her I needed to take a few hours off today, she asked why. And when I told her it was private, she got concerned. Not, like, wanted-to-hire-an-investigator-to-tail me, but more like, worried-my-ex-was-up-to-something-and-wanted-to-help.

Which is a really nice thing. It's a sweet thing.

But it made it awkward for me to explain where I was going. It's not like I could really say, "I've had this persistent pelvic pain since my divorce, and I'm worried my ex gave me an STD. Now that I've said I love you to your son, well. I want to make sure the old car is ready to take out for a drive whenever that happens."

Oh my word. Even thinking about saying that to Mrs. Earl makes me blush. But it's not like I really want her worrying about what's causing me to take off work, either. Overall, I really like working with my boyfriend's mom, but nothing's perfect.

"Donna Ellingson?"

"That's me." I stand up so forcefully that the nurse holding my chart steps backward.

Her brows draw together.

"Sorry," I say. "I got a little anxious while I was waiting."

She nods. "That's not uncommon. Come with me."

After waiting in the lobby for nearly forty minutes, I'm almost shocked when the doc shows up moments after I'm shown to an exam room.

"Why are you here today?" She asks. "It looks like. . ." The doc scans the chart. "Just a checkup?"

I swallow. "The thing is, I got divorced a while back, and I wanted to make sure. . .nothing was wrong."

"STD screen. Got it." She checks a box on my chart. "And?"

I blink. "Isn't that enough?"

"You said *a while ago*. In my experience, people usually suspect STDs right away, or they experience symptoms that lead them to come in if they do have them. Since you're not reporting any, I'm assuming something else prompted you to make a visit now."

"Oh." I look down at my feet. "Well. I'm also dating

someone new, and I really, really like him. I have a son, but having him wasn't exactly easy."

"Easy?" The doctor raises her eyebrows.

"I lost three babies—two before and one after having Aiden."

This time, it's the doctor who looks a little surprised. "I'm so sorry."

"I have really heavy periods, and I have endometriosis, and while you were getting my pap smear and STD test and whatnot, I thought you might just kick the tires a little and make sure everything's alright."

"What did the doctors say when you miscarried?"

I shrug.

"It would be really helpful—"

"I don't know," I say. "My husband didn't want any more kids, so he didn't want me to go see any."

"You had three miscarriages without seeing any doctors about why?" There's the judgment I expected.

"I saw an ER doctor each time," I say. "But they always referred me to specialists, and we never went to see any of them."

The doctor walks across the room and sits down on the chair next to me. Her eyes are kind. "What other symptoms have you had?"

I really don't need kindness right now. I'm already fighting my hardest not to cry. I inhale sharply to try and stave off any tears. "I filled out the form." I sniffle.

She nods, releases my hand, and flips through the chart again. "Erratic periods. Intermittent heavy bleeding during periods that lasts up to nine days?" Her eyes widen. "Significant discomfort during and after periods?"

I nod.

"Alright, well, while you're here, I'm going to

suggest a real workup. We had two patients cancel this afternoon, so I should have time. Do you have insurance? Or will that—"

"Just do it," I say. "I'll pay whatever."

The doctor stands up, her eyes meeting mine. "Alright." Her smile isn't very enthusiastic, but it's genuine.

That's when I discover that waiting in the doctor's office *is* the stressful part. Those miscarriages during my relationship with Aiden's dad were sad. They were devastating, really. But since my marriage was such a wreck. . .they were also a relief. I wanted another child, but I didn't really want another child with *Charles*. So there was always an element of anxiety that went along with any possible pregnancy.

But now that I'm free of him, now that I have an amazing boyfriend, now that I can get answers for what was going on, I'm really, *really* nervous about what the doctor might say. An ultrasound and a CAT scan later, it's nearly dinner time. Will's texted me twice.

And I'm still waiting.

When the door opens and the kind lady doctor finally walks back in, her face isn't cheery. She looks downright stoic.

"Did a patient die in surgery?" Yes, my joke is lame.

But at least it makes her laugh. "All my patients are fine," she says. "Also, there's good news. You have no STDs."

"But the bad news?" Because when someone says 'there's good news,' there's always bad news as well.

"You already knew you had endometriosis."

For some reason, that makes tears well up in my eyes, but I nod.

"And you know that it can cause infertility in as many as fifty percent of the women who deal with it."

"But I already had one child."

"You did, when you were younger than you are now," she says. "The scar tissue increases with age, making implantation increasingly more difficult."

That sounds ominous. "I'm still young."

She forces a smile.

Now I'm getting really nervous.

"The ultrasound also showed fibroids."

"Is that from the endometriosis?"

She shakes her head. "They're usually not too concerning. A lot of women have fibroids and never even realize they do. That's why we got the CAT scan." She frowns. "The three miscarriages was the tip-off for me. You have something called submucosal fibroids, which can cause infertility on their own, but when combined with the endometriosis. . ."

"What's the treatment?"

She licks her lips. "The thing is, we can remove certain fibroids, but when they're submucosal, the removal causes even more scar tissue."

Which is the problem caused by the endometriosis. All the scar tissue already makes it hard for the fetus to properly attach. "Basically, my uterus is like the surface of the moon. Pitted and not compatible with life."

She doesn't even feign a laugh. She just sits down next to me again. "We don't really know. Plenty of women who don't seem likely to conceive and carry a child still do."

Women who don't seem likely to conceive or carry a child.

The words roll through my brain on repeat. Three miscarriages. "I guess this is where I'm supposed to be grateful that I have Aiden." But the words feel like sawdust in my mouth. "And I am. I love him."

"Some women aren't able to have any children at all."

"Are you married?"

I shouldn't have asked. I can see the surprise and defense in the woman's face.

"I'm sorry," I say. "I know it's none of my business. But I was married to a horrible jerk, and now I have the best boyfriend in the world, and things are going really well, and I want a big family. I came from a smallish one, and my best friend has four—soon-to-be five—kids, and I guess I wanted that too. And the guy I'm with, he would be the best dad." And now I'm bawling like I'm on death row and I'm not getting a last meal. "I'm already this train wreck he inexplicably likes, and his mom had to give me a job, and he keeps having to step in to help me with my ex, and he's amazing with my son, but I really, really don't want to be the reason he can't—we can't—have any more kids." The bawling has somehow evolved into heaving sobs, and tears are rolling down from my cheeks onto my pants, and I'm sure the doctor is regretting sitting next to me at all.

She turns toward me and pulls me against her.

And now I'm crying on the lapel of some doctor who isn't paid nearly enough. She pats my back slowly. "It's alright. It's going to be alright."

"When your doctor tells you that plenty of women experience miracles, basically, it doesn't feel like it's going to be alright."

"You don't have to deal with this right now," she says. "You have plenty of time. Years and years, yet."

But when I finally get home, when I pull up in the driveway of my adorable little house, the one that Amanda Saddler gifted Aiden and me, it doesn't *feel* like I have all the time in the world. When Beth opens the door, and Aiden's head pokes out above her, and I notice that Will's truck is on the curb. . .it feels like

27

every second I have is precious, and I've been wasting them.

If Aiden's the only kid I'll ever have, then every moment of his childhood means more, somehow. I think about how the toddler years are behind me, about how I'll never experience my child learning to walk again, or learning to say 'mama.' I'll never again change a diaper. I know people hate changing them, but I didn't even realize that I'd changed my last when I did it.

Which is why I'm totally sobbing like a lunatic when Will taps on the window of my car. "Hey, what's wrong?" His face is so concerned, and his eyes are so earnest. Eyes we'll never see in a child of our own. Eyes I can never give him, not the way I want to.

I shake my head and keep on bawling.

He pulls on the door handle.

It's locked.

He pulls again, and taps, and says, "Donna. Open the door. What's going on?"

I can't quite do it.

"Mom said you left and didn't say why?"

Oh, no. He already knows something's wrong. No wonder he's worried. It's not just Donna being Donna. He knows that I may have an actual reason to be this upset.

I hit the unlock button.

Only, now Aiden and Beth are right behind him.

"Is something wrong?" Beth's face is cloudy, her eyes filled with concern.

Aiden's voice is far too adult-sounding when he asks, "Mom? Why are you so sad?"

I swipe at my cheeks. It's a wonder I have enough water in me to make any more tears after my ridiculous meltdown at the doctor's office. "Nothing. It's fine.

Everything's fine." I force a smile. "I just saw you three waiting on me, and I got emotional. It happens to moms sometimes."

Beth looks like she wants to call me out, but she just narrows her eyes and compresses her lips and takes Aiden's arm. "Let's go inside, buddy. The mac and cheese is almost done."

Oh, good. I'm upset I won't have any more kids while the one I do have is basically being neglected. Mac and cheese for dinner when I should have been making something. . . Not that this is abnormal. I regularly flake on dinner and we eat junk-food-adjacent processed trash. Maybe the unlikelihood of me having more kids is for the best.

And I'm spiraling again.

"Now that the peanut gallery has gone back inside, care to share?" Will wipes my face with his hands so gently that I can't help thinking how careful he'd be with a baby.

"I can't have kids." Okay. Well, that's one way to explain my afternoon.

"What?" His entire face looks confused. "What are you talking about?"

I stare at the steering wheel. It's freezing cold outside, and we should go inside, but I can't seem to move. "I spent the afternoon at the doctor's office. I had an ultrasound and a CAT scan that I can't afford, and I found out that between my endometriosis, my uterine fibroids, and the three miscarriages I had before and after Aiden, it's very likely that I'll never have another child." My voice is so small at the end that I'm not sure whether he can even understand me.

"Donna."

"I think we should break up."

Will starts laughing. "Donna."

I slam my hand against the top of the steering wheel so hard that the horn actually lets out a small chirp. "Why aren't you listening?"

Beth and Aiden poke their heads out again, but Will waves them back inside. Beth looks annoyed, but she drags Aiden back.

"I am listening, Donna. I know you're feeling particularly upset, and I know those were hard things to hear, but do you know what I just heard?"

I can't even turn my head. This steering wheel feels like the only thing that's real in my life.

Will carefully drags my chin toward him, forcing my eyes to go along with it. When I see his face, his beautiful, calm, somewhat amused face, my heart breaks all over again. "Will."

"Donna, you're healthy and strong, and you're totally fine. You're not dying. You don't have cancer. You have a job and a boyfriend and a very healthy and strong and happy son. You have a niece who's a delight whom you're currently raising because your brother's the worst, and you don't even need to have more kids. We haven't even talked about it. Maybe I don't even want kids."

"You do, though."

"I have one already, as far as I'm concerned."

"Aiden has a father." I know it's a mean thing to say, but it's also true. "A crappy father, but he has a dad."

"That little boy needs a decent dad, and I'm fine with being his fallback." Will shrugs. "You know what I *do want*?"

I shake my head slowly.

Will sighs, and then he releases me, and he drops down on one knee in the dirty-snow-encrusted mud on the edge of my driveway. He pulls a ring out of his pocket.

"I've been carrying this stupid ring around for weeks. I didn't want to do a big, huge, overwrought proposal. It always feels like those people are trying too hard. And I didn't want to steal the thunder from Eddy and Amanda with their engagement."

I can't believe I'm looking at a diamond ring.

"I didn't want to rush you, either. So I just waited, and waited, and waited. But for some reason, *this* feels like the right moment. When you're sad, and when you're worried, and when you've had a bad day. That's the time for me to say that, Donna Ellingson, I have loved you for years, and now I want to love you in the broad daylight while holding your hand. I don't care whether you have ten children with me or whether we just adopt the world's cutest dog. Or eleven ugly dogs. Whatever you want, whatever God has planned for us, that's what I want to do. As long as it's with you."

And now I'm crying all over again.

"Please, please, *please* take this ring and say you'll marry me, you ridiculous, adorable, tenacious woman."

I confess to Will that I'm even more broken than he knew, and his reaction is to propose, with a ring he's been carrying around for weeks. "You think this is the right time?"

He stands up. "Yes, because loving someone means being there when they're sad and scared. It's not all flowers and fancy meals." He looks down at his wet, muddy knee. "And maybe I'm not supposed to kneel in the mud, and ideally you wouldn't be gripping that steering wheel like it's a rope connected to a helicopter that's going to get you out of a deep chasm in which you're doomed to die."

I laugh.

He leans against the side of my car, his eyes still intent on mine. "I don't want you to think I didn't give this any thought. Actually, I waited for years for the perfect moment to ask you out. You left for school and then got married before I ever asked. When you came back, I waited for you to get over the divorce and be ready to date. I've learned something in all that waiting."

"What?"

He drops his head down until it's right next to mine. "I've learned that there are no perfect moments, or at least, there never have been for me. So I just take the crappy, imperfect moments I get, and I do my best to make them as great as I can." His mouth shifts closer to mine then, his eyes dropping to my lips.

Will always makes the regular moments we have pretty amazing by taking things slowly. When his lips finally close over mine, my heart swells.

This man loves me.

He loves me when I'm puffy and bawling.

He loves me when I'm complaining and angry.

He loves me when my niece is stuck feeding my kid macaroni and cheese.

He loves my kid when he's being a spoiled brat.

He proposes when I'm throwing myself a huge pity party.

And he never misses a beat, even when I deliver bad news.

He's like the solid steel and concrete foundation of a commercial building. He's like the steel beams under a huge bridge. He doesn't sway with the wind. He doesn't shudder in a storm. He's solid. And he's unfailingly kind.

When his hand cups my jaw, dragging me out of the car and against his long, lean body, my insides start doing somersaults, and I know just what to say.

It's simple, really, the idea of turning this imperfect

moment into a perfect one. I think I can do just what he said. I think we can turn this day of bad news into a memory that's good. It'll take just one word.

"Yes," I say.

Will beams.

And through my tears, I smile right back.

Forget a bad boy who rides a Harley or a Casanova who unclasps a bra by glancing at it. I've found myself a man who takes horrible days and makes them sunny. That's what I really needed in my life.

And now that's what I'll have forever.

❧ 4 ❧

HELEN

When I had to drive out to start Harvard business school, I knew the trip was going to be long—forty-five hours, to be precise, from San Francisco, California to Cambridge, Massachusetts. It's also a very boring drive. Nevada and Utah are desert. Wyoming and Nebraska are empty of, well, everything, including people. Unless you love pigs, Iowa's a waste of time, too. Without anything I wanted to see or do on the way, I wanted to get that drive over with as quickly as I could.

Actually, that's really been my *modus operandi* for the majority of my life. If something needs to be done, do it efficiently and get it over with as painlessly as possible. I looked it up while I was in undergraduate and discovered that sleeping less than six hours a night was shown to cause an increase in amyloid-beta, a protein that causes brain plaque.

I always get my six hours and not a minute more, so I stopped in some town in Iowa and slept. Then I woke up and kept right on driving. I recall two things from that trip: the unsatisfactory presence of cockroaches in the hotel room where I stayed, and my vigilance in watching the gas tank. I only exited the freeway on that drive to refuel. I bought food and went to the restroom whenever I ran out of gas. I've always been like that. When I have a goal, I despise being delayed, sidetracked, or put off.

That's the only reason I've been borderline obsessive about stupid David Park and his smirk. It's not because of David, *per se*. He's just a freeway exit on the way to my real goal: complete domination and control of the place my sister now lives so I can keep her safe.

David made it sound like I'm some kind of petty tyrant, but really, when I thought Abigail was sick, it panicked me. What if she really had been in trouble? What if she died? Her life may be disappointing to my parents, and if I'm honest, a little disappointing to me. She has so much unfulfilled potential. But even so, she's the closest person to me in the world, genetically. She's probably the only person I know who has the same capacity that I do, mentally. Sure, some of it has probably atrophied through complete and total non-use while she wasted years changing diapers and doing other mundane tasks, but she's still smarter than most anyone else I meet.

One thing I can control is eliminating anyone who might try to push her around in Manila. The best form of security in life is massive amounts of money. Very few things can mess with someone when they hold all the cards. I mean to make sure that Abigail and her bevy of children are as safe as evil Aunt Helen can make them.

"Here are the plans for how we could set up the 'Ranch Experience.'" I drop the mock ups, projections, and sketches on the table. I know Abigail was delighted that Mandy's still alive, but Amanda's has been inconsistent. She's angry, but also happy. The unpredictable way in which she reacts to Mandy is obnoxious. The two of them keep insisting we're all equal partners, but then they outvote me two to one on everything. Unless I remind Amanda of Mandy's departure. Sometimes then, she'll vote for me.

At the end of the day, the legalities are on my side. I bought things fair and square, so if I wanted to, I could toss them out on their ear. The only thing that has kept me from doing that already is Abigail. She has an irritating level of attachment to. . .well, it feels like she's attached to most everyone I've met, but these two more than any others.

"I thought you said David refused to sell?" Amanda Brooks looks smug. There are very few things in this world I hate more than someone who's acting smug.

I roll my eyes. "I knew he'd do that. It's how things are done. But after I call his sister and explain what poor business decisions he's making—"

"Whoa," Amanda says. "Your grand plan is to *tattle* on him?"

I shrug. "When people are acting irrationally, it's sometimes the only way. Like you'd do with any other unruly dog—leash them."

"But you can't leash him," Mandy says. "He's a grown man." She smiles then. "I've always been Team Eddy, but that doesn't mean I can't appreciate David Park for what he is. Grade A—"

"Okay," I say. "Let's not start objectifying our enemies."

"Is he our enemy?" Mandy asks. "We're catering to the women, and he can cater to the men. We could be like peanut butter and jelly."

I sigh. "In an area this small, we don't need two separate resorts. The smart play is—"

"His is already built," Mandy says. "So if there can be only one, are you proposing that we buy it, run him out, and then just shut our operation down?"

I sigh. "No."

"Then what?" She leans back and sucks air through the holes in between her teeth. "Because it sure sounds like it."

"We move forward with this as planned—building a women's retreat—and then after buying his facility, we can advertise them together. Run the two locations like two prongs of the same company. If they want a family experience, a work retreat, or a guys' trip, they can head for Dutch John. If they want a women's retreat or an empowering experience or whatever you're calling it, they can come to the Manila women's resort." I nod. "Happy?"

"I only want to do this one," Amanda says. "Let's just leave David alone, and—"

"It's eleven at night in Seoul right now, but I'll call her once it's a decent hour. After she understands what I'm willing to pay—"

"Why are you wanting to buy his resort?" Mandy asks. "You didn't seem to care until you found out he was running that dude ranch over here, and—"

"That's the issue." I may have started off by wanting the ranch that's next door to my sister. But David Park's stupid, smug face is even worse than Amanda's. More obnoxious. More invasive. "Initially, he was staying in Dutch John, but now he's invading my space, and if he'll do that, who knows how far he'll go? Why doesn't he just buy a ranch over on his side if he means to leave us alone? I don't want him here, and that made me not want him around at all."

37

"Ranches don't go up for sale very often," Mandy says. "What will you do if his sister *doesn't* take your side? He's her brother. You're no one to her."

"I'm Helen Fisher." I straighten in my dining table chair. "I'm not *no one* to anyone." I shake my head. "But once she sees the numbers, she'll realize I'm right. If he wants to have a ranch experience, he should do it right next to his dumb retreat."

"Those are only projections, though." Amanda says. "Won't she give him the benefit of the doubt, at least until he gets it running? It's not like he has to do much. He could start bringing customers over in another few weeks, probably."

Amanda's right about one thing. If David's sister is as stupid as he is, or if she's bull-headed in her loyalty, this might not go easily. It could turn into a more protracted battle. I'm guessing by his reaction that his relationship with his sister is complicated, but if it's not, I'll need a plan B. I may as well come up with one just in case.

That's when it hits me.

"We have another ranch we can use already." I stand up.

"What?"

"Ethan's ranch. I bet he'd love to have a little extra revenue coming in from offering guided tours."

"But he can barely handle the ranch work. He currently needs his stepdad's help," Amanda says. "The last thing he'll want is extra chores and people traipsing through—"

"I'm going to at least talk to him. If David Park won't take the easy exit, I'm going to have a plan B that will force him out."

"This is crazy," Amanda says. "You're worrying about something that—"

38

I grab my sketches and projections and stuff them into my briefcase. "You guys go over the approvals and the timeline for the contractors and see what we can expedite. I want to open in the spring."

Mandy's spluttering as I walk out the door.

I take a lot of delight in annoying those two. I can't decide whether it's because they're obnoxious, or whether it's because they're Abigail's best friends, and I'm a jealous brat. Luckily, I'm self-aware enough not to care. Does it really matter, as long as I'm enjoying it? The Epicureans got a few things right, and focusing on things that bring you pleasure is one of them.

As I climb into my car, I think it through. Working with Ethan might be even better than taking David Park's ranch away from him. If I collaborate with Ethan, he can earn extra money, and I'll have a reason to help my nephew out. It could be a win-win. And if we can put David Park out of business in the process, that would be a bonus.

Besides, the Ellingson ranch is nearby, but Ethan's is as close as it gets. If we get the resort up and running, we could use golf carts to take people over there. They could walk if we paved a little path. I almost feel bad for driving to and from these meetings. Or you know, I would, if it was more than twenty-five degrees in this wretched town right now. I can't even drive my sportscar in this mess—I had to buy a Range Rover. I zip my coat up to my neck and brace myself before opening the door.

It's not currently snowing, which is nice, but it's already blanketing *everything*. So when Ethan's not inside—the other kids are at school, presumably—I have no idea where else to look for him. He doesn't answer when I call, but it goes right to voicemail. The cell reception around here is terrible.

I'm walking back to the house when I notice footprints in the light snowfall from last night. Ethan must have cleared the pathway, but I can see where these steps branched off. It's not toward the barn, either. It's heading in the direction of Steve's place.

If that really is where he went, why would Ethan *walk* to Steve's? Surely in this weather he'd drive that crappy old truck or take one of the four-wheelers. Right?

Unless he's doing something else.

"Ethan?" I try calling his name a few more times, but there's no response.

Of course there isn't. We're living in the land that time forgot. I sigh and turn back to my car. But as I open the door, it occurs to me that Ethan was clearly walking wherever he was walking alone. No companion steps are next to his. What if he's doing a cow thing that's new? What if he had an injured animal he was trying to help? It's not like he could *call* us for help if something went wrong. Cell phones are notoriously unreliable around here.

It's probably fine. I'm just paranoid with animal stuff because I know nothing about it. Ethan's much more competent on a ranch than anyone else I know. He's a natural with it.

But if he does need a hand. . .or even if he doesn't, if I just walk a little ways, he might be right there, like, untying a cow that got tangled in. . .well, they don't have barbed wire. But, you know, something that's tangly.

I should just head back and wait for him.

But something keeps bugging me. What if Ethan's not okay? I hate this nagging feeling of concern. It's not like me to worry about other people when I have no reason to be worried. That's Abby's job, not mine.

I shiver in the strong headwind.

And that decides it for me. It's freezing cold, and I'm wearing the nicest Prada snow boots money can buy, and the thickest sheepskin coat that Overland sells, and I'm still shivering. I should at least walk a little ways to make sure my nephew is alright.

His footprints are ridiculously easy to follow, thankfully, because I'm not any kind of tracker. I'm about to turn back—it feels like I've walked practically to Steve's by now—when I finally hear his voice. I open my mouth to call his name when I realize that he's not alone. There's another voice, too. It's a woman's.

"I said *hot* chocolate," she's saying. "But this is barely warm."

"That's not my fault," Ethan says. "The microwave only gets it so hot, and I couldn't find a mug, so I had to haul it in those little paper cups."

Someone's giggling. I really hope it's not Ethan. A lot of what they're saying is muffled and I can't quite make it out, but it sounds private. Clearly he's not in any distress, and I think about turning around and heading home, but I *did* come over to talk to him, and I did walk a long way, and he *is* right there.

"—reason you're so cold is that your coat isn't zipped."

There's some kind of scuffling sound, like someone's stumbling.

"That's a rude thing for you to say, when you know why it's not zipped."

"Let's go shopping," he says. "I know you're not ready to tell people, but pretty soon you won't be able to avoid it. Plus, I think maternity clothes are cute."

Maternity clothes?! What in the world *is going on?*

I definitely need to think about what I just heard and figure out what it means, and then I need to tell

Abby. Right? Right. Right? I've never felt more confused or unsure in my entire life. Ethan. . .knows this girl who's pregnant. He thinks she should tell people about. . .*their baby?*

Well, he sure is his father's son. He got some girl pregnant before he's old enough to make good decisions, and before he has the means to support a child. Before he's even started college.

This is a disaster.

I wonder how Abby will react. She'll probably ask me to book the circus again. Oh, no. Am I going to have to sit through a baby shower for my poor nephew and pretend that it's good news? I'm definitely not in any condition to talk to Ethan right now, so I turn to leave.

And that's when I step on the most vindictive stick in the entire field. It's buried under snow. It should be soggy, not snapping with the vigor of. . .well, a teenage boy, I guess. It's so loud that Ethan immediately says, "Who's there?"

I've never wished that Manila was a forest. I mean, it's a cattle ranching area. There are some trees, but it's mostly grazing land. But at least if there were lots of trees, the stick would make sense, and I could *hide* behind one of the big stick-making trees or something. As it is, once Ethan pokes his head around the small and cultivated grove of trees he and that pregnant girl are standing behind, there's nowhere to hide.

"Aunt Helen?" His eyes are wide.

"Uh. Yes. I saw your footprints, and well." I spread my arms wide. "How's life?"

"So you obviously heard me talking about maternity clothes."

"Mater-na-what?" I shrug. "No idea what you're saying."

He arches one eyebrow.

"Just tell her," Beth says. "You're right. I've been sticking my head in the sand, but eventually people will find out." In spite of her brave words, Beth pulls either side of her jacket together more tightly as if covering her belly will somehow cover her secret.

"Is it a boy or a girl?" I cringe as I ask.

"I haven't decided what to do with it yet," Beth says.

Oh, thank goodness. I figured that my sister's son wouldn't even *consider* all his good options. "I have a private jet," I say. "So technically, you don't have to tell anyone."

Beth's mouth dangles open.

Ethan's brow draws together, and then his jaw drops too. Which means they were definitely *not* considering abortion. "Listen, I know your mom isn't someone who would ever consider—"

Ethan's scowling when he explains. "Beth can't decide whether to keep the baby or put it up for adoption. Those are the things she's debating between."

"Don't you get a say?" I ask. "I mean, you should at least consider every option. It doesn't mean you have to take it. But no one would ever have to know. That's all I'm saying."

"I appreciate your willingness to help." Ethan's snippy tone belies his words. "I really do, Aunt Helen, but for now, if you could just—"

"I won't tell your mother," I say, "if that's what you're worried about."

"Mom knows," Ethan says. "And Steve does, too."

That's a surprise. "She does?" No wonder they're not considering all their options. "That's too bad. I wish I'd found out first. But even so, if you want to live in my New York apartment for a few months or something, so that people around here don't have to find out, you're welcome to—"

"It's not Ethan's baby," Beth blurts out, her eyes wide. "It feels like you should know that, and it seems like you're assuming it is."

Now I'm really confused. "Oh. So, you're what? Good friends?" Something horrible hits me. "Wait. Whose baby *is* it?"

"No one you've ever met," Beth says. "I barely know him."

That actually makes me like her more. I didn't figure I'd find many open-minded people around Manila. I wonder what kind of personality it takes to be willing to live the way you want to live when everyone here is so provincial. "Good for you."

She scowls. "No, not good for me. It was a stupid mistake, but look." She sighs, like *I'm* the one with poor judgment. "I better get back. I have to work."

What kind of work could she be rushing off to? A waitress? A janitor? The second she's gone, I'm going to make Ethan make *some* kind of sense of all this.

"I'll see you for dinner?" he asks.

She nods.

But the second she's out of earshot, I can't help pouncing. "So are you dating? Or not?"

Ethan starts walking toward the house immediately, like I'm an insurance salesman he can't shake. I'm forced to trot after him. Prada boots are not made for trotting. "Ethan Brooks, turn around and talk to me."

My nephew turns around, but he doesn't look inclined to chat. His eyes flash. "You barged into my breakfast date, upset my girlfriend, and suggested she get an *abortion*. So pardon me if I'm being a little rude."

"If no one has suggested an abortion before now,

then I'm certainly not going to apologize for mentioning it. The woman carries every ounce of the responsibility for pregnancy, and really most all of the bad risk of—"

"I'm aware," Ethan says. "But Beth isn't all women. She's not a cause or a crusade. She's a person, my girlfriend—"

"Yes, you said."

"And that's a pretty upsetting thing for you to imply, that we're being irresponsible."

"Oh, I think it's irrefutable that she was irresponsible." I can't help chuckling. "But I never blame the woman. It's totally unfair that they're the only ones who suffer."

"Aunt Helen," Ethan says, "it's not my baby, but if Beth decides to keep it, it will be. While she's trying to decide what to do, she's trying to keep it quiet. She doesn't want everyone pressuring her about it. Okay?"

"If it's not yours, why would you date her?"

His eyes are steady and entirely calm as they meet mine. "I love her. Some people don't have just two settings: attack or run away. Some people know how to stick around for the long haul, wherever the road goes."

I think my teenage nephew, whose girlfriend is pregnant, just lectured me on how to live my life. It should tick me off. For some reason, I find it utterly hilarious. "Alright, Ethan. Alright." I pat him on the shoulder and walk back to the house by his side.

He probably needs extra money more than ever before, especially if she keeps the kid, but for some reason, I don't bother asking him about the ranch tours. Maybe, even for me, having a baby puts some things into perspective.

Is he right? Am I someone who runs away?

In business, they call me a bulldog. I go for the throat and never take prisoners. Maybe in my personal life, I've been a bit of a lone wolf, but that doesn't mean I run from things.

Does it?

When my phone bings, I can't help my smile. My team never fails to come through. It's David Park's sister's phone number, email address, and physical address. The next few hours are long as I wait for eight in the morning to roll around in Korea, but I make good use of them. It gives me some time to assemble all my documents on David's retreat, his American holdings, and every weakness I've been able to identify. He's a pretty conservative guy, businesswise. He's been able to be, since he was born to a wealthy family, but even so, I found a few things.

I'm a little surprised when Ji-Hye answers on the first ring. I know a few Korean phrases, but not many. "Annyeonghaseyo," I say.

"This is an American number," Ji-Hye says in English, thankfully. "Is it about my brother? Is he alright?"

"Uh, yes. I'm calling from the United States," I say. "David's fine, but I am calling you because of him."

"Who is this?" She doesn't sound very happy, which is hardly a surprise. I'd be ticked, too, if someone I didn't know called my private number and just started talking about Abby.

"I'm actually calling to ask for your help." I inhale and exhale slowly. People evaluate your importance by how quickly you rush things. I'm not a beggar, and if she hangs up on me, she'll discover that quickly. "My name's Helen Fisher. I own the largest private equity firm in the United States."

"Why are you calling, Helen?"

"I've known David for a while. We went to Harvard Business School at the same time." I pause again. "But he's really getting on my nerves right now, and when I get annoyed, I get. . .destructive."

"What do you want from me?"

"Your brother has just built a resort in a small town called Dutch John. It's in the middle of nowhere—near a natural landmark called the Flaming Gorge. He came out here because he liked a friend of my sister's, but she's getting married. My sister also lives here, which is why I've taken an interest in the area, and I don't play well with others."

"The town's too small for the both of you?"

Lots of impressive business people in other countries learn English. Most of them don't learn it well enough to really understand when and how to use our dated clichés. I have a newfound respect for Ji-Hye. "Something like that. I've offered him very generous terms of purchase for a small ranch he bought very close to my sister's home. He's refused me, repeatedly."

"What about his resort?"

"I'd happily buy it as well, but I don't really care whether he keeps it or not. I just want him to sell me the ranch and leave us alone."

She makes a soft sound that I assume means she's considering my offer. "Would you say my brother is your enemy, Helen Fisher?"

Is she getting defensive? "That's a strong word," I say. "He's a nuisance." I sigh. "Have you heard of Disney?"

Ji-Hye laughs. "I live in Seoul, not Timbuktu."

"Disney's famous for pursuing copyright infringement cases, both small and large. If you're a little old woman living in a tiny town and you dress up as one of their characters and start earning money for it, the second they hear of it, and they're always searching, they'll sue you. They do this to protect their ongoing intellectual property rights. No matter how minor, no matter how small the case, Disney's expensive lawyers march in and treat it like a murder trial. Everyone always folds. They all know they can't go against Disney, because Disney has deep pockets. They can outlast any of these people who might want to stand against them."

"And?"

"I'm twice as vindictive and nearly as rich," I say. "Your family is very wealthy, but this isn't a fight you want your brother to pick for you."

"I feel like we may have something in common, Miss Fisher." She pauses, too, clearly another control freak like me. "Maybe several things. But the most relevant at this point is that my father is about to make a decision about his successor. He's been waiting for years for David to return home and get married, and the pressure on my brother to finally cave is about to rise. Korea's not very progressive yet, and fathers want their holdings to be run by their sons whenever possible. As I'm sure you can understand, that's frustrating to me."

"I might murder him, if I were you."

"I don't think I'll need to go quite that far." I can practically hear her evil smile. "But if you managed to send me anything you could turn up that would demonstrate his incompetence, the weakness of his position in America, or the ways in which he might have mismanaged the company—such as building a resort in a ridiculous location, for instance—I would appreciate it."

"Appreciate?"

"Is that backwards? How about this? I'll sign the papers that will sell you the ranch, and then I hope that you'll show your appreciation."

We talk about a few more details, but I'm smiling as I hang up the phone.

❧ 5 ❧

AMANDA

For most of my life, I've been almost painfully embarrassed about my parents. After Paul proposed, we went back to meet his parents. I wasn't surprised that such gracious, well-spoken, intelligent people had raised someone as brilliant and talented as Paul. If anything, I was surprised by how considerate and empathetic they were.

Paul was a genius, but he wasn't especially kind.

But after we got back to New York City, he asked me when we should go back to visit my family. I changed the subject. He brought it up again a few days later, and I realized that I might not be able to avoid introducing the man who meant to marry me to my parents.

I did what anyone in my situation would do.

Just before the trip I set up to see my parents was set to happen, my family became deathly ill with a stomach bug. We ate the cost of the tickets, and I felt a bit guilty about the lie, but if I hadn't come up with a way to prevent Paul from meeting my parents, I'm absolutely positive we'd never have gotten married in the first place.

Who wants to marry someone, especially someone who's already not good enough for them, when their family is worse than a literal millstone around their neck? They're more like a toxic-waste-filled barrel of garbage that has always been hiding, waiting to drag me down with them.

I only escaped by cutting the chain and never looking back.

Only, now I'm starting to wonder whether that was less of a necessity and more a sign of my own cruelty. Mom's been coming over every day and helping out while the repair shop works on their car. Today alone, she wiped the counters off, swept and mopped the floors, and now she's scrubbing toilets. She used Fabuloso, that floor cleaner, for all three things, but at least she's trying.

"Mom, you don't have to do that."

"You're paying for our hotel," she calls back. "It's the least I can do."

I wonder what happens to counters when they've been coated in floor cleaner. And toilets, for that matter. Is it bad for the plumbing?

At the same time, my dad's cleaning out Mandy's shed—the place where she'd moved most everything she didn't want to have burn when she set her own barn on fire. She couldn't really go out there and clean it out beforehand, so it's now full of a strange mix of things Mandy valued and also old corroded tools and rotting boxes of farm equipment.

"Dad really doesn't have to go through all that stuff, either."

"You know he and your brothers go crazy when they can't do something with their hands." Mom's not even standing up to talk to me. She's still face down, scrubbing the side of the toilet.

Also, she's making no sense. In the years I was home, I don't recall my dad or brothers ever doing much that could be considered 'using their hands,' unless she means changing the TV station by pressing a button on a remote or dumping piles of trash on the floor.

I do remember them drinking beer. Lots and lots of beer.

"Last summer, they spent their evenings building a new animal shelter, you know."

Is Mom just making things up now? There's no way they did anything like that. "Uh-huh," I say. "Neat."

She finally comes out of the bathroom at the same time that Mandy turns out of her room and shoots down the hall. Why does such an old lady move so fast? She plows into Mom's elbow, knocking the dirty-water-and-Fabuloso bucket sideways.

Water careens out of the bucket and splatters all over the flooring. At least Mom's language when she's shocked comes out just as I remember it. Of course, that makes me cringe big time.

It also sends Maren and Emery shooting out of their rooms.

Emery can't stop fast enough to avoid the spill, so she slips on the puddle in front of her room and pinwheels her arms, trying to avoid falling backwards on her butt. At the last second, she grabs the door trim, clinging to it like a victim of the Titanic clutching the closest life raft. Her feet splay outward as she slides slowly to the ground.

"Now it looks like you peed your pants." Maren's smirk is pretty familiar. Just when I think the two of them are getting along a little better, Maren's bratty flares up.

Emery's face scrunches up, turns bright red, and I realize that a meltdown is imminent.

"Knock it off, Maren. Help your sister." Mandy's glare is as effective as a slap, and Maren springs forward to yank Emery back up to her feet. "And you," Mandy spins around to glare at Emery. "Go change. No one should have wet pants this time of year."

"I'm so sorry," my mom says. "I didn't realize this hallway was a rocket launching facility."

That's actually pretty funny. I can't really help my laugh.

Mandy doesn't seem very amused, but she can get over it. It's not like she scrubs the toilets. Now that Abigail and her army of hard-working minions don't live with us, I'm the one who gets stuck doing it. If my mom's efforts mean that she needs to exercise a little more care when she comes flying out of her room and into the hall, well. She should be doing that anyway.

"Hey, when's your next doctor appointment?" I ask.

"Thursday," she says. "Why? Are you taking me?"

"Of course," I say. "When have I not? Other than that time you left me and went to California."

Mom's watching our interchange like a bloodhound scenting a fox, so I drop it. I like tormenting Mandy—I feel like she deserves it. I'm still upset, and I don't think she realizes how hard her supposed death hit me. But this probably isn't the time for it.

Luckily, Abigail arrives before Mom can pry. Roscoe does his job as our doorbell, barking and jumping up on the door the second he sees her from the windows set along the sides of the front door.

"You're going dress shopping?" Mandy asks.

I nod. "Abby has been working like a crazy person,

trying to get all her cases taken care of before her baby comes, but she finally found a time."

"Isn't it due in like, March?" Mandy asks.

"No, sooner than that. I think it's the end of January." I grab my purse. "But she's got the holidays coming, too, and the kids have all kinds of things they're doing. Plus Whitney's in the school play, like Emery, and Izzy has a horse show Steve's taking her to. Abby's not sure how much time she'll have as things get closer, so we're stuck going on a Saturday."

Mandy shrugs. "It's not like Salt Lake City will be such a bustling metropolis that you can't deal with it on a weekend."

I snort. "No, I guess not. It's just the closest city with any decent bridal boutiques."

"You could fly," Mom says. "I'm sure plenty of fancy places would love to have you wear one of their dresses."

She's not wrong. "But Abby's pregnant, and commercial travel—"

"There's always Helen. She's got a jet." Mandy's voice is flat. She loves Abby to the moon and back, but she's never been delighted with Helen. Now that she's part of our business deal, things have only gotten worse. Even so, it's hard to deny that Helen brings some perks.

I open the door. "Hey, Abby. You ready to go?" I don't really want Abby to hang out chatting with my mom for very long. I'm not sure why I don't want the two of them together, but it feels like a bad idea.

Her hand's lifted like she's about to knock.

"Roscoe's a good early warning system." I ruffle the top of his back as he shoots past me to lick Abby's hand.

"Looks like your family's all here," Abby says.

"Should we reschedule? I don't want to get in the way of family time."

"Oh, we aren't going nowhere," my mom says. "Don't worry. You can go, and we'll stay here and watch the girls."

Abby's face is marvelously calm—she has a killer poker face. Mandy, however, looks a little ill. "I already told Amanda that I'd keep an eye on them," Mandy says.

"I'm almost seventeen." Maren has come out of her room again and she's leaning against the couch. "And Emery's almost thirteen. I really don't think anyone needs to watch us."

Mandy snorts.

"Mom and Dad are leaving soon anyway, I'm sure," I say, hoping Mom will take the hint. "They've been hard at work since breakfast this morning." I made them breakfast in an attempt to pump them for info about why they're really here. Unfortunately, other than watching them eat all the pancakes and fried eggs I tossed on the frying pan, I got nothing out of them.

"Your dad's cleaning out the shed?" Abby looks impressed. "It's pretty cold outside today, but at least he has a warm coat finally."

She must have seen them downtown, probably going to work or lunch. I'm a little embarrassed that they hung around improperly dressed for so long.

"They're wearing my dad's old clothes." Mandy's trying to suppress her laugh, but not very successfully.

"That's why they all look like old men. . .from the eighties." Abby's grinning.

"Hey, my dad was pretty trendy." Mandy mutters something else I can't quite catch, but I do get a few words. *For the area.*

I actually find it pretty humorous too, seeing my

freeloading brothers wearing coats borrowed from a much smaller, much older man that were probably not really in style thirty years ago, either. Luckily, they were carefully stored in mothballs, so they aren't full of holes. They do smell like mothballs, though.

It's not a scent that I really enjoy.

Or even tolerate well.

Which makes it funnier that they're essentially marinating in it. I wonder whether it'll make them more eager to finally come clean about what they came for. Or maybe it'll be bad enough that they'll just go home.

I'd accept either one.

"If you don't need me to watch the girls, maybe I could come to the dress fitting," Mom says.

"Actually," Abigail says, "a few of the boutiques we have appointments at only gave us a dressing room big enough for two people." She frowns. "I thought Mandy might want to come, but they told me they couldn't accommodate a larger party. I don't mind sending you in my place, though." Her smile looks genuine.

"Oh, I wouldn't even think about taking the maid of honor's spot." Mom looks pointedly at Abby's belly. "Unless you're worried about making such a long drive."

"She's not." I grab Abby's hand and shoot out the door.

Roscoe's still out here with us, but he doesn't panic when I leave anymore, thankfully.

"That was quick thinking with the 'only room for two' thing," I say. "I can't believe my mom was trying to oust you."

Abigail shrugs. "If you'd rather take her, I don't mind. Or we can just tell her we called and the places that had limited space said she can come. I just thought I'd give you a graceful out if you wanted one."

I head for the car. "Oh, I did want one. I was impressed."

"I've had years and years of practice with my family." Abigail sighs. "Believe me. They're even more dogged than your mother when they want something."

Dad and Xavier wave as we head for the car. "Drive safe," Dad says, as if he's ever spent a moment worried about my safety.

I just half-heartedly wave and then hop into the car.

"It looks like they're making an effort," Abigail says.

"I mean, they've been here for a really long time," I say. "This is the first time they've really been this determined."

Abigail arches one eyebrow.

Color rises in my cheeks. "Look, I know what you're thinking, and I'm not sure you really understand—"

"I'm not sure you do know what I'm thinking." Abigail leans against the window, like she enjoys the feeling of the cool pane of glass against her face. I mean, she is pregnant. She's probably hot a lot more often right now.

"Well, I'm sure you'll tell me."

That makes her laugh. "Yes, one thing I'm terribly bad at is keeping quiet."

"Spit it out, then."

"I think it's brave of you to welcome them back." I wait for her to elaborate, but she doesn't. This may be the shortest piece of advice she's ever given.

Actually, it's not even advice. It was just a compliment. "That's it?"

She shrugs.

"Isn't this where you tell me that I'm not really letting them in? You could say that I should give them a chance to be the family they haven't been in the past? Or you could remind me that people change?"

"Eddy must be saying that stuff already." Abigail laughs. "In my experience, people almost never change."

I didn't expect her to say that. I mean, it's probably true, but it's a pretty depressing thought. It sounds more like something I'd say than something she would. "Then why do you put up with Helen?"

That makes her laugh again.

"I'm kind of not kidding. She's horrible."

"I've never been in business with her," Abby says.

"I think the world might collapse under the weight of both of you working together."

"Actually, it almost happened."

"What? When?"

"A long time ago." Abby turns to look out the window again and sighs.

"You planning to share?"

She shrugs. "I mean, there's not a lot to say. She had already started her company. She told me that she was having trouble finding legal counsel for it, or at least, counsel she could trust. She'd had a lawyer try to cheat her or something. I told her when I graduated, I would come work for her. Nate and Robert were clerking for a big firm, but I went and worked for her over the summer. It was actually pretty cool. We got along better than I expected."

"And then?"

"Ethan," she says. "I got pregnant, and Nate and I got married, and that was the end of the Fisher sisters taking over the world."

"Oh."

"I'm not sure whether it really would have been great once I was a lawyer, telling her no on things and giving my professional opinion. I was more like a glorified file girl that summer."

"Did she resent Ethan? Or Nate?"

"I'm not sure," she says. "I didn't ask her what she thought. She was—she's always been this fireproof superhuman, and I didn't even really think about what she thought about it. My whole world had shifted in a moment, and Nate and Ethan became the center of it." She shifts her hands until they frame up her belly. "Isn't it funny how everything changes when you become a mother?"

I think about that.

Nothing changed for my mom, I don't think. She certainly didn't act like a mother ought to act. I'm terribly afraid that like her, I didn't change much either. I told myself that I was doing what was best for my girls, ensuring their independence, but was I really exercising the same brand of selfishness as my own mother?

"You're quiet," Abby says. "Are you and Eddy thinking about having kids?"

My laugh is so loud that it startles Abby.

"I'll take that as a no."

"It's a heck no," I say. "I'm done growing small people."

She's smiling. "Fair enough."

"I still don't understand how you can be a mother, a wife, a businesswoman, and still have the patience to deal with Helen now that she's back."

"I used to think she was superhuman, but now, as a seasoned mother, as a younger sister with a little more perspective, I've come to realize that Helen is profoundly lost."

Lost.

I think about that word. She's not in a place where no one can find her. We know exactly where she is. Which means Abby's saying that either Helen doesn't know where she is or that she doesn't know what she wants. "Do you really think you can do anything to help her?" In my experience, people like Helen won't let anyone do anything for them. Not that I've really ever known anyone like Helen.

Even Paul was more human than Helen.

Abigail's words this time are slow, as if she's still forming them in the nanoseconds before they spill over. "I hadn't thought, until this moment, how similar the two situations were."

"What situations?"

"Well, twenty years ago, when I found out I was pregnant with Ethan, I told my sister I couldn't work with her. I told her I was getting married."

"Okay."

"And now, she's back. She came to stop me from marrying Steve." She freezes, and blinks. "I wonder if she did that because she thought she might have a chance at. . ." She shakes her head. "She just thought it was stupid of me to marry Steve. But now that she knows him, she's seen that he's as good as Nate in his own way."

"What else were you thinking?"

"It's stupid."

"Nothing you think is ever really stupid."

She chuckles. "I mean, I was just thinking that maybe Helen showed up because she was jealous or something. Like, we had this chance to be partners, and Nate ruined it, and now that he's gone, maybe we could be close again, and then some new guy shows up before she has a chance to talk about it."

It may be the most brilliant thing she's ever said. "People think about jealousy as being another man for a woman, or another woman for a man, but I think jealousy drives more of our actions than we realize," I say. "You might be right."

Abigail shrugs. "Well, here I am, married and pregnant again, this time in the right order, and once again, Helen's here, acting like a hurt puppy."

"This time, though, instead of just giving up, Helen stuck around."

"I don't think it's really because of that. She hasn't mentioned a word about us working together," Abby says. "I'm sure the last thing Helen needs is a B-list lawyer looking over her big, complicated acquisitions, her corporate restructuring, and her hostile takeovers."

"I can't figure out why she's bothering with a tiny little retreat out in the middle of nowhere either."

"To be honest, I thought she might have a secret crush on David Park." Abby smiles. "I mean, you didn't want him, but he might be perfect for her, don't you think?"

"Helen and *David*?" Now I can barely talk for laughing. "That would be like a lioness dating a friendly goat."

"Oh, come on. David's hardly a goat. His family's wealthy, he's well educated, and he runs their entire American book of business."

"There's no way that the same person would like your sister and me," I say. "We're like oil and water."

"Are you, though?" Abby holds up a finger. "You're a beautiful woman." She adds another. "You're a successful businesswoman." She raises one more. "You're opinionated."

"Okay, but that's where it ends."

"I guess." Abby's brow is furrowed.

"Can you even imagine poor David, involved with someone like Helen?"

Abby frowns. "My sister's very honest about who she is and what she wants. She hasn't placed value on the same things as us, but she's not evil."

"Do you really think she might change enough to be able to have a healthy relationship with anyone, though?"

"I think that selfish people are usually selfish. I expect it of them. Takers take. It's what they do. What worries me more than takers who take is takers who suddenly start acting caring and kind."

"What does that mean?"

"You're obsessing about Helen, when she's only helped you so far. I know she's probably hard to work with, but it's not like she's a bad asset to have in a company."

"And?"

"Your parents, however, have never brought you anything but grief. While I'm impressed with your willingness to welcome them back, their ongoing presence has been far more concerning to me. When selfish people start doing something uncharacteristically thoughtful, start looking for the real reason."

Unexpected anger floods me. With a sister like Helen, Abigail's going to criticize my family? But instead of yelling at her like I would have a year ago, I try to step back.

Was she trying to hurt my feelings?

She openly and honestly acknowledged Helen's strengths and weaknesses. She told me a lot about their past. She told me she's trying to help her sister who's lost.

She told me she was impressed by my bravery. . .and she's worried about me being hurt by the very people who have hurt me more profoundly than probably anyone else.

She's my sister.

She's my best friend.

Maybe instead of being all angry and defending people whom I also distrust, I should try listening to her.

I think about what she said again. She doesn't trust them, and it made me mad that she's acting like I might not realize they're users. "I did look into things," I say. "That's why I asked for your friend's number. They don't have any criminal charges pending, and while they're about to lose their trailer, trust me. It wasn't ever worth much. They're probably better off losing it and starting over."

"Sometimes we're just missing one little piece of information, and then we can make sense of the puzzle."

"I guess," I say.

"But, I will also admit that while change is not common, it is possible."

"Am I an idiot for hoping that maybe they aren't trying to play me?" I hate how pathetic I sound.

Abby's hand drops on top of mine. "Not at all."

"Really?"

She squeezes my hand. "You've lost a husband, you've fended for yourself, you've met someone new and then had the faith to trust them. You've made friends and bonded with new family, and you're growing into a better mother and friend every single day. I'm proud of you, Amanda. Wanting to see the best in your family is just an extension of the rest of your changes."

The rest of the day goes really well. We find half a dozen dresses that might work, all of them from excellent designers. I may not have found the perfect dress, but it's better to find a few that work than just one that you're set on when you're relying on them comping it for publicity.

When we get back home, my dad's still there. He and my brothers are finally closing up the shed.

"Wow, you're still here?" I glance at the setting sun. "You've been working for like ten hours."

My dad pulls the beanie off his head, his greying hair flying up at strange angles. "I know, sugar bean, but the thing is, we got some news today."

I cringe at his stupid nickname. "What news?" My heart sinks. This is the moment I've been waiting for, the moment when I find out why they really came. They've done one moderately nice thing, so they think the time is right to ask for whatever it is they really want. I swallow and nod. "Just go ahead and ask already."

"My friend Ed found us a job." His shoulders droop. "And the car's fixed. I know work's going great for you, but it's been rough for us lately. I wish we could tell them to hold it for us until the new year, but they'd find new people in a snap."

My dad and my brothers have been working as an electrical crew, apparently. I pity the people whose houses they wire, but I guess it's honest work. Mostly.

"Okay." But, what's he asking for exactly? Does he want me to front him enough money so that they can stick around? That's not so bad. I could talk to Eddy. I might even do it. I mean, they're annoying, but they are my family.

Mom's head pokes out the door. "You're back." She beams.

"I hear that you're leaving." I hate the waiting. "So how much money do you need to—"

"Your dad and brothers have to go back and work," Mom says. "But if you don't mind, I'd like to stick around and help with the wedding." She's beaming at me, like this is some lifelong dream come true.

When I turn toward Dad, he's looking all encouraging. And other than paying for their hotel, food, and car repairs, they aren't asking for anything else. Even when I wait an awkward amount of time, they never ask me to pay them to stay.

"Do you need gas money?" I finally ask. "Or a loan to help you keep the house?"

Dad shakes his head. "No, Ed said they'd send me an advance on our first paycheck, so that'll hold us over."

I can't believe what he's saying.

"We can come back for the wedding," Roy says. "Dad made 'em promise." He's not even really my brother. He's a stepbrother. I didn't think it really mattered to him whether I got married, much less whether he was present for it.

I blink.

"You'll forgive us, right?" Peter asks.

"Of course," I say.

"And you'll look after yer ma until we get back?" Dad asks.

"Maybe people can change," Abby whispers.

I hate how desperately I hope that she's right.

❧ 6 ❧

DONNA

When I was in college, I stayed in the residence hall in a room I shared with an assigned roommate. The one assigned to me my freshman year was obsessed with gaming and spent thousands of dollars on a game console, multiple laptop screens, and extensive special gear. Other than classes, which she often managed to get notes for online, she almost never left the shared space.

She barely even left to eat.

She ordered Chinese food and pizza regularly, and sometimes she'd even pay someone to bring her burgers. This was way before Uber Eats and whatnot sprang up. Her refusal to ever leave the room meant that I never really had a moment to myself in my own home. I didn't care too much—at least, not until I got a boyfriend.

Once Charlie and I started dating, it became much more irritating. He had a roommate too, and that guy was a shut-in, practically. He was a biomechanics major, and he was obsessed with getting into medical school at Harvard. Since I was a respectful human being, I never brought my boyfriend back to my room, and he never took me to his. It just didn't seem polite. That meant that we made out in cars, in movie theaters, in the park behind a tree, and anywhere else we could.

It was a bit of a double standard, respecting my roommates but not anyone out in public. I was young enough that didn't even occur to me.

In all the time we dated, we never, ever spent any time on a bed. It's not that I was a saint or anything. We just didn't have access to one. Of course, I assumed that as an adult, it would be different. I have a credit card. I pay taxes. I have a car that's no work of art, but it's paid off. I can do whatever I want, and whenever I see Will, what I *want* involves him and me and somewhere that no one else is watching.

Only, I also have a son.

And a niece who lives with me.

Will has a great place, of course, but in a recent ice storm, a tremendous amount of snow managed to cave in the roof, and now he's temporarily living with his wonderful parents. It's awesome he has that option, but it means that I'm channeling my inner college student yet again.

Will has a lean build that makes me swallow every time I see him. He has amazing eyes I could fall into. His biceps, when he picks up a gallon of milk, or when he opens a window, or when he does most anything at all, leave me almost breathless. His low chuckle when I make a joke, his possessive gaze on me when he thinks I look nice, they're all things that make me want to shove him up against a wall and kiss him.

And he just asked me to marry him.

Then he went home after a quick peck on the cheek like a good high school kid should. I can tell he's as irritated as I am when, almost the moment I reach work, he turns up.

"Hey." He grins. "Aiden's at school?"

I nod. "I already went by the ranch for Mr. Park, too. He said I have maybe three or four more days of odds and ends, and then I'll be done working for him."

"That's exciting," Will says. "Right? Are you still feeling good about working here?"

"Yep."

"That wasn't very enthusiastic." His brow furrows.

"I like the work so far. It's rewarding, and most of the people are really nice. But I'm worried about working with your mom."

"Worried?"

"She never corrects me. I have to drag the truth out of her if I've messed something up. I want to do things the right way, and I need her to tell me when I don't."

Will's lips compress, which is what he does whenever he's thinking about something. "Let me think about that one. Mom won't want to ever tell you that you're doing the wrong thing, because she likes you so much."

"I'm glad she likes me, but she's also my boss."

He nods. "Beth's at work?"

The fishing tours are done for the season, so she's waitressing at Brownings every afternoon. It frees up her mornings for the photography classes she's taking.

"She's doing her online course."

Will nods, and then his eyes slide upward, slowing down at my legs, and then widening when he takes in the straining buttons of my uniform blouse.

I can feel the heat rise in my cheeks. "Your sister's uniforms are a little small."

He crosses the room in three strides and wraps an

arm around my waist. "I'll say." His head lowers over mine, his eyes fixated on my mouth.

"I'm getting some new ones," I say.

"No rush." The curve of his lips is devilish.

"Ha."

"Although, the last thing we need is for all the guests to—you know what? Let's rush that order." He's grinning now, and he does my favorite thing ever. He kisses me while he's smiling.

I always liked his smile.

I'd never thought about how it might feel to have someone I loved smiling with joy while he kissed me. His lips aren't as full. They aren't as soft. But I know the reason why. I know he's happy, and we're happy, and that joy reverberates between us in a way I can't really explain.

Everything about Will makes me happy, so when he deepens the kiss, pressing my back against the wall behind the check-in counter, I let out a little sigh. The rest of the world always disappears when Will touches me, but I think it's gotten worse since he proposed.

"I bet there's a room that's free." Will's voice is husky.

That makes my heart flip over.

"There are some perks to my mother owning the hotel, you know."

Someone behind us clears their throat.

And then they giggle.

I stiffen. "Will," I say against his mouth.

He nips at my lip.

"William Earl."

"You know what?" the throat clearer says. "I'll come back."

The voice is familiar, and my brain shoves against

the fog my boyfriend's—my fiancé's—mouth has created. Why do I know the voice? Then it hits me.

It's my future mother-in-law.

Will's mother.

I practically bodycheck him to escape and swipe my hand across my face, just in case he smeared my makeup. "Mrs. Earl. I am so sorry."

She shakes her head, blushing as much as I am, I'm pretty sure. "It's fine."

"What can I help you with?"

"Tina called in sick," she says. "But it's fine. You stay here, and I'll clean the rooms."

"Absolutely not," I say. "Maybe we split them up?"

"That's what I was going to suggest." She's looking at the ground, but then she glances up to grab the clipboard with the cleaning checklist on it. As she does, her eyes lift up my body, freezing somewhere halfway up.

She's staring at my ring.

"Sorry, Mom," Will says. "I just had a hotel-related question to ask, and your new employee was so charming. . ." As if he's just noticing that his mother is mimicking a marble statue, Will clears his throat. "Mom? Earth to Mom."

"Are you?" She finally moves, her eyes lifting to her son's. "Are you. . .engaged?"

"I was going to call," he says, "but it was kind of late by the time I thought of it." He keeps talking, but I can't hear a word.

Because his mother's screaming so loudly, and jumping up and down so enthusiastically, that no other sound is audible. "Oh, William! Oh, William!! You're getting married! To the girl of your dreams! We're going to have a wedding!" And then she goes supersonic, and no one can understand her but the dolphins. You know, if there were any dolphins this far inland.

"Alright, Mom. Alright." Will pats her shoulder. "Breathe, Mom. Try and breathe."

She hugs him, fiercely, and then she releases him and spins toward me. Her face is bright red, and tears are streaming down her face, and it hits me. This delight, this joy, this overwhelming happiness? I have no family to react that way. No one I can even call, really.

I mean, sure, Aiden and Beth were happy for me. Abigail and Amanda will be delighted too, I'm sure. But my mother's gone, and my lousy father, too. My brother probably won't even come. I'm not sure whether I want him to. Even if my mom was here, I doubt she'd react like this. She didn't love Charles, but when I told her we were getting married, she simply smiled softly and said, "Wonderful."

When Mrs. Earl's arms go around me, it's like something inside me that's been broken is glued back together. It's not perfect. It's not like new either, but it's better than it has been in years.

Marrying Will would have been the right call for any number of reasons, but gaining a new family right along with him is icing on an already delicious cake. "I'm so happy you're pleased."

"Pleased?" Mrs. Earl lets me go so that she can wrap her hands around my cheeks. "My girl, if you knew how long I'd prayed for this, for my Will to be happy, for him not to be alone." She beams. "And when I think of the tiny Wills and itty-bitty Donnas that will be running around."

"Mom," Will says, a warning note in his tone.

She waves at us with both hands. "I know, I know. I

71

won't pressure you. But you're not exactly young. Don't wait too long, alright?"

"Donna and I already talked it over, and if we decide to have more children—don't forget that we already have Aiden—we'll probably adopt. There are lots of kids out there who need a great home. Biologically producing a child isn't the only way."

Mrs. Earl looks a little disappointed for a split second, and then she rallies. "Well, whatever you decide, I'm still delighted. You hear me? Aiden is the finest little boy I've ever met, and if you have a little Donna, a little William, or a completely different family shape that you two choose, I'm just giddy for that, too."

I'll give her this. She's genuinely happy for her son, even when what he wants isn't what she wanted him to want. I need to remember that and apply her wisdom to my life when Aiden is old enough to want something more complicated than goldfish added to his mac and cheese.

Thinking about Will stepping up to protect me and shield my heart just makes me love him more. "Mrs. Earl," I say. "The thing is—"

Will takes my hand and shakes his head.

"It's fine," I say. "Your mom's been amazing, and I think she should know."

"Know what?" Her eyes widen. "Please tell me no one's ill."

"Nothing like that," Will says.

"Well, sort of," I say. "I have had quite a few miscarriages in the past, and the doctors aren't positive that I'll be able to have another child." My voice breaks on the word child, and I'm about to cry again.

"Oh, Donna." Mrs. Earl hugs me again. "Sweetheart, I lost three children in a row after having Will's

sister. It was the hardest eighteen months of my life."
She releases me and her eyes are so tender it hurts.

"I'm so sorry."

She shakes her head. "I had two amazing children and a man who loved me. I had what I needed." She sighs. "And you have Will and Aiden."

"I'm not sure what the future holds, but we really appreciate your support."

"If you do decide to adopt, did Will happen to tell you that my sister runs an adoption agency in Salt Lake City?"

Okay, that was fast.

"We haven't even set a wedding date yet," I say.

Mrs. Earl shakes her head. "Of course. Right."

I do admire her enthusiasm. Engaged to adopting in five minutes or less. I am sure that, for someone who loves family and children as much as Mrs. Earl does, waiting this long for her son to find a match was hard enough.

"Well, you tell her that if she hears of a sweet little girl who needs a home, you've got a great family for her." I wink.

Mrs. Earl's practically bubbling with joy as we split up to clean our respective rooms.

"A little girl, huh?" Will asks.

"I already have a boy." I arch one eyebrow.

"I could do a little girl, too." Will tosses his head at the checklist. "Need a hand?"

"Like you have time."

"I have some brakes to replace, but the ranch chores are pretty minimal right now. I've already taken out the hay and I made sure the water was de-iced."

My amazing fiancé helps me tuck sheets on beds, scrub bathroom sinks and counters, and change a light-bulb before he finally leaves. "Good luck," I say.

"Brakes are a breeze." He blows me a kiss on his way out.

I manage to go through and clean up the room assignments and complete the details on an online booking before his mother catches up to me.

"Looks like you had some help," she says. "Will has always been the sweetest about coming by to see whether I need anything when he has time in the morning."

"You trained him well."

"I hope I didn't upset you earlier," she says. "I say things without thinking sometimes, and I never want my carelessness to upset you."

"I hope your son and I didn't scar you. I'll be sure not to ever act that inappropriately here again." What if, instead of his mother, it had been a guest? I cringe internally.

"Really, it's fine. We're a small town. It's a small hotel. I know it's not the Ritz Carlton."

It feels like the right moment to address it. I hope I'm not wrong. "When Aiden was really small," I say, "he was kind of a spoiled brat."

Mrs. Earl's mouth drops open. "I can't believe that."

"You should. I had a lot of trouble dealing with him most of the time."

"But he's such a good, sweet boy."

"He'd demand an ice cream cone for breakfast," I say. "He'd refuse to eat anything else. Or sometimes he insisted on wearing pajamas, day and night. I couldn't talk him into changing them."

"Those things aren't too bad," Mrs. Earl says.

"I was at the park one morning where I'd met a friend, and she asked me why he was still wearing long-sleeved pajamas. I told her I hadn't been able to convince him to change."

74

Mrs. Earl looks confused.

"She told me that I was his *mother* and not his friend." I still feel pretty silly thinking about this. "I told her that I wanted to be his friend as well. I had a husband who was a real jerk to me. You met my parents, and you know my brother. I didn't really have anyone in my family who liked me, and I wanted that, desperately."

"Oh, Donna."

She's about to start comforting me, and I need to finish making my point first. "But Mrs. Earl, that's when my friend taught me something. Kids need boundaries. He liked me *more* for making him feel safe. For telling him no when he wanted something inappropriate, and for being his mother and not his pal."

"Good for you," Mrs. Earl says. "A lot of mothers I've met still haven't figured that out. It must be why Aiden's such a wonderful boy."

"I'm glad you think that because, right now, I'm going to tell you the same thing."

She looks shocked. "But Will's grown."

"About me," I say. "I'm going to be your daughter-in-law, and I'm delighted about that. But right now, and especially when we're here, I'm also your employee."

Her eyes widen, understanding dawning.

"You've been letting me eat ice cream cones for breakfast and wear long-sleeved pajamas. I wish you wouldn't. Like Aiden, I want to be a good kid. I want to do things that are healthy for my long-term longevity at this job. So when you see me doing something like ordering the wrong conditioner, please stop me. When I carelessly enter something in the wrong place or the wrong way, fuss at me. I'm not made of porcelain. I can take it. And in this circumstance, I want you to do it. I think it'll make us happier as family, too."

Mrs. Earl smiles. "Will really is a lucky guy. You're smart, beautiful, and kind. And if you ever make out with my son behind the reception desk again, I'll dock you a day's pay."

Now I'm smiling as well. "Thanks."

"You're welcome." She points at the check-out invoices. "And while we're talking about this, you've been filling these out all wrong."

Oh, boy. The rest of the day is pretty brutal, but I asked for it. And I'm glad that my future mother-in-law is someone who listens.

❧ 7 ❧

HELEN

My parents aren't the kind of people who finish each other's sentences, but they're almost painfully alike. They both run their departments at Stanford. They both love being in charge, making other people feel stupid, and creating new ideas that will awe and impress their colleagues.

They both love to read.

They both love to schmooze, as long as it's 'their' kind of people.

They are perfect for academics. They met when they were both getting their PhD, and I think it was *like* at first sight, even if you couldn't really call it love. They never seemed very passionate, but they also never really fought, at least, not that I can recall. At every step, when I was growing up, if I asked one of them something and they said no, the other would be sure to say the same thing.

I didn't think I wanted a relationship like that. Actually, it was about the worst kind of matchup I could imagine when I was in school. When I met Oliver—we nearly came to blows in Econ 220 over the ethics of the debt ceiling—it was *just* what I thought I wanted.

His family had as much money as mine had brains. He had been a swimmer in high school, and he still had the broad shoulders he'd developed from swimming butterfly. And when he told me he loved me, I thought he really meant it.

It hurt when he refused to even pitch my business idea to his dad. I wanted to crawl into a bottle and never come out after he dumped me. Six months later, when he and his dad did the very thing I'd pitched to him?

My despair changed quickly to rage.

I probably owe Oliver a big old thank you card, to be honest. There are very few things that motivate me like a desire for revenge, and I knew that the best revenge was a life well lived. I'm sure he thought the daughter of a couple of academics wouldn't be able to execute the idea I'd shared. Or maybe he just didn't want his father to know a girl had the idea instead of him.

Either way, it taught me that I can't ever trust a guy unless our interests are entirely aligned. In reality, I think it's stupid to *ever* trust a guy. Even when they don't mean to, they can destroy a girl's future with barely a second thought. Like Abby. My business was well on the way to being the megalith that it is, and she could own half of it today, if only she hadn't thought Nate looked great in his stupid acid wash jeans.

And *again*, she's met a guy and saddled herself with another baby.

I mean, don't get me wrong. Her kids are great, for kids, and they're pretty smart, too. But their priorities are all out of whack. Mom and Dad took things too far, but at least they set us on a path of excellence. What's

Abigail's plan for Ethan? Is she really going to let him stay here and push cows around his entire life?

What I really can't understand is why Abby's not freaking out about Ethan's decision to work a ranch instead of going to college. It's not like he's decided to delay grad school or something. He's earning his undergraduate degree *online*, like he's a complete loser. If I see an online college on someone's resume, it goes straight into the trash, do not pass go, do not collect a single, solitary red cent.

More than anything else, Ethan may be the reason I'm still here, insisting on developing out this retreat. I plan to give Abby my share to run so that even if her legal practice here evaporates, which it could with a very light breeze, she'll have something to feed her many children. I mean, I suppose I could set up a trust, but people value things more when they feel like they're earning them.

It's stupid, but I actually feel a little bit of excitement when the enormous trucks roll up to pour the concrete. They've been framing up the footings for the resort complex for a week now, and we're finally going to have slabs. Amanda is, of course, taking the dumbest photos ever, smiling and waving alongside the best looking of our beer-gut, rotten-toothed contractors. I suppose she's pretty decent at photo editing, or she wouldn't have been able to make anything with her little account at all.

Still. What's the point?

I've had multibillion dollar deals that went together faster than this venture, so maybe that's why I feel happy about something so small. At least I don't have to fake my smile when Mandy waves me over to pose for the photo of the three of us in front of the Gold Strike sign that arrived just in time.

"Say cheese," Amanda reminds us.

Moments after our photo's taken, but before the concrete actually begins to flow into the first of the molds, a large pickup truck pulls up and a man in a white hardhat leaps from the passenger side. He practically sprints toward us, waving his hands. "Wait."

I eye him like I'd eye a cockroach in my apartment. Not with any joy, I'll tell you that. No one who rushes in screaming is here for anything good. "Who are you?"

"I'm from the county, and I just heard you were pouring concrete, but you can't. Your application had errors. It shouldn't have been approved."

It takes nearly an hour for us to get to the bottom of things, but the alleged errors are ridiculous. That alone tells me who's to blame. The horrible thing about small towns is that the people running them are absolute tyrants. I'd almost rather build in a third world country than in a small town. At least the government leaders in Kabul and Mumbai are honest about taking bribes.

They also have a lot more to lose.

When I watch our concrete trucks roll away, without a single speck having been poured, I'm ready to light David Park's head on fire. Unfortunately, because we aren't in India or Afghanistan, that might get me thrown in jail.

I settle for storming into his place of business instead.

The same little man who couldn't stop me before stands up and holds up both his hands, palm out. "I've been told you're not allowed to just walk back—"

I ignore him and keep on walking.

"Hey," he shouts.

I can't help my smile. How far will David Park go? He has a security staff onsite. Will he call them?

Before I've finished the thought, men in dark suits with earpieces shoot through a side door and step in front of the stairs. They cross their arms.

"Come on," I say. "Are you being serious?"

They don't have sunglasses on, so I can see the doubt in their eyes.

"What kind of threat do I really pose?" I put one hand on my hip. "Your boss told you that under no circumstances am I to be allowed to pass. Right?"

The man on the right nods. That means he's the boss.

I turn to address him. "Why do you think David almighty Park has blocked my entry?" I tilt my head. "It's because he did something horrible to me that was likely also illegal. He knew I'd show up at his stupid little office to complain, and he's lucky I'm not bringing more people with me." I wave my free hands. "I really, really need to yell at your boss, so you're about to have two options."

The man who nodded swallows. The other man, the taller one, shifts a bit. They glance at each other.

"You're looking at a black belt who trained so that she could walk the feral streets of New York City without terror. I'm perfectly capable, even in high heels, of knocking you both down and crawling over you to that stairwell. Or you can step aside and tell Mr. Park that you didn't catch me in time—scramble the feed just in case he's obsessive." I wave at the cameras. "Or you can try to stop me and see what kind of assault charges you're stuck dealing with." I drop my voice. "But I have billions of dollars, and that means I have the capacity to drag a legal battle out until it has created generational debt." I drop my voice. "I strongly suggest that you choose option A."

The key with things like this is not waiting for

them to think about it. Make their choice for them. I push past both men and practically jog up the stairwell. David almighty Park thinks he can hide after pulling that stunt? He must be kidding.

When I reach the office suite upstairs, I don't slow down. I push right past the secretary's desk and head for the back corner in a beeline. Only, he's not there. If anything, all this running around is making me angrier. I pause for a moment and ball my hands into fists as I think about where else he might be. If he was alerted that I'm here, would he really have run? Is he that big of a coward?

If so, why did he escalate this fight to begin with?

"Helen."

I spin around, forcing my hands to relax. I want to look as calm as possible. Or at least, not anxious.

David Park's standing in the hall behind me, smiling. "To what do I owe this honor?"

"Honor?" I start toward him with very little idea of what exactly I'm going to do. "You just fired a shot in my direction, David, and I'm not sure you really have any idea what you started."

"Whoa there, tiger." David throws up his hands.

"Are you really going to play dumb?" I roll my eyes. "If you didn't do anything, then why did you have two guard dogs waiting for me downstairs?" I step right in front of him, our faces less than a foot apart, and I'm still fuming.

A smile creeps across his face. "Let's talk in the conference room again." He tosses his head behind him.

"You sure you don't want witnesses present?" I can't control my glare.

He laughs. "I'll take my chances."

I storm past him, slamming my shoulder into his arm as hard as I can.

He follows me inside and then closes the door behind us. "For the record, you fired the first shots," he says calmly.

"Excuse me?"

"My sister, who has never once taken any interest in what I'm doing here, ordered the sale of the Ellingson ranch." He sighs. "You called her and made that happen."

"I warned you that I would." I sit down and cross my legs.

"And I told you that I wouldn't sell that property."

"If you have a boss, you have no real power." I can't help my smug smile. "Face it, David, you can thumb your nose at me, but in a few days, we'll be pouring concrete and your stupid little prank will have been meaningless. So why piss me off?"

David inhales slowly, and then he stalks toward me, unconcerned, a lazy look in his eyes. "I was warning you." He sits on the table top, which is only possible because he's stupidly tall. "I'm not a toothless lion. My sister already wanted to slap me on the hand, which is the only reason she didn't ignore you entirely, but that doesn't mean that you can bully me. I have more than a trick or two up my sleeve."

"What does that mean?"

David stands up, shifts, and sits in the chair next to me. Then he spins it until he's facing me directly. "Let's start over, Helen."

"Says the person who just punched me on the nose." He must have lost his mind. "Nice try."

"You wouldn't have respected me if I hadn't done something," he says. "But I have some information you'll want. We could be friends, you and I."

I stand up. "I think we're done here."

He doesn't stand. He just smiles at me. "Why did you come, if you weren't looking to kiss and make up?"

"*Kiss*?" I ask. "Are you kidding me right now?"

"Speaking of kissing, how long have you been dating Kyle?"

Why's he asking me that? What does that have to do with—he said he had information. Is it about Kyle? I've never trusted him, but he's undeniably competent, and since I've been spending so much of my time here, I needed someone competent to run the day-to-day operations of HF Group. "We aren't dating."

"He was your date to the wedding."

"You don't get along with him. I know."

"I'm surprised that anyone gets along with him. I feel like he'd eat his own grandmother for dinner if he thought she'd taste good."

"He's not that bad," I say, but I don't really mean it.

"You have him managing your group while you're gone. I assumed that meant you trusted him."

He's not asking. Why is he telling me something I clearly already know? Unless. . . "What's your information, exactly?"

"Oh." He lifts his eyebrows. "I thought we were done here." He grins.

I want to slap it off his face.

"Feel free to show yourself out. You obviously know the way."

"David." I fold my arms. "What do you know?"

"I'm sure it's nothing that will surprise you."

"Then why did you say it was information I'd want?"

He stands, too, and once again we're standing face-to-face. "A friend of a friend is on your board. He told

84

me *you* were delaying an acquisition, but that your dear boyfriend Kyle is rushing it forward."

"Kyle is neither dear nor my boyfriend," I say. "And there's no way that he—"

Is there?

Would he be brazen enough to work against my direct orders? My time and focus being here isn't the only reason I'm delaying the major acquisition that was on the books. The company we're acquiring isn't very valuable, but they have one subsidiary that's developing technology we need. However, I can't push for the change of legislation required for that tech to take off if I own it already. Plus, the euro's on its way down.

I need six more months.

Why would Kyle rush something I specifically told him to delay?

The answer's fairly obvious. He's convinced the investors that I've checked out, and he thinks I'm derelict. He's stepping in and taking action to show them that he can do what I haven't.

The only reason he would do that is to convince them to oust me. Is he that idiotic? Does he really think he can take my group away from me? Even if I've been a little distracted, *I'm* the one who has made them all a killing. I'm the one who has selected every single project we've taken on. I'm the one who has wined and dined all my investors. There's no way that they would.

. .

But David's looking at me with something close to *pity*.

"What else?" I ask.

"I said it was a friend of a friend," he says. "My friend is the one who owns the Hagemann Group."

The company I'm planning to acquire. "And?"

"He was complaining that if the owner wanted to

drag her feet she could, but that he figured he'd just find a new buyer. Only, before he could start looking, Kyle came to him and said he'd keep it from being a problem."

To save the deal, Kyle's rushing forward, and my board's watching him save the day. Which means there's no way he's not using this to undermine their confidence in me. David almighty Park actually had valuable information. Inside knowledge that he shared with me. . .like a chump, for nothing.

"Why would you tell me all that?" Maybe he thinks it'll distract me. "I can fire Kyle from here. He's not a stakeholder. Not a significant one, anyway."

David's eyes are pretty intense. I'll give him that. "I thought you were just like Kyle when we were in school. Birds of a feather and all that. But you're here, obsessing over this little retreat your sister's friend is building. . .because you care about Abigail. I thought that maybe you misunderstood some things about me, too."

And now I owe him.

Obviously.

"Your sister was all too happy to help me out," I say. "Your dad's naming a successor soon, and she wants to both keep you here and make you look bad."

He frowns.

"I'll refuse to send her the files I prepared on your American operations, and now I've warned you of her plans. We're even."

"I'll set up a call with my friend so that you and he can announce that although the acquisition is delayed a bit, you're still moving ahead. You can use that to mollify your board."

I suppress the urge to slap him. "Stop suggesting ways you can help me."

"Why?"

"Because that leaves me *indebted*. I hate it."

He laughs, and then he drops back into his seat. "Oh, that." He shakes his head. "I don't keep track with my friends."

"We aren't friends," I say. "We're barely acquaintances."

He rolls his eyes. "Helen."

"David?" I sit on the top of the table this time, hoisting myself up with a small hop. "I don't have friends. It gets too messy." I lean toward him a little. "And I always keep track."

"How exhausting," David says.

"I find it to be far less stressful," I say. "So now that you're helping me yet again, what do you want for it?"

He leans back in his chair and smiles. "What do I want from the great Helen Fisher?"

I scowl. "A ceasefire here," he says. "Don't try to make me sell the Ellingson ranch or my beautiful new retreat."

He's irritating, but if I agree to it, then I won't need to see him anymore. I hate that, in just one move, really, he's beat me. I marched in here last week determined to make him back down, and now he wants me to wave the white flag. I grind my teeth, thinking about whether there's something else I could offer.

"And." He beams.

"And?" I splutter. "You're saying you want me to surrender *and* something else, too?"

He nods slowly. "The ceasefire is irritating, and maybe even a little embarrassing, but only between you and me. No one else knows about it."

"Mandy does," I say. "And Amanda Brooks."

He shrugs. "So tell them that I agreed to promote your retreat as well as mine for free."

"But you're not going to—"

He shrugs. "Different demographics. It makes sense. I had already worked up an ad campaign for couples. The girls can come stay at your place, and the guys can come be manly men at mine."

I hate him. "Why do you have an answer for everything, like you—"

"Like I know you, Helen?" He taps his fingers on the table only inches from where I'm sitting. "I think I do know you, a little bit, and I'd like to get to know you better."

Heat rises in my cheeks. Is he suggesting that we go on a date? "You like Amanda Brooks," I say. "You moved here and built this retreat so you'd have an excuse to pursue her."

"I was bored." He stands. "She intrigued me."

Past tense?

"But that's not what I'm saying anyway." His grin this time is devilish. "You thought I was asking you out?" He snorts. "I want the use of your brain." He taps my forehead with one finger.

An electric current flies up my spine.

I want him to touch me again.

Right now.

I inhale sharply.

"I want ten consulting sessions where I can pick your brain about what I need to do."

"Because of your dad's upcoming selection?" He's a little shrewder than I thought.

He shrugs. "Will you do it?"

I hold out my hand. "Ceasefire."

He shakes his head. "I want the consulting sessions, too."

"You're not doing me a big enough favor," I say. "I

88

could have ousted stupid, greedy Kyle and smoothed things over with Brett on my own."

"Fine. Four sessions."

"Done," I say.

This time, his smile is broad enough that it reaches his eyes. I hate how they sparkle, which makes me nervous. "I look forward to doing business with you, Helen Fisher."

AMANDA

One thing no one has ever accused me of is not having an opinion. As an influencer, it's been my job for years now to tell people what I think about products. I'll eviscerate certain things and love others. I like to think my good taste has been instrumental in the success of my account.

However, now that I'm planning a wedding, I need to choose food that the majority of the guests coming will enjoy. That feels. . .hard. Abigail has been my go-to for over a year now when I need a second opinion, and as a pregnant lady, she can put the food away. She's already gained enough weight that I'm afraid to ask how much.

It makes her the perfect person to accompany me on this dinner tasting so we can select the menu for Eddy's and my reception. Of course, Eddy got called away on some horse emergency. Why do horses always manage to gash themselves at the most irritating times?

I'm glancing at the clock for the third time—Abigail's never late—when the door finally opens. I hop to my feet. "Thank goodness. They've been pretty flexible, but—" Only, it's not Abigail. It's evil Abigail. "What are you doing here?"

Helen looks ready to march into a boardroom or something. She's wearing her usual business suit with stilettos, covered in a stupidly posh overcoat, as if that makes her clothing appropriate for the brutal weather we've been having.

"Abigail's doctor called this morning. Her something or another levels were high at the last appointment, so they're making her go in for some kind of repeat. . ." She throws her hands in the air. "I don't know. She insists it's not a big deal, but she can't go with you. Believe me, I do not want to be here either, but it was better than having her delay her medical care to taste some tacky tacos or whatever you're thinking of serving."

I draw my shoulders back and glare at her as powerfully as I can.

"Are you constipated?" Helen slides her purse off her shoulder. "I might have something for that."

I want to stomp my foot on hers. "No, I'm not. I'm angry. What on earth would make you think your help would be preferable to none?"

"Excuse me?" Helen's eyes narrow. "Are you saying I'm not capable of expressing an acceptable opinion on your wedding reception food?"

"I'm saying that I already tend to pick things that are too fancy for this area and its inhabitants. The last thing I need is Miss New York Snobbery to weigh in."

She laughs. "Ah, yes. Manila, Utah in all its glory. Why do you care what they want to eat? They're lucky to be invited at all."

"Why are you even here?" I grab my purse off the counter, determined now to go alone. "I have no idea what you're after, messing around with this retreat like you have some place in Manila. You hate the people who live here, you despise small town life, and no matter how long you spend here, you're never going to fit in. You threw a baby shower with a *circus*, for heaven's sake. If you've ever heard of anything more absurd, I'd love to hear it."

"People loved that circus."

"Yes, human beings can't look away from a ridiculous spectacle." I cross my arms. "But that doesn't mean they liked it. And similarly, they will never like you."

"You know," Helen says. "I think I've been more than generous with you. My sister says you're a decent human being, all evidence to the contrary, and she said you have good taste. Since working with you, I've seen no indication that either thing is true, and I'm really baffled that David Park liked you."

"Yes, well, cyborgs have trouble understanding humans. Always have."

"Alright. I'll just let Abby know that I offered my services as your wingwoman or whatever and that they were declined." Helen sniffs.

Is she. . .disappointed? Did I somehow hurt her feelings?

No way.

Nothing ever bothers Helen.

She really isn't like a regular person.

"You know." She's got one hand on the door. "If you think I will never fit in here in Manila, what makes you think that Abby ever will? Or you?"

"Why do you think she doesn't already?"

"You think I would never be able to live here because I'm a Stanford educated, Harvard business degree wielding captain of industry," she says. "But my sister went to Yale and Harvard and she has one of the most brilliant minds I've ever seen."

"And that's what will keep you from ever being welcome here," I say. "You think you're better than everyone else, that your mind is so superior to theirs that they're practically beneath your notice. But your sister Abby, big-brained though she may be, has a correspondingly big heart. She uses her education and gifts to right wrongs and eliminate injustices. She doesn't lord it over people and make them feel small. That's why, though you may not have realized it yet, she's already one of the most important people in town. It's why she belonged almost the very second she arrived."

"It's also why she's being run ragged with stupid problems that are beneath her."

"People love her," I say, "because she loves them. It's actually pretty simple."

Helen stares at me, but not with her should-be-patented terrifying glare. No, she stares at me as though she's analyzing me. It's the same look she turns on proposals for the retreat when she's deciding where the weak points are.

And then without another word, she turns and leaves.

Why does every single interaction with her feel like the most hideous argument of my life? Like I'm trying to catch a hurricane in a hydro flask? Or like I'm trying to stay on a miserable bull for a few more seconds before it breaks my back?

I'm nearly shaking by the time I reach my car, and that's when I realize that I'm a little more like Helen than I'd care to admit. Mandy's meeting with some people from the county to convince them to re-grant our approvals, and Abby has a doctor's appointment that I really hope is just routine. Other than the two of them, I really don't have anyone to ask to come with me. I mean, I could ask Donna, but she's engaged now too, and she's probably plenty busy planning her upcoming wedding and dealing with a new job.

Abigail seems to know everyone. Her wedding was jam packed. Ours probably will be, too, but only because people like Eddy. I can taunt Helen about how people love Abby because she's lovable, but I'm not really the most welcoming person either.

If I'm being honest, the reason I hate Helen is that I'm jealous.

Abigail loves me. I know she does. She would have happily come with me and shared her opinions on things. She loves my girls, and she does everything she can to help and support us. But she loves Helen, too, and I hate that she has a *real* sister who is now here.

I've gotten used to telling people that Abigail's my sister, but now when I say that, they say, "Oh, wow. Helen and Abby look so much alike, but you look totally different."

Or they say, "I had no idea she had two sisters."

Like I'm a phony.

Like I'm second best.

Like I'm inherently less important to Abigail than Helen.

A tap on the fogged-up window of my car startles me. What time is it? Are the girls home? But when I open the door, it's not the girls. There are hours yet before they'll be done with school.

The person standing outside my car door is my mom.

"Did you want another somebody along?" She swallows. "I'd be happy to come."

Why didn't I think of her?

Probably because of all the people in the world, she's the one I've worked hardest *not* to care about the opinion of. I mean, mostly her opinion has been hurtful. She didn't care about me enough to help me with anything or even pay attention to what I was doing when I was a kid. And then once I got older, she only cared what I was doing inasmuch as it meant I might have money for her to steal.

Only this time, when I offered them money, they didn't take it. And Dad and my brothers are working, and she stayed here to spend more time with me.

It feels surreal, to be honest.

"Um, okay."

On the drive to the resort—David Park's resort is hosting the reception, of course, and the chef there was insistent that they have first pass at the catering job—things are pretty awkward. I'm not sure what to say, and Mom clearly has no idea either.

"You didn't see your brothers much while they was here," she finally says. "They wanted to get to see you more."

"You could have let me know you were coming in advance," I say. "Then I might have been able to make time to do some things. You know, show them around."

She frowns. "Maren sure is big. She's just like her mom."

"You're saying I'm big?"

"No." Mom shakes her head. "I mean, she's beautiful and really has a lot of opinions for a young woman. She's hard to boss."

"Maren's a mean-girl brat. I can't believe you think I was like that." That's not entirely fair. She's gotten a lot better since being around Izzy, but still.

"It's all coming out wrong," Mom says. "I'm trying to say something nice."

My hands grip the wheel tightly. "I know you are. It's just weird, a compliment coming from you."

She sighs.

"Just be patient, okay?" When I glance her way, she's staring at her hands where they're folded in her lap.

"I know I'm a bad mother."

And now she's putting me in the position of having to argue with her. Well, I won't. Bad was a nice word for the kind of mother she was. Neglectful, selfish, embarrassing. They'd all have been insufficient to address the breadth of her deficiencies as well.

"For years, I left you alone cuz I didn't have a right to show up and crow about your success. I didn't help you with them none. But then when I saw you getting married again. . ."

"That's when you what? Why are you really here? You have to want money, right?"

"Amanda, that's not fair."

"Two months after Paul and I got married, you showed up. You guys wouldn't leave, not until Paul bought you a car and gave you a pile of money to pay off your credit cards."

"We didn't have a choice," Mom says. "You know your dad had a drinking problem back then, and we owed some scary guys."

I'm tired of hearing all her excuses. "What do you really need this time?" I ask. "If you just tell me, maybe I can help." And then I'll finally understand why they came. Even sweet, forgiving Abby doesn't buy the act.

Mom's face looks hurt when I finally glance her way. Well, too bad. I refuse to apologize for the truth.

When we reach the taste-testing, she has her forced smile firmly in place. "Ain't this the nicest place for a wedding I ever seen?" She's looking around like a schoolgirl.

Which might be fine if she was Maren, but a nearly seventy-year-old woman acting like she thinks she's a teen?

It's embarrassing.

This type of absurdity is at least known territory.

She gives me her input on the food. She hates all the frufru things, which is probably exactly what I needed to hear. No mussels, escargot, or caviar. She practically gagged when she saw the Wagyu tartare. She liked the burrata, which they paired with fresh peaches and tomatoes, layered on toasted French bread, but she said, "Why did they have to ruin the peaches like that? Someone should tell them that peaches don't go with tomatoes."

All in all, I probably selected a better menu with her help, given the majority of the audience will probably share her culinary close-mindedness.

When we head for the car, Mom's head is down. She's almost shuffling as she walks, probably because of the intermittent ice patches. But for the first time, when I look at her, I see a frail old woman.

I was so busy when I was growing up tallying her shortcomings that I never really considered what her life was like. Maybe she hated missing my activities. Maybe it gutted her to always be begging me for money.

But what if I was the only person she knew each time who had any?

"Thanks, Mom," I finally force myself to say. Because above all else, she was at least trying today.

I'm climbing into the driver's side when movement catches my eye. It's David Park, waving. I stand again, closing the door. The last thing I need is loads of questions from my mom. It took enough convincing from me to get Eddy to agree to this as the venue. If Mom misunderstands something and sets him off again. . .

"I didn't know you were coming," he says. "I hope they treated you well."

"Of course," I say. "Your chef's better than I expected, even. I told him I don't need to meet with anyone else, and we have a final menu."

David beams. "I'm happy to hear it. I sort of poached him from California. He's a few years away from retirement, and that's perfect timing. See, California has this horrible claw-back thing on retirement funds. If the professional works for five years or more outside of California before retiring, they won't insist on being paid taxes out of his or her retirement savings. I heard that he wanted to work somewhere else for five years before retiring, and I used that to convince him that Utah would be just the place."

"I hope he doesn't hate it."

"He's a big hiker. I kind of glossed over the lack of shopping and amenities and spent a lot of time oohing and aahing about the Gorge."

"It is a spectacular view." I can't help my half-smile. "Will you miss it?"

"Miss it?" David's eyebrows rise. "Why?"

"Helen said—" I snap my mouth shut. "No reason."

He grins. "I can imagine what Helen said, but we've come to terms." He looks shockingly smug. Very few people look that way after an interaction with my new business partner.

"I thought you hated her."

"I hated her date to that wedding. Kyle is the worst kind of person."

"So is Helen."

"Oh, I'm not so sure," he says. "She's a tough nut, to

be sure, but I think if she cracks, she might not be so bad after all."

I can hardly process what he's saying.

"But listen, I won't keep you." He glances at the windshield. "It looks like you have someone who came with you." He squints. "It's not Abby, is it?"

I shake my head. "It's a friend who came to help me pick food. Abby's at a doctor's appointment."

"She's having another kid, huh?" He whistles. "Greedy, isn't it?"

I laugh. "You sound like Donna. You want kids?"

He shrugs. "I'd love a dozen, but you know, they're a little hard to come by when you only want them with the perfect mother." He sighs. "All the ones I'd be willing to take get snapped up."

Just another reason we weren't a good fit. Eddy gets that I am *done* with the tiny-human-making. At least David's a guy. He can marry someone half his age and have his twelve kids if he wants. I hope he does.

"You should ignore Helen's taunts and head back to California," I say. "There are way more women there who might be decent mothers."

He bites his lip. "I'll keep that advice in mind, but for right now, I've just negotiated myself a pretty decent opportunity."

I can't help my curiosity. "With Helen?" When he doesn't immediately say no, it makes me nervous. "Because she's got partners. She can't just go around selling and buying things on her own."

He smiles the half-smile I'm most used to seeing on him. "She didn't buy or sell or trade anything that wasn't entirely hers."

Now I really want to know what he's talking about. But my mom chooses that moment to open her door. "Who's this?"

99

"We better go."

Before David can be the polite soul he is, I wave at Mom, climb in the door and turn on my engine. His eyes are wide when we tear out of the parking lot. The last thing I want is for David Park to meet my mother. I'd like it if at least some of the residents of the area didn't connect me to her, and he does not want to be on her call list when she does need money.

"He was handsome," Mom says.

"We used to date," I say. "Kind of."

Why did I say that? I'm an idiot.

Mom pelts me with questions the entire way home. I'm not sure why it makes me blush so much, or why I tell her so much about our history. How he pursued me when Eddy was on tour, how he took me to Abby's wedding, and how Eddy showed up and they nearly came to blows.

"How exciting," Mom says. "You do take after me." She looks almost proud.

"What?"

"Your dad wasn't my only suitor, you know." She tosses her hair.

"Um, yeah, how could I ever forget *Roy's dad?*" I cringe saying it. The year Dad was in prison, Mom made a new boyfriend, and when Dad got out and he ran off his competition, the loser she was dating left his son with us.

Roy's been part of our family ever since.

If you're in a bad enough situation that joining my family is a step up, let's just say your life must be in dire straits. Maybe that's why Roy was always my least obnoxious brother. I wonder whether he thought he might get kicked out. He's also never understood why I ran away and never looked back, so he's not that bright.

My mom's still comparing our love lives, and I feel ill.

The rest of the way home, I'm subjected to the most terrifying stories about the guys Mom dated. Objectively speaking, my dad still sounds like he was the worst prospect. She's either exaggerating, or she had very poor judgment. I don't bother asking which— it's unlikely most of what I'm hearing is even true. Instead, I just smile and make little comments here and there, forcing myself to pretend to enjoy it.

The funny thing about pretending is that sometimes you forget you're doing it. That long drive becomes, possibly, the best time I've ever spent with my mom. When I drop her off at the hotel and Eddy calls, asking me to come by, I'm almost sad.

"Thanks for your help today," I say.

"No problem." She smiles. "It was my honor. I hope I didn't embarrass you too much."

That kind of stings. I never realized she knew she was making me cringe. "Not at all," I lie.

"That's nice of you to say."

For the first time in a very long time, I actually feel kind of lousy about the anger I harbor against my mother. By the time I get to Eddy's, I'm actually wallowing in it. "I might be a bad daughter, too," I say when he opens the door. "But if so, isn't that also her fault?"

"Good to see you, too." He's smiling when he presses a kiss against my lips. Eddy's arms wrap around me and it's like I can breathe again. I don't really have to worry about whether I'm a bad person.

If someone like Eddy likes me, I can't be that bad.

"That menu you sent sounds perfect. I kind of expected more seafood soufflés or something."

I laugh. "Mom steered me away from anything really good."

"Sounds like she was the perfect assistant." He takes my hand and drags me into the family room. "If it's something you think is classy and perfect, it will probably be widely under-appreciated around here."

I sigh and drop into my favorite spot on his big comfy couch. "Mom said the same thing, but less politely."

"I'm sure she meant well."

"I'm beginning to worry that she might," I say softly.

He chuckles. "Worry? Wouldn't that be a good thing?"

"Have you heard of that internet thing, 'who's the jerk?'"

"Do you mean who's the a—"

"Yes, that." I roll my eyes.

"Sure. I've seen the posts. People posting about situations to have people comment and say who was wrong."

"I've always been sure of a few things." I hold up a finger. "The earth is round." I hold up another. "Gravity keeps me from being able to fly like I should."

He laughs.

I hold up another finger. "You can never have enough money."

He nods. "Sure, sure."

"And my family is a total loss."

He looks sad, this time. "You know, I grew up thinking almost the same thing."

"Your sister's great," I say, "and your parents adore you."

"That's true," he says. "But they fight constantly. Do you know how embarrassing it is to have your parents arguing over who melted the chapstick when you're at a track meet?" He covers his face with his hands. "Or shouting at each other in the grocery store about whether they should buy mayonnaise or Miracle Whip?"

"What's Miracle Whip?"

"Mom's from Georgia. She swears by it."

"Okay."

"Look, all I'm saying is that family is complicated, and a lot of people think theirs is the worst. Maybe yours isn't as bad as you thought, but that doesn't mean you're a villain. Your mom's here, trying to make amends."

I think about that.

"Maybe you should let her."

"It's hard, though."

"You forgave Mandy for faking her death."

I mean, I kind of did. I still get so angry about it sometimes that I can't look at her. Other times, I wake up in the middle of the night in a cold sweat, terrified she really did die. "I think I wasn't equipped to *not* forgive her."

"Well, if you can try and get over that, maybe you should try and get over your mom being a little neglectful."

"She disappeared for weeks at a time," I say.

"Alright, a lot neglectful."

"She sold my school books and bought alcohol with them."

He cringes. Sometimes I forget that he had some substance abuse problems too.

"Anyway, I'm going to try."

"Speaking of fresh starts." He smiles full throttle.

Sometimes it still catches me off-guard, like a front door slamming on my hand. Like a car backfiring. Like that moment the biscuit can finally pops open.

He's so unbearably handsome, and he loves *me*.

"What? Did something from our registry come?"

"Wait, did you put my address down?"

"I've been meaning to tell you that," I say. "I've thought about it, and I've talked to the girls, and we know your office is close, so it makes sense for us to move here after the wedding."

"Is Mandy going to be okay with it?" Eddy looks genuinely concerned.

"She's a big girl. She'll get over it."

"You know, parents whose kids are about to leave for college are always talking about not having that much time left." He's mocking me right now. Maren can be a pain, but she leaves in less than a year, and it's starting to freak me out.

"You don't say."

"But have you considered that, with your mother and with Mandy, you may not have much time left?"

That nearly stops my heart dead. "Mandy hasn't slowed down."

"Some people, like animals, don't. They run until the last second, and then. . ." He brushes his hands together.

"Stop." I shove against his chest.

"I'm just saying." He takes my hand and squeezes it. "I've been thinking too, and if you want me to move in with you there, I'll do it."

My heart swells. Neither of us wanted to move, but now we're both offering to do it. We may not be Steve and Abby, but we're not such a mess. "Still. I think it makes more sense for us to move here. I even told Mandy, and she took it reasonably well."

"Oh, good." Eddy's grin is back. "I didn't really want

to move in over there. With all the resort stuff, it's gotten even less appealing."

I can't help laughing. "Well, that was a very believable faux offer."

"Was it obvious I was offering because you'd already said you would come here?"

Now I'm really laughing. "That is so *us*."

"What?"

"I was thinking we're kind of turning into Steve and Abby, all selfless and loving."

"Don't compare me to that boring old man again, please and thank you." Eddy tickles me.

I squeal and kick out, bumping Snuggles. That's when I realize she didn't even hop up to come and lick the tar out of my hand when I got here. "Hey." I sit up. "Is Snuggles alright?"

"Why do you ask?" Eddy's staring at me intently.

"She's just lying there." Now I'm actually worried. He's a vet. Surely if something's wrong, he already knows.

"She has been sleeping a lot more than usual lately," he says. "So I decided to run a few tests." He sighs. "So after Roscoe's attack, you remember me saying you ought to get him neutered, right?"

"Yes, but then we had thing after thing. It's on the list. Didn't you say you don't really do those?"

"I'm a large animal vet. I definitely don't." He sighs. "If he had been humping things or if he was ever aggressive, we'd probably have prioritized it."

"Oh, no. Are you saying?" I look down at the snoozing wolf-dog.

He waves at Snuggles. "She's definitely pregnant."

"Wait, your dog wasn't spayed?" Now I'm sitting straight up. "You've got to be kidding."

"Haven't you ever heard the painter's house is

always the last one to be painted?" He looks embarrassed, at least. "I kept meaning to make an appointment and take her into Vernal, but it just didn't happen before I left, and then when I got back I was trying to win you back."

"And now the wedding."

"Which may be preceded by a litter of Roscoe's babies, unless I'm mistaken. She hasn't really been around anyone else."

"That we know of," I say. "But don't you think that we're going to be paying a single dime of pup support until we get a paternity test."

He's laughing, but I can tell he's a little stressed.

"It's Roscoe," I say. "I'm sure those puppies will be angels."

"Have you ever been around a young border collie?" he asks.

I shake my head.

"They're like tornadoes wrapped in fur."

He's probably exaggerating.

Right?

🎇 9 🎇

BETH

When I was really small, if I had a big decision to make, I would look for a daisy. In a pinch, any flower would do, but daisies were best. "He loves me. He hates me. He loves me. He hates me." That's the game my friend Hannah taught me when we were in kindergarten.

It was supposed to help me decide whether someone liked me, but it kind of became my go-to decision-making tool. It might sound absurd, but I felt like, if there was a God, this would be an easy way for him to talk to me. Surely he could control what kind of flower I would find, and I'd have a fifty-fifty shot of getting it right. If he just put the right number of petals on the dumb flower, it was like he was telling me what to do.

It worked when I had to choose between art and music. (Art, hands down.)

It worked when I had to choose which dress to wear on the first day of school.

And it worked when I had to decide whether to buy my mom a scarf or a pair of sunglasses for Christmas. She wore that scarf nearly every day the winter after, so clearly the daisy was right. That one was especially hard to find, given the time of year. I actually wound up stealing the daisy I used from a bouquet of flowers at the True Value. I felt bad about that one for a while.

But as I look at the pile of massacred daisies that Ethan gave me, ostensibly to cheer me up, I realize that my methods might be a bit too juvenile for my present situation. It may be time for me to update my process.

"Whoa. Should I read into this?" Ethan's standing in the doorway of my room, staring with eyes as wide as saucers. No, dinner plates.

The pile of discarded daisy petals does look a little ominous.

"What's wrong with me?"

"Do you pull the heads off of dolls?" Ethan asks. "Or what about the wings off bugs?"

"Stop," I say.

"To complete a full diagnosis, I'm afraid I'll need more information. How long has it been since you last skinned a cat or any other small furry creatures?"

I stand up.

Ethan takes three steps and wraps his arms around me. My belly has a clear and definite bump now. There's a baby in there, and I don't even know whether I want to keep it.

Whether *we* should keep it.

"Yesterday, I made my decision," I say.

Ethan's arms loosen and he leans back enough to meet my eye. "You did? That's amazing!"

"And then today, I changed my mind again."

His shoulders droop. "Oh."

"And round and round we go."

"My mom had her twenty-week ultrasound," he says.

"Wasn't she twenty weeks last month?" I'm keeping a lot closer track of that sort of thing now that I've got a baby of my own. It's a strange thing to be thinking.

"Actually a few weeks before, but she was a little late doing it," he says. "I was thinking about that the other day. That's when they found out it was a boy, and I think you need one of those. Aren't you almost twenty weeks?"

"In three days," I say. "But the thing is, I don't want to go to the doctor until I know what to tell them. Am I keeping it? Am I putting it up for adoption? What do I do?"

Ethan swallows. "Maybe knowing the gender would help."

I think about that for a moment, and then anxiety floods me. "I already feel really guilty about the idea of putting it up for adoption. How much worse will I feel if I find out it's a girl? Or a boy?" I shake my head. "I don't think it'll help me for it to feel even more real."

"Beth."

I look up into his gentle, empathetic eyes. "You should be getting prenatal care."

"I'm taking the vitamins you bought."

He coughs. "Swiped from my mom."

"Same thing."

"If I bought them, who knows who might notice?"

"They'd assume they were for your mom."

"It is so weird that my mom's pregnant the same time as you."

"It's not so weird because of her." I point at myself with both hands. "I'm the freakshow."

"Stop." He catches my hands and presses them against his chest. "You're *my* freakshow."

Ethan always knows what to say. If he'd said I wasn't the strange one, I'd have argued. If he said nothing, I'd feel awkward. Leaning in made me laugh.

Which gives me an idea. "I know I said I didn't know what I wanted, and you said you'd be supportive of whatever I decide, but. . ."

"What?"

"What if you made the decision?" Why didn't I think of this before? "You're so smart, and you're an unbiased third party."

"Hardly."

"You do have my best interest in mind." I clap. "Yes. I like it. You decide for us both."

"Alright," he says. "We keep it. Him. Her." He shrugs. "Let's keep it."

I frown. "But—"

"No? Okay, then we put her up for adoption. Or him."

I blink. "How can—"

He backs away from me slowly, waving his hands at me. "Nope. I'm out. Sorry. Your call again."

I laugh until I start to cry. "I can't decide. When I work up the resolve to keep it, then I start thinking about how many things I won't be able to do. How much responsibility it'll be. How I might let him or her down. I think about how this was not part of the plan. And, worst of all, I think about how I don't really want to raise a child that *he* helped make."

Ethan presses his lips together, clearly unsure what to say.

"But then when I think about finding a good family for it, and I think about a mother and father who want a child and can't have one, I get excited. I'd be doing this huge thing, and I'd also probably be doing what's best for this child. But what if he or she wonders later why I gave them up? What if this kid thinks it's because I didn't love it? Or worse, will it think it's because it wasn't good enough?" I shudder. "I can't do that to a baby, either. And once I meet the little person, I'm sure I'll want to keep it."

"So whatever choice you make, you undo it moments later."

"Something like that."

"What happened to the flowers?" Ethan asks. "Ritual sacrifice to the decision gods?"

I snicker. "No." I'm a little embarrassed to tell him. "There's this thing, where you pull the petals off."

"He loves me, he loves me not?"

"Wait, you've heard of it?"

His brow furrows. "Beth, literally everyone has heard of it."

"Oh. Well anyway, sometimes I do that to make decisions. Keep it. Give it up. Keep it. Give it up."

"And what did the flowers say?"

I shrug. "I lost track. Doesn't really matter—I didn't like either answer."

Ethan sits on the corner of my bed. "But Beth?"

"Yeah?" I sit next to him.

He places a hand on my stomach gently, quietly, and he waits. The baby kicks, and he smiles. "Those are your two options."

I slump. "I know."

"You have to choose one of them."

"I know."

"And you really, really need to go get some prenatal care done."

"I know that, too."

"Good." He stands up. "Then let's go."

"Excuse me?"

"I made you an appointment, and if we hurry, we won't even be late."

"You. . .wait. You did what?"

"You heard me. I made you an appointment at my mom's OB. Steve says he's the best, and they both know about you already, so you don't have to worry about that."

"But—"

"Let's go." He lifts me up under my armpits. "Let's go see this baby on the monitor, and maybe that will help you make a decision."

Ethan's a good person. A really good person. So good that I don't really deserve him. He makes jokes and sings songs and makes fun of his singing all the way to the hospital. And then while we wait, he starts making lists of the most awful, reprehensible baby names I've ever heard.

"We can*not* name him Adolph."

"Not Adolph. Geez. *Adolfo*," he says. "With an f, and an o at the end. It's a subtle difference, but I don't think an Adol*fo* would ever slaughter millions of innocent people just to solidify his power so he could conquer the world."

"Hitler jokes are not funny."

He sighs. "I know. If Michael Scott taught me anything—"

"He didn't teach you anything," I say. "He's a fictional character."

He plows on, undeterred. "It's that jokes about Hitler aren't funny. But I keep finding myself trying to do the impossible."

Like helping me make decisions.

Like holding my hand while we wait for the doctor.

Like making jokes when I want to cry. Or puke. Or both.

"Thank you," I say.

"For never giving up?" He grins. "Okay, here's one I thought of the other day."

I punch his arm.

"It's going to be alright," he says.

"You know that, why? Because of my marvelous track record of excellent decision making?"

He snorts. "You did choose to date the best guy in town."

"That's true." More surprising, he chose me right back.

"Elizabeth Ellingson."

"You didn't give them a fake name?" I practically hiss.

"They wanted insurance information," he says. "Lying on that is fraud." He drops his voice. "Besides, everyone's going to find out soon." He glances pointedly at my baby bump.

I can't hide it much longer. I've noticed people looking at me strangely, like they think I might be gaining the freshman fifteen without being an actual college freshman. Before too long, they're going to realize I'm gaining all the weight in one particular area. Actually, I've been a little shocked no one has noticed before now, especially Donna. She has been distracted. Maybe that's why I've gotten away with it. Or it could be that no one in a million years thought I'd get pregnant. . .

After we go back to the room, we hurry up and wait *again*. When a doctor finally comes into the room, judging by his white coat, he asks me a lot of questions that make me feel really guilty.

"This is your first prenatal care visit?" Arched eyebrow.

"How long have you known you were pregnant?" He taps the chart with the stylus.

"Why did you choose to wait this long to be seen? Do you have a family history of problems with your pregnancy?"

"Hey," Ethan finally says. "Is this the Spanish inquisition, or did you plan to check on the baby before you put her in the stocks and let people toss tomatoes at her?"

The doctor smiles then. "It's good to see an involved father, even if your anger is misplaced."

I brace myself for Ethan to explain that he's not the father. Only, he doesn't. "I'm hoping we can get the twenty-week ultrasound done soon. She's at twenty weeks in a few days, by our calculations."

The doctor nods. "We do those in house. Usually people book them pretty far in advance, but. . ." He clicks on a few things. "Sometimes we have cancellations." He looks up. "I'll let you know what I can find in the next few days."

A blood draw, one pee-in-a-cup, and a few more forms later, and we're being ushered into a smallish room with a big machine. There are cords draped all over like it's part of the rise-of-the-machines, and there's a kid who looks barely older than me sitting next to it.

"I'm Natalie," she says. "I'll be doing your ultrasound today."

"Wow," Ethan says. "When he said he'd see what he had, it didn't occur to me that we might get in today." He blinks and shakes his head. "That doctor was cooler than I thought."

Natalie laughs. "Well, this machine is new and so am I."

"Wait, do we want an ultrasound by a new ultra-sounder?" I ask. "Is this like, your first time ever?"

Natalie laughs. "I'm a little slower than the other techs, maybe, but trust me. I've done hundreds of hours of training, and the ultrasound is just a machine that takes images by wave technology. It's harmless to your sweet little baby, even if I am slow."

And that makes me start bawling.

My sweet baby.

Unlike the judgy doctor, she just assumes this child's a blessing. She's the first person, other than Ethan, to act excited for me. For us. "Thanks."

Natalie's eyes are wide, now, and she reaches a tentative hand forward, toward my forearm. "Are you alright?"

I laugh, wiping at my tears. "I'm fine, I swear."

Ethan takes my other hand. Poor little Natalie shows me how to lift my hospital gown up and shove the waistband of my pants down, and then she squeezes some gel, which is surprisingly warm, onto my exposed belly. "Now, as I mentioned, I'm a little new, so sometimes I'm a little slow finding the right—oh!" She clicks some buttons and freeze frames an image, and even to me, it's clear what I'm looking at.

It's a profile photo of the baby in my stomach.

"What a little darling. Look at her, posing."

"Wait, is it a girl?" Ethan asks.

Natalie shrugs. "I mean, I don't know yet. Usually we kind of call it a boy, then a girl, then a boy, until we know."

"I don't want to know the gender," I say. "Don't tell us."

"Oh." Natalie nods. "Alright. Some people like to be surprised."

"I'm not keeping it," I say. And just like that, I

realize that the reason I delayed this visit is that I know I shouldn't keep him or her. I want to. Or rather, I don't want to give this child up. But I also don't want to be a lousy mother, and I don't want to resent him or her for the rest of my life.

Natalie's eyes are soft, but she just nods and gets down to work. She takes images of the baby's internal organs. She photographs its brain. She takes images of blood flow and its tiny heart. And then she takes some screen shots of what I think might be the sex organs.

I wish it looked like more than blurry lines to me. I wish I knew what I was seeing.

"So it's a boy?" Ethan asks.

Natalie's lips compress.

"A girl?"

"She said she doesn't want to know." Natalie ducks her head.

"But *I* didn't say that," Ethan says.

I laugh. "It's fine," I say. "You can tell him."

"After you leave the room?"

Now that I've made a decision and said it out loud, I feel galvanized. "No, you can say it in front of me. I guess if it's a girl I might look for different parents than if it's a boy."

"Why?" Natalie looks genuinely interested.

I shrug. "Maybe for a girl, a girlier mother, or a more protective-looking dad. If it's a boy, I'll want a dad who wants to go outside and play with him. A father who'll be a great example."

"Well, start looking for girly mothers, then," Natalie says. "This baby is definitely a girl."

Something about the news makes me cry, which is embarrassing. I decided not to keep her, but it feels like I'm closer to her than ever before. My little girl.

"Let's call her Natalie," I say as we're leaving the hospital.

"Natalie?" Ethan asks.

"It's just a temporary name, and I like the idea of calling her after the first person who was excited for us."

"Even though there is no 'us' for this little baby," Ethan says. "You still feel good about that?"

I nod. "It's the right thing, for her and for me."

"Alright." He squeezes my hand.

I wondered whether, when I made my decision, he really would agree with whatever I chose. It seems like he will. On the drive back into town, he asks me a lot of well-considered questions.

Have I looked into adoption agencies? Have I considered whether I want her to go to a family where she'll be an only child, or where she'll have siblings? Do I want a placement for her that's close or somewhere far away? Do I want an open adoption or one that's closed?

He has clearly given this more thought than I have.

We're nearly back to Donna's when my stomach growls. Since becoming pregnant, I'm hungry *all the time*. No wonder I've gained so much weight. "Hey, can we stop and grab some ice cream?"

"It's twenty-five degrees outside," he says. "How about we grab some sandwiches?" His eyes light up. "Or we could go by Brownings. They have a pre-turkey-day special, and it has gravy on top of—"

"Natalie wants ice cream."

He sighs. "Oh, Natalie. You're so picky, and you're going to make your mother really, really cold." He freezes.

And so do I.

I mean, I *am* her mother, even if I'm giving her up.

But no one has ever called me that before. *Natalie's mother*. So cut and dried, like I'm a high school graduate. Like I'm a photographer. Like I'm Ethan's girlfriend.

I'm Natalie's mother.

The words are still tumbling around in my brain when I trot into the True Value and practically sprint to the back of the store. It is freezing outside, and I didn't bother zipping my coat up all the way, so it's gusty, too.

I'm actually not sure my coat will work for much longer. I wonder where people buy maternity clothes when they live in Manila. It's not like we have a department store. I'm tossing three pints into my little hand-held basket instead of two, depressed at the thought, when I hear a familiar voice.

"Beth."

It's Hannah.

I turn around slowly.

Her eyes drop to the ice cream. "Wow. Someone has a weird craving." She laughs.

"It's for Ethan's family," I lie. "They do these ice cream nights."

"You're really together, then?" She looks surprised. "I heard you're taking online classes, and my uncle told me you were doing a great job with his tours, but I kind of figured you'd change your mind and decide to leave for college anyway."

I shrug.

"Looks like you've been going to a few too many family ice cream nights." Her giggle's irritating. She looks totally different than she did in high school. I heard she went to a community college in Salt Lake, so it's not like she's really flying high. But I guess it's better than just staying here, doing nothing.

"Time with Ethan's family is the best part of my week."

"Beth?" Ethan's trotting down the aisle. "Did you find the ice cream?"

Oh, no. Hannah's on him like white on rice. "Ethan! So this really is for your family's ice cream night?"

Ethan frowns, but he's his mother's son. "Of course it is." He reaches past me and grabs a pint of Rocky Road. "Make sure to get that. It's Gabe's favorite." He winks at me.

"Well, I better run. Mom just wanted me to pick up some cornbread. You have to make it a few days before you want to make the stuffing, you know, or it gets all goopy."

"What's she talking about?" Ethan asks. "Remind me not to eat her stale stuffing."

I laugh.

I'm not in a hurry to race to the register, since Hannah's checking out, so I kind of shuffle my way forward, my eyes caught by the new gift display. Traditionally, Manila's shopping game is not strong. There just isn't anywhere to buy something for someone if you didn't have time to plan a trip into a bigger town like Green River. So if you have a bridal shower, a birthday party, or a holiday like Christmas or Valentine's Day coming up, you're kind of in trouble.

I guess they've heard our complaining. There's now a five-foot section labeled 'gifts.' Right in the upper right corner of it is a tiny little pair of pink fleece boots.

For an itty bitty baby girl.

My hand shifts without thinking. I tug them off the metal prong and turn them gently toward me. My fingers brush against the soft fleece, and then I compulsively press them against my cheek.

The profile photo of Natalie pops into my mind. "She's posing," the brand new ultrasound tech had said.

I have no idea what I'm doing, with this pregnancy or in life. Ethan has no idea how to be a father. My parents will hate the idea of me keeping her, and they'll be worse than useless in helping me raise a child.

If I have a baby, online classes will become my only option, and I can forget about going to workshops. I won't have the money for it, for one, but I also won't have the time. New babies need regular sleep routines, diaper changes, baths, you name it. You can't just head out on a trip and expect other people to watch them. No matter which way I look at it, I should really find little Natalie a better home than I can provide, with a more competent mother. But holding those pink booties and thinking of that profile photo, I can't do it.

"I want what's best for Natalie," I say. "That has been my number one priority since before I knew she was, well, Natalie." I sigh. "But my heart hurts right now, because I want to keep her."

And Ethan whoops and picks me up, spinning me around. Then he kisses me right on the mouth. "So do I. Let's do it."

🐿 10 🐿

DONNA

There are many things that I like waking up to in the morning. Since moving into this tiny house on the edge of town, I've actually grown reaccustomed to a lot of morning experiences I never had anywhere I lived while I was in California.

The pleasant chirping of birds, for instance.

I'm sure California has plenty of birds, but not near where I lived. I mostly heard honking and shouts when I was on campus, and once we moved into San Fran, it was even worse.

The fresh breeze, when it's not the middle of winter, inspires me to often leave my window open all night.

Once, right after moving into this new house, I even woke up to the sound of snapping twigs from a deer and its fawn outside, having breakfast on my front lawn. They bounded away right after we made eye contact, but it was fun to see the wildlife that's completely at home here, in Manila city-proper.

But if I had to choose my least favorite thing to wake up to, it would be a phone call from Charles. Or

Patrick, I guess. So when the incessant ringing wakes me and I see my brother's name on my caller ID, I roll over and try to go back to sleep. Usually he'll leave me an angry voicemail or send me a nasty text and then ease up for a bit. Not today, though. Today, he calls back three more times in quick succession.

I stuff a pillow over my head like I've seen people do in movies and television shows, but that just keeps me from being able to breathe and makes my face hot.

"Oh fine," I shout. "You win, you stupid jerk."

I'm swiping 'talk' when Aiden's head pokes through my door. "Mom?"

I wave him away. "It's fine. Mom's fine."

"You are, huh?" Patrick sounds even angrier than I am. "Well, that makes one of us. How dare you keep this a secret!?"

"Keep what a secret?" I yawn mid-what, so it comes out sounding more like 'Keep whu-hayut a secret?'

"That my daughter's *pregnant*!"

I drop my phone.

It takes me a moment or two to relocate it from where it's hiding beneath the mountain of puffiness my duvet has turned into. "Patrick?"

"—laughable, given how you belittled us for being bad parents. I can't wait to see what Aiden does. I'm sure that whatever it is, it'll land him in jail like his father. Or maybe he'll overdose on drugs and die, thanks to your *stellar* parenting."

Patrick, as always, deserves a nice hard slap from a two-by-four. He always takes things too far, like his measurement for what's appropriate just broke off and he never bothered to replace it. "Stop ranting for a moment and go back to what you said before."

"Are you really going to pretend that you don't know what I'm talking about?"

"Are you sure she really is?" I think about the bulky sweaters and jackets she's been wearing. She's also started wearing a lot of scarves and hoodies, even around the house. But that's just a teenager, finding her style, right?

Could she be pregnant?

"Who would the father even be?" I ask. "And wait. How do *you* know?" There's no doubt in my mind that Beth would never confide in her father about something she hasn't yet told me.

"Well you see, Donna, I know because I got an insurance statement, so I was hoping the responsible adult she was living with, you know, the one who said I was a miserable father and a terrible example, might have some answers for me about things like who the father might be. My assumption is that it's that unwashed disgrace who stole Jed's ranch from us."

"Actually, you cost them their ranch," I snap. "They are such great people that out of the kindness of her heart, Amanda Saddler set your horrible injustice straight."

"I'm sorry," Patrick says. "Your high horse is in a ditch right now, Donna. Once you've hosed it off, call me back."

This is definitely one of the worst moments of my life. My horrible, selfish, obtuse brother is calling me out. And he's justified. "I'll look into it."

He's talking again, but I don't have the energy to deal with any more, so I hang up. I know I should be eating crow and apologizing and whatever, but first I need to know what exactly is happening under my own roof.

I normally throw on whatever clothing is near the top of my drawers and call it good, but today, that feels insufficient. For women, clothing is a little like armor, and I need to be ready for battle. I try on a dozen blouses before I find one that says both 'you can trust me,' and 'how could you?' Then I'm thrown into a tailspin about whether I should pair a skirt and heels with it, to tell her that I'm the boss here, or pants and cross my legs, to show her we're still friends.

By the third pair of pants, I realize that I'm just stalling because I'm afraid. I have an elementary-school-aged little boy. I'm not equipped to be advising a teenager who has probably gotten pregnant.

And what if it's my fault?

Was I delinquent in keeping an eye on her?

Beth seems so put-together and sensible compared to her father. She's kind, empathetic, and polite, and she's dating *Ethan Brooks*. Is there a dreamier guy she could be dating?

How could this happen?

I mean, I know how it happened. But I'm still spinning. I text Mrs. Earl and tell her I'll be a bit late, and then I square my shoulders, give myself a little pep talk, and push through my door into the tiny hallway.

Ethan's already here. He and Beth are laughing. It looks like he cooked again. That boy gets up, feeds his animals, takes care of the other ranch-type things, and then books it over here to eat breakfast with Beth most mornings. Is he really the kind of kid who would have unprotected sex with a teenager? Clearly I'm a bad judge of character. First Charlie, and then this.

"Are you pregnant?"

Apparently, when I'm confused, I just blurt things out. I clap a hand over my mouth, as if that may change the reality of what I just said, or the possibility that it's true.

"I am." Beth's voice is quiet, but it's not scared or nervous. She clearly didn't just find out.

"And is Ethan the father?"

Ethan beams. "Yes."

Beth shakes her head. "No."

"What?" I rub my hand across my face, but I can't hide from this. I drop my hands back to my sides. "*How?*"

"Ethan's not the father," Beth says. "It was a boy my parents dragged me out on a boat with."

"Oh." Does that mean this isn't my fault? "So, when is the baby due?"

"I had my twenty-week ultrasound a few days ago," she says. "And I'm due on tax day."

"April fifteenth?" I shake my head. "Oh, Beth. How did this happen?"

"We're excited," Ethan says. "We decided a few days ago to keep her."

Her. It's a girl.

I want a little girl so badly that I could sob right now, and Beth didn't even mean to get pregnant. Why is the world like this? People who don't want babies have them. Meanwhile, I probably won't be able to have one at all.

As if my brain is too occupied processing other things, the rest of the words Ethan just said register. "Wait, we, as in you and Beth?" I mean, they are dating, and he clearly knew about all this.

Ethan nods. "At first Beth wanted to put her up for adoption, but then we saw these little pink shoes. . .and." He throws his hands into the air. "She changed her mind."

She got pregnant from some guy she met on a boat.

She decided to keep it because she saw some pink shoes?

Oh, yes, this baby's in good hands. "Okay."

And now I have to call my brother and tell him he's going to be a grandfather. I feel sick.

"Are you alright?" Beth stands up. "You don't look very good."

"Yeah, you're really pale." Ethan stands, too.

"I'm fine." I swallow and breathe in and out a few times. "I'm totally fine. I have to get my son ready and off to school." Yes. I can focus on Aiden. The child I have. The one who is already mine. Not the baby girl that a few days ago Beth didn't even want.

Getting Aiden ready to meet the bus takes eleven minutes, and Beth and Ethan are still in the kitchen when I come back inside. I'm going to have to get used to dealing with this all the time. I may as well find out everything I can right now.

"Your dad knows," I say.

Beth's head snaps up, her pupils dilate, and her breathing gets shallow. "What? Why?"

"Didn't you wonder how I found out?"

"I thought maybe you overheard us," she says.

I shake my head slowly. "Your dad called me. Apparently the insurance sent some kind of statement to him, and voila. Better than a baby announcement."

"Oh, no."

"Did you think he'd never notice?" I ask. "I mean, he's not the best dad, but he's got eyes."

Beth sighs. "I figured I could put him off for a while, and let's face it. We both do better when we don't see each other."

"Where are you and the baby going to live?"

Beth glances back toward Ethan like he might have the answers.

"My mom and Steve are remodeling his house, and when they're done, I'll have the ranch house to myself. We'll get married, and then she can move in."

"We'll get married?" Beth's face is incredulous, like he just suggested the craziest thing in the world.

"If we're keeping her, don't you think we should?" Ethan looks entirely serious. He wants to raise a baby that's not his, marry the mother, and provide a home for them all to live in. He's like a fairy tale prince on a white horse, charging in to the rescue. Except with a cowboy hat and very nice Lucchesse boots.

Beth would probably be fired as a princess in two seconds flat. She looks utterly unimpressed. "Ethan, we talked about this."

"But that was before you said you wanted to keep her," he says. "It's different now, isn't it?"

She sighs.

"It's not?" Ethan drags his chair closer, focused only on Beth. "Then what am I going to be to this baby? If we aren't getting married, if I'm not really going to be helping, then I'm what? Your boyfriend? Just some guy who's hanging around?"

Beth inhales and stares out the front window. "It's complicated, Ethan. I don't want us to rush through things that are supposed to be these big, well-considered decisions."

"Like having a baby?" He arches one eyebrow. "Because that's already happening. I just don't understand why you're upset at me for wanting to be there for you and the baby."

"It's not the right reason to get married," Beth says. "And it's not the right way to do it, either. My dad married my mom to save her from her parents controlling her life, and he ended up making things worse." Her voice drops to a whisper, and I feel a little bad for standing here, watching. "I don't want that for us."

"You think I do?" Ethan's eyes flash. "None of this has been done the way I wanted it to be done." He stands up. "The difference is that I put on my big boy pants and decided what I wanted to do about the situation we're already in. I've been patient. I've been supportive, but it's time for you to decide what you want, Beth, and then tell me whether I'm part of it." He turns, notices me, and startles, like he'd forgotten I was even here. After a moment's pause, he strides out the door.

I've never seen this side of Ethan.

Judging by Beth's expression, she may not have seen it either.

The sound of the door closing is pretty final. Beth looks like she's been socked between the eyes. I pull up a chair and sit down next to her. "It's a lot," I say. "I'm sorry you're dealing with this."

"With what?" Beth's hand drops to her belly. "The baby?"

"Of course, that," I say. "But I really I meant Ethan throwing a fit."

Beth laughs, but it almost sounds like she's crying.

I place my hand on the one of hers that's still on the table.

"He's being honest," she says. "If you knew how supportive, how patient, and how considerate he's been for the last few months. The last year, really." She shakes her head. "Ethan's not the villain."

"Are you implying that you are?"

Will chooses that moment to tap and come in the front door. I force a smile, but he can clearly tell something's wrong. "Ethan just shot out of here like he's answering a 911 call." He scans the room for signs of emergency.

"Everything's fine." I glance at Beth and tilt my head, asking for permission to tell him.

She shrugs.

"Beth's pregnant, and Ethan's trying to get her to decide what the next few months are going to look like."

Beth stands up. "I'm eighteen. I'm supposed to be working a part-time job, trying classes, and planning a few months ahead, tops. But Ethan wants to get married, pick out China patterns, and plant tulips behind a little picket fence."

"Hey," I say. "Picket fences are cute."

"Tulips?" Will's eyes look nervous, like a rabbit caught in the garden. He opens his mouth and then closes it again.

"Beth has decided to keep the baby," I say slowly. "But Ethan's not sure where he fits into all that."

"As the father, wouldn't he have a say, too?" Will's talking slowly, like he's trying to find a safe spot to step in the midst of an active minefield. "Or is that not what people think these days?"

"He's not the father." Beth's voice is flat. "I guess it's going to be a question everyone asks, but I'm already tired of talking about it."

I shake my head at Will.

He mouths the word, "What?" at me. As if I can really explain that he should let me handle things.

"If you decide you don't want to keep the baby," Will says, "Donna got some bad news of her own last week. Docs say she probably can't have kids. We'd love to have it."

My jaw nearly drops to the floor. "It's not a puppy, Will. You don't just put it in a crate and give it to your neighbor who has a rat problem."

"Who said anything about rats?" Will asks. "I was just saying that if Beth doesn't want it, but she wants it to have a great home, we have that right here." He turns toward Beth. "A great home, I mean."

"William Earl, I love you to the moon and back. Usually, everything you do and say is polite, caring, and considerate, but right now, you're even worse than Ethan." I point at the door. "Get out."

His shoulders fall. "I'm sorry, Beth. I'm not trying to be an idiot. Sometimes it just comes naturally, I guess. Congrats on the baby." He bobs his head. "No matter what you decide, I really mean that. Babies are always a blessing."

The second the door closes for the second time, Beth bursts into tears.

"Oh, no." I stand and pull her closer, wrapping my arms around her. She sobs against my shoulder for a long time. Long enough that my shoulder goes to sleep and starts tingling. Long enough that my left foot starts to go numb.

I want to help her feel better, but if it takes much longer, I may need to call the paramedics to move me out of the kitchen. Just as I'm working up the nerve to say something to Beth, she drags in a ragged breath and releases me. "Thank you." The whispered words make it worth it.

My poor little niece.

"I haven't been through what you're dealing with," I say. "But I was barely older than you when I married a man whom I thought was dynamic and brilliant and loved me." I walk into the family room, hoping she'll follow me.

Thankfully, she does. "And?"

"You've met Charlie," I say, my tone as flat as a two-days-open soda.

"Oh. Right."

"We make a lot of decisions when we're young, and some of them have consequences that we can't imagine at the time. I actually think you're smart for taking your time with this one."

"You don't think I should just marry Ethan?"

"He's what? Twelve?"

Beth laughs.

"But honestly, if you were telling me that the idea of setting up house with that handsome, earnest kid was your heart's desire, then I'd be all for it. It's so much easier to raise a child as a partnership. Or, you know, I think it is."

"He didn't help at all? Uncle Charlie, I mean?"

I shake my head. "That was my job as the woman." I sigh. "But none of that matters here. What does matter is—" Something hits me then. "Does the father know? Because if he shows up later, demanding the baby. . ." Custody battles are the actual, literal, honest-to-goodness worst thing in anyone's life. Or if there's something worse, they've got to be awfully close.

"He knows," Beth says. "Or rather, I called him. He insists it's not his baby."

"What a standup guy." I plop onto the edge of the sofa.

Beth shrugs. "It might be easier."

"Depending on what you decide to do, you may need him to sign off on paperwork. I hope—"

"As long as it's a paper saying he has no responsibility or legal connection to the baby, he'll sign, I bet."

"Well, that's something."

"But do you think I'm stupid for wanting to keep her?" Beth sits down next to me on the sofa. "The baby, I mean. I don't have anywhere else to live, and I don't want to get married because of a mistake. Does that make sense?"

"It does. It's like getting first place because the

actual first place winner was disqualified. You may have won, but it's for all the wrong reasons."

Beth tilts her head.

"Okay, I'm not Abigail, but I gave the analogy a solid effort."

She laughs.

"Look. What I'm trying to say is this. You have a place to live here, and even if you decide to raise a newborn in your room, that's still true."

"Can you really not have kids?"

"Do you remember the night Will proposed?"

Beth's eyes widen. "The night you were crying in your car?"

"I'd been to see a doc, and they said that between my endometriosis and the particular kind of fibroids I have, it's very unlikely. Plus, as people get older, it gets harder and harder anyway."

"And you want more kids?"

"I'm not sure this is the best time to be talking about this."

"I didn't even think about giving her to you." Beth's voice is small, and her gaze drops to her hands. "Or maybe I did, but not for very long. I want to stay here, living with you. But it would be too hard, if you had my baby. But maybe Will's right."

My heart lurches in my chest. "Right?"

She looks up at me. "I don't want to give her up, but mostly because I want to make sure she has the best family. One that loves her as much as I do. How well can you really ever know a family you're considering for adoption?"

I can't breathe.

"But you would love her. I know you would."

I nod.

A tear rolls down her cheek. "If I gave her to you, I

would need to move out. I think it would be too hard, otherwise."

"Beth."

She shakes her head. "I think maybe that's what I need to do. It's the first answer that hasn't immediately fought back. It's not like I really know what I'm doing in life, and it's not like I have the best job here or whatever."

"This feels like a pretty dramatic decision, and there's no reason you have to make it right this moment."

"Ever since I found out I was having a baby, I've been wrestling with this. Keep the baby. Give her up. Keep the baby. Give her up. No matter what I decided, it felt wrong. But this feels right, giving her to you." Tears are streaming down her face, now. "If she ever asks me why I decided not to keep her, I can tell her. Because who better to raise my beloved child than the best mother I know?"

And now I feel pretty guilty. Because the day started out badly, but now it's taken a turn toward sunshine and rainbows. Not for Beth, I guess, but definitely for me. Is it wrong to profit from someone else's misery?

It feels a little bit wrong. But it also feels surprisingly good.

I was once on my way to a meeting with investors on Stone Street when a clearly high man in a ripped t-shirt jumped in front of me. I do not have a black belt in anything—that was a bluff—but I didn't miss a beat.

"I'll give you one hundred dollars in cash," I said. "And you don't have to try to mug me, or even lay a hand on me. Then we can go our separate ways. Deal?"

The man had grinned a gap-toothed grin and nodded.

I handed him the cash and made it to my meeting on time.

Another time, I was doing due diligence on a deal in Brisbane when a spider the size of my forearm leapt out from under my car. A group of investors were watching me, and I didn't even scream. I'd done my research and I knew that huntsman spiders don't bite humans. I shooed it away—my heart beating wildly in my chest—and got in my car.

When an interloper tried to snake the deal, the Australian syndicate within the company insisted they would stick with me. The fearless American, they called me.

But looking at this pile of stuff?

I want to turn tail and run.

"Aren't these too small?" I extend my finger and poke the rubbery end of the tiniest little bottle I've ever seen.

Abigail laughs. "That's not for me, idiot. We just found out that Roscoe's having puppies."

"I'll admit that I'm not the most observant when it comes to animals, but isn't he a boy dog? What kind of bizarre experiments is your friend's vet boyfriend doing?"

"Roscoe fathered puppies," Abby clarifies. "And it's not my friend. She's my sister-in-law, Amanda, and her *fiancé* did not perform any experiments. He has a female dog, and Roscoe spent a little too much time around her without the proper surgical preparation."

"Apparently," I say. "That's a terrible plot twist. So why do you need to have teeny tiny bottles?"

Abigail smiles. "Hopefully they won't need them. Most puppy births are uneventful, but my neighbor bred Pomeranians, and once she had to dropper feed one of her puppies all night long before it got strong enough to latch."

"And you got them because. . ."

"Eddy's a large animal vet." She grabs a bag and starts sticking things into it, including the tiny bottles, what looks like a heating pad, and a big jar of puppy formula. Maybe I should have noticed that one.

"Okay, but they're his puppies, right?"

Abigail sighs. "They are, but I'm trying to show my support." She smiles. "And, they promised my kids that they can have one of the puppies."

There it is. "That's a mistake. You're about to have

a baby."

"I know." Abby sighs. "We've missed having Roscoe around, though, and if you've learned anything about our family yet, you should know that when something seems hard, we just double down and make it harder."

But she's grinning ear to ear. Abby has always thrived with more things on her plate than anyone else could ever hope to eat, much less digest. "Fine."

"You let go of that one quick." She narrows her eyes. "Do you want a puppy too, Helen? Amanda's not your biggest fan, but if I beg—"

"Don't even *think* about it." She must be out of her mind. A baby border collie? I'd rather scalp myself and make a wig out of it. Giving me a dog I don't want is just the kind of thing Abby would *love* to do. "In case that wasn't clear, I do not want a puppy. I will never want a puppy. The day someone gives me a puppy is the day it gets abandoned in a weighted bag down by the river. Am I clear?"

Abby rolls her eyes. "You pretend to be this unfeeling monster, but I know it's not true." She taps her finger on my nose.

Which makes me sneeze.

And that makes her laugh.

"You're the unfeeling monster," I say.

"But you're the one who came in here to help me set up the nursery. If that's not big-hearted, I don't know what is."

The reality is that, I just found out that I'm supposed to give her some kind of baby gift after the baby comes, too. Or rather, I found out that Amanda and Mandy are. I can't let them get her something without getting her something better myself. Since I already bought everything I could think of for the shower, I have no idea what else she might need. I figured the only way I'd come up with something great is if I can see what she has and doesn't have.

And that's why I'm sitting in here, in the room that blue vomited.

Apparently, setting up a nursery involves assembling a crib. After we try for a half an hour, strip two screws, and mash Abby's finger, we give up.

"Well, Steve will surely thank us for our efforts." I can't help my droll tone.

Abby scrunches her nose at the pile of mess we've stuffed back into the now-opened box. "It's the thought that counts?"

"You know, most clichés, like that one, are just dead wrong."

"I think he'll appreciate that we tried." Abby folds her arms and glares at me.

"Yes, I'm sure he'll be delighted that his job is now three times harder. Maybe he'll shiver with delight that his wife tried, and failed, to do a task he now has to fix."

"What would you have done if your husband was tired and busy? Just let him deal with it alone?"

"First, I'd never have a husband. Second, I'd never need to be assembling stuff in a nursery. But *if* I were ever in an alternate universe and that scenario existed, I'd hire someone," I say. "Then nothing would be messed up, and my theoretical husband wouldn't be working harder because of my ineptitude."

"I get it now," she says.

"Get what?"

"Why Amanda hates you."

I lift my nose. "I'll take that as a compliment. Your *former* sister-in-law is a self-absorbed, self-righteous, inconsiderate—"

"Hello, pot. It's the kettle here. Yes, I have your

reservation for eight o'clock on the books. We'll be ready for you."

This time I'm the one glaring. "I'm not self-absorbed. I'm over here helping you with your nursery."

"She's planning a wedding, which I have done nothing to help with."

"I know. I keep getting stuck as your fill-in. Speaking of, did that doctor test thing go alright?" I glance down at her belly. It's big. It appears to be fine.

She laughs. "It's fine. The alien I'm growing in my womb is A-OK."

I nod. "Good to hear. But are you a little annoyed it's another boy?"

This time, her laugh is loud. "You are the prickliest, most obnoxious sister anyone has ever had." She sits down on the squishy, oversized rocker in the corner of the room and sighs. Then she wipes the laughter-inspired tears from her eyes. "No. I'm happy to have a boy."

"Really?"

"Really," she says. "The girls are awesome, don't get me wrong. But I also love the step-on-bugs, poke-things-with-a-stick, throw-a-ball-as-hard-as-I-can little boys. Trust me. A little boy has a lot of wonderful things to recommend it. Plus, there aren't enough amazing men in the world. I have the chance to add one to that pile."

I can't argue with her logic there. I've found an awful lot of the lousy ones. Our next task is sorting through clothing and pulling off tags so we can wash them before little bits wears them. "Is this really necessary?"

"Baby skin is sensitive. If I don't wash it before I put it on him, he might get a rash."

"Please let me hire you a nanny." I yank a tag off without breaking the stupid plastic connecter thing again. "Ugh. Then they can do this kind of crap."

"I already told you—"

"I know, quality time, blah blah. You have to change his diapers so he'll know to ask you whether to smoke pot later on."

That one earns me a stuffed elephant to the head, which I probably deserve.

But I've been here two hours, and so far, it looks like she has everything she needs and then some for this little crumb cruncher. When my phone bings, I whip it out of my pocket like it's a lifeline. Please let it be my golden ticket out of tag-pulling and wipe warmer installation.

DON'T FORGET. BROWNINGS IN AN HOUR.

I swear under my breath. Talk about the opposite of a golden ticket. It might be the only thing I want to do less than baby prep.

"What's wrong?" My sister's eyes are intent, like she's ready to draw her sword and slay the dragon for me. It's cute. Unnecessary, but cute.

"Nothing," I say. "I just have to go meet David almighty Park at Brownings."

"Wait." She straightens in her glider. "Why are you meeting him?" Is that a smile tickling at the edge of her mouth?

"It's a work thing."

"What kind of work thing?" Abby bites her lip, as if she has more she wants to say, but she's stopping herself.

I roll my eyes. "Whatever you're thinking, don't. We went head-to-head on the Ellingson ranch, and—"

"Which I hear he still owns."

My nostrils flare. "Yes, but only because he did me a favor, and I decided to let it go."

Now she's smiling for real. "Magnanimous."

"Stop."

"Stop what?" She shrugs. "I just complimented you."

"Stop smiling that stupid, knowing grin. You've done that since we were kids, so don't think I don't see it."

Now she's beaming. "Helen, I don't understand why you can't call a spade a spade."

"I owe him a favor, so I'm going to review his business plan for him. That's all."

"You're going to. . ." Her eyes widen. "Whoa."

I stand up. "What does that mean?"

"I thought maybe you were having some fun on the side with the only person here who might possibly understand what you are. But you're *reviewing his business plan*?" She whistles. "This is more serious than I thought."

"Shut up." This time, I'm the one who throws the elephant.

"You're totally going on a date."

"Are you going deaf? Did the doctors miss something huge? I said I'm *reviewing his business plan*." And now I'm roaring like an insane person.

Abigail has never looked more smug in her life.

"It's not a date."

"Okay."

"It's not."

"The lady doth protest too much, methinks."

"I hate you, and I hate Hamlet, and if you don't stop, I'll. . ." I stomp my foot. No one in the world ticks me off like Abigail does. Except maybe David almighty Park.

140

"You'll what?" She lifts her eyebrows. "You'll start a hostile takeover of Charles Schwab where all our retirement savings and the kids' college funds are?"

"Do you really invest with Schwab?" I can't help my lip curl.

"Oh, come on. What's really going on with you and David? Because for you, reviewing a guy's business plan is like Netflix and chill to anyone else."

"I have no idea what that means," I say, "but David almighty Park helped me out. You know how much I hate being in debt, so I'm going to help him enough that he can never say that I owe him again." I shrug. "That's it."

"Alright," she says. "If you insist."

"What now?"

"You're calling him David almighty Park, and you're pretending that's an insult, right?"

"Pretending?" I roll my eyes. "How has my lawyer sister not grasped the nuances of sarcasm yet? I'm *mocking* him."

"Are you? You've used it enough, and with a very distinct tone, that it almost sounds like an endearment. Like a mother calling her kid a stinker."

She's still laughing when I storm out.

Which means I'm almost twenty minutes early when I pull up to Brownings. I plan to just sit in my car, but then I see him. David almighty Park—which is definitely not an endearment—happens to glance out the window. When he sees me, his eyes light up, and he lifts his hand.

He's so handsome that I want to put my car in reverse and head back home. So what if Abby's still there gloating? I should *not* be sitting at dinner with this man, going over his business plan. Thanks to Abby, no matter how I say that in my mind, it sounds dirty. My mouth's as dry as a Bordeaux Cabernet Sauvignon, and I feel like I've been backed into some kind of cage.

When he waves, I realize that I can't leave.

He would certainly press to know why, and that would be worse than Abby's mocking. I'll just have to endure this one meeting, and then I can put him off when he asks for the others. Maybe I can send him my recommendations via email instead. Honestly, he'd probably get a more thorough evaluation that way.

Only, when I get inside, I notice he's sitting at the table without a single folder, paper, or even a notepad.

"I thought we were doing our first consult today." I haven't sat down yet. If he even sounds the tiniest bit like thinks this is a date, I'm gone.

"We are, aren't we?" He kicks my chair out and points.

I try to imagine him doing that with Amanda, and I can't even fathom it. She'd be mortally offended. "But you don't have files, papers, or anything at all."

"I thought you had a photographic memory," he says. "Do you need me to have files?"

I shake my head. "But I figured you'd want to write some of my thoughts down."

He shrugs. "I have a decent memory, too."

"Fine," I say.

"Fine," he says.

And now we sound like dueling parrots. "What are you eating?"

"Generally speaking, I like to glance at the menu first."

"Is it your first time here?"

He shakes his head.

"Then let's see that photographic memory at work. What's on the menu?"

His eyebrows draw together. "I don't know, maybe a column with burgers, and one with sandwiches?"

I close my eyes. "The top reads 'Browning's Drive-in and Flaming Gorge Motel.' Then below that, there's a blue box with a phone number. Underneath there's a pink box that says Burgers on the left, Sandwiches on the right. The burgers are as follows: Cheeseburger, Double Cheeseburger, Bacon Cheeseburger, Double Bacon Cheeseburger, Pastrami Burger, Jalapeño-Bacon Cheeseburger, which is missing the tilde over the n, Mushroom and Swiss Burger, Bleu-Bacon Burger, spelled wrong, and then a space, and then French fries. The sandwiches—"

"Stop," David says. "Alright. I believe you. Geez."

"You didn't before?"

He pulls a face. "I mean, I did, but I thought it was only for things you're trying hard to retain."

"Nope." I tap the side of my head. "I have basically stored nearly every dumb thing I've ever seen up here."

"Your future husband's in for a real treat."

"I won't ever have a husband," I say. "But assuming I'm not being argumentative, what do you mean?"

"You'll recall every single mistake he ever makes."

"And that's why I'll never get married," I say. "Men assume going in to things that they'll be making mistakes. Doesn't that seem problematic? But besides that, I'd never be able to afford a divorce."

Instead of laughing, he looks sad. "If you can't afford a divorce, who can?"

His tone really bums me out. "I was kidding."

"So you do plan to get married some day?"

"Oh, I wasn't kidding about that. I just meant about that divorce thing."

He's looking at me with sympathy now, and I hate it. "You're not married, either."

The waitress shows up then, handing us menus.

"She doesn't need one," David says, "but I still like to browse my options and try new things."

"An optimist," the waitress says. "I like that."

As unimpressed as David seemed to be with my photographic recall with the menu, he's at least that impressed by my suggestions for his company. In fact, once I start making them, he begins asking more questions than I anticipated.

"You'd actually have sold off the entire factory?"

"Semiconductors have been reporting one of the lowest profit margins of any sector in the past few years," I say. "You should have seen that coming with the shortage in—"

"But what about my supply chain? I need to have them or I can't manufacture—"

"That's the reason that when you sell it, you insist on a ten-year contract as part of the deal."

"Ten years?" David whistles.

"Indexed for inflation," I say. "And you should make sure that part of the sales terms hold your company as the priority client, regardless of sales volume or profit."

He moves from one section of his company to another rapid fire, but finally, as he finishes the last bite of his French Dip, he stops. "No wonder you never do consults."

"How do you know I never do them?" I ask. "It's not like I have a website."

"I might have heard that you didn't before I asked for one." Is he blushing? "But you agreed to do some for me."

There's no way I'm going to touch that. "Now that we've had one, don't you agree that this one time was as good as four consults with—"

He throws his hands up. "Hey, now. You can't go

144

back on our deal. You said four, and I mean to get all four."

"But what more could we talk about?"

"I'm going to draw up a plan to put all these suggestions you just made into action. I certainly need your input on the implementation. Or are you saying you think I can handle the execution as well as you would?"

I roll my eyes. "And then what? Will you need me to look over your shoulder as you present the plan to your board, too?"

"Would you do that?" He looks entirely earnest.

"David," I say.

"Say it again." He smiles.

"Say what?"

"My name." He leans toward me, his elbows on the table. "I don't think you've ever said it without swearing directly after."

That makes me laugh.

"David, listen."

"I'm listening." His eyes are far, far too intent for a casual conversation over sandwiches. "I always listen when you talk."

"We aren't dating." That's not at all what I meant to say, but after his weird demand that I say his name again, it feels more important.

Instead of laughing at me, or agreeing that it would be absurd, he just leans back and folds his arms across his broad chest. "Tell me the stock prices on my company won't fall when I announce the sales of two of our biggest subsidiaries."

"Oh, they might," I say. "But your business will be stronger in the long run, and in another month or two, once it becomes clear why you did it and that you've strengthened your positions, the stock will soar."

"But the reason I asked that is that people might worry."

"I mean, sure, they might." He changed gears fast. "Helen."

Something inside my chest flutters at the sound of his voice, like the rich purr of an expensive sportscar.

"You're saying we aren't dating because you're worried that we are."

Oh, shoot. He's smarter than I thought he was. I can feel the heat in my cheeks. When his leg brushes against mine, it feels. . .*intentional*.

"David, let me rephrase. Just as people might have worried the stock will fall, with reason, us going to dinner, or spending another hour or two together over the next few weeks, might confuse outsiders. But I want it to be clear between us that we are not dating."

He sits up so quickly that my heart pounds in my chest. His head leans toward mine, his eyes staring at my mouth. And then his head drops slowly, his hands bracing against the table on either side of my body. His lips are a hair's breadth from my mouth when he whispers, "What if I don't feel clear about it either?"

In that moment, something my sister said comes back to me, practically flashing in neon letters in my brain. *I thought maybe you were having some fun on the side with the only person here who might possibly understand what you are.*

Some fun on the side.

He knows what I am.

That's what I do. That's always been what I do. Kyle. Thomas. Braxton. I love them and leave them, and I never look back. Why in the world didn't I think of this earlier?

Because of all the men I've ever *had fun* with, David almighty Park may be the most interesting. And also, the best looking. Without warning, like a sidewinder striking, my hand whips behind his head and drags his mouth against mine.

He reacts quickly, like he was just waiting for me to attack.

What I don't expect is the jolt of lightning that shoots through me, from my mouth outward, burning a path through me. It's almost like he's claimed me. *Property of David almighty Park.*

Oh, no, no, no. Helen doesn't play like that.

I lean in, matching his energy with my own.

Until a strange sound distracts me. Someone's rapping on the table. My brain decides to engage enough that I identify that the sound's coming from the knuckles of our waitress against the table top.

"This is a family place," she hisses.

Whoops.

I stand up, leaving a two-hundred-dollar tip in the hopes that will keep me from being banned. With only three restaurants in the entire town, I really can't cause problems at any of them.

David's smiling like the cat that caught the fattest mouse in town.

For some reason, it only makes him hotter.

Which annoys me.

"Let's go," I say.

He follows me out without complaining about not getting to pay the check. Thank goodness. I can't handle one of those guys, not even as fun on the side. When we reach my car, I point at the passenger side. "Get in."

"What?" His eyes light up. "Why? Are we going somewhere else to make out more?"

Is he kidding? "I figured we should find a hotel."

"A *hotel?*" His shoulders droop. "Are you serious?"

I've never in my life had a guy be disappointed by that suggestion. "I was, yes. But now, I'm sensing that's not something you want."

"Helen, why would we go to a hotel? That was such an amazing kiss that I clearly forgot where we were, but I barely know you."

"Do you really need to know me?" I don't even try to disguise the disdain in my tone.

"Yes." He frowns. "And what's more, I *want* to get to know you, maybe more than anyone I've ever met. You're terrifying in all the best ways."

"Not interested." I unlock my door and open it.

"You're not interested. . .in getting to know me?"

I nod.

"But you would want to find a hotel." His voice is flat. He's clearly upset, but I can't for the life of me figure out why. It's not like I said he's uninteresting.

"David, I'm picky, okay? Even for something like this." I wave my hand between us.

"And what is *this* to you, exactly?"

"You're here for a while, and so am I. Does it have to be more complicated than that?"

"You're profoundly screwed up." David shakes his head, pivots on his heel, and heads down the street.

I'm not sure four words have ever stung me quite so much. For some reason, as I drive back to Abby's, I'm crying. Me. Helen. Captainess of Industry. Queen of Business. Destroyer of Companies. Rebuilder of the Broken Conglomerate.

Crying.

Over David almighty Park.

If he thinks I'm doing those other three consults now, he's lost his ever-loving mind. I will never talk to that jerk ever again.

❧ 12 ❧

AMANDA

I hated Thanksgiving as a child.

For most of my life, I counted on the school to provide a somewhat decent breakfast and lunch for me. I mean, sure, the meat was questionable, and the produce was almost always from a can, but canned peaches aren't so bad. They were usually swimming in sugar, at least.

And when you're hungry, you're not very picky.

I'd also never really had anything better, so the hamburgers at school tasted pretty good. The corndogs were fine. The Tuesday before Thanksgiving, they'd make a really good, really big turkey dinner. It had the stuffing you get in a big gelatinous blob, and cranberry sauce that came from a can, and the mushy orange yams that came soaked in that thick syrup.

I loved it.

But the actual day of Thanksgiving, the day on which we were meant to count our blessings and say prayers and all that? I was always at home on that day, and if I was lucky, I'd find a hot dog that I could microwave myself. If not, well. Let's just say that one year, I found out what it means when a can looks like it's eaten too much and needs bigger pants.

I wound up trashing the clothes I was wearing when that can of mushroom soup exploded. I could not scrub the smell out, no matter how many times I tried. Whenever Thanksgiving draws near, I swear I can still smell that same odor.

And right now, I am staring at the recipe that Abby sent me for green beans. Sure enough, it calls for cream of mushroom soup.

"Hey," I say. "What could I substitute for the cream of mushroom soup in the green bean casserole?"

Mandy rolls her eyes. "I bought it. It's in the back corner of the can cabinet."

We have a can cabinet? *Focus, Amanda.* "Yeah, but say I had an aversion to mushroom soup. Then what could I use instead?"

Mandy arches one eyebrow. "Why would you have an aversion to mushroom soup?"

"Yeah, why do you?" Maren puts her hand on her hip. "Is it really unhealthy or something?"

I hate that she's already calorie counting as a junior in high school, but I really don't have the bandwidth to argue with her about that right now. "Maybe you can mix this up for me." I'm practically gagging just thinking about that smell.

"I'm making the stuffing," Maren says.

"I can do it," Emery says. "Here." She holds out her hand for the recipe.

"You just add water to make the stuffing." I glare at Maren. "Emery's making the rolls, the sweet potato casserole, *and* the mashed potatoes."

"Yeah, yeah," Maren says. "Emery's perfect, blah blah. But in case you didn't notice, the rolls came out of that bag, so maybe her halo isn't exactly gleaming."

She points at the orange *Rhodes Rolls* bag that's almost floating on the top of the trash can. Somehow it stuck to the side of the trash bag, staying visible even though the bin is mostly empty.

"Still, I think you should make the green beans." Otherwise, I'll feel guilty about Emery doing everything.

"I'd rather not," Maren says. "You're the one who volunteered to host Thanksgiving. I told you it was a stupid idea."

"But Donna's house is too small, and Abby's pregnant," I say. "I certainly wouldn't have volunteered otherwise. Believe me."

"Don't look at me," Mandy says from where she's leaning on the edge of the kitchen table. "I usually buy the nicest TV dinner they have. And I've already done my part." She holds up a bottle of wine.

My mom breezes into the room—which is about right. She's been up around eleven a.m. every morning this week since I told her to just come stay with us. "Did someone say green beans?"

We all look at her like she's out of place.

Because she is.

It hasn't been as awful to have my mom around as I thought, but even during her time here, she's steered clear of the kitchen. My girls make the meals now, mostly, thanks to Abby's kids training them and my general failure at all things cooking-related. Maybe I got that from my mom. . .

"Did you know that Mom started a cookie company?" Maren can't help her snort. She's never going to stop talking about that one.

"You did?" Mom's eyes light up. "Ooh, where is it? I'd love to go."

"You'd need a very precise time machine for that,"

Maren says. "Not only did it already close, it was barely open before it did."

"That's a cryin' shame," Mom says.

"Here." Emery hands my mother the very recipe she just took from me. "Mom doesn't want to make this now that she saw it has mushroom soup in it."

Mom spins toward me. "Is she still fussing about that?"

"That?" Maren looks like a hound who just scented a big, smelly fox. "What is *that*, exactly? Be specific."

I shake my head. "There's no need to—"

Mom claps in delight. "So one year, we were busy celebrating on the porch out front. The weather was great."

I consider telling them that celebrating means she and Dad were piss-drunk, but I decide not to share.

"Anyhow, the boys had gone to a friend's house or something, I think. And then your dad and I hear this huge *bang*, and when we rush inside." She starts laughing. Then she points. Like I'm a carnival side show. A court jester.

My mom's mocking me in my own home.

I'm not even surprised. It's actually her behavior of the past few weeks that has been more shocking.

"She was covered, head to toe, in mushroom soup."

"Rotten mushroom soup," I explain. "Mom never bothered cleaning out the pantry, and I didn't know that when a can swells up, it's because it's full of bacteria."

Maren's nose scrunches up.

Emery covers her mouth like she can smell it.

"Bacteria makes things smell really, really bad." I shake my head. "Haven't been able to touch mushroom soup since that day."

"But you ate Aunt Abigail's green beans last year."

Maren's looking at me in a superior way that really chuffs.

"I didn't know what was in them," I say. "It's the rotten smell that really throws me off, but when I've tried opening mushroom soup, it just overtakes me."

"Well, you're in luck," Mom says. "My recipe for green beans doesn't have no mushrooms of any kind."

"Did you bring your recipes?" Emery asks. "That was smart."

Mom taps her head. "I got it locked up in here."

"Oh." Emery's too kind for her own good. I'm quite positive that Mom's green beans will be terrible. In all the years I lived at home, I never ate a single thing she made, because she rarely cooked. But when she did, nothing she made was ever edible.

Or even edible-adjacent.

"It's fine, Mom. I can—"

"Oh, no, I insist," she says.

"Let your mother make her green beans." Mandy has a look on her face that makes me nervous. When she goes out onto the porch to put up the Thanksgiving wreath we took down for the most recent snowstorm, I follow her out.

"What was that face for?"

"What face?" Mandy's making her best Bambi eyes, but I'm not buying it.

"Why did you take her side?"

Mandy hangs the wreath, and then turns toward me slowly, her face a picture of delight. "Amanda Brooks, what part of today do you think is going to taste good?"

"Excuse me?"

She pins me with a stare. "You heard me."

"It's Thanksgiving," I say. "Abby gave us her recipes."

Her laugh-turned-bark grates on my nerves. "Abigail

gave you her recipes. That would be like me giving my pig Jed the ingredients to a soufflé and being upset when it tasted like a bowl of pig-licked mush."

"I may not be Abby, but I'm better than a pig. I can read, for one."

She arches one eyebrow.

"It's Thanksgiving," I say.

"And I plan to enjoy the car crash as much as humanly possible." She jabs me in the stomach. "And you should, too."

"Why do you assume that the first time I host Thanksgiving, it'll be a car crash?"

"You should have listened to me and Helen and had it catered." Mandy shrugs. "Don't take this the wrong way, but most things you do are a bit of a car crash. People love stopping to look at those. It's entertaining."

"Do you really think this entire day is going to be a mess?"

"Emery's store-bought dough will probably be just fine, assuming we don't burn the rolls. And Eddy's bringing pie, so I bet those are fine. Abby and her kids are coming with a turkey, thank heavens. But I bet the mashed potatoes are lumpy—"

"We decided to use the boxed kind."

"Even better." She's beaming. "I bet Abigail has never had those in her life."

"Look," I say.

"No, you look. One of the beauties of a large family is that you have a lot of oddballs, and it makes for great stories, like your exploding mushroom soup."

"That traumatized me."

"I'm sure it did." Mandy cocks her head sideways. "Do you know what humor is, girl?"

"It's stuff that's funny."

"Yes, but *why* is it funny?"

I have no idea what she's saying.

"It's funny because it's something horrible. Something we shouldn't talk about. But for some reason, it's been made okay."

"What?"

"When I get bad news, sometimes I laugh about it. It's a nervous reaction our body has."

"Okay." I'm starting to freeze to death, but if we go back inside, Maren and Emery and my mom will hound me again. I rub my hands on my upper arms.

"Why are racist jokes funny?"

"They're not." I scowl.

"That's right!" She slaps my shoulder. "Because now we don't just get nervous about them. We all agree they're wrong. So they're *not* okay anymore. But someone who's fat making jokes about their own weight? That's fine. Someone making jokes about their own religion, that's also okay. A black man can make a joke about black people—it's okay, because he's a part of the group being targeted so he can't really mean harm. Your trauma from back then is funny precisely because it's been a long time since it happened. You have to laugh about it so you can stop crying."

"You're saying it's good that this Thanksgiving is going to be really bad."

"I'm saying that, as a group, we have some rough edges right now. Your mother. Helen. Ethan and Beth." She drops her voice down low. "Something is going on with those two. I don't know what, but I've heard Abby whispering, and. . ." She shakes her head. "Mark my word, girl. Something." She tsks.

"Alright, well."

"Let your mother make her horrible green beans,

and you're investing in a hilarious joke for a future Thanksgiving."

When we walk back inside, my mom's scooping *Crisco* out of a jar and dropping it into a pot.

"Oh, no. Forget everything I said," Mandy whispers. "We need to get rid of those discreetly."

"Too late." I'm barely able to suppress my laughter. "I'll get *you* an extra helping so you're fully in on the joke next year."

She jabs me in the ribs, but it's worth it.

About ten minutes before everyone's supposed to arrive, as I'm changing into a cable knit sweater and spraying on some perfume, it occurs to me that my mom may not have something nice to wear. I zip down the hall toward her room, which is open a hair, but when I hear her talking, I pull up short.

Are Maren or Emery in there, getting some grandma bonding time? My greatest hope has been that they, without the damage I've had from years of neglect and indifferent behavior, might be able to actually get to know her. That they might learn a little something about where I came from.

"—told you that I can't help you with that. No, I'm not going to ask her for money. Not this time."

There's a pause.

"Because I said so. You're working, and that should be enough for now."

After the next pause, she raises her voice. "I already said no." She spins around then, and sees me.

"Hi." I wave awkwardly.

Her eyes widen. "Oh. Hey, dumplin."

"Can I come in?"

She glances at the floor as if she's embarrassed the room is a mess. In all the years of my life, I've never seen any room she has inhabited that would not rival a pigsty for filth. And we have an actual pig living in this house.

I feel a little bad for using a pigsty as my comparison. Jed's really pretty clean.

She waves me in, kicking at piles of clothes as I walk through the door. I try not to think about how many dust bunnies she's kicked her dirty clothes through.

"I wasn't trying to listen in, but I couldn't help hearing."

"I'm sorry," she says. "Your dad's just been a little stressed out."

When were they not? "Mom, to be honest, I've expected you to ask for money since the moment you arrived."

She sighs. "I know."

"I'm sure you owe plenty of people." Because they always do. "How about this? You've come and you've stayed longer than I ever thought you might." I force a smile. "But I have money saved, so how about I give you ten grand, and you head back home?"

Her eyes widen.

"Would that help?"

"We couldn't possibly—"

"And I can start sending you a thousand dollars a month." I haven't checked with Eddy, but I doubt he'll mind. Some people have child support. I have crazy-parent-keep-away money. Is that really so bad?

"Amanda." Mom reaches her hand out like she's going to set it on mine.

My entire body tenses up. We are definitely not in a place where she can comfort me with her touch. She freezes and drops her hand back to her own lap. "That's a very nice offer, and you know we always wind up in a tight spot." She inhales sharply through her nose. "But this time, we decided not to ask, and I ain't changing." She shakes her head. "No, ma'am."

I must have temporarily suffered some kind of brain fog. "You're saying no?"

"Yes. I'm saying no." She leans a little closer. "But if you could not mention the offer to your dad, that'd be really good."

"Mom." She's never tried this strategy before, and frankly, it's a good one. "Alright. Fifteen thousand now, and fifteen hundred a month for the next year."

It might be worth that forever, if they don't come back and cause problems again. Honestly, I bet Mandy spent close to two grand on their hotel rooms for the two plus weeks that Dad and the boys stuck around. Maybe more. She kept telling me that she got a deal for being friends with the hotel owner, but isn't everyone friends with her? I mean, she knows the whole town. If that's really her business model, how can she keep the doors open?

But even when I push again, Mom still turns me down. "Let's just go out there and celebrate being together for Thanksgiving." Mom smiles. "It's our first Thanksgiving together since you left home."

I don't mention that I didn't leave home. We were all evicted, and I landed on the couch of one of my friends, which was a huge step up at the time. "Alright. We can do that."

When I leave, I realize that I didn't even offer to loan her something to wear. I guess the conversation we had was both more important and more honest than the one I had planned.

After the tornado of people arrive, I lose track of any coherent thoughts.

Abigail, Steve, and their five arrive—his daughter's in town for Thanksgiving this year. I can't believe there will be six the next time she comes out. Abby must have lost her mind.

Next come Donna, Will, Beth, and Aiden. When I go to hug Beth, she yanks back like I'm carrying the plague. "Sorry," she says. "I have a little cold. Don't want to get you sick."

I guess she's not worried about Ethan, though, because they're holding hands and she keeps leaning against his chest.

And finally, Eddy makes it. "Sorry." He's unwinding his scarf when I realize he's not alone. He's got Snuggles on a leash. "She was freaking out when I went to leave. I tried to calm her down for almost twenty minutes, but no dice."

Roscoe rushes to her side, licking her face.

She growls at him an awful lot, but I guess like me, she's more growl than bite. At first, the pair of them circle the room like they're on guard duty, but after a few moments of hand sniffs and licks, they calm down. Then, a bit later, they wander off and lie down in a big pile in the corner of the family room, by the Christmas tree.

Thank goodness.

"Oh, no!" I spin around, looking for Jed. Roscoe's gotten used to Mandy's pig, but Snuggles might try to eat him.

"I put him in my bathroom," Mandy says. "Even if someone inadvertently opens my door." She glares at Aiden and Gabe. "He still won't get loose."

"Smart," Abby says. "You never know with this many kids what hare-brained things they'll do."

Helen breezes through the door five moments later and looks around the room. "I need some men."

"Excuse me?" Eddy looks at Steve, who shrugs.

"To help me carry things, obviously." She rolls her eyes like they're the idiots.

They follow her out, and Mandy catches my eye. "You could see where we were confused by that statement." Her conspiratorial grin may be the best thing about her. "I mean. I could use some men, too."

A moment later, when Eddy and Steve return, each toting large boxes, I'm the one who's lost. "What is that?"

"Abby said she was making the turkey, but Steve insisted on doing it." She waves her hand near her face. "Pregnancy gag reflexes and all that."

"Okay."

"So I asked what I'm supposed to do, and she said *nothing*, which I guess is fair. I'm not known for being a cook. But then it hit me what I could do."

"Which was?" Abigail stands up and walks into the room. She's not waddling, but her belly's pronounced. I don't miss that at all.

"What did Dad's friend always bring when he came for Thanksgiving?" She's beaming at Abigail.

"Chocolate covered cherries?" Her eyes light up.

I hate it.

"You didn't." Abby's rubbing her hands together.

Helen nods. "You betcha. I almost forgot how much we loved them. Remember when we each ate an entire box and Mom screamed for like an hour?"

"She never screamed," Abby says. "Except for that year."

"I got everyone their own huge box." Helen gestures to where the guys put the boxes on the exterior wall. "So when we're all done with dinner, you can each grab yours."

"I hate cherries," I say.

"You ate them on that cheesecake," Abby says.

"Cherry Coke is your favorite." Maren's a traitor.

"And you love cherry vanilla ice cream." I didn't expect it from Emery.

I narrow my eyes. "It's a new thing. I burned out on them."

"Great. Then can I have yours?" Eddy's an idiot. I'm marrying an idiot.

"Hey," Mandy says. "Let's eat."

A knock at the door has me smiling. I wondered whether he would actually show.

"Isn't everyone here?" Abby's eyes cut my direction. "Please tell me you didn't invite my parents again."

With my mom here? I think that if our crappy but opposite parents met, they might explode. "No." But I do rush to the door and swing it open. "It's—"

"David almighty Park," Helen says, her face flushing bright red.

And I finally have something to be thankful for on this fine day of gratitude. I hit paydirt.

She looks absolutely horrified.

She deserves it.

"Cherries." I can't help muttering to myself as I practically dance into the kitchen. "Who brings gifts to Thanksgiving?"

My mom turns toward me. "What, dear?"

"Nothing."

"Your friends are all so nice! That's about the sweetest thing I've ever seen anyone do. Did you know that chocolate covered cherries are my favorite food in the world?"

My mom even sucks at hating the people I hate.

"Alright." I gesture to get all the tiny conversations all over the house to hush. "I'm just delighted to be hosting Thanksgiving this year."

"Along with me." Mandy has reached my side, and

she's beaming. Difference being, I think she's actually delighted.

"Steve, set the turkey on the edge of the counter there, right next to the plates. And then if you could start slicing that, we can start loading up plates."

Abby clears her throat. "Steve?"

He's looking at her.

"What?" I have no idea why she's—oh. It finally hits me. "Would you like to say grace, Abby?"

"If you'd like me to."

After my nod, she does, and a more beautiful prayer I'm not sure I've ever heard. I actually feel a little bad forgetting about it. Once it's over, everyone starts to load up their plates, kids first, followed by adults. Although a lot of things were brought by others, like the turkey, a spinach and bacon salad, a fluffy pink cranberry salad, the pies, and the stuffed mushrooms, I'm still proud of the things we provided.

I grab one of Emery's rolls, and then I scoop up a spoonful of her sweet potato casserole. The pecans are chopped a little inconsistently, and it's a little wet, but it looks great otherwise. Abby's right next to me, and I can feel her eyes watching me.

"You did really well," she says, as if she knew I'd be nervous. She probably did. She always knows everything.

"Thanks," I say. "Maren made the stuffing." I feel a little bad for that disclaimer, but she is pregnant. She should know what she's eating.

Abby takes a hearty spoonful of that too, as if to show her support of our efforts. "I could eat stuffing by the vat right now." She makes a feeble half-smile.

"And I made the green beans," my mom says.

When I glance down into her pot of canned green beans, it's even worse than I feared. She didn't drain any of the water from the cans, so they're all mushy, watery, and floating in and around the pepper she added liberally are little chunks of what I recognize as lard.

"You know, I read a whole article a few weeks ago on how bad butter is for you," my mom says. "And especially since you're pregnant, I didn't want to add to all the butter everyone else was using." She glares at Maren, as though you can make edible stuffing without butter.

"How thoughtful." Abby's nose only crinkles a bit as she scoops up green beans and puts them onto her plate.

"It's our old family recipe," my mom says. "Amanda ate this every year growing up."

I never ate green beans made by my mother a single time in my entire life. That doesn't stop her from putting a huge spoonful on my plate this year.

Mandy's smarter, though. She acts like she's forgotten something, hops out of line, and circles back to the end. Now she'll make it through without having to take any, I'm guessing. She's a genius.

"Don't worry about running out," my mom's telling Steve, who's eying the green beans askance. "I can make more in a jiff."

"Oh, great." He puts almost as many as Abby did, and I just have to force myself to move along. With all those other things on their plates, I'm sure it'll be fine. Plus, it's not like they're toxic. No one ever died of mushy, over-salted green beans. Not even when there are chunks of fat floating in them.

And then we're all sitting down, the kids at a card table that's partially blocking the hall bathroom, and the rest of us at a long table that runs from the kitchen to the family room. Gabe and Aiden are sitting at a tiny table Mandy bought for crafting, but they seem jazzed about it. The dogs are circling and whining a bit, but no more than I expected with this many people all holding plates of food.

Maybe the best part of the day so far is when Helen sits on the far end of the table as far from David as she can get, and then Eddy boots David. "I'm sure you won't mind if I sit by my fiancée?"

"Not at all." David picks up his plate, dances around the edge of the sofa, and sets it right across from Helen.

The glare she gives him fills my heart with joy. I shouldn't care so much about taunting her, but I just can't stand her stupid displays. So what if she and Abby shared some Thanksgiving stories about cherries and getting yelled at. Her precious sister lives right by me, by choice.

But when Eddy slides his free hand into mine, and I glance at the kids' table where Maren and Izzy are chatting, and where Olivia, Steve's daughter, Whitney, and Emery are laughing, my heart eases. I should really try to be nicer to Helen precisely because I live by her sister. I get to enjoy all the things she won't, whenever she decides to go back to her regularly scheduled life.

I really do have a lot to be grateful for this year.

Abby's just finishing her stuffing when my mom glances at her plate. "You haven't tried your green beans yet."

"I was saving them." Abby always knows just what to say. Then she forces a smile, which is almost impossible to recognize unless you know her, scoops up a spoonful and. . .

"Wait," I say. "We should eat them at the same time." I shoot her an apologetic look. At least if she's suffering through this, she won't be alone. I muster up my courage and scoop up a spoonful as well.

A moment later, I nod in her direction and we both shove the spoonfuls into our mouths.

You'd think that, after years of eating cold cans of whatever happened to be in the pantry, horrible school lunches, and microwaved hotdogs, I'd be ready for this moment. But the thing is, there have been so many years in between where I've refined my palate. People pay me to evaluate restaurants on my Insta. I've literally eaten at some of the best places in America.

Not even the very clear image of watery, mushy, lard-seasoned beans prepared me for what I just stuffed in my mouth. Mom must've added some extra ingredient. My teeth are still chewing, but my throat has closed off. I can't quite put my finger on what it is, until. . .

"Did you put a raw egg in this?" Abby asks the question around a mouthful of food, but then she finally forces the green beans down.

"Yes." Mom's actually smiling. "I used to have the hardest time getting my kids to eat enough protein, so I got in the habit of adding eggs to everything. Their oatmeal, their grits, and sometimes, even their breakfast cereal."

We never, ever, ever had enough money to buy breakfast cereal, and for the first time in my life, I'm thankful for that fact. I can't think of anything that would be more disgusting than what's in my mouth right now, but breakfast cereal with a raw egg in it?

That sounds just as bad.

Sadly, knowing what the slimy element in my mouthful of masticated goo is does not help me swallow it.

"Why aren't you swallowing?" Mom looks genuinely confused.

Helen's actually laughing.

Eddy pats me on the back.

Mandy's covering her mouth with her hand.

Digging deep for some strength I didn't realize I possessed, I finally choke it down. The second I do, the smell of rotten mushroom soup washes over me, as if it was summoned from my memory. That explosion's like the gift that keeps on giving.

Or maybe it was just the swallow that broke the camel's stomach. Because on the heels of my memory, I realize that I'm about to puke my guts out. The bathroom's blocked by the kids' table, and there's no way I can get down the hall, through my room, and to my bathroom in time.

I do what anyone in my place would do and vault over the sofa to reach the front porch. At least the place where I'm projectile vomiting everything I've eaten today is easy to sweep once it's frozen.

My weak stomach appears to be interesting enough that Steve comes rushing out. "Abby said I should check on you." He looks dubious.

I wave him away right as another wave hits. "Go."

But Eddy's coming out, so Steve can't really go in. And then Maren and Emery are shooting out too, followed by Mandy, and then the entire family has poured out of the front door to stare at me in my lowest moment.

When I finally manage to stop, and I'm wiping my mouth with the back of the sleeve of my cream, cable knit sweater, I turn to Mandy. "What's that you said about bad stuff happening?"

She laughs. "This will be a really good story later."

"Much later."

But I'm almost laughing now.

Until Maren shrieks.

We all spin around just in time to see Snuggles pull the entire turkey down from the edge of the counter. As it slides off, the handle of the roasting pan hits the sweet potato casserole pan, which bumps the bowl of stuffing on its way down. The stuffing slides sideways, careening into the gravy boat, and they all splatter forward and then downward, spraying the pies with both stuffing and gravy.

We all race in, but it's too late. The kitchen's a disaster. "The only thing that salvages this mess," Eddy says, "is that you each have an entire box of cherries."

"The pies." Helen looks almost as sick as Abby.

"I'm so sorry, guys," I say. "If I hadn't distracted everyone, the dogs would never have done that."

"Dogs?" Ethan's petting Roscoe. "He would never."

Eddy laughs. "You're right. Roscoe's the gentleman here. It's Snuggles who's to blame." He crouches down and rubs her head. "But in her defense, she is pregnant. Maybe the puppies were craving turkey."

That makes everyone laugh, and a few moments later, we've broken open the boxes of cherries, and everyone has stuffed their faces with them. Ironically, it's Gabe who alerts us all to a tiny detail we should probably have noticed before.

"Hey. What does li-qwer mean?"

"What, bud?" Ethan ruffles his head.

"The cherries have a lot of ingredients, but the first one is li-qwer."

"Do you mean liquor?" my mom asks.

Abby meets my eyes with a look of horror.

David Park bursts out laughing.

Abby spins around to face Helen. "Did you just get my kids wasted?"

"Oh, no, did you eat any?" I ask. "You're pregnant."

"Luckily, my stomach is tiny," she says. "I was doing dishes while I waited for my stomach to make some space." But then her eyes widen and she glances at Ethan. "Not to worry, though. Even if I *had* eaten a handful, it wouldn't really do anything to harm the baby."

That was weird.

"I love these cherries." Gabe's swaying a little as he pops another one in his mouth.

His mom snatches them out of his hand and grabs his wrist. "Sorry, Mister. I'm cutting you off."

Mandy's cackling so loudly that my mom's starting to get agitated.

"This is a Thanksgiving we won't forget," Mandy says.

"Listen up, Archers and Brooks, load up in the car. It's time to let you all sleep it off." Abby's shaking her head on the way out. "At least I'm safe to drive." She pauses on the porch. "Helen, maybe you better come with me."

Helen's so busy glaring at David that I'm not sure she even heard Abby. But then she whips her head around. "Yes. Let's go."

Maren's belting out an Adele song at the top of her lungs while they gather up their things and disappear, and all I can think is, the day is finally over. We are very blessed, but sometimes it feels like we're a little *too* blessed.

Luckily David's not a big cherry person, so he offers to drive Donna, Will, Beth, and Aiden all home. The house is trashed, but it's finally mine again. I had enough cherries that I don't even feel that upset about the whole thing.

"I mean, it could have been worse," I say.

Eddy sticks around until the kitchen's mostly clean and the food's in the fridge. That's when it finally occurs to me—the worst fiancée in the world—that Eddy's in AA.

"Oh, no. Did you eat cherries?" I clench my teeth. "I will kill Helen."

"I realized, a little late, sorry, that Helen bringing all that made you mad. I didn't eat any as a show of solidarity."

I close my eyes. "Thank goodness."

"I'm fine." He presses a kiss to my cheek. "Thanks for caring."

Once I know he's alright, I collapse on the sofa, my head sinking into the down throw pillow on the corner. I close my eyes. "Oh, good."

"Ah, ah, no way. You don't get to lie down here. The last time you fell asleep on the sofa, I heard about that kink in your neck all day." Eddy's arms slide underneath my neck and my knees, and suddenly it feels like I'm floating. He carries me into my bedroom and lays me down on my bed. "You'll wish you'd brushed your teeth in the morning, but I can't fix everything."

"It's fine." I smile. "Thank you."

"I hope you had a good Thanksgiving. Hosting's a lot. I'm proud of you."

"Maybe next year, you and I will host."

"That's fine, but promise me. Your mom is *not* making the green beans."

"Or anything else." I sigh. "She's embarrassing."

"No one judges you by her," he says. "You have lots of people who love you."

"I offered her money to leave," I whisper, "but she turned it down."

"How much?"

I tell him, and he grunts. "Hm. Well, good for her."

"What do you think it means?"

"Maybe she's changed," he says. "It's rare, but it happens. The Amanda Brooks I met would not be laughing today's mishaps off. She wouldn't be meddling in people's love lives, either, but you're doing both."

"What?"

"Isn't that why you invited David?" His eyebrows rise. "Please tell me you invited him because you noticed the spark between him and Helen and not because you like him yourself."

I roll my eyes. "Please. I've only ever liked you."

"Good answer." He kisses me, and then he stands. "When I count my blessings, Amanda, you're at the very top of the list." He blows me a kiss and then ducks out.

As I drift off to sleep, I think about what he said. Could my mom really have changed? Her cooking skills clearly haven't improved, but could she really not want my money? Could she be here because she loves me?

I hate how much I want that to be true. For years, I've been safe. Nothing my family did could hurt me, because I didn't expect anything of them. But if I start to hope. . .

That's the scariest part.

✤ 13 ✤

DONNA

After I left home, I moved into the Stanford dorms. They were small, they were cramped, and they smelled. On top of that, I had a roommate who made me a little nuts. When I moved out, it was to live with Charles. After our separation, I moved home and lived with my dad, caring for him until nearly the very end.

Which means this little house that Amanda Saddler gifted me is the very first home I've ever owned. It's also the very first place I've ever lived that was entirely mine.

"It's too small," Will says.

"Your place isn't any bigger." I frown.

"Well, it wasn't," he says. "While I was fixing the cave-in, I had them add almost a thousand square feet."

"You're converting the garage, like Abby and Amanda did over at the Birch Creek Ranch."

"They gave me the idea," he says. "It won't be enough, but it's a start, and I still have my nice garage for my project cars. So even if we have to park outside for a while, it's no big deal. Or you know, it won't be, after spring hits."

"Aiden needs a room," I say.

"The new baby will need a room too." Will can't say the words without the corner of his mouth turning upward.

His elation makes me smile, too. "Right."

"And if you can convince Beth to stay, she'll need a room."

"Do you want her to stay?" I whisper the words, a little embarrassed to be articulating them. I'm sad she's insisting that after the baby's born, she needs to leave, but part of me is also relieved.

I mean, will she really be my baby if her actual mother is living in the same house? Not really, right? I'll just be the free babysitter she found to watch the child so she can live her carefree life. Beth's only eighteen, so I get the desire, but I never had the life she's describing. I went from student, to married, to miserable, and then after having Aiden, miserable and trapped with my kid's father.

Will, however, seems to suffer from none of the selfish feelings that I do. "Of course I want her to stay. Do you really think she'll be better off in Seattle with her parents?"

"I mean, not with Patrick and Amelia, but she'll definitely have more opportunities in Seattle. She's studying photography, and there are only so many times she can photograph the Gorge or the tourists who visit while they're holding a fish, right?"

"Sometimes the everyday things are the most beautiful," Will says.

"That's just something boring people say."

Will laughs. "Well, I think she's better off here, where people love her. But you're the fancy college girl, so if you think she should go to college and experience what's out there, then maybe you're right. Maybe Seattle really will be better."

"How can she even decide what breakfast she likes best when she's only ever had eggs?"

"I still love eggs," Will says, "and I've had lots of different things, but I do see your point." He slides some papers in front of me. "Just take a look at these."

I glance down at the sheets in front of me. "What exactly are. . ." But then I realize exactly what they are. "Who drew these?" They're nearly perfect sketches, as far as I can tell, of both the house I'm sitting in, and of Will's old farmhouse, which he inherited from his grandparents.

"Steve helped me come up with a little more space than just the garage," he says. "And we also talked about how, on the lot this house has, we could add two rooms and a bathroom here. Or we could add one room and another living area. I just need you to decide where you'd rather live, and then you can see how each of them could be renovated so that—"

I cover his wrist with my hand. "I love you, Will Earl."

His eyes snap toward mine. "I love you, too. I have loved you for a very, very long time now. I just want to make you happy."

"The next few months are going to be really busy, and probably also really hard."

He twists his wrist, entwining his fingers into mine. "A wedding, a new baby, and a home remodel." He's grinning again. "The most exciting few months of my entire life. . .other than the day you moved back into town."

"I remember that day. It was not exciting. It was depressing. Everyone I saw either blinked and stammered, or they swore and shouted. They all heard I was back, and no one knew why, and they all wanted to know. No one had the nerve to just ask."

"Except me. I didn't care why you were back," Will says. "I was just happy you showed up without that stupid guy you married."

Without even looking at the sketches in more detail, I tap the one of his farmhouse. "This one."

"But you should look at the kitchens before you decide," he says. "The problem with the old farmhouse is that they didn't really build pantries back then, so to add one, we'll have to sacrifice part of the breakfast room. And the plumbing—"

I press one finger to his lips. "William Earl, I want you to be close to your animals, your fancy garage, and your parents. There's more space for our future together and whatever it holds. I choose the farmhouse."

"But you love this house."

"I do," I admit. "But what I loved about it was that it's mine. It was a place I didn't have to answer to anyone else about. It's a place where I can be safe with Aiden, a place where I can decorate any way I want. It's a place that felt permanent, or you know, semi-permanent." I glance around the room at the curtains I picked out that Will helped me hang. At the throw pillows on the sofa in the family room. At the little fence around my front lawn. "It was a place I chose, and it's a place I'll remember fondly, but now I'm choosing you—us. I'm choosing to move to a place that's always been your home, near the parents who have always been there for you and who have welcomed me. A place we're going to change into exactly what we want—together."

"Are you sure?"

I nod.

"Alright, well, in some ways that'll be easier. I'll move in with my parents, and you can stay here while we tear the place up."

"It's almost Christmas," I say. "Is this really the best time to go tearing things up?"

"The baby's due in mid-April, right?"

"Sure."

"And what if she comes early?"

Early? I hadn't even considered it. "It's Beth's first baby. They usually don't come. . ." Then I think about my friend whose baby came eight weeks early and spent weeks in the NICU. And one of the kids in Gabe's class who said he came a month early, but went home from the hospital right on time. "Oh my gosh. What if she comes early?"

"When were you thinking for the wedding? My mom's asking, and I was also wondering when we could mention about the baby."

I close my eyes and inhale slowly. "Okay. Amanda's wedding is right after Christmas. I was thinking March for ours, but that doesn't really give us much space for baby stuff, does it?"

"Maybe we shoot for February, and I can try and have the house ready by March."

I'm nodding.

"What are you guys doing?" Beth's rubbing her eyes as she walks out of her room. Her eyes drop to the table, and she leans closer to get a better look. "Oh, wow."

"Will and Steve drew up these sketches."

"Because he knows about the baby," Will says.

Beth's eyes fly wide. "Wait, what did you tell him about it?"

Will freezes. "What do you mean?"

175

"Did you tell him that I'm giving you the baby?"

My sweet fiancé's Adam's apple bobs a little when he swallows. "I told him that after your baby was born, we'd need more space."

Beth's mouth is moving, like she's talking to someone inside of her head. "Okay, but you didn't say it was going to be *your* baby, right?"

"What's going on?" I ask. "Did you change your mind?" My heart contracts, like someone just told me Aiden's standing on the edge of a cliff. How can I care so much about a baby I've never even seen? I need to stop being so ridiculous and remember that this entire plan is predicated on the whims of an eighteen-year-old. The rug could be yanked out from under us at any point.

"I didn't change my mind," Beth says. "But I haven't told Ethan yet."

Oh.

"If he hears you're the one getting the baby, then I'll have to explain that I'm moving, and I don't know how to do that yet."

He won't follow her to Seattle. Or, at least, I can't imagine that he will. He's been pretty set on running the ranch here.

"But you have to tell him," Will says. "Right? I mean, it's not like your plan is to have the baby and disappear like smoke."

Beth glares at Will. "Of course not, but he's going to be so disappointed."

He's going to be wrecked. Oh, my heart goes out to poor Ethan, who has done everything right, every single step of the way. "Are you sure you want—"

"I'm sure." She inhales and then exhales slowly, her face relaxing. "Aunt Donna, since the day I found out I was pregnant, I've changed my mind every single day, sometimes every hour, about what I wanted to do. Keep the baby. Give her up. Keep her. Give her up. Run away to Europe. At no point have I felt any sort of peace about any decision, not until I decided that I'd give her to you."

"Okay," I say, my heartbeat slowing down a hair.

"You are her mother." Her hands drop to either side of her small belly. "Once I said it out loud, I realized it was true. I mean, I'm her mother, but you're her *real* mom. Kind of like how Amelia's my mother, but you've been much more of a mom to me than she was." A tear wells up in her eye and runs down her left cheek.

My heart swells. I've never said anything like that, but I've felt it before. I felt it the day she asked if she could move in with me. I felt it when she told me she was pregnant—that worry, the worry a parent would feel for her child when she was in a tough spot. To hear Beth say it out loud. . .it feels legitimate now. As if it's not all in my head.

"I haven't even wobbled since I decided to give her to you two. Everyone in the world deserves parents as good as you will be."

Now I'm crying, too. "But Beth, are you sure you have to leave?"

Will stands, picking up a piece of paper. "You shouldn't! I'm adding two more rooms to the existing three bedrooms in that house. We'd have plenty of space for you to stay."

"I feel at peace with you keeping this little girl." Beth wipes at her tears. "But I don't think I could live there, watching you both do what I couldn't. I don't think I could live my happy, carefree teenage life while you're doing all the work I should be doing for her. I'd feel. . .I don't know. Guilty, maybe. Or left out."

"Alright," I say. "That's fine. But if you change your mind—"

"I won't." She shakes her head. "But thank you for wanting me to."

Will takes two steps and wraps an arm around Beth's shoulder. "Our offer always stands. Next week, next month, next year. When you want to come back, you'll have a room. You'll have a place. Always."

Her crying redoubles. So does mine.

Which is right when Ethan walks through the door. "Whoa, what's going on in here?"

❧ 14 ❧

BETH

My Aunt Donna likes to make plans. I watch her with her lists, with her calendars, and with her paperwork. She tallies the costs of things. She sketches out the sequence in which events should happen. It's probably why she was good at her job at the retreat build-out before, and it's definitely why she's good at helping run Mrs. Earl's hotel.

But the thing about making plans is that something always comes up that wrecks them.

I had a plan, too.

Now I have a baby.

And a boyfriend whom I love.

Sometimes the things that wreck your plans are the best things that happen in your entire life. Occasionally, it's even something you never thought could happen. My biggest problem for the past few months has been that I couldn't see a clear path for both me and for my daughter.

How can I give her the family she deserves? How can I find a place where I can also thrive? If I keep her here, everyone will know she's not Ethan's baby.

Everyone will know she was the result of a one-time mistake. That'll be her story.

I hate that story.

I want to change it. Since the fishing tours dried up, I've just been working a few shifts a week at Brownings. I throw a big apron on during each shift and so far, no one has noticed. If I can stop doing that soon and just hide in Donna's house until the spring, maybe I can have the baby and people can just assume she and Will adopted with no specifics about where. When I head out for Seattle to take some photography classes, she'll have a good story, and it won't strangle mine.

It's not a bad plan, but there's collateral damage.

Ethan's the brightest patch of light that has ever shone on my life. He's the freshest breeze. The joy in my misery. He wanted us to try dating, to see whether what we have would work, but his promise has always been forever.

I just don't see how we can work, not here. Not in Manila.

The bad thing about small towns is also the good thing about them. There are so few people that they know everything about everything. They gossip like nothing else in the world. And in this place where most everyone goes to church, there's more judgment than anywhere else I've been.

Not that I've been many places.

So the one remaining piece in the puzzle of how to resolve my plan-wrecking miracle has been figuring out how to tell Ethan. "It's not goodbye," I practice saying in front of the mirror. "We're just hitting pause." Tears roll down my face as I say it. There's no way he's going to understand.

Ethan and his family are the kind of people who see a problem and muscle their way through. They work, and they fight, and they slay dragons. The Ellingsons don't slay things. They don't attack things head on. We slink away and circle back around later. We hide and hope and wait.

But when I hear people talking outside, I have to at least peek out and see what's going on. Will isn't usually over here quite this early.

"Of course I want her to stay," Will says.

I realize he's talking about me.

"Do you really think she'll be better off in Seattle with her parents?" He sounds so irritated at the whole idea, like my departure would be the worst mistake ever.

"I mean, not with Patrick and Amelia, but she'll definitely have more opportunities in Seattle." Aunt Donna sighs. "She's studying photography, and there are only so many times she can photograph the Gorge or the tourists who visit while they're holding a fish, right?"

She's right about that. There are so many things I'm learning in even just my online classes, but I'm kind of limited here. No downtown area. No parks. Just big open ranches, broad sky, and lots of cows.

"Sometimes the everyday things are the most beautiful," Will says.

Donna laughs and slaps his arm. "That's just something boring people say."

I love watching them. I wonder whether that's how Ethan and I look. I hope it is. They're so effortless and carefree around one another. No guarded looks or pensive thoughts before each word they speak. There are no fraught secrets or ultimatums like my parents. There's no manipulation like with my grandparents.

Just joy and support and teasing.

"Well, I think she's better off here, where people

love her," Will says. "But you're the fancy college girl, so if you think she should go to college and experience what's out there, then maybe you're right. Maybe Seattle really will be better."

Donna's brow furrows, like she's not at all sure, but then she nods. "How can she even decide what breakfast she likes best when she's only ever had eggs?"

"I still love eggs," Will says. "and I've had lots of different things, but I do see your point." He pushes some papers in front of her. "Just take a look at these."

Donna squints, shifting the papers slightly. "What exactly are. . ." But then her eyes widen and her mouth forms into a little 'o.' "Who drew these?"

"Steve helped me come up with a little more space than just the garage," he says. "And we also talked about how, on the lot this house has, we could add two rooms and a bathroom here. Or we could add one room and another living area. I just need you to decide where you'd rather live, and then you can see how each of them could be renovated so that—"

She grabs his arm. "I love you, Will Earl."

My heart flips inside my chest. I should not be watching this, but it's helping me, too. How nice would it be to have parents who adore each other? Parents who are both smart, hard-working, and capable. That's what I'm doing for my little girl. That's why I haven't wavered since choosing Donna.

"I love you, too. I have loved you for a very, very long time now. I just want to make you happy."

"The next few months are going to be really busy, and probably really hard," Aunt Donna says.

I duck back into my room then. Really busy months for them as they do everything necessary to get ready for this baby. As they get married. As they work and play and visit.

I realize that I don't really want to hide in this house for all those things. If I don't want anyone to know I'm pregnant, I'll miss all the fun stuff. Their wedding. Amanda's wedding. Christmas parties.

My parents finally know the truth about most of it —Dad threatened to drive down here until Aunt Donna got on the phone and talked him down. They're not happy, but they're relieved I'm not keeping it.

But how am I going to tell Ethan? As soon as I do, he's going to realize that it'll be awkward for me after she's born. He'll ask about my plans. My plan to hide and leave will impact him, too. He'll be stuck inside as well. . .

I finally force myself back out into the family room, and I reassure Aunt Donna and Will that I'm not going to change my mind about the baby. They're as great about it as they always are, trying to convince me to consider sticking around. Will even wraps an arm around my shoulders and says, "Our offer always stands. Next week, next month, next year. When you want to come back, you'll have a room. You'll have a place. Always."

It makes me cry, and Aunt Donna and Will are crying too, but in a good way. Happy tears, mostly.

Of course, that's when the door opens and Ethan walks through. He takes one look at Will and me, both of us with tears rolling down our faces, and he asks, "Whoa, what's going on in here?"

I scramble around for anything I can say that won't force the truth right this very moment, but I've never been good at that sort of thing.

Aunt Donna's eyes keep panning from Ethan back to me, and she looks sick.

"I'm giving my baby to Aunt Donna," I say. "And Will."

"Oh." Ethan nods. "Actually, that makes a lot of sense. Did you decide that a few weeks ago?"

I straighten my shoulders, Will drops his arm, and I step toward Ethan. "I did."

"Why didn't you tell me then?" He knows. I can tell by the way he's standing, by the stiff way he's holding his head, that he knows there's more.

"Can we go for a walk?"

Ethan glances at the door to Aiden's room, from which he will emerge any moment. "Yeah. Let's do that."

I'm sure Aunt Donna and Will breathe a huge sigh of relief when we step outside, but I almost wish I could carry them in my pocket. Aunt Donna's great at smoothing things over.

"Alright, that's the part I'm not getting. I thought that, if you've stuck with the decision to give Donna the baby for a few weeks, you'd be happy, but you look. . .sad." He takes my hand. "And you've been crying."

"I'm mostly happy," I say. "I was crying because they love me, and I know they'll love this baby." My free hand rests against my stomach. I have no idea why that makes me happier. It's not like the baby knows.

"That's good." He walks with me then, both of us heading out toward the creek that runs just past town. Ethan knows me well enough not to press for more. If he pushes, I'll just do what Ellingsons do best. Hide deeper.

But eventually, he has to be told. And now that the Band-aid's half off. . . "I don't think I can stay here, after I have the baby, Ethan."

He stops walking, his hand stopping me, too. "Why not?"

I sigh. "Can you imagine what it would be like, me living in the same house with them?"

He shrugs. "Sure. I've been in a house with a baby before. When Gabe was born—"

"It's not the same."

"Not exactly."

"Not at all." I try to pull my hand away.

But he won't let me. "No. Not this time."

"What?"

"If you have that baby and you have to leave, fine. Last time you had big news, something you didn't want to tell me, you hid. You wouldn't let me near you. You wouldn't tell me what was going on, and you kept it all to yourself. But now we're together. You love me, and I love you. That means we share what we're feeling. You've told me you're worried that after the baby comes, you won't be able to live here."

I nod.

"That's fine, but you don't really know what it'll be like, and you aren't leaving yet. So you've told me what you want to do, and I'll keep holding your hand, rubbing your feet, bringing you breakfast, and taking you on dates right up until this little girl makes her glorious entry into the world."

"But Ethan, what I'm saying is that I want to keep this a secret. No one can know it's my baby. That means we'll be hiding for months."

"Okay, so we'll go for walks and I'll get a lot of takeout."

"And after the baby's born, I'm moving to Seattle. I'll take photography classes. I'll live—"

He kisses me then.

Not a peck on the lips to keep me from talking. A real kiss. His arms slide against my cheeks, they pull my face toward his just as his lips ignite feelings inside of me that I've rarely felt before.

And then he releases my mouth, and his hand slides

back into mine again. He upends my world, and then he goes back to walking.

"Ethan."

"If you talk about moving again, I'll just kiss you. It's a win-win for me, so feel free."

My free hand tightens into a ball.

"Okay," I say. "Maybe you need time to think about it, to process that—"

And he spins me around and kisses me again, this time longer, more intently than before, which I hadn't thought possible. He runs one hand through my messy hair, and then he sighs against my mouth. "Definitely a win."

Alright. I'll let him process for now. But no matter how many amazing kisses we share, he won't be able to change my mind. Ellingsons may run, but we're also very stubborn. We do exactly what we want, we just do it quietly.

At least he'll have time to prepare, and greedily, I'm delighted that he reacted so well. I put off telling him, because I wanted more time to spend with him before the end. And more time is apparently exactly what I'm getting.

15

HELEN

I usually spend Thanksgivings alone. It's a great time for me to catch up on things I've fallen behind on for work, because everyone else takes off. It's like getting a head start in a foot race, for instance. A dead zone for other people, but a bonus round for me.

Twice in the past few decades, I've accepted my sister's invitation and joined her family.

She always had a room ready for me with fresh sheets, a clean floor, and a connected bathroom. She made sure the kids didn't bug me too much. She prepared the food. Every year there was a gleaming turkey, cornbread dressing, green bean casserole, sweet potato casserole, fresh rolls, mashed potatoes and gravy, and several different salads. She'd make her famous stuffed mushrooms. I'm sure they're unhealthy, because nothing with that much cream cheese and bacon can be good for you, but they're addictive.

Things were perfect, but I never really felt like a part of the group.

I was always the person people forgot was there

until I said something. I never got the inside jokes. I never got asked to pass anything to anyone. They'd literally ask the person next to me, but not me. It was probably because they didn't want to put me off. It was probably well intentioned. But I always felt like the most outside of the outsiders.

So this year, on my third ever Thanksgiving with Abby's family, I wanted to bring something that everyone would love. I thought back on our Thanksgivings as kids, and the one that stood out the most, the one that was the brightest in my mind, was the one where Mom's cousin brought us each a box of cherries. We ate them all on the very day of Thanksgiving, and both Abby and I had tummy aches that night.

I'd get my inside joke, and I'd be giving presents to everyone, including the people I was sure didn't want me there, like Amanda. She may have been the host, but who doesn't love a good present? I ordered them to be overnighted from the nicest chocolatier I could find online. Okay, fine. I had my assistant order them from the nicest chocolatier he could find online. Still, it was my idea, and I paid for it. When they arrived, I lovingly stroked the shiny blue boxes.

And then when I gave them out, Abby's eyes sparkled. She remembered that year. Everyone was delighted to eat as many as they could. Which is how, on my third Thanksgiving Day, I inadvertently managed to get my sister's kids drunk.

My sister who rarely even drinks so much as a glass of wine.

It makes sense—any adult that really had more than one or two would have immediately noticed the liquor, but the kids who were pounding them who had never had a drop?

Not so much.

I've been trying my hardest ever since to not think about it. I certainly don't plan to ever bring it up. Unfortunately, Amanda thinks it's hilarious to bring it up over and over. I thought working with her might be good. The more I got to know her, the more I hoped that I'd fit in with Abby's friends here.

That might be a lie.

I didn't want to fit in. That's never been my style. I wanted to take over. But Amanda isn't keen on anyone taking over. Instead, she's been taking every pot shot she can. So when she shows up at Abby's house unannounced on the Saturday after Thanksgiving, I don't even pretend to be happy to see her.

Not that she cares.

"With barely more than three weeks until the wedding, my final selection for the table centerpieces is due today, and Eddy got another stupid emergency call. Some dumb cow got stuck somewhere stupid." Amanda makes me help her carry twenty different floral arrangements into the house, because you can't 'really see' the arrangements from the car, apparently.

Now Abby and I are both stuck staring at them.

"They all look the same," I say. "Red flowers, white flowers, pine cones. Greenery." I squint. "Oh, and that one has candy canes."

"That's why I didn't come over here to get your opinion." Amanda isn't glaring. No, instead, she's using her I'm-half-kidding voice so that Abigail won't get mad. "I get more than enough of that at work."

"But you did make me help carry them all in."

"That's because Abigail's pregnant, idiot."

Why can't she carry her own stuff in? Because she's Princess Amanda, and doing things herself never occurs to her. That's why.

"I think this one." Abigail leans toward the oval

one, brushing her fingers against the huge white magnolias. "But maybe I like it so much because of the Southern touch. I know that's not really your thing."

"Why do you have to decide now?" I ask. "It's not like they're going to make the flowers in the next few days. You could have just waited for Eddy to resolve the cow emergency, and then he could have picked between white, eggshell, ecru, and snowy."

"What?" Amanda asks.

Abby giggles, her hand half-covering her mouth. "She's making a joke about how women always bug their husbands to choose between four different colors of white wall paint."

If Amanda could bring herself to just stick her tongue out at me, it might be easier on her than maintaining that uncomfortable facial expression. "You're so clever," she says. "But I have to pick now, because the next three weeks are the hot time for Christmas flower delivery. To get my arrangements for free, I have to post a sneak peek for my wedding so that other people will want to race out and buy the same thing for their Christmas parties, obviously."

"I'm so sorry I didn't know that," I say. "As someone who buys my stuff, I'm not familiar with the intricacies of freebie-seekers."

Amanda's face turns an even darker shade of red, and I suppress my smile.

Abigail ignores us. "If you don't want magnolias, I vote for the white lilies with the cranberry clusters and poinsettias. Against those crisp white tablecloths, they'll really stand out."

"I do like the magnolias," Amanda says. "But do you think people will say it's not really on theme?"

"Isn't the theme Christmas?" I exhale and barely keep from shaking my head. "They're all on theme."

As the doorbell rings, I'm dodging a kick from Amanda, so I decide to answer it.

"Who is it?" Abby asks, turning.

A deliveryman hands me a brown package that's wrapped with festive Christmas tape. "It looks like a gift." I walk across the room and hand it to her, but as I do, our eyes drop to the address at the same time.

"It's for you," Abigail says. "Who even knows you're here?"

"My assistant," I say. "And maybe a handful of other people." But no one who would send me a gift, I don't think.

"Ooh, it's a surprise." Amanda rubs her hands together.

"You're excited that I got a surprise?" Maybe she thinks we are friends after all. Maybe I'm just not good at interpreting—

"With the way you treat people, it could be a dead rat." Her eyes widen. "Or a bag of candy with razor blades in it."

Abby glares at her, so I'm chalking that one up as a win. "Here." She hands me some scissors.

"You want me to open it right here?" I know Amanda was kidding, but I have gotten some unfriendly mail before from people whose companies I've disassembled, and now I'm nervous to open it. I doubt they would be able to find this address, but who knows?

"Come on." Abby's looking at it like there might be a puppy inside. "It's exciting."

Could it be from her? I slice the top open, and then I lift off the paper. Resting inside, underneath some beautiful packaging, is a large bottle of rum. Ambassador, the bottle says. The brand is Diplomatico.

"I hate rum," I say. "Who would send me this?"

"Oh, there's a card." Abby snags it and opens it toward me so we can both read it.

For our next date, let's make cherries.

-David

"Oh, Helen. You said it wasn't a date!" She drops the paper, which flutters to the ground.

"Wait, who's it from?" Amanda's looking from Abby to me and back again like she's going to explode if she can't find out.

"It's *not* a date," I say. "I'm totally serious. He's just being funny."

"Oh, I'd say he is making a joke, at your expense. He wants to make cherries." Abby's grin keeps widening, and then disappearing, and then widening again as if she wants to suppress it, but she can't quite manage it.

"Who?" Amanda asks. "Who are we talking about?"

Abby kicks the paper toward her.

I practically toss the box on the ground and dive for it at the same time. Sadly, with Abby's nudge, Amanda's closer, and she gets to it before I do.

And then my phone starts ringing.

Amanda's already reading it, so I decide that maybe I can use the phone call to get out of listening to her react to it. "Hello?"

It's my assistant, Roger. He's one of the few truly capable people in my life. "I hate to bother you, but I thought you ought to know."

That's not a good first line. "About?"

"Someone named David Park sent everyone at headquarters a huge box of cherry cordials."

He wouldn't really do that, right? "He did what?"

"They all had the same note with them." Roger clears his throat as if he's preparing to read something.

"If you see her, tell your boss she owes me. Happy Holidays, David Park."

I'm going to shoot him and then I'm going to tank his stock. And then I'm going to buy more than fifty percent and fire him. No, wait, I'll buy a competitor and put him under. "It's just a joke," I say. "Don't worry about it." I pause. "Actually, send them all a huge box of the most expensive truffles you can find from me, with the message, 'I always pay all my debts. Helen Fisher.'"

"Wait, send truffles to David Park?" Roger asks. "Or to your employees?"

He's probably right. Sending more things to my employees will just keep them thinking about it. I want to stab David Park in the eye right now. This is my *job*. How dare he mess with my image? "Actually, don't do anything. I'll take care of it." I hang up, lean over, and grab the bottle of rum. Then I head for the door, grabbing my coat and purse on the way.

"Where are you going?" Amanda asks. "Are you really dating David?"

I pivot on my toe. "By tonight, there won't *be* a David Park for anyone to date."

Amanda's spluttering something or other to Abby as I walk out, but I can't be bothered with that right now. My brain's revving the engine, thinking of ways to retaliate. The fastest and easiest way would be a tweet. I open my phone to think of just what to say.

As one of less than a hundred female billionaires in the United States, I have more than a few followers on my very inconsistent Twitter account. But if I tweet something, Elon will call and want to know what's going on—he follows his own platform pretty closely for any content from his inner circle—not to mention a dozen other work acquaintances who might call. I really don't want to talk to any of them.

Plus, if anyone in the financial world happened to hear about his irritating cherry stunt, any kind of tweet I make will just confirm the rumors circling about me and stupid David Park.

That's the last thing I need.

Anyone whose name is associated positively with mine winds up with soaring stock prices. I want the opposite. I want to punch David almighty Park in the throat, but realistically, I should treat this like training a dog. I should bop him on the nose so he knows that this sort of thing isn't acceptable.

I'm closing down Twitter when a tweet on my feed catches my eye.

Helen Fisher trawling for sushi? It's a photo of the two of us at Brownings, and I'm laughing. It was posted by the man I just fired, our long-time business acquaintance, Kyle Saunders.

How did Kyle get his hands on that photo?

He must be having me followed.

The only thing that pisses me off more than David Park messing with me is Kyle acting like he caught me doing something embarrassing. Also, it's offensive that he's highlighting David's ethnicity in such a childish way. It downright infuriates me.

When David Park's car rolls down the drive and pulls in next to mine, I decide that he's lucky. Three minutes ago, I was devising ways to claw his eyes out or tank his stock prices. Neither one would have improved the chances that his father would name him as successor.

But now?

My hatred for Kyle after his attempt to steal the board, as well as his tackiness on social media, has made my small-fish enemy into a friend. I open my door and lean against my car.

"Oh." David startles, and he shifts until he's facing me. "You're already out here."

"I was coming for you," I say.

"That sounds ominous."

"Until I saw this." I swivel my phone around and show him the tweet Kyle Saunders just made.

"I hate that guy." A muscle in his jaw twitches.

"That makes two of us."

"So?"

"Well, I obviously plan to call Hank with BCG, where I hear he was thinking of going next, to tell him to steer clear. I'm also going to short the stock in KlinePeter Holdings." I can't help my smile.

"I heard he was heavy into that."

"When others see me doing it. . ."

"You're terrifying."

"You should thank him, really," I say. "I was at least this angry with you before I saw his text."

"But mine was funny," David says.

"It might have been if you hadn't told me I was profoundly broken," I say.

"Actually, I think I said you were profoundly screwed up."

"And that's better, how?"

He shrugs. "I just like accuracy, that's all."

That makes me laugh.

"I'm glad Kyle was so stupid that you aren't mad at me anymore."

"Oh, I'm still mad at you." I walk toward him, my Prada snow boots crunching against the old snow. "I'm just angrier with him. And that's why. . ."

"Why what?" David's staring at me intently, like he can't wait to see what I say next, which is a little intoxicating.

I need to focus. This is just the first step in a new

strategy. "You know that what we agreed upon were not dates." I lift my eyebrows. "I agreed to do some consults."

He shrugs. "Potato, potahto."

"You were promised access to my business expertise."

"You did invite me back to your hotel. Was that because you had your files there?" His half-grin is killer. "Or did you just need access to your laptop?"

I press one finger against his chest, right above the spot where his zipper ends. "Kyle's trying to use you to embarrass me."

"And what about me?" he asks. "I'm the raw fish in this scenario."

"You're not even Japanese."

"Right? He could have at least called me gimbap."

I laugh, flattening my hand against him for balance, and then my heart rate spikes. Because the chest I feel under my hand is firm, muscular, and solid. "I'm about to tweet a response."

David's brows draw together. "You're what?"

I spin, leaning back against him, and snap a photo of us with my free hand.

I'm smiling, but David's not. He looks intense in a way that only the hottest Asian men can manage. His jawline is flawless, his eyes are smoldering, and his skin looks luminescent.

It's perfect.

"What are you doing?" David looks. . .wary.

"I hope you're ready for this."

"For what?"

"When I go trawling, I always reel in my catch." I type out a tweet. **Correction. Helen Fisher caught David Park. And he's just as delicious as he looks.** "Are you ready for your stock prices to soar?" I swivel the phone around to face him. "Because now those three consults have been upgraded to dates. We have a fake relationship to sell, at least long enough to make Kyle look like an idiot."

"Is he your ex?"

I roll my eyes. "He wishes. He tried and tried to get me to make something official. He was an arm to hold at parties when I was bored." I pause. "I've never, not in twenty years of dominating the business world, publicly announced a relationship of any kind."

"I think that makes me your first boyfriend." David reaches out and taps the button on my phone to send the tweet live. "This should be interesting."

❧ 16 ❧

HELEN

Every time I talked to Abby while she was in school, she had a new boyfriend. Or at least, that's how it felt. I often wondered how much more impressive she'd be, how much more progress she'd make, if she wasn't so distracted by all the social and relationship drama. But now that I finally have a boyfriend of my own, or at least, now that people *think* I do, I almost get the attraction.

I shouldn't be scrolling through comments or checking all the text messages that are pouring in, but I can't seem to help it. People I haven't heard from for years are calling and messaging me.

Reporters, too.

Do people really care more about you when they think someone else does? Are humans really all such lemmings?

"I can't believe I had to find out from Twitter," Abby says. I hate that she, more than anyone, is as delighted as she is.

"Oh, please," I say. "I told you already. It's not real."

"Then why are you changing clothes?" She arches

that stupid eyebrow into that expression of hers that scares everyone but me. "He's just sitting outside waiting on you, and you're in here worrying about what shirt to wear." She shakes her head. "That's not something I ever thought I'd be saying to my self-possessed sister."

I'm not about to tell her that mostly I just came back to change my undies. He may have shot me down the last time I asked him to a hotel, but I'm not about to go on a date, fake or otherwise, in the grandma panties I'm wearing. You never know what might happen in my life right now, clearly. It would be just like David Park to change his tune when I wasn't prepared.

"I need to take a few more photos," I explain. "So get out, and let me put the dumb blouse on."

"Get out?" She rolls her eyes. "As if I've never seen your boobs."

"Abby, I've got to pee, too. Or did you want to watch that for some reason?"

She huffs, but she finally leaves.

Once I've finally changed, I start to think about where I'm going. David Park's waiting outside in his car, and we're going on a *date*. Not really, of course. It's just to stick it to his family and also to stupid Kyle.

But even so.

It's a date.

I've been to events with people before. I've taken business partners and rivals both, depending on my goals. But I've never really been romantically entangled with anyone, and it feels. . .well, it's making my heart race like I'm a high school senior or something equally stupid. Not that I was this idiotic then.

What is wrong with me?

I force my heart to stop racing, so that I can go out

there and pose for a few stupid photos. Then I can answer any questions he has about his business plan, and we'll be down to just two more meetings. Easy peasy.

When I walk outside, I'm prepared to exchange a few more quips with Abby and head for David's car. Only, he's waiting inside, chatting with her himself, his feet kicked out and crossed at the ankle, his eyes lit up. He's acting like he really is my boyfriend and he's worried about securing my sister's approval.

"Let's go." I kick the bottom of his shoe. "And I'm sure I told you to wait outside."

David tilts his head and pulls a face at Abby. "See? What did I tell you?"

She laughs. "You're not wrong. I'll be curious to see whether you can snap her out of it."

"Out of what?" I scowl.

"He said you treat him like a dog," Abby mock-whispers. "He said you're always ordering him around and chastising him for any missteps."

"I didn't say it exactly like that." He's smiling, though, so he said *essentially* that.

"Let's go, Fido," I say.

"Oh, come on," he says. "At least give me a cool name, like Killer."

"More like Sunshine," Abby says. "You're way too friendly and egalitarian to be called Killer."

David grabs his chest. "You two are both horrifying. Have you ever heard that?" He shakes his head. "Never mind. Everyone's probably too afraid to tell you."

Abby's still laughing as we walk out the door.

"Killer?" I roll my eyes. "Really?"

"You know, other people find me very intimidating." David marches a little too quickly to his car, and I realize that he's annoyed.

As I'm climbing into my side of his car, I think about it. He's from a powerful family in Korea. He likely grew up with a lot of people who were jealous of him. Then he came to America and went to some of the best schools here. He graduated from Harvard Business School somewhere near the top. Close enough to be annoying, anyway.

And yet, he's never overly aggressive. He maintained his integrity in business, never doing things he deemed to be predatory. I might think that's weak, but to some people that would be considered the opposite.

Strong.

He stuck with what he believes.

He never cuts out the little guys.

I'm not planning on learning a whole new moral code for him or whatever, but maybe in his own way, he is a Killer. "Fine."

"Fine what?" He turns his BMW sedan on, and backs down the driveway. "Fine, you'll stop treating me like a dog?"

I snort. "Hardly. But I can try calling you Killer."

He sighs. "I should've known."

My assistant Roger calls me then, with some urgent questions about the due diligence we're still moving through. I almost make David pull over, but I decide that if I can't trust my honorable fake-boyfriend, even though he knows the principal manager of the company we're acquiring, who can I trust?

Plus, it's fairly routine stuff. I doubt his buddy would be shocked we're looking into it. By the time I get off the phone, I realize that we're downtown.

Downtown Manila, that is.

Being in the heart of Manila's like. . . Well. It shouldn't be called downtown. It's not even a town. He's stopped in front of the R-Hideout, the tiny hotel-lodge thing that Donna's boyfriend Will's mother runs. "What on earth are we doing here? You can't really mean for us to go to Brownings again. How many bad burgers can you really eat?"

"You're so snobby." David points. "Look around for a minute."

"At what, exactly?"

In that moment, as if he timed it, lights click on up and down the street. Christmas lights basically blanket the entire tiny road, from the ram statue in front of R-Hideout, to twinkle lights around all the pillars and posts and along the rustic rooftop. Every single tree, every single bush, and every roofline is lit up.

The carwash has little critters and snowman figurines dancing across the front. The True Value hardware store that also doubles as the worst market ever has the porch line, the handrails, and the roofline outlined, and on top of that, Santa and his elves are in a sleigh on the top of the building. The church building by the Green River street sign is lit up like a torch. Even the snowcone/fireworks stand has reindeer in front of it and lights strung along the rooftop.

With the layer of snow blanketing most of the ground, which you can't tell is dingy now that the sun has gone down, it looks almost. . .magical.

"Alright," I admit. "It's kind of pretty."

"You're so used to being awed only by earth-shattering things that I thought it might be nice to just take in the cute decorations right in front of us." David hops out and jogs around the car. Before I can stop him, he's opened my door. "Milady."

I slap his hand. "Knock it off."

"I knew you'd be a pain."

I sigh, but I climb out and let him close the door behind me. "I'm not a monster. I can see that it's cute."

As we walk the length of the road, our breath puffing out in front of us, the lights blinking and twinkling, and music blasting from half of the stores, I realize that he was right.

I frequently miss the beauty that's right in front of me.

I'm always too busy focusing on the work that lies ahead to bother looking for anything lovely at all. Is that why people like it here? "I'll admit that this isn't that bad."

"I'm glad you'll admit that," he says. "Because look."

We've stopped in front of the abandoned building next door to my sister's legal office. "Um."

"I hear this used to be a post office," he says. "My crew said it was a real mess inside."

"I think Mandy owns this," I say. "Why would your crew—"

"Just wait." He pushes the front door open.

Inside, I expect to see a somewhat dilapidated old post office setup. Instead, I walk into a Christmas wonderland. "Whoa, Killer. What's going on?"

Once we walk past the arbor of Christmas flowers that look like every one of Amanda's floral arrangements are having a block party, we enter the main room. There's a table with candles in the center. The tablecloth's immaculate. The centerpiece is even tasteful. . .a few poinsettias, a few pinecones, and a little gnome.

As we get closer, I realize it's actually two gnomes, and they're kissing. Underneath mistletoe. Gag me.

"What do you think?"

"All this for a burger?" I shake my head. "It's a cute idea for a fake date, but you went to way too much work." It is pretty impressive that he set all of this up here, in the middle of nowhere. I realize that he must have set it up when he ordered the cherries. There's no way he could have planned this after I announced that we were dating.

Which means this wasn't fake. . .to him.

"Ah, ah." He picks up his phone and taps away. Less than thirty seconds later, three people walk inside from the front door. Where were they hiding when we came in? The only people I saw looked like regular townspeople.

"Sorry we didn't see you, sir." The first man is tall, and he's fairly young. There's no way he's a local. "The first course is deep-fried langoustine with creamed uni and nasturtium." He hands us a card.

"No way," I say. "This can't be. . ."

"Have you been to Atomix?" David smiles.

"Killer." I shake my head. "You couldn't have convinced the chef from there to bring food out here. I don't believe you."

David leans closer. "The chef's my cousin." He presses a finger to his lips. "Don't tell anyone, but I gave him the startup capital that got that place started."

I remember then that it's a Korean place. What are the odds? "That's nuts."

"Chef Park sends his apologies for not coming himself," the tall man says. "But the Mayor was eating there tonight. He thinks his sous chef should be able to prepare the menu he chose adequately."

Adequately is an understatement. Maybe it's because we're eating it in the center of an old, abandoned building. Maybe it's the quaint but also over-the-top Christmas decorations. Or maybe it's the company that I'm growing to not hate, but we share one of the best meals I've ever eaten.

Briny caviar served over a bed of delicate baby arti-
chokes and some of the freshest cheese curds I've ever
tasted. A whole turbot, braised and then grilled in a
rich seafood stock. And it's all finished off with a light,
perfectly balanced strawberry bingsu, with freshly
grated orange zest on the whipped cream.

Just like in the restaurant, at the end of the night,
we each have a stack of cards that give context to the
menu items, and also each one has historical information about their country and culture.

Of course, that's when I realize that I didn't take a
single photo.

"Wait," I say, as the tall man's ducking out.

He turns back, eyes scanning our table. "Is something wrong?"

"Not at all." I hold out my phone. "Could you snap
a photo of us, though?"

When I try to tip him as he passes my phone back,
he shakes his head. "I can't accept any gratuities.
Believe me, Mr. Park pays me well."

"Nice try," David says.

"Well." I lean back in my chair and pat my belly.
"That did not help my metabolism, but I think it was
worth it. I've missed New York's more robust dining
options."

"I'm glad you enjoyed it."

"Pretty decent for a second date," I say.

"Wait, is that an admission that our first meal was
also a date?"

I roll my eyes. "Before you take me home, did you
have a business plan you wanted me to look over?"

"Before we go home?" He glances at his watch. "It's
barely past eight p.m."

"Right, but what else is there to do?" I wave my
hands. "I mean, really."

"I thought you might say that, but I chose tonight for a reason."

"Because we just officially told everyone we were dating?" I laugh. "Good call." And then I remember that he planned all this before he knew that I'd announce we were dating. He planned this, and sent my employees cherries, and sent me rum with that card about our date.

He leans closer. "Tonight is Manila's famous Christmas Ball."

"Christmas ball?" My brain churns furiously, trying to think of what kind of ball this area might have that would have something to do with Christmas. A cheese-ball? Knowing this town, it would be the size of a punch bowl or something even bigger. Then I envision some kind of weird ball dropping like on New Year's, but it's a huge beach ball instead. Only after my brain pitches out all those weird ideas do I finally realize what he must be saying.

"A ball, as in a dance?"

He nods.

"You have got to be kidding."

"Not at all," he says. "They love to dance here."

"We're not in high school, Killer." Of all the ridiculous. . . "Just take me home."

"Absolutely not," he says. "You liked seeing the lights and you loved the dinner. Now, give me the benefit of the doubt, and let's go try their dance."

"I am not dressed for that." I gesture at my puffy coat, pencil pants, and snow boots.

"Correction," he says. "You're not dressed for a New York City ball. You're probably overdressed for a Manila, Utah ball."

"And that's my point," I say. "I'd be overdressed in my pajamas."

"Helen, if you can't get over yourself, you'll never be happy anywhere. Not in Manila, and not anywhere else either." David walks away as if he doesn't care whether I follow.

With as big of a jerk as I've been, he may not.

Is what he said right? Am I the problem? I look up and down the street I admired two hours before. The cheap, yellow and rainbow lights are just as tacky as they were before. The storefronts are just as sad. The huge gaps between the buildings on Manila's Main Street are just as painfully wide as they always have been.

But maybe none of that matters.

David's walking past the brightly lit crèche, his broad shoulders wrapped in the finest charcoal wool, his hair perfectly combed and styled. He'll be the best-looking and richest person in that dumb old church cultural hall.

And unlike me, he might not even notice.

Would I be happier if I took each day as they came? If I could figure out how to appreciate what each place and time had to offer, and I didn't spend so much time judging everything? I sigh long and slow.

He might be right.

He's already inside, the warmth of the light spilling outward from the door he just disappeared through. And now, thanks to my own willful fit, I'm stuck walking into a place where I know almost no one alone. Maybe I should just go home.

I belatedly recall that he's my ride, and it's not like there's an Uber here. So now my options include calling Abby or Ethan, going into that dance alone, or sitting here in the cold until David finally emerges. I wonder how many local girls will beg him to dance with them while I'm hiding out here.

Some of the women out here are actually kind of cute. I mean, they'll have no idea what he's saying or what he's doing or who he is, but they're not terrible to look at. Why does the idea of all of the cute little farmers dancing with him and batting their goopy, dime-store mascara-covered eyes bother me?

We're *fake* dating.

I refuse to go rushing in there because I'm sort of jealous. I'm *Helen Fisher*. I don't cave and follow people around. I whip out my phone and call Abby.

"Hello?" It's noisy where she is.

"Hey, Abs."

"I can hardly hear you. Are you okay?"

"The thing is, I kind of need a ride."

"Oh, well, where are you? I'm not at home, but I can—"

Someone else is talking to her.

"Sorry. Steve was asking who it was."

"Where are you?" I feel guilty for calling her. My sister spends most nights at home with her kids and her new husband. Usually a drive down the road and back wouldn't cause her any frustration. "You know what? Never mind. I can just call Ethan."

"You need to talk to Ethan? He's right here."

"Wait," I shout. "Where's here?"

"Manila has this Christmas ball every year," she says. "It's a cute little town event, really." Abby's talking to someone else again. "Helen? Why am I talking to David Park right now? Where are you, exactly? Did he ditch you? Should I kick him in the shin right now? Because I may be pregnant, but I swear, I can still kick the ever-loving fire—"

I swear under my breath and hang up.

But at least I know that there will be a few people there I know. The worst part is that, as I walk past the stupid manger scene, baby Jesus is smirking at me. I just know he is.

He should be.

I'm pretentious.

Snobby.

And I'm about to look like an idiot, because now everyone knows I didn't want to come, and that stupid David Park left me alone because I threw a baby fit.

Also, they can clearly see that I lost our tug-of-war.

"Hey," David says the moment I walk through the door. "Did your call finally end?" He holds up his arm as if to wave me over.

I glance at Abby and then back at David.

"Did you get so distracted you didn't see which way he went?" Abby's laughing at me alright, but not for the reason I thought she would be. "Helen, you get so focused on work stuff that sometimes, I worry you'll walk off the edge of a cliff. You're not a good multi-tasker. It's a good thing you usually have a driver."

Steve's laughing.

David's laughing.

And now Amanda and Donna are approaching, also both laughing. "Did you hear what just happened?" Donna's face is bright red.

"About Mr. Crenshaw's pants?" Steve's laughing even harder. "Did you know that same thing happened to his dad, but like, twenty years ago?"

"What are they talking about?" I ask, hoping Abby will clue me in.

"Mr. Crenshaw has a black suit he wears every year, but only for this," David says. "He's the head elder in the church here. But this year, apparently he gained a bit too much weight, and his wife told him it wouldn't fit."

"Okay."

"Well, he was determined to prove her wrong," Amanda says. "He told everyone that his wife didn't pay any attention to how he looked, and he insisted that he hadn't gained a pound."

"And?"

"They were doing the same line dance they always do, to 'All I Want for Christmas,'" Will says, just arriving, but clearly also in on the joke.

"You can line dance to that?" I can't even imagine it.

"Oh yeah," Donna says. "In another five minutes, they'll be line dancing to 'Last Christmas.' Just wait."

"Uh, okay." Maybe we can escape before then. If I get roped into that, I'll never be able to live it down.

"Anyway," Steve says, clearly unhappy with how slowly the story's being told. "He did that part where you kick and twist-turn, and his pants split right up the back."

"That sounds. . .unfortunate," I say.

"Oh, it's better than that," Abby says. "You told it all wrong."

"I was saving that part for you." Steve's beaming at her, which is annoying, but also kind of cute. He does it all the time, like he thinks she's a movie star or something.

"To squeeze into the suit, Mr. Crenshaw had to get rid of everything that wasn't strictly necessary," Amanda hisses. "*Everything.*"

Donna snorts.

Will barks a laugh.

"We were on the front row," Abby says, "because Steve's a judge this year." She makes a gagging sound.

"Let's just say, at first, I thought he was wearing hairy pants," Amanda says. "And we all got a new appreciation for what his wife deals with." She pulls a hilarious face.

And that's when I can't help it. I start laughing, too. I wasn't even there.

I don't know Mr. Crenshaw, or his wife, and I don't care what she has to deal with. But the idea of all of them standing around and staring while some poor man's pants split up the back? It's pretty funny.

"Sounds like my work call really ruined the night for me."

"Oh, we're just getting started." David reaches for my hand right as I hear the opening bars of "Last Christmas."

"No way," I say.

"Yes." He's smiling broadly when he takes my hand.

Everyone's smiling by the end of that song, including me. The people here may not be business moguls. They may not own very much at all, but they are much happier than most of the people I've met in New York City, and to be honest, I have a lot more fun dancing with them and gossiping than I ever did back there.

Or at least, I do right up until David's taking me home and his phone rings. I happen to glance at the caller ID. It says Noona.

I'm not an expert at Korean, but I know that word means older sister. I wonder whether he's told her that I told him about our plan. I'm assuming she watches his social media closely enough to have noticed that we're now dating. Does she know it's fake?

"Hello?" David answers it, to my shock, on his car phone.

She says something in Korean that I don't understand. I catch one word. Oma. It means mom.

"We just started dating. Tell Mom not to be too excited yet."

"You have me to thank, you know." His sister switches to English, which makes it way easier for me to be nosy.

"I'm sorry. In what way did you have anything to do with me finally getting a girlfriend?"

"She called me. Your girlfriend, I mean."

My heart skips a beat. He clearly didn't tell her that I already came clean.

"I figured that out when you randomly filled out papers for the sale of the Ellingson ranch." He exhales. "Tell me something else, or I'll stick with my position that you didn't help me get the girl at all."

"I made her think that you were being cut out—I told her Dad's choosing a successor soon, and that I needed her help to make sure it's not you."

"And how did that help me?"

I can practically hear Ji-Hye's smile through her tone. "Oh, Ji-ho, you know nothing about women. She's one of the richest women in the world. Do you think she got there by flirting? No, she takes people down. So when she called me, that meant you had done something right. You had attracted her attention. I just made you more desirable, by telling her you were a viable option for running the family business."

"But I would never take that from you, as you know."

"But *she* doesn't know that."

"She does now," David says.

I can't help laughing. "Hi, Ji-Hye."

"You have me on speakerphone?" She switches to Korean then, and she speeds up a lot. I'm pretty sure she's bawling him out.

"Calm down," he says. "Whatever you did, it

worked. Because things are going great. Tell Mom that, okay?"

"I wasn't actually trying to trick you," Ji-Hye says. She starts muttering in Korean again. "When are you coming home for a visit?" She drops her voice. "Because when you do, Ji-ho, I'm going to kill you with my bare hands." She hangs up.

"Pretty sure your family now thinks we're dating for real," I say.

He shrugs. "You have your reasons to say we're dating, and I have mine."

We pull into the driveway before I can ask any other questions, but as I head back into my room, I can't help thinking about how many things I thought I knew about David Park that turned out to be totally wrong. He's pretty competent about business, even if he's not as aggressive as I am. He's a good brother, and he doesn't want to go home and take over their company. He has a decent sister, and she likes him. He fits in with the small-town people in Manila, including Amanda and Eddy, who had to dislike him at first, based on how he pursued her.

I'm beginning to feel a little bad about this fake-dating thing. For a split second, I consider. . .but no. That's not me.

I don't date people for real.

🌿 17 🌿

AMANDA

Sometimes I can snap a photo at just the right time and in just the right lighting, and I immediately know it's magical.

That's how I got started on IG, to be honest.

I had these two darling girls, and I took a gazillion photos of them. When I would feel really proud of one, I'd post it on IG. At first, only my friends followed me. But then, one day, in a very un-photo-worthy moment, I came into the room and saw that Maren had opened most of my nail polish.

And painted it all over the wall.

Blobby flowers.

Streaks.

A heart.

And the word Mom.

Before I started to cry, I whipped out my camera and snapped a photo. Maren looks half deer-in-the-headlights, half proud-as-peaches, and Emery's in the corner, looking very nervous.

But the central focus of the photo is the messy, toddler-painted word, Mom. I put that photo up with just one hashtag. #Momlife. It went viral. I wasn't the only mom out there whose kid had made a tremendous mess. It's frustrating—and expensive—to clean up after something like that.

Those moments are fleeting, too.

The sweet little word she painted contrasted with the epic amount of work that her mom was about to have to do in order to deal with her cute moment. It sort of encapsulated what we all struggle with. The messy joys of motherhood.

In the best of times, Instagram is like that photo.

It highlights the beauty in the mess. It focuses on the things that matter. It makes us laugh. Smile. Cry. And feel.

But since making my account into a business account, the more common type of post I make is not effortless. It's not super insightful. It's just one more shiny, bright photo in a line of shiny, bright photos.

It's a slog.

That's how this wedding feels, to be honest.

When Eddy arrives, I practically sprint for the door. "Ah, you're here. Tell me what you think about these invitations?" Snuggles is just as excited as I am. She races round and round the room with Roscoe—we call the excited racing their laps.

"Didn't we already send the invites out?" Eddy's eyebrows rise. "Because we're getting married in like two weeks."

"Two weeks and three days." I may be a little frantic about the time. It feels like sand escaping through a hole that's clearly too big.

"Okay."

I shake my head. "They all went out, but the invitation company wanted three shares on social, remember?"

Eddy blinks.

"This is the last one, and now I can't think of an angle to take the photo. Or maybe the background's no good."

"They don't want it to be super Christmassy, I assume?"

"Why wouldn't they?" Now my heart's picking up. It's going to be really hard to make them *not* look Christmassy. I can't include all our invitation details, because I want those to be private, but I need to have some part of the invitation visible. "It has poinsettias on it!"

"Oh, no," Eddy says. "I don't know. I was just asking."

"It's resting on a stack of Christmas cards," I say. "I hope they don't mind if it looks Christmassy!"

Eddy drops a hand on my shoulder. "Amanda."

"What?" I bat it away.

"Amanda." He grabs my shoulders with both hands, and then he waits until I finally meet his gaze.

"What?" I do not have time for this. "I need to get a post up this morning, so that I have time to do another one this afternoon. I'm running out of time to post all this junk, and they complain if their post is made too close to someone else's."

"You need to calm down," he says. "It's great that we got all this stuff for free, but we have plenty of money. Maybe you just tell these people that you'll pay for the stuff."

"It's too late for that now," I say. "I've already signed the agreements." My voice sounds a little frantic, even to me.

Eddy drags me in for a hug. "I love you."

He does? The woman who's shrieking and who just slapped his hand away?

But he must.

He keeps me like that, pressed against his chest. His breathing isn't fast. His heart rate isn't elevated. He's clearly not stressed. Probably because he doesn't have to do any of this stuff, and the holidays are a notoriously slow time for large animal practices. The horses and cows are mostly inside barns, eating hay and doing nothing. Other than some lameness exams, he's got nothing to do.

"Is it safe for me to release you yet?" I can feel his chest shaking a bit as he chuckles. "Or will you fall back into panic mode?"

That's why I love him. When I'm frantic, he calms me down.

He releases me slowly, and then he turns to the invitations. "I love this. The last two you did were stylized, with Christmas-themed items by the invitation, but this one looks like it just arrived at someone's house, along with these other cards, all of which look just a little shabby next to it."

"Right?" I inhale and exhale slowly. "I'm going to tag it #luxe. It looks luxe, right?"

He brushes a hand down the side of my face. "Just like you, yes. It looks deluxe for sure."

"Ew." I nip at his hand. "Not deluxe. That sounds like you're saying I'm big. Luxe is short for *luxurious*."

"Did I mention that I'm a vet?" He shrugs. "I don't know fancy words."

"That's why you need me."

Jed's scratching on the door. Both dogs are pretty good with him, but he gets a little anxious when they're both here, racing around. I open the back door and let him out. He's been staying inside more with the cold weather and the construction that's moving ahead on the retreat building behind us in fits and starts, so it'll be good for him to get out on a nice, sunny day like today. Maybe he'll even go rummage around in what's left of the garden, under the nasty old piles of dirty snow.

If we get really lucky, the last of it will melt today.

I duck back inside, once I see that Jed's happily rooting around, and focus long enough to snap a few photos. I manage to edit one and post it in under five minutes, which feels like a huge win.

"Let's do something fun today," Eddy says. "We could drive down to Vernal and catch that new movie Maren was talking about."

"Without the girls?"

Eddy shrugs, and then he smiles that devilishly handsome rockstar smile I can't ever seem to resist. "They don't have to know."

"Know what?" My mom pops out of her room.

My cute fiancé nearly stumbles backward into the wall. "Oh. You're home."

Mom swallows. "Where else would I be?"

"I'm here too, champ." Mandy breezes through her door and into the family room. "Did you think you had her all to yourself?"

"And I invited your parents over too," I say. "We have to finalize the seating chart."

"It's a wonder that so many people get married," Eddy says. "You'd think the wedding would sour more people on it." He drops into an armchair. "Fine. Let's talk about the seating chart, but tomorrow—"

"Tomorrow you're choosing the gifts for the guests." Mandy looks like she's having way too much fun.

"Wait, why do we have to give them anything?" He frowns. "It's our wedding."

"Abby and Steve gave us those cute painted horseshoes, remember? They had little gems on them and they said, 'Thanks for coming to our special day.'"

"That was a *gift?*" Eddy snorts. "I thought Steve was just trying to clear out his old horseshoes. And mine looked like it was painted by Gabe, who does not have a future as an artist. Just saying."

I kick the bottom of his boot and sit down next to him. "Be nice."

"Great, well, if that's our measuring stick, I've got a huge pile of horns near my dumpster. Had to dehorn a bunch of goats last week that Old Ulysses never got around to doing. We could have Emery paint those, and they'd look way better than those dumb horseshoes."

My mother looks ill.

"He's kidding, Mom."

"Am I?" Eddy shakes his head. "We're giving these people dinner. We're entertaining them. We're the ones getting married. If you don't think they'll like painted horns, maybe we just skip getting them anything at all."

Mandy says, "Or you could give them all a bag of cookies. I bet you even have some cookie labels left around here somewhere."

"You, shut up," I say. "Neither of you are funny."

"Why's that funny?" Mom asks. "I bet they'd love her cookies."

Luckily, before I have to kick both of them, the doorbell rings. As I open it, Eddy's mother's already fussing at her husband.

"—told you not to ring the doorbell. It's rude. Someone might've been sleeping."

"No one's sleeping," Eddy's dad says. "Her kids are at school." He's glaring.

"Come on in," I say. "Not a single soul's asleep

around here, no matter how much they might need a nap." I glare at Mandy and Eddy.

"Wow, everyone is here," Eddy's mother says. "I didn't realize."

"It made more sense to have us all here together to do the seating chart," I say. "As you may already know, we have about three hundred people coming to the wedding, if the RSVPs can be trusted."

"Three hundred?" Eddy's mother's eyes widen. "Is every single person in Manila coming?"

Sadly, that would be the right number of people if every single occupant turned out.

"I have a few friends from New York City who are flying out," I say. "Eddy has some friends and co-workers from his tour, as well as a few buddies from vet school."

"Okay," his dad says. "Can't you just kinda group them in together?"

"I have two friend groups," I say. "I have one group of friends I know because of my first husband, Paul. They don't work, and they mostly like to gossip about one another."

"And?" Mom asks.

"The other group is mostly influencer friends, and you can't seat them all together, either. So I'll need to kind of sprinkle my people around. But we should make sure they're not sitting by people who will. . ." Hmm. How do I say they need to be by people who aren't totally rural without being offensive?

"Basically," Mandy says, "we need to put Eddy's fancy friends by Amanda's fancy friends, but not all together, or they'll fight. Like two roosters thrown in a box."

I nod. "Something like that, yes."

"Great." Mandy grabs a piece of paper, and she

starts drawing rectangles on it. "So you have the tables on the right side here, here, and here." She points, and then she grabs another piece of paper. "Then the tables in the front." And one more. "And the ones on the other side."

"I think the family should be front and center," Eddy's mom says.

"Great," my mom says. "This table seats ten. How many people are in your family?"

Eddy's mother turns to look at her husband, sending him a meaningful glance I don't quite understand. "Well."

"The two of us," Eddy's dad says. "And Eddy's sister and her boyfriend. My brother and his wife and their three kids. One's married."

"I think that's ten," Eddy's mom says.

"Oh." Mom sighs. "Well, you could have that front table, I can sit just to the right of that."

"Abigail will be there." I feel a little bad sticking her with my mom, but she seems to do fine with everyone. "We could have her, Steve, her four kids, Beth, Donna, and Will."

"But then there's Aiden," Mom says. "And I'm out of room again."

"You and Dad and the boys can take this table," Eddy points at the third in the front section. "I have a few friends who can get a little rowdy, but I bet you and Mandy can keep them in line."

Mom shakes her head. "Your dad and brothers can't come. They're running behind on the contract cuz of weather, and there are penalties. They asked me to tell you."

That's a little surprising, since they've been so gung-ho, but it's not really a shock. It's more bizarre that Mom's still here. Even so, I'm surprised by how disappointed I am. It's not like I really even wanted them here. Mom's constantly saying embarrassing things, and it'll be even worse when my New York City friends arrive. But. . .

"Gabe's small," Mandy says. "So are the other kids. I bet we can squeeze an extra chair or two at that table."

"Or that," Eddy says.

Squeeze an extra chair or two? That's about the Mandiest thing I've ever heard.

"I don't think that's going to look very elegant," Eddy's mom says. "And the theme certainly seems to be elegance."

"That's not a theme. Besides, you shouldn't butt in," Eddy's dad says. "You're always butting in when people don't need your opinion."

"Alright," I say. "Maybe we can have the waitstaff do two smaller tables of eight. Then we could have the kids at one table, and the adults at the other. Everyone will fit."

The rest of the seating chart goes about like that, with every snag being compounded by Eddy's mom and dad arguing about it. It feels symbolic, somehow, of this entire wedding. By the time we finish and Eddy's parents finally leave, I'm ready to collapse into an Amanda-shaped puddle on the floor.

"See? One more task done," Eddy says.

"Yes, and the kids come home in. . ." I glance at my watch. "Thirty minutes."

"It would have been way faster without my mom and dad," Eddy says. "Next time, just leave them out."

"They're the only ones, other than you, who know a lot of the locals."

"Me and Mandy both do," Eddy says.

"I wanted them to feel involved," I say.

"They're not that bad," my mom says. "I mean, you can tell they love each other."

Does my mom have ears? Eddy and I both turn toward her at the same time. "Excuse me?" I ask. "The two people who just left? Is that who you're talking about?"

She shrugs. "I mean, they argued, but some people just do that. Neither of them said anything really mean."

Mandy's brow furrows. "You're right. They do argue, and they cut each other off, and they disagree, but they never call names. You could almost call it bickering, like what siblings do."

"I hardly think," Eddy says, "that you could say it's out of love or affection."

"Abby's kids do that too, sort of," Mandy says. "They pick at each other a lot. I mean, this is a little more picking, and a little less joke-like, but maybe she's right. Maybe it's not that bad."

"I do not want us to ever interact like that," Eddy says.

I shake my head. "Never ever."

"At least we're on the same page." He shudders. "Because even if they don't hate each other, it's not nice a nice atmosphere to be around."

"Alright, I need to take photos of the bridesmaid dresses," I say. "So once the girls come home, let's get the three of you into them."

"I thought it was cute when Abby put me in one," Mandy says. "But now I'm starting to feel like I'm the comic relief."

"That's crazy," I say.

"Is it?" Mandy ducks into her room and comes bouncing back out, holding the dress we chose. "Abby let us choose any dress we wanted in the right color.

223

You have me wearing *this*." She holds the dress against her chest, and I take a good look.

I mean, I've seen it before. I picked it.

It's a flattering enough cut for her, and everything looks good on teenage girls, so I thought it would be fine. It's bright red, A-line, and it has embroidered pine trees along the flouncy skirt.

It might look a little young.

Eddy snickers.

"Do you want me to kick you again?"

"When did you kick me?" Eddy takes a step away just to be safe.

"That's it." Mandy shakes her head. "I'm not wearing this."

"Oh, come on," I say. "At least let me get the photos today. My Insta feed loves you. If you hate how they come out, we'll find you something else before the wedding."

But after we get some shots, out by the pine trees in the front yard, I see what she's saying. She definitely needs something else, a dress that's more age appropriate.

"Fine," I say. "We'll pick a new one."

She shakes her head. "Told ya."

Just one more thing to do. By the time we finally finish, it's time to make something for dinner. And when everyone's eaten, and we've cleaned up, I want to curl up into a ball and cry.

"You okay?" Eddy nudges my slipper with the toe of his boot. "You look exhausted."

"I hate this," I say. "I wish we could just elope."

"But we're almost done, right?" Eddy asks. "Besides. You, elope?" He bursts out laughing.

"What's funny about that?"

"Miss Instagram herself?" He shakes his head. "No way."

"I've done all this before," I say. "You'd think I'd be smarter the second time around."

He tugs on my arm until I sit up. Then he tugs me against him. I collapse into my favorite spot against his chest. That earns us a few exaggerated 'ewwws' from the kitchen, but they should be getting used to it. "The difference is that this time, you're marrying someone you love." His voice is a warm hum against my cheek.

"That's true," I say. "But I don't think this is helping me love you more."

He pushes me up far enough that I can see his face. "Are you kidding?"

"Didn't you just say this stuff is a drag? You're surprised people survive the wedding."

"I was kidding. Mostly."

"We're almost there, but I wish I could go back and just *not* do all this stuff. I wish we could just, I don't know, make our own invitations, and pick wildflowers."

"There aren't any flowers growing wild. It's winter."

"You know what I mean," I say. "I wish we hadn't invited our old friends, who are going to make fun of Manila. They won't understand us or what we're doing."

Eddy stares at me then. "Is that really what you want?"

I think about all the invitations that have gone out. The people who have bought plane tickets.

My fiancé is someone who fixes flat tires for me, who buys the shoes I walk past and touch and say, 'these are nice.' He's a man who grabs Drano the second I mention that a drain's moving slowly and fixes it. Do I really want him to insist that we call this off

225

with two weeks to go? A wedding in his town with all his friends and family?

No.

That would be too big of a mess. I started this, so I need to finish it.

"I'm just grumbling," I lie. "It's fine."

And the thing is, it will be fine. The wedding itself may not be what I want, but I'll be married to Eddy at the end. That's the most important part.

"I thought you were still doing Instagram because you liked it." Emery perches on the edge of the sofa, her eyes wide. "It seems like you hate it now, though."

"I did like it," I say.

"When adults do what they like for money, sometimes it's great," Eddy says. "But sometimes it takes the thing they like and ruins it."

Maren drifts in and sits down, too. "What do you mean?"

"I love writing songs," Eddy says. "I've always loved it. But lately, when I send a new song to my manager, I always cringe."

"Why?" Maren's looking at him intently.

"I write what sounds good. I write what I'm feeling. But my manager wants me to write what will sell. So I'll get the song I loved back with notes like, 'needs more romance.' Or sometimes he'll say, 'too repetitive.' Last week I sent him a song, and he said, 'It's too whiny. You're not a country star.'"

"Ouch," Maren says.

"Doing what you love for work can make you hate it," I say. "He's right about that."

"Is that what happened with the cookies?" Emery asks. "Did making them for a job make you hate them?"

"No, that's when your mom was in her 'copy

Abigail' phase," Mandy says. "I don't think she really made cookies before or since." Her cackling restores a bit of my joy.

Even if it's at my expense.

These are the people I want at my wedding.

Abby. Her kids. Mandy. My kids. Eddy. His bickering parents.

And my mom. That one surprises me, but it's true.

I wish I could go back and realize this a few months ago, but it feels important that I've at least learned this about myself now. Bigger isn't always better. Sometimes it's just bigger.

"Hey, does she usually pace like that?" Mandy's looking at the entryway.

Where Snuggles is pacing.

"Oh, no." Eddy sighs. "I guess it's better than the day of the wedding, right?"

"Wait, what's happening?" Maren asks.

"I think Snuggles is about to have puppies." I stand up and walk toward her and Roscoe. He's sitting down, but he looks nervous.

"I better get her home," Eddy says. "Sometimes they're in labor for a full day. But with bigger dogs, it's usually not that long."

"Oh, wow," I say. "What do we do?"

"Depends on whether you all want to see it."

"Could she have them here?" Emery looks like she usually does on Christmas morning.

"She could," Eddy says, "but it would be better for her at my place. She's more at home there. Plus, I have a big whelping box set up."

"To the car," Emery yells.

I'm digging around for sleeping bags and blankets when my phone rings. In all the chaos, I almost don't hear it. "Can someone grab that?"

"It's Steve," Mandy says. "Does he call you very often?"

Never. I drop the blankets I'm holding and answer. "Hello?"

"Hey," he says. "I don't want to alarm you, but I wanted to update you. Abby had an ultrasound today, and they found that her amniotic fluid levels are low. Very, very low. They've given her a steroid shot, and they want to deliver the baby tomorrow or the next day."

"Oh, no." My heart races. "That's not good. How early are we?"

"Eight weeks," he says. "They're checking for evidence of a fluid leak right now."

"Are you in Green River? I'll be right there."

"Nah, the OB's in Vernal—we're at Ashley Regional," he says. "But it's okay. You don't have to come. We know you've got kids and a wedding to plan."

And puppies coming too, but I don't even mention that.

Abby matters more. "I'll be there soon."

18

DONNA

Back when we were married, Charlie usually saved his anger and abuse and manipulation for me. But one thing he did yell at Aiden for was being too loud.

My sweet little guy who loved to sing along to shows, who loved to exclaim with joy when he built the biggest Lego tower in the world, always got really quiet and nervous right before Charlie came home for the day. I didn't even realize it was stressing him out until it had already changed his behavior.

He was afraid to be too loud.

He was nervous to take up too much space.

He didn't feel safe in his own home. In his own skin.

So it fills me with joy when he gets dropped off and runs into the kitchen, slinging his backpack on the floor, and shouts, "Guess what?" He's practically bouncing.

It feels like I have a little bit of the old Aiden back. It's the same feeling I get when I see a sprout coming from the base of a plant I thought had died.

"Oh." I belatedly realize that he actually wants me to guess. "Um, did you get a present at school from a friend?"

He shakes his head.

"Did you meet Santa Claus?"

"No. Mom, Santa's super busy right now." He rolls his eyes like I'm the idiot.

"Okay, well, you may have to tell me."

Ethan comes out of Beth's room. "Hey, dude. Welcome home." Beth told him she was leaving after the baby's born, and he's still here, whenever he's not working, around the clock.

Ethan and Aiden high-five.

"Guess what?" Aiden claps his hands. "I have good news."

"Oh," Ethan says. "Is it about the school play?"

Aiden's smile widens. "Yes. How did you know?"

"Gabe said he was trying out, too."

My sweet son starts nodding so hard that I worry he'll scramble his brains. "Yes, yes!" He bounces more.

"Did you get a part in the play?" I didn't even hear about the play. Ethan's a better brother than I am a mom. How sad.

"I got the *best* part!" He jumps in the air. "And Gabe got the other best part!"

"Oh." I wonder what that means.

"I'm young Ebudneezer Scrooge, and Gabe's old Ebudneezer Scrooge."

"He got Ebenezer?" Ethan asks. "Because that's what he wanted."

"Yes." Aiden nods again. "We both wanted it, and it was Gabe's idea that maybe we could both share it. Isn't that totally awesome?"

"It really is," Ethan says.

Especially because there's no way my son would

have beaten Gabe. He's only a year younger, but he acts much younger, and he doesn't read nearly as well.

"Since Gabe's older," Aiden says, "we decided he should be the older one, and I can be the young one." He grabs my hand. "They're both kinda selfish and greedy, Mom, but don't worry. An angel tells us to be better."

"An angel?" Beth pokes her head out. "Wow, they've changed that story."

"Well, I think it says a ghost," Aiden says. "But me and Gabe decided an angel would be better."

"Is the teacher letting you say angel?" Ethan's eyebrows rise. "Really?"

Aiden shrugs. "I don't know, but the Angel of the past is our friend Hannah, and she said she really wants to wear wings."

I can't help laughing. This play is going to be *interesting*. "I can't wait to watch it."

"They're throwing it together pretty fast," Beth says. "Isn't school out in like a week?"

Aiden frowns. "There's not that much to do. You just read the stuff on the paper."

Wow, this play is going to be amazing.

Ethan glances at me, and then at Beth. His eyes are wide. "We really cannot wait, dude. You're going to be great."

Will's parking his car in the driveway, and when he comes in, Aiden starts all over again. "Hey, guess what?"

After a handful of decent guesses and a few really bad ones, Ethan and I take pity on him and spill the news.

"Wait, an angel?" Will's face is priceless. "My mom is going to *love* this version."

"Right?" Aiden asks. "The writer should have

known that an angel's better than a ghost, but good thing Gabe and I know."

"Why's an angel better?" Ethan is clearly having as much fun with this as I am.

"Ghosts just float, and they can't touch anything," Aiden says.

"Right," Beth says. "Geez, Ethan."

"Plus, angels have halos and they can go to heaven." Aiden walks off then, as if there's no contest.

When I start making dinner, since it's my night, Will, Ethan, Aiden, and Beth start playing cards. Aiden's gotten pretty decent at playing team spades, honestly. It didn't even occur to me that a kid his age could play games like that, but he loves it.

This is a life I never thought I'd have.

Sautéing onions and ground meat while my fiancé, my son, my niece, and her boyfriend are all laughing in my kitchen. It almost feels too good to be true.

I'm nearly done with the ground meat when Aiden asks, "Why are you making dinner so early? I just got home from school."

"Well, today's my day off. I've been wanting to make a few freezer meals for Abby, so I figured, why not get started today?"

"That's so thoughtful," Beth says.

"She's done a lot for me, and people like her usually don't get much."

"You'd think people who are always helping other people would get lots of help," Aiden says.

"Why wouldn't everyone help her?" Beth asks. "I bet they do."

"People don't help women like Abby," Will says. "She's too competent. They help people who look like they need help. The more capable you are, the more often you're left to handle things alone."

Will probably knows because his mom's just like that.

"Donna's like that too," Will says.

"What?" I shake my head. "No way. I'm a mess."

"Oh, no, he's right," Beth says. "You are."

When the phone rings, I grab it without thinking. "Hello?"

"Miss Ellingson?"

"Yes, that's me," I say.

"I'm Garett Young, calling about the Navajo Cliffs. I'm a forestry service employee. The cliffs are part of the Ashley National Forest."

I inhale sharply. This is my top pick for our wedding venue, but I'm not sure whether they'll be open for weddings in February. "Great. I'm so happy you called me back."

"I'm afraid I have some bad news."

"You're not open in February?"

"We really don't recommend making any plans like that before June. Mother Nature's fickle, and while we do take bookings for May, they're not always a good idea."

I sigh.

"If you could move the date back—"

"Unfortunately, that won't work. But thank you so much for calling me back."

"Of course. I'm sorry I don't have better news."

When I hang up, everyone in the kitchen's staring at me. "You're getting married in February?" Aiden asks. "Isn't that really cold?"

"Amanda's getting married the day after Christmas, silly," Ethan says. "February is the month of Valentine's Day. It's a great time to get married."

"Not around here." Aiden frowns. "Why don't you

pick the summer? Then you have more time. And you can do the waterfall place."

Navajo Falls is where I took him camping right after his dad went to jail. He loves it there. "Luckily, there are lots of great places around here," I say.

"What about David Park's retreat?" Will asks. "Isn't that where Amanda and Eddy are doing their reception?"

"It's booked," I say. "All four weekends in February are unavailable. I guess we could look at mid-week, but it'll be hard for everyone to come."

"As long as you're there." Will jogs over to where I'm standing and wraps one arm around my waist. "We can get married anywhere. Any time. Whatever you want."

"Let's do May," Aiden says. "Or June."

"Your mom's going to pick a time that makes her happy." Ethan ruffles Aiden's hair. He knows why we're hurrying.

It might be silly, but I want to be married when we adopt our little girl. I've done plenty of things wrong in my life. I want to get everything right that I can this time.

"We could use a barn," Will says. "I've seen pictures of that, and we have a barn. Lots of our friends do, too."

"It's too small," I say. "I want to invite your whole family and all our friends."

"How about the County Fairgrounds?" Beth asks. "You could bring in heaters."

It's not a terrible idea. "I'll look into that."

"How's the wedding stuff coming?" Beth asks.

I shrug. "Not great. It's hard to throw something together in two months, and being in the middle of winter makes it harder." I shake my head. "Not all of us

234

have people leaping through hoops to get us to use their stuff, either. I should have started an Instagram account."

"I don't know," Ethan says. "Aunt Amanda doesn't always seem that happy about it. I think she wishes she was just paying."

I laugh. "The grass really is always greener."

"I guess so," Ethan says.

"Well, our grass is going to be plenty green," Will says. "Don't worry. I'll call Mom's buddy about the fairground and let you know what they say."

"Yes, that might be our best bet." My phone rings again. I flip off the gas on the stove, and pick up, again without looking. I'm barely conscious of the fact that someone's calling Ethan at the same time.

"Hey," Amanda says.

"What's up?"

"Have you heard about Abigail?"

My heart starts hammering in my chest. "Have I heard what?"

"She's in the hospital. Her amniotic fluid's low, and they're giving steroids. Looks like it's baby time."

"It's two months early," I say. "That can't be right."

"No one told him that, apparently."

Oh, no. I'm worried for Abigail, of course, but something else occurs to me. I've been assuming this baby will come on time, in April.

What if she comes early?

Is February even soon enough?

"Donna?"

"Yes, sorry. I'm sorry. What did you say?"

"Are you going to go see her? She's in Vernal. Ashley Regional Medical Center."

Ethan's standing up across the room, and he's racing for the door.

"I have Ethan here," I say. "I better check on him. I imagine we'll all be going."

"Right," Amanda says. "Well, I'm going to go alone. Snuggles is having puppies right now. My girls are going to stay to make sure Eddy has what he needs, and I'm driving over to check on Abby."

"If you head over here, you can ride with us."

"Wait, Mandy wants to come, too."

"Both of you can fit, I'm sure," I say.

After I hang up, Will looks around the room. "We may need to get a bigger car," Will says. "You know, soon."

Ethan's already outside, unlocking his car.

"Wait." Beth left the door open when she chased after him. "You're not safe to drive."

"You need to stay inside," he says. "You're showing too much now. If you go out, everyone will know, and then you'll have to answer all the questions you don't want to deal with."

"I'm coming," Beth says. "And I'll drive." She jogs back to the house, throws a big sweater over her maternity dress, which I bought her online, and slides her feet into her clunky snow boots. "Ready."

"I guess we'll see you guys there," I say.

"Should I stay here with Aiden?" Will asks.

"No!" Aiden grabs his coat. "I want to come. You're talking about Gabe's mom, right?"

I nod. "Her baby isn't supposed to be born for a while, but he may come a little early. If that happens, the doctors there will take really good care of him, okay? But he may have some special tubes and wires connected to him to help him breathe."

Aiden's lip trembles and his eyes widen. "Okay."

"But don't worry. That little boy's daddy is a doctor. They know what to do. Okay?"

236

Aiden nods.

I can't help thinking about our February wedding the entire ride over. Mandy and Amanda ask me things about three or four times that I don't even hear, but Will covers for me pretty well.

"Ethan's probably there already," I say, as Will makes the turn to head for the hospital.

"Is this the best place for them to come?" Mandy asks. "I mean, do they even have a neonatal unit?"

"Neonatal?" I shrug. "Not sure, but they're closer to Salt Lake from Vernal, so it's probably better than Rock Springs if something goes wrong."

"Everyone stop talking about worst case scenarios," Amanda says. "Maybe we'll get there and everything will be fine."

"She's over forty," I say. "That's why we're talking. But hopefully it's fine."

"Age isn't everything," Mandy says. "Abby's in great shape."

When we arrive, the nurse at the ER doesn't look very pleased, and Ethan looks like he might punch her.

"This woman, Abigail Archer," the nurse is saying, "she's not even in active delivery. She can't have more than two people in the room with her."

"Well, we'll just wait in the closest waiting room, then," I say. "Can you tell us where that is?" I place one hand on Ethan's wrist, which is shaking a little bit.

"That's not protocol." The woman frowns. "You folks ought to head back home. They'll call you if they have news."

"It's fine," Steve's voice surprises me. Thank goodness for his level head in times like this. "I talked to the charge nurse," he says. "The floor's not full." He's standing behind the nurse's station, waving us over.

"Whittni said it's fine for them to go back?" The

crabby woman who was waving us off looks unsure now.

"She told me to tell you not to worry." He smiles. "You run a tight ship, which is why we came here, but our little boat is full of sailors, and they all fret."

The woman heaves a sigh. "Fine. Follow him, I guess."

So we do, like scared baby ducks.

The idea of the mighty Abigail being sick or having a problem is a little disconcerting. "Is she alright?" I ask.

Everyone's head swivels toward Steve.

"I told you guys that you didn't need to come," he says. "She's going to be fine. We have excellent treatments for this sort of thing. They didn't find evidence of a leak, and the baby seems to be alright. But with such low amniotic fluid, they're worried about complications. They're still wanting to give him a few days to develop his lungs a bit, and then they want to induce."

"They want to?" Mandy asks. "What does Abby want?"

"You're a smart lady," Steve says. "She's currently fighting with them. She's absolutely convinced that this little guy is not ready to come out yet."

That sounds more like the woman I know.

"She's not someone who backs down easily." A smile's playing at the corners of Steve's mouth.

"So what do you think?" Amanda asks.

"As a father?" Steve stops and turns. "Or as a doctor?"

"Both," I say.

"As a doctor, I think we should play the odds. Give him the steroids, then deliver. That's what the book says to do."

"But as a father?"

238

"I'm absolutely terrified, and I want to run around screaming."

That makes me smile, but it's not the right mood.

"You're a great dad," Will says. "But your doctor hat might be more helpful here than your father one."

"We have some awesome doctors on the case," Steve says. "I'm happy, for once, to be here in another capacity."

It must be strange for him to be in a hospital but not be in charge of the medical care of the patient at issue. Steve opens the door, and Abby's voice hits me like a flyswatter to the face.

"But I already said that I want to delay as long as possible."

"Right, but we think putting it off more than a day or two—"

"You're just nervous," she says. "Any bad outcome will be on you."

The woman looks about the same age as Abby. "A bad outcome is bad for everyone. By definition."

"I want to hear from Doctor Peters," she says. "I'll wait until we do."

"He's going to say the same thing."

Abby crosses her arms. "Then when he does, we'll make a decision."

The woman rolls her eyes and spins on her heel. She nearly crashes right into Will before realizing we're all here.

"You can't all be here," she says.

"Whittni says it's fine," Steve says.

"Whittni doesn't run the hospital." The woman folds her arms.

Steve scrunches his nose. "Actually, you might be wrong about that."

The woman, surprisingly, laughs. "Fine. But you can

only come into this room two at a time. Otherwise, you wait next door."

Steve nods.

The doc lowers her voice. "Too much stress is bad for her. Got it?"

"Yes, I'll remember that the next time I want to pick a fight." Steve's smirking.

"I wasn't picking a fight. I'm advocating for that baby."

"Okay," Steve says. "My mistake."

The doctor looks really annoyed when she finally leaves.

He and Ethan go inside, and Izzy, Whitney, and Gabe head out. We shepherd them all next door with us.

"So here's what happened," Izzy says. "Mom came to her doctor appointment alone, because we were at school, right?"

Aiden's hanging on her every word. Actually, we all are.

"And then she calls Steve, who's always totally calm, and after he answers, he sits up really straight, right?"

Amanda frowns.

"And then he's like, 'Grab your bags and a few snacks, and let's go.'" Izzy nods slowly. "And Whitney and I got Gabe's stuff too, and then we got in the car, and we came straight here. By the time we got here, they'd done more tests, and they were saying they needed to give Mom a steroid shot."

"But I don't understand what's wrong." Gabe looks even more worried than Aiden.

"So here's the deal," Izzy says. "Babies are stuck in the mom's stomach, so they're like, swimming in this stuff called amniotic fluid. They need it, and they like, pee in it, too."

All the kids say 'Eww,' including Whitney, who probably just heard all this when Izzy did.

"But if they don't have enough, then that's bad." Izzy's clearly worried about her mom, but she's also loving that she's the one whom everyone's listening to.

"How low is hers?" I ask.

"It's supposed to be five or more," Izzy says. "Usually it's around twenty. Mom's is a two or three."

Aiden, my sweet little boy, starts crying.

"Oh, no," Izzy says. "Don't cry."

"I was jealous that Gabe was getting another brother, and now he's dying because of me."

Will grabs Aiden under the armpits and swings him up in the air. "None of this is your fault, bud."

Instead of pushing away, like I expect him to, Aiden grabs Will around his neck and hugs him tightly. He's gotten so big, but he's still so small. After a moment, Will sets him on the window seat in the hospital room and sits down next to him.

"Dad says the baby's gonna be fine," Gabe says. "He said not to worry. He never lies."

It's cute, hearing Gabe call Steve 'dad.'

"Plus, he's a doctor," Whitney says. "And doctors know about this stuff a lot more than we do. That's why I'm not worried." She folds her arms across her chest, and I realize that Whitney and Izzy are more alike than I thought.

"So if he's going to be fine, then when will he come home?" Aiden asks. "When will he be old enough to play with?"

Gabe shrugs. "Probably a year or something."

"Until he comes home?" Aiden asks.

"Until we can play," Gabe says. "I bet he comes home faster."

"Let's hope so," Mandy says. "Can you imagine the hospital bill for that?"

I suppress my shudder.

"I really wish I could have a little brother." Aiden slumps.

Apparently now that he's decided Abby's baby is fine, he's back to jealousy. Kids' moods swing so fast, I can barely keep up.

"You're going to have a little sister," Beth says. "It's not quite the same, but it'll be cool too."

I freeze.

She told me we weren't telling anyone. It made me a little nervous, to be honest. I was worried she might change her mind. But now she's announcing it in front of everyone.

"What, now?" Mandy cuts her eyes toward me. "Donna, are you pregnant?" She lowers her head a bit and squints. "You are a sly dog, William Earl."

Will laughs. "Donna's not pregnant, no."

Mandy's head snaps toward him. "Then what's Beth talking about?"

"I'm pregnant," Beth says. "And I've decided to give my baby to Donna and Will." She smiles. "Also, it's a girl."

I suppose this is a decent time to tell everyone. We're all here.

Except Abby, Steve, and Ethan. They already know, though. And Amanda's fiancé and her kids, I guess. "Where's Eddy? And the girls?"

"Snuggles is having her puppies," Amanda says. "They're all pretty excited, but they're also nervous about Abby. I promised them I'd call with updates."

"You could've brought the dog here," Aiden says. "I want to see the puppies!"

The idea of a wolf dog giving birth in the middle of

a hospital seems particularly funny, or maybe I'm just stressed. Either way, I start laughing.

"It's not stupid," Aiden says.

"No. Not at all." I crouch down next to him. "I'm sorry for laughing. They don't allow dogs in hospitals, though, not ever."

"Oh." Aiden frowns. "That's dumb."

"Some people are allergic," I say. "And dogs aren't always calming. Their barking might keep sick people awake."

"I doubt Snuggles would want to have puppies here, either," Izzy says.

Aiden frowns. "Why didn't you tell me I'm having a sister?"

I look at his sweet little face. I'm so used to thinking of him as a baby that maybe I didn't give him enough credit. "Beth wanted us to keep it a secret for a while, and I was trying to do that."

"Is that why her stomach's so big?" He glances sideways at her. "Because I thought she was eating way too much."

Beth laughs. "That's true too, munchkin."

Now everyone's laughing.

"Why is Beth giving you her baby?" Aiden asks. "Why doesn't she keep her baby?"

Ah, kids. We love them so much, but they make things more complicated in every way.

"I'm not ready to have a baby," Beth says. "I didn't plan things out right, but I love this little baby a lot. I wanted to give it the best parents I ever met, so I picked your mom and Mr. Will."

Aiden's forehead crinkles up. "Mr. Will's not even a parent yet. Maybe you should give her to Miss Abby and Mr. Steve instead."

Mandy coughs, probably to cover her laugh.

"Not everyone can have the very best parents in the world," I say. "Some people have to settle for just pretty good ones, like you are."

"You're really good," Aiden says. "And Mr. Will's really nice. I just don't think he knows a lot yet."

"I have faith he'll learn," Beth says. "When they don't know something, maybe you can help."

Aiden nods. "Well, I hope she's cute. Because I'm really cute, and I would hate if people didn't tell her that. She might get sad."

Beth's lip is twitching.

"Don't worry, though. Even if she's ugly, I'll tell her she's cute." Aiden smiles. "Since she's a baby, she won't even know I'm lying."

"Good idea," Will says. "But I wouldn't worry too much about that."

"What does your husband look like?" Aiden asks, his neck craned so he can look up at Beth. "Because if he's cute, the baby probably will be, too. You're pretty."

"My. . .husband?" Beth snorts. "Um. So. . ."

"He's very handsome," I say. "Don't worry."

"Yes," Beth says. "He's super handsome."

"She's not married, dummy," Izzy says. "She's Ethan's girlfriend."

"We may need to have a talk with him soon," Will whispers. "I call not-it."

"What's the talk about?" Gabe asks. "Maybe I can tell him."

It feels like we should have talked this over beforehand.

"Probably not," I say. "But let's revisit this all later, okay?"

"Can I come, too? Because I have some questions." Gabe glances at the door. "Let's do it before Dad and Mom come back."

Now we're all laughing.

Given all the madness of the past few hours, I think that's a pretty good thing.

"I do wish you were having a boy," Aiden says with a small sigh. "But I guess a sister's still cool."

"Sisters might even be better," Gabe says.

"Why?" Aiden looks confused.

"They don't steal your Legos as often." Gabe sighs. "Just don't leave them out on the floor, cuz babies will eat them."

"Maybe we should write some of this down," Will whispers.

"Boys are better than girls. Everyone's pregnant. Puppies coming too. Babies swallow Legos." Mandy's shaking her head. "I need to sit down. I'm not sure I can take any more news." She glares at Amanda. "How about you? You pregnant, too?"

Amanda shakes her head, her face stricken. "No way."

"I think you've now heard all of it," I say.

Of course, that's when Helen shows up, dragging nurses behind her like she's just wrestled them for the right to enter.

She looks downright angry. "What in heaven's name is going on, and why are these idiots telling me I can't come back when you're all here?"

❦ 19 ❧

HELEN

When we were growing up, if Abby had a torn cuticle, she came to me. When she had a school project that was confusing, when she started her period, when she liked a boy. All her problems.

She always came to me about them.

I mean, I can't blame her. My mom wasn't exactly very warm or welcoming. But I think she also knew that whatever it took, I would do it for her. If I had to crack heads, they'd be cracked. If she needed me to threaten a teacher, I had done it before. If she was worried Mom or Dad would be upset, she knew I would keep her secret safe.

After she went off to school, she called me a handful of times. Once it was about a boy, once she needed money, and another time, she was stuck and I called her a cab.

But after that, she quit calling.

I mistakenly assumed it was because she didn't have any emergencies. It wasn't until years later that I realized why she really stopped. She had found someone she trusted more, someone who was there for her, someone better than me.

But then that guy died.

I thought, when that happened, that she'd call me again. When I heard about Nate, I wrapped up my main project, just so I'd be ready when she called.

Only, she didn't.

She had moved on, and that kind of hurt.

By the time I stopped waiting for her call and decided to just show up, she'd already met a new person. And that idiot got her pregnant. Now that stupid baby's putting her at risk *again*. Worst of all, I'm apparently the last person in Manila to find out about it.

"You're saying that she has something called intra-hepatic choleostasis of pregnancy?"

Abby doesn't look very worried. "Say that five times fast, I dare you."

It's nice that she's making jokes, but they're totally inappropriate right now. I need answers.

"That's right. It's a condition that presents from itchiness, and after we diagnosed that—"

"Wait, when did you diagnose that?" I glare at Abby. "This is the first I'm hearing about it."

"A few weeks ago," the doctor says, glancing at Abby.

My sister shrugs. "It's not a big deal. They gave me medicine for it."

"It actually is a big deal," the doctor says. "It causes spontaneous miscarriage in the last few weeks, which is why we told you that we planned to induce at thirty-seven weeks."

"Steve knew," Abby says. "He wasn't too nervous."

He grunts.

This doctor looks miffed. I suppose I did call her in

here to explain something again that everyone else has heard. "Look, the point is, her condition can cause calcification of the placenta, which we think may have begun, and that causes low birth weight and failure to thrive in utero."

Abby brings her hands up around her stomach. "They were doing an ultrasound today to check the placenta, and that's when they discovered my amniotic fluid's low."

"Which means?" I ask.

"It means I'm being monitored," she says. "It means that my baby still needs more time, but to be cautious, we're doing steroid injections and monitoring him."

"We strongly recommend that you deliver him in two days," the doctor says.

"Helen," Abby says.

My phone starts ringing. It's David. I press the red button. He'll have to wait.

"You can take it," Steve says. "It's fine."

"No." That's how he squeezed me out in the first place. He always acts like I have things that are more important, and if I take the bait, it implies that I'm not putting her first. "It's fine."

"Look," Abby says. "I've been seeing a doctor when he's here once a week. He's a neonatal specialist, and I called him. I'd like to wait to hear from him before we decide anything. My amniotic fluid level is the only new scary thing, and it's right on the wobble line."

"Respectfully, it's not on the wobble line," the doctor says. "It's a two—"

"Or a three," Abby says.

"And anything under a five is concerning."

"See?" Abby says. "Concerning. Not terrifying. It could be an error by the ultrasound tech. It could be a misread. I've been on the monitor for two hours, and the baby has been fine this whole time."

"Okay," I say, "but—"

David calls. *Again.*

I glare at my phone.

"Who is it?" Abby stretches as tall as she can get and peers over my lap. "Is that the handsome Mr. Park?"

I turn my phone over. "Maybe." My cheeks heat up.

"Ooh, answer, or I'll call him."

"You can't," Steve whispers. "The battery died, remember?"

"Then you'll give me yours." She holds out her hand.

"Come on." I groan, but I flip my phone over and answer, just before it would have gone to voicemail.

"Where are you?" David asks.

"Huh?"

"I said I'd come by around seven."

It's eight-oh-four. I groan again, but this time, I actually feel really bad. "I'm so sorry. Listen, Abby's in the hospital, and I completely forgot about—"

"Is she alright?"

"That's debatable," I say. "She insists she's fine, but some of the doctors disagree."

"That's not true," Abby yells. "I'm fine."

"She sounds like her normal self," David says. "Which hospital?"

"Vernal," I say. "Ashley whatever."

"I'll be there in an hour."

"No, no, don't bother coming," I say. "The nurses are already flipping out because of how many people are here."

"Nurses love me," he says.

I'll just bet they do.

"Trust me," he says. "I'll see you soon."

Why am I smiling? How stupid. I kill the smile and hang up.

"You like him." Abby has never looked more self-satisfied in her life.

"He's going to get yelled at by that scary nurse at the front desk," I say.

"She's not a nurse," Steve says. "She's the clerk, and they're paid to yell at people."

"Well, anyway, I bet he can't even get through. That's why I was smiling."

"Sure," Abby says. "Whatever you say."

An hour and three minutes later, David Park breezes through the door, hands Steve a big black box, and then grabs a chair.

"What's this?" Steve asks.

"Open them," David says.

"Chocolate covered cherries!" Steve slaps his leg. "Brilliant."

"Those are booze-free." David crosses his heart, like he's a twelve-year-old girl.

I kick the box, spilling cherries all over the floor.

"Hey," Steve says. "Those weren't yours."

"Oh, don't worry," David says. "I'm prepared for sour behavior from her. I have a dozen more boxes outside. I've already given everyone next door a box of their own, too. And the staff. I'm actually thinking of investing in that little chocolate company, I've been giving them so much business."

"You're the worst," I say.

But for some reason, I don't really mean it.

"As fun as it is for you all to be here," Abby says, "they're not letting me go tonight, and that doesn't mean you all need to stay. Why don't you guys head home, and maybe in the morning I can talk some sense into Dr. Peters?"

"What did you want to talk to me about?" A doctor in his early fifties is leaning against the door, his blocky glasses low on his nose. "Because I'm not supposed to be here for another two days, you know."

"I was going to talk to you on the phone tomorrow," Abby says. "What are you doing here now?"

"When the board of directors for your hospital calls and asks for a favor, you drive straight through. You're lucky I was in Heber City for my son's birthday."

"You—the—*who* called you?" Abby turns toward Steve. "I told you we could wait. No one was suggesting we deliver him today."

He shrugs. "It wasn't me."

I raise my hand. "I put my assistant on it."

"I should've known," Abby says. "I'm so sorry, Dr. Peters."

"You know, I wouldn't have pegged you for a high roller," Dr. Peters says, "but I'm glad they called, honestly. Monitoring you is good, but I think we can wait and see for a bit. The baby's not in any distress, and I'm not sure we're in a 'better out than in' scenario. At least, not yet."

"They already gave me steroids," Abby says.

"That's good, actually. I'll probably have them give you another round in a day or two. I'd like to repeat the ultrasound tomorrow, and maybe again the next day. But I'm not in a huge rush to deliver this little baby unless something changes. Eight weeks early isn't horrifying, but it's also not ideal."

"No, it's not," Abby says. "Thank you for saying that."

"What are those?" Dr. Peters is staring at the floor.

More specifically, he's staring at the chocolate-covered cherries we haven't had time to clean up yet.

"They're cherries," Steve says. "My sister-in-law *startled me*, and I dropped them."

"Thank goodness," Dr. Peters says. "They look like little poops. At least I don't need to send out the alert that we have huge rats."

Both guys laugh with him at that one. Why do men always think anything to do with poop is funny?

"I'm so sorry," David whispers, as the doctor leaves. He's looking right at Steve.

"For what?" I ask. "Why should you be sorry?"

"Now that Abby was right, and now that Helen dragged that poor doc in to confirm it, they're going to be even worse than usual."

Steve laughs. For some reason, Abby does, too.

I'm not smiling—someone has to play the straight man—but it feels good, being a part of the team that helps fix a problem in Abby's life. I may not be the first person she calls, but I can still show up a bit late and throw my weight around.

I still have a place.

I know we ought to let Abby rest. I should head home now, but instead, we stick around for a while longer. We talk, we eat stupid cherries, and I order milkshakes for everyone. And for the first time in a very long time, I'm a part of a group of people. . .that may not be right.

It feels like *family*.

But eventually, it's nearly midnight. The kids have school, and they're exhausted. Steve rounds everyone up.

"I'll take them home," I say. "You can stay."

"Are you sure?" he asks.

I nod.

"Thank you." He sounds like he means it.

"Should we call Mom?" I ask on my way out the door. "Or I could text Dad."

Abby shakes her head. "Nah, they'd just worry. There's nothing for them to do. Besides, I think everything will be fine."

A year ago, that would have been me.

I'd be the one she's not calling or texting, because there's nothing I could do to help. I'm only here right now because I've been living here. Because I know her friends and family, and because I'm close.

Maybe that nonsense Abby's always saying about not hiring a nanny and changing diapers yourself so that the kids will know to turn to you for help is actually true for adults, too. Could doing grunt work really be the key to effectively caring for someone?

It seems insane.

Crazy enough to be right.

❦ 20 ❦

DONNA

When I was in elementary school, we always performed the actual nativity. It's appalling that the school was basically pushing Christianity, I know, but Manila's not exactly a culturally diverse place, so I didn't even know enough to realize it was insular. Now that I do know that not everyone celebrates Christmas, I'm still not interested in rocking the boat.

If other parents passed around a petition for a less Christian Christmas play, sure, I'd sign it. But I'm not about to break out the picket signs and Sharpies myself. Especially since my son is *so* delighted to have landed the lead. Or, splitting the lead.

No explanation of Aiden's could have prepared me for Gabe, in full old-man makeup, as Ebenezer. He is the perfect crochety old man. He's holding a cane, he's hunched over, his hair is grey, and he's using a shaky voice. It's absolutely brilliant.

When Aiden appears, it becomes glaringly obvious that my son's riding his bestie's coattails. Aiden's playing the young man, at least. So if his diction's bad, and if he giggles too much, well, he's a little kid. He sure does look cute, though, in his little top hat and breeches.

"I can't believe Abby's missing this," I whisper.

"Shh." Amanda points at her phone, set up on top of the back of a chair, clearly streaming.

I shrug. "It's not the same," I whisper.

Amanda nods. "Gabe is so stinking cute, right?"

"Oh my word, he's amazing."

Right then, he says the line we all know.

"If they would rather die," he wheezes, "they had better do it, and decrease the surplus population."

Somehow, that little nerd memorized all his parts. Meanwhile, Aiden keeps reading his off of slips he tucks into and pulls out of his sleeve.

"Aiden, too," Amanda says. "He's also just darling."

"Isn't he?" Will asks.

"Oh, hush," I say. "Anyone with eyes can see that Gabe's better."

"It's an elementary school play," Will says. "Who cares? They're both nailing it."

I realize that he's right. My competitive nature sometimes causes me to worry about things I should let go. "They are." I think about all the things I fret about that don't bring me joy. I actually spent a bit of time being jealous of Abby, who's in the hospital right now, because she can have another kid and I can't.

From that moment forward, I focus on how adorable Aiden looks and stop comparing my life to anyone else's. It's a little easier to keep that resolve when the ghosts are performing. The teachers apparently insisted that they keep the words for the play the same, but they didn't argue with the little kids who wanted to wear angel costumes instead of ghost ones.

Instead of chains, the ghost of the future's shaking

a lute, which makes no noise, but the laughter from the audience is plenty loud.

When the play ends, Amanda sighs. "That was a nice little break." She slides her phone into her purse. "Back to the grind."

"You mean the resort? I thought you were temporarily on hold again thanks to the weather?"

Another snowstorm's on the way, and it feels like we've already had two winters' worth.

"Are you worried about the weather wrecking the wedding, now that it's only a week away?"

"I'm just glad that Mandy has a generator," she says. "Eddy has one too, so if you guys need somewhere to go. . ."

"Will has one, and so do his parents," I say. "So don't worry about us."

"It'll really stink if Abby can't leave the hospital." Amanda looks genuinely worried about her, and not just because it might throw off her wedding.

"For Christmas and for the wedding," I say. "I bet her kids are missing her, too."

Amanda's face falls. "This whole wedding feels like a mistake, to be honest."

"A mistake?"

Amanda shrugs. "I mean, there are still a lot of things to do, and I'm running out of time, and Abby's in the hospital, and I just feel like." She throws her hands into the air. "I don't feel like a bride, and I don't feel Christmassy." She bursts into tears.

"Oh, no," I say. "Whoa."

Aiden chooses that moment to show up, and I notice that Gabe just reached Ethan, Beth, Steve, Izzy, and Whitney on Amanda's other side. Even Eddy, Mandy, Maren, and Emery are gushing, telling him how great he did. Poor Amanda swipes at her eyes and forces a smile.

But after we've gushed over Aiden and gotten photos of Aiden and Gabe, I tell Will that I need to go to Mandy's house.

"To Amanda Saddler's?" He looks skeptical. "Today's Aiden's last day of school, and his dad's coming to get him."

Shoot. "Not until the morning. I'll get back as soon as I can, but I need to lend a hand."

"Your friends are stupid," Will says. But he's smiling, and I know he's not upset.

"I'll be back soon."

Amanda's surprised when I pull up right behind her car. She waves the others in and approaches my car as I'm climbing out. "Everything okay?"

"I just thought I'd offer my help. Surely there are party favors to fold or tie ribbons to, or who knows what. I have hands, and I'm not afraid to use them."

Amanda grins. "That's so nice, but it's Christmas. I can't possibly—"

"I insist. Just an hour or two."

Moments later, Amanda's running through all the details with me. "I'm just worried I've forgotten something." She's shown me the floral arrangements she chose, which are perfect, the selections for the reception food, also amazing, and the adorable little Christmas ornaments they're giving each guest. "I just need to slide a photo of us into each one," she says. "And then stuff them back in the boxes."

"Is that the dress?" I point at a huge, puffy white bag hanging from the window in the corner. "Can I see it?"

"Oh, right, yes." She crosses the room and unzips it, and a massive ivory silk dress falls out, with the most stunning golden, sparkling crepe overlay, piled up on one side and cascading down at an angle to entirely consume the hugely full skirt.

It's exactly the dress I would pick.

I am entirely in love.

So of course, I can't help gushing. "That is the most beautiful dress I have ever seen."

Amanda shrugs. "Really? I thought it was alright, but I kind of envisioned myself in something in more of a mermaid style, maybe with a flare right at the bottom."

I drag my eyes away from the dress and stare at Amanda, my mouth still open.

"No?"

"Why would you pick this one if you wanted a mermaid style?"

She sighs. "Mermaid was last year's theme, I guess, and this year Vera wanted to go another direction. Every single dress we saw was huge and fluffy, like this one." She runs her hand down it absently. "I mean, it's fine, right? I feel like a brat, complaining about a Vera Wang gown that I got for free, but it's not really what I had in mind."

"I don't think that's terrible. It is your wedding. . ."

Amanda collapses on her bed. "I guess."

I perch on the edge. I know I'm not Abby. I'm not nearly as close to her as all that, but I've known her for a while now. Amanda's not effusive, but she gets excited. She seems. . .almost depressed. "Why are you getting married at Christmas if you don't want to?"

"I do want to get married. I don't have any reservations about that at all." A single tear rolls down her cheek. "But everything around us has gone wrong. None of it is really *my problem*, so I can't even be disappointed. But the thing is, I don't really have a lot of family." She looks at her hands.

Other than Abigail.

"I know this sounds dumb. We weren't even friends a few years ago. But she's stuck in the hospital, and I'm worried about her and the baby, and it feels *wrong* to be throwing some big party. And I don't want to get married if she can't come."

I open my mouth, but before I can say a word, she crashes right along in typical Amanda fashion.

"My mom's here, I know, and I guess that's neat. To be honest, even after all this time, I keep waiting for her to. . .I don't know. To disappoint me. Does that sound awful? I don't care if she does come, but I can't really trust her. So that leaves three hundred people I barely know, and only a few I care about."

Now she's really bawling, and I feel like Abby or Eddy or someone else who has a name ending in y should be here handling this, but too bad for Amanda. The B team is the only one not benched. "So cancel it," I say.

She looks up then, and she quits crying. But then she starts to hiccup.

"Cancel it," I say.

She shakes her head. "So many people already have plane tickets, and my mom's here, and Eddy will be upset."

"He might be upset. The plane tickets thing, well." I shrug. "It's your *wedding*, Amanda."

"But it's just one day, and the marriage is the important thing."

I flop back on the bed. "I keep telling myself that, too. My wedding is at least as big a disaster as this one."

"Why?" Amanda's peering down at me now, and with the light behind her head, she's almost glowing.

Is it because she sort of resembles an angel that I completely break down and tell her all my stuff? I ramble on and on about how I wanted a big wedding this time, full of all the people here in Manila that Will loves, the people I left when I married stupid Charlie. I want my new in-laws to have the exact party they want. I want Aiden to really be able to welcome Will as his father.

But I also want to adopt this little baby. I tell her about my infertility issues, and about my fears that we'd never have any other kids. I tell her how worried I am about Beth insisting that she has to leave, and about my secret fear that Beth might change her mind.

"And now that Aiden knows, I'm especially worried." I close my eyes. "What if she *doesn't* change her mind, but then she hates me forever because of it?"

Amanda flops back on the bed next to me. "I have no idea what to say. I'm not Abigail."

I laugh, but my laughter turns quickly to tears. "Neither am I."

"My advice may not be very good," Amanda says. "I'm a little selfish, as I'm sure you know, but I do know Beth a little, and I know you a little more. You're both really good people. That little girl is lucky to have both of you. She has a happy home right now, and that's more than either of us had. So for the adoption, with how much you love each other, I bet it works itself out in the best way."

She's not telling me I have nothing to fear. She's not telling me Beth won't change her mind, or that she won't resent me for taking her baby. But she is telling me that the baby will be loved, and I guess maybe I lost sight of that.

Isn't that the most important part?

Family can be messy. And messy is uncomfortable. But the worst part isn't when it's messy. It's when it's hollow. It's when there's no love there to smooth over the mess. She's right—Beth and I may have some bumps ahead of us, but we love each other, and we both love that little girl.

"Thanks," I say. "As an Abigail fill-in, you're not terrible."

Amanda laughs. "That may be the nicest thing anyone has ever said about me."

That makes me laugh, too.

"And one more thing." Amanda sits up, and then she pulls me up. She's looking right at me, intently, when she says, "I need a favor."

"Okay." Now that neither of us is crying, I'm beginning to feel a little guilty for not being home when it's Aiden's last night with me for a week.

"I want you to take my wedding."

"Excuse me?"

"I don't even want it. It's become something I don't recognize."

"What are you saying?"

"You love the dress. You like the Christmas wedding idea. You're worried that February won't be soon enough." Amanda smiles. "You actually *want* the whole town to be present. And anyone whom we didn't invite that you want, you can put in the empty seats from my New York City friends who won't come."

"Amanda." I'm already shaking my head.

"Hear me out." She's smiling, and it looks like a peaceful one, not an awkward, smug, or giddy smile. "We can blame the storm. We can tell people we'll reschedule."

"But then you'll wind up in the same boat that you're in now."

She shakes her head. "I'll just elope. The people who matter can still come. And hey, maybe my dad and brothers can make it too if we put this off. Actually, this is perfect."

"But you got all that stuff for free because it was for your wedding."

She shrugs. "They wanted me to post about it. Other than the gown, I've posted about everything. I can still snap a photo of that. . .on you. And when I announce that we're postponing our wedding, well. That'll be such a crazy announcement that will get so much interaction that Vera Wang will forgive me. I'm sure of it." She shrugs. "Or if not, you might have to pay them for the dress."

"Which would be totally fine." I look at the gorgeous gown I was jealous of a few minutes ago. "You know, growing up, I always wished I had a fairy godmother. I figured mine must've been a drunk or something." My laugh's a little forced. "But maybe she was just dealing with her own stuff up until now."

"I like that," Amanda says. "I get to be a fairy godmother." She tilts her head. "Does that mean I should wear something white and fluffy to your wedding, and maybe stick a tiara in my hair? I think I know some kids who could loan me their wings."

"Maybe on a day other than my wedding that used to be your wedding."

It starts to sink in, then. "Will Eddy be upset?"

"You know, probably because he's a vet, Eddy rolls with things remarkably well. And I'll tell him we can still take the honeymoon."

That reminds me. "I wonder if I can get stupid Charlie to switch weeks with me so Aiden can be here for the wedding. Then he could go stay with him while we go on a honeymoon."

"Will Manila survive us both being gone for a week?" Amanda's beaming. She looks three times as happy right now. If anything was going to convince me to take her wedding, this is it.

"I can't believe you're doing this," I say.

"Since I'm giving you a wedding," Amanda says, "do I have to get you a present?"

I can't help laughing. "I think you're covered."

"You better go tell Will, and I'll call Eddy." Amanda walks me out, still talking about wedding details she hadn't mentioned. "Oh! And I can give you these ornaments. You just need to print up photos and replace ours and they'll be from you guys instead."

"Oh, great," I say.

"What are you talking about?" Mandy asks.

"I'm giving Donna my wedding," Amanda says.

I expect Mandy to be disappointed. "Glory be," she says. "And I'm not a bridesmaid in your wedding, right?" Her eyes look practically desperate.

"No. . .?"

She cackles then, and I realize that I picked the right answer. "Hallelujah, it's a Christmas miracle." She points at Amanda. "I was about to come shout at you. That new dress we ordered came in, and it's worse than the last one."

"You can put it in the rag bag now for all I care," Amanda says.

"What a brilliant idea." Mandy turns toward me. "And now you'll be married with plenty of time to deal with that new baby."

"Exactly," I say.

"What did you just say?" Amanda's mother's

standing in the hallway in a ratty Metallica t-shirt and striped pajama pants.

"Oh, hey, Mom. You know how I've been all stressed out about the wedding?"

Her mother shakes her head. "No. I forbid it."

"What?" Amanda looks confused.

"You have to get married in a week. I've been here helping."

"Mom," Amanda says, "I've already decided. And I am *so* much happier. This is the right call."

She shakes her head. "No. Either you get married, or I'm leaving."

"That's alright," Amanda says. "You can leave. I know you miss Dad and the boys."

Her mother's voice goes almost supersonic. "I should have known you'd pull a stunt like this. You've always been a spoiled, bratty diva." She says a few more choice words I could have done without hearing, and then she ducks back into her room.

Amanda looks like she's been sucker punched.

"She's probably drunk," Mandy says. "It's been a long few days."

I'm not sure how to react to that, but when Amanda walks me out to my car, I try. "If you're rethinking the wedding—"

Amanda shakes her head. "Not in the slightest. My mom has never been the most steady, and frankly, it's a miracle we've gotten along for this long."

I'm not even sitting in the drivers' side yet when Amanda's mom walks out of the house carrying a bag. "Take me to the airport," she says.

"What?" Is she talking to me?

"Mom, stop."

But her mother won't look at her. "If you're stealing

my daughter's wedding, the least you can do is give me a ride."

"It's dinner time." Mandy's on the porch, zipping up her jacket. "I'll take you, you terrorist."

"What did you call me?"

"A terrorist," Mandy says. "Did I stutter?"

Amanda's mother splutters. "How dare you—"

"Your daughter might be upset about your little ultimatum, but I'm not. So get in the truck, and I'll drive you to the closest airport. You can sit there or go to an airport hotel, your choice, until you get on a flight out."

"Amanda." Her mom crosses her arms. "Are you just going to stand there and let me leave?"

"Yes." Amanda's nostrils flare. "Mandy's right. You're being unfair, and I won't cave. It's my wedding, and I have every right to manage it as I see fit."

Amanda's mother looks like a toddler who has been called out. Like she can't believe that if she doesn't eat her green beans, she won't get cake. Finally, she stomps her foot and heads for the truck. I can't seem to move as Mandy stalks along behind her, unlocks the truck, and climbs in. They pull down the drive, and then they're gone.

"At least she's leaving before the storm hits." Amanda shrugs and goes back inside the house.

On the way home, before I've even called Will, I call Charlie. He refuses to budge one inch, of course. Not a huge surprise. "You really thought I would give up *Christmas* for New Years?" He scoffs. "You must think I'm a real idiot. Like you're really planning a wedding for a week from now."

"Forget it," I say. "I'll pick him up on Christmas day, at five p.m., as planned. If you're one minute late, I'll sue for full custody."

"You wouldn't have a prayer."

"You know that I would," I say. "After your shenanigans over the summer, and with my lawyer, you'd lose your chance to see him at all." I'm not convinced he'd care, but his parents do, a little, I think. He needs them to like him, since they're funding his entire lifestyle.

When I get home to see Will, I'm actually really nervous. What if he's upset? I was so delighted, and it felt so. . .lucky. . .that I didn't stop to think. Should I have called him?

Yes.

I'm a terrible fiancée.

What if he's angry? What if he's upset? What if he's—

When I walk through the door, he's playing hide-and-go-seek with Aiden. "Well, he's not under the sofa."

Aiden's giggling from inside the coat closet, which is his favorite place to hide.

"Ah, finally, his mom's back. Honey, any ideas where Aiden might be hiding? He's stumped me this time."

I burst into tears.

How could I have just decided about a wedding without asking him? He's such an amazing guy. Too amazing. Better than I deserve.

"What's wrong?" Will hops over the coffee table to reach my side faster.

"Mom?" Aiden pokes his head out of the coat closet.

"I'm afraid I've done something really stupid," I say. "I could still get out of it, I'm sure." Right? I bet I could. "You know how stressed I've been about the wedding, and the baby, and—"

266

Will takes my hand. "It's going to be fine. Just tell me what happened."

"You know I went to help Amanda, and I loved her dress, and her flowers, and the food she chose, and then. . .Amanda offered to give us her wedding." I bite my lip.

"What?" Will blinks. "I'm not sure I understand. Is she loaning you a dress?"

I shake my head. "She's been wanting to call hers off."

"She's dumping Eddy?" Will looks sick.

"No, no, nothing like that. She's just, it's complicated. But she feels like it's not what she wanted. She wants something smaller, something without a lot of people and pressure."

"Okay. But what did *you* do?"

I sit down on the sofa, pulling him down next to me, and I start from the beginning. "I went over there to help her, right?"

He nods.

And then I lead him through what happened, step by step, including how her mother reacted. "So really, maybe she'll change her mind and we don't have to do it anyway."

Will scratches the scruff on his jaw. "So, assuming Amanda doesn't change her mind, we're getting married in a week?"

"The day after Christmas?" Aiden asks. "You'll be my dad, then?"

"Well, I mean, you'll still have a dad," Will says. "But I'll be married to your mom, and you can call me Dad anytime you want."

"Will I get a special present?" Aiden asks. "Because when Mr. Steve married Miss Abby, he got the kids presents. Gabe told me."

Will laughs. "Steve's a smart man. I'll have to look into that."

Aiden nods.

"Well, if you're worried about me being upset, you don't need to worry. If this makes you happy, I'm all for it. My parents won't mind, either."

"Are you sure?"

"They'll probably need to watch Aiden, right? The week after Christmas?"

"For our honeymoon," I say. "If your dad can manage the ranch without you and your mom can manage the hotel and Aiden." I cringe. "It's probably too much, right? Maybe Charlie can—"

"Donna." Will's grin is practically wolfish. "They'll manage."

Tomorrow will probably be a whirlwind of last-minute plans, and also that storm's supposed to hit tomorrow night, but at least for tonight, it feels like my fairy tale carriage has arrived. My prince is definitely by my side.

My happily ever after is staring me in the face, and I love it.

✿ 21 ✿

AMANDA

The first time a reporter called me, I was on cloud nine. . .actually, it felt more like cloud nineteen. Cloud nine wasn't quite high enough. I figured that if someone wanted to write about me, it must mean that I was a person of note. I was giddy at the idea that the media cared about my life.

Part of that was my desperate need for validation, of course.

But part of my excitement was that I was moving up in the world of influencing, and I knew that would be a good thing. I was tired of paying off one credit card with a cash advance on another. I wanted a steadier income and more reliable sponsors, and having a news outlet talk about me and my life, well, it felt like a way to boost my following.

It did get me new followers. I was right about that.

The article they published actually said a lot of things about me and my Instagram account, and lots of people looked me up as a result. The problem is that the reporter also said quite a few critical things. Unfortunately, they happened to be mostly true. Although some people defended me and attacked him, what he said still hurt.

Even now, I can still recite several of the lines by heart.

"If you're the type of person who values form over substance, if you like to lick the frosting off the cake and throw the only part with any nutritional value in the trash, you might love Amanda Brooks' Instagram account, *Champagne for Less*."

He used my account to highlight everything frivolous and absurd about social media, using discount shoppers who nevertheless want designer goods as his most striking example.

"In a society where we mistakenly value wealth and extravagance, some people make a living showing wannabes how to achieve their shallow dreams without entirely breaking their rapidly diminishing bank accounts."

Sure, some of the things he said were inspired by my silliness or excess, but mostly it was a setup from the start. After that, I learned pretty quickly to develop a thick skin. Several thousand new fans followed my page after the release of his article, which was a net gain, but the cost was extra haters. It's like anything on social media, or really anything to do with notoriety. It always cuts both ways. As you gain recognition and as your fan base grows, so too do your detractors.

One of the best things about my new job working with Mandy is that, unless I decide I want to take on a project, I'm free to do as little or as much with my Instagram account as I *choose* these days. I no longer rely on it to feed my girls or to buy extravagant things, like clothing and shoes, that I don't need.

Ultimately, Eddy and I decided not to announce that we weren't getting married. We figured that we could announce it on the day of our wedding and still share photos of my dear friend's wedding instead. That way, the people who provided us wedding items would receive the maximum amount of buzz about the stuff they provided and hopefully not be upset.

Eddy was remarkably unfazed when I told him about the wedding. "I thought you might do something like that." He shrugged. "You looked more and more stressed and less and less excited. The last thing I wanted was for any of this to make you miserable."

We both spent about thirty minutes copying and pasting text messages to our family and friends who lived out of town, and it was all over pretty painlessly. Even the girls were unsurprised.

"About time," Maren said. "All the details were getting, like, super annoying."

"But you're still getting married, right?" Emery asked.

"Probably in the next month or so," I said.

"We just didn't realize that we wanted a very small, very quiet wedding until we got down the path." Eddy shrugged. "It was starting to ruin the whole thing, with all the details and people and opinions."

"And the puppies," Emery said.

The puppies have actually been my salvation. They look a little bit like sea turtles when they use their floppy legs to schlep their way toward their mom when they're hungry or cold. Nine little puppies, all but two of which look almost just like Roscoe. Those border collie genes are strong.

Eddy has handled the hard part, sleeping next to the whelping box and listening so that when one can't find a place to eat, he can help it latch.

The most surprising part to me is how involved Roscoe has been. I didn't think he'd be allowed to stick around, but he stays in the room with the puppies night and day, leaving only to go to the bathroom. He hasn't done a lot with them, but he watches over them and he keeps bringing food to Snuggles, as if she can't just hop out and eat from her normal dog food bowl.

The first day, he brought a bird—how he killed it, I don't know. He's never done it before. I didn't even notice he was holding it in his mouth when he came in. Eddy couldn't stop laughing because Snuggles ate it, making a tremendous mess in the corner of his bedroom.

Thankfully, Snuggles has been fine with me, the girls, and Eddy doing most anything around her and with the puppies. Emery has practically set up camp in here.

It's helped my empathetic little one to play with them. She was the only one who was really devastated about my mom leaving. Poor, sweet Emery didn't even see my mom's abandonment as a possibility. She's so young that she'd barely spent an hour with Mom before this trip, and she didn't really understand the history of abandonment Mom has.

I'm actually holding a sleeping puppy when Mandy bursts through the door.

"Shh." I lift my hands to show her why I'm shushing her.

"Cute," she says. "But maybe pass that one off to Mom and follow me outside."

That's strange. Usually Mandy, who likes the puppies but misses having us at her place, would grab a puppy too and plop down next to me. Something must be wrong.

Is it Abby?

I left my phone in the kitchen, so I wouldn't have heard any calls. The puppy wakes up when I set her inside the whelping box, but Snuggles is on the job immediately, licking her and guiding her to a snack so she can go back to sleep.

I practically sprint out of the room. "What's wrong?"

Mandy cringes a little.

"Is Abby alright?"

"Amanda Brooks, you have grown up."

"Excuse me?" I look around the kitchen, but no one else is here. "Are you talking to me or about me?"

Mandy cackles. "When you got here, your first question in this circumstance wouldn't have been about Abby."

"I wouldn't have been sitting in Eddy's room holding a puppy, either," I say. "But if you don't tell me what's wrong, I might still explode."

She inhales slowly and then sits down.

That's not good.

"The girls are fine?"

Mandy shrugs. "Sure, but you should do a google search on yourself."

That doesn't sound good. I whip out my phone and type in my own name, my hands trembling as I do. A dozen stories pop up, as well as one video. I force myself to click on the video.

It's an interview.

With my mom.

"So you're the mother of Amanda Brooks," the talk show host is asking. "The mastermind behind Champagne for Less, and the fiancée of Eddy Dutton, a rock singer who's just experienced a huge revival."

My mom beams. "Yep, that's my little girl."

Oh, no. This is not good at all.

I pause it. "Can you just tell me what she says?" If I watch it, I'll never be able to forget any of it.

Mandy's eyes are sad. "She basically says that you and Eddy have called off the wedding, and then she gives. . .reasons."

I close my eyes and try to stay calm. "Why would she do that?"

But as I ask the question, I realize she must have been paid to do it. That must be why they came in the first place, so they could sell the inside scoop on the wedding. I flip open a new tab, and sure enough, the articles have loads of photos. Several of them even have video clips of me shouting, presumably *at* Eddy. The stories she gave them do not paint an attractive picture of me.

They also supposedly act as evidence that Eddy's an abusive alcoholic.

I mean, he *is* an addict, but he's also been sober for a long time. The yelling from that one video of him came from the vet visit he took my dad along on. He was yelling at a cow that kept stepping on his foot. He was pretty sure it was intentional.

It must have required some really clever editing to get it into the shape it's now in. I wonder who Mom paid to do that.

"She really tricked me this time," I say. "When she refused the money I offered." I whistle. "I'm so stupid." I let her *live* with me, and I let her and Dad and my brothers come over and work around the yard, while all of them were snapping photos and making up stories.

"You don't look very surprised," Mandy says.

"I've been a little light on details about my past," I say. "Let's just say that this isn't very surprising. Actually, the biggest shock is that she was creative enough to think of this."

"She did mention that she watched your engagement on YouTube," Mandy says. "Maybe that gave her the idea."

"Or someone could have reached out to her, I suppose." That's probably more likely. Mom wasn't ever much of a self-starter. She wouldn't have the first idea of who to call, and she wouldn't have been likely to know what people might pay, either.

I hope she got a lot. She'll need those thirty pieces of silver the next time she has an issue, because she's never getting another red cent from me.

"I'm assuming Eddy doesn't know?" I ask.

Mandy shrugs. "Haven't seen him, but I saw this as soon as I opened my laptop this morning."

Of course she did.

"He'll hear about it soon. I imagine his manager's not going to be pleased." I stand up, cross the room to the mirror in the hall, and then I smooth my hair down with my hands. It's very obvious that I've been spending too much time with puppies and not enough time outside of Eddy's house.

"You look fine." Mandy stands too. "You should go find that boy."

I hug her. "Thank you."

"You'd have seen it soon enough yourself."

"Thanks for coming to me when you saw," I say. "And for helping me find a job that doesn't rely on the popularity of my social media accounts." My heart swells. "This isn't a nice surprise, but it would have wrecked me a year ago. Now, I have the luxury of trying not to care."

Mandy nods. "Not only that. I'm proud of you, girl."

"Proud?" I frown. "Because none of what she said is true?"

She shakes her head. "That's a given. I'm proud of you because you let her in enough to hurt you like that."

That makes me bawl. "I was an idiot. I should've known."

She pulls me tighter against her. "No, you were brave. You've been hurt before, many times, and instead of shutting her out, you're healthy enough to invite her in. Her nastiness isn't your fault. It's not on you. You're strong now, and you know your worth."

I realize that what she's saying is true, but it's because of her, of Abby, and because of Eddy. "I have people who love me. That's why I could let her come stay. That's why I'm fine."

Mandy smiles. "You do have people who love you, and you know none of the stuff she said matters." She taps my phone. "So don't let it wreck your day. You hear me?"

I wipe at the tears on my cheeks, and I point at the door. "I'm gonna go find Eddy."

She swats my backside as I leave. She's a very strange old lady.

Eddy's bent over a horse's hoof when I finally find him. His sister was spot on, as usual. My irritation that he was almost forty miles away is more than offset by the fact that he doesn't look upset, which means he doesn't know yet. At least I'll be here to hug him if he's hurt by it.

I mean, he for sure will be, right?

Just another bad thing in our lives that's my fault.

"Sore hoof?"

Eddy drops the Clydesdale's hoof. "White line, sadly."

"That's bad?"

He nods. "But we have some great treatments." I wait while he explains the options to the draft horse's owner, a nice lady named Linda. None of the options sound very good to me, but thankfully, I'm not a draft horse with a sore hoof.

I zip up my coat, and while I wait, I can't help scanning a few more articles on my phone. Mom and Dad sure were busy. I wonder how much money they made. Will they try to contact me? Or will they realize that bridge is now entirely and completely burned?

"You alright?" Eddy's eyes are full of concern when he finally walks toward me.

I shrug. "I'm sure you haven't heard yet, but my parents—"

"You saw?" His lips purse. "Sorry about that. I thought with the puppies, you might not be checking."

My jaw drops.

"I knew I ought to tell you, but you looked too peaceful and happy this morning."

"Eddy, did you read what they said about you? It's absolutely horrible." For the first time, I think to check *his* social.

I absolutely adore Amanda Brooks, who will soon become Amanda Dutton. We've postponed our wedding for a short time due to both family emergency and holiday stress, but very soon we'll share photos. Anything else you hear or read is a tall tale.

A tall tale. It's so very *Eddy*.

He wraps an arm around my shoulder. "You told me we should get rid of them. I encouraged you to let them stay. I'm so sorry."

"Is your manager furious?"

Eddy shakes his head. "All press is good press,

remember? They've just released a statement saying that your mother and you aren't close and that while she took some photos and videos, they were taken out of context and don't reflect our reality."

I open my mouth, and then I close it again.

"Are you upset? I should have told you about it earlier, and then we could have had a call with them together."

I shake my head. "No, you did great. I'm actually surprised you're not angrier."

"Oh, if your mom was still here. . ." He chuckles. "I'm just not ticked at you."

I lean my head on his shoulder. "I can't wait to marry you."

"I have a suggestion."

"Okay." I straighten so I can see his face. "You sound worried about it."

"I've been thinking about it for a while. I know you still make money from the Insta posts and your blog, but. . ."

"But what?"

"I know you spent years building all of that, and I'm not saying it's not impressive. I know it is, but it doesn't seem to bring you joy lately."

I can't argue with him about that. It used to be fun. Then after that, it was my whole world. I relied on it. I obsessed over it. It was security and terror and inadequacy, all in the same place.

"But you have another job, and my vet practice is doing fine, and I've been making money off my music, too."

"Okay."

"We're about to get married. I'd be happy to sign a prenup saying all my money is your money if that makes you feel better." He grins. "But I think that maybe we should delete our social media accounts."

"Have you run that idea past your manager?" I frown. "I doubt he'd sign off."

"He was the first person I asked," Eddy says. "When he was coming up with his statement, I realized he's pretty good at that stuff. I asked if I could just hand my account off to him with a notice that it's now run by my label."

"Do you trust them to run it?"

He shrugs. "I don't really care what they say. I mean, they can post videos on there that I send them from time to time. That's the only thing I use it for. But then you and I could go off grid."

"Off grid?" I lift my eyebrows. "Do I look like the kind of girl who lives without manicures and facials, much less electricity and running water?"

"I meant figuratively, obviously." He ducks and kisses my nose. "You look like the kind of girl who can think things over and let me know."

I shake my head. "No, you're right. This has been a long time in coming. I've had countless heart-to-hearts with sponsors, telling them what they can and can't dictate. I've had horrible ups and downs for years, and the media's always pushing for information I don't want to share. I hate it. You're right."

That night, after Eddy's done working for the day, and after I've had the time to notify a few of my influencer friends, I gather my kids and Mandy and Eddy, and we all watch as I delete my Instagram account.

It's terrifying, and it's exhilarating.

Until I met Eddy and Abigail and Amanda Saddler, I'd never have felt safe enough to do something like this. But now that I have. . .

For the first time in years, I feel utterly *free*.

HELEN

Christmas wasn't very magical when I was a kid. Mom and Dad are academics, and as such, they had to explain that they didn't believe in creation myths, or celebrating the birthday of a deity they didn't believe in, but that culturally Christmas was significant, so when we were older, they let us get a tree, and they also bought us each a few presents.

If they mostly gave us things like sets of encyclopedias, protractors, and scientific calculators, well, they are who they are.

Every year, when people start putting up tinsel and trees and decorating with twinkle lights, I still hear Mom's voice in my head mocking it. I hear Dad talking about how ridiculous it is that we celebrate an event that very likely didn't even happen by buying things people neither want nor need.

"Even if there was a baby that was a god who was born, would he want us to be giving each other presents?" That's what he'd say. Every year. As if we hadn't heard it dozens of times.

The idea of celebrating Christmas always made me feel like. . .I don't know. As if the act of celebrating it was evidence that I was a halfwit, a dupe, and a superstitious idiot. So when my friends had parties, I'd go and hear myself repeating the same things Dad and Mom had said to me. I didn't really want them to be true, but no one ever could refute them, and I was more afraid of being a dupe than of being a scrooge.

Abigail being stuck in the hospital has given neither of us anything to do, and we've spent a lot of time talking about things. I still can't believe she walked away from Mom and Dad and immediately started going to church.

"Without them sitting next to me, dissecting everything, church made me really happy," she says. "You should try it sometime. You might find that it's not as ridiculous as Mom and Dad said it was, if you give it a chance."

"You really think God made the very problematic, very imperfect Earth and then, what? Just wandered away?"

Abigail sighs. "You can't argue with faith, Helen. Faith is believing in something you can't see, touch, or hear. Faith is not knowing, but believing nonetheless. I feel peace and happiness when I believe, so I believe."

She's right. You can't argue with faith. It's like trying to pick a fight with a wind gust. Instead of trying, I change the subject. "Okay, we've made plates of cookies, but the kids are still insisting we wait until tomorrow to deliver them. They're all in the freezer, waiting."

"Did you decorate the house?"

I nod dutifully. "I will warn you that no one could recall quite where you put some things, like the gnome family, and although Izzy took charge, the other kids aren't convinced they got it right."

"As if it matters." But she's smiling.

"It does to them."

Abby's kids are struggling without her. You can see it in their eyes, in their slow, forced movements, and in the way they all snap their heads around to look toward the door every time it opens, hoping against hope for a miracle. Christmas isn't the same without her there.

She's the heart of that home.

I know, because I miss her in the same way. That's why I've spent so much time sitting in this boring hospital room.

"Alright, so the things I told you I ordered?"

I nod. "All wrapped and labeled."

She winces a bit, but it's unnecessary.

"Roger came in for three days. I had him do it." My gay assistant is a hundred times better at wrapping than I'll ever be. I tried wrapping two packages and immediately called for backup.

"Well, that's good." Abigail leans forward. "Even the big green—"

"Even that one," I say. "You don't have to worry."

"We've spent exactly one Christmas in a hospital," she says. "And that was when people were still hopeful about Nate. They thought he might recover. We sang songs. We watched movies. We wore Christmas pajamas." Her voice drops to a whisper. "Not long after that, he died."

I was too busy to even show up for a visit that year.

Or maybe I just didn't want to be there for all that misery and sadness. Either way, Abigail was alone with her kids with all that, and I can't even imagine what it must have been like. "I'm sorry."

"I can't stay here," she says.

"You have to stay here."

An hour later, Steve's off shift, and he and Dr. Peters are arguing with Abby.

"I know the fluid level's still below a five," she says. "Believe me when I say that I love this baby more than anyone, but my amniotic fluid has been hovering between a four and a five for almost two weeks. It's not going down. The baby's not in distress."

Dr. Peters sighs. "If it wasn't Christmas, would we even be having this conversation?"

Steve looks as if he's given up on arguing. I can't tell whether he's scared of Abby, or whether she has convinced him.

"This baby may not be growing as fast as we'd like, but he's not failure to thrive, and my condition has been stable. My husband's an ER doc, and my sister bought a monitor and an ultrasound machine. Steve can check on things at home just like you have been here."

I was initially opposed to the idea of her leaving, but I've been here a lot. She spends a few hours on the monitor and a few hours off. They draw blood once a day. They do her ultrasound once a day. I don't know why Steve couldn't do most of that from home.

"You have to call me twice a day," Dr. Peters says.

Abby sighs heavily and nods, and then she freezes. Her eyes widen, and a smile spreads across her face. "Wait, you're saying yes? I can go home?"

He sighs. "You seem to have been right about everything so far, and although you're high risk, you're right that your husband can check you as well as the techs here. If he promises to do that—wait. Do you have Christmas Day off?"

Steve bobs his head. "My sister-in-law's getting married." He clears his throat. "Or, she was. And now our friend's getting married. So yeah, I swapped New Year's to get off."

"Wait, a wedding?" Dr. Peters frowns. "No dancing, and she can't be on her feet for more than five minutes at a time."

"I can go to the wedding?" Now my sister's really happy. "Oh, Dr. Peters. Thank you."

"Don't thank me." He points at her belly. "Be smart, and take it easy."

"We'll see that she does," I say.

"I'm counting on you," Dr. Peters says, "because I think her husband's scared of her." He's half kidding.

It takes nearly an hour and a half after that before we're finally discharged, and then it's another hour and a half to drive home, because Steve drives like my grandma. If she was recovering from a recent trauma that made her scared to drive. Also, if she was still alive.

"I'm never letting you drive again," I mutter for the fiftieth time.

"We just got out of the hospital," Steve says. "Do you really think we should endanger her life?"

I can't help spluttering. "Excuse me?"

"I've been going five over the whole way home, but some of us see the wrecks that happen when people drive like you, and it's not what we need to experience firsthand on Christmas Eve."

"Who do you think will be the most surprised?" Abby asks as we turn into the homestretch.

"My money's on Izzy," Steve says. "That girl is your most devoted fan. She made all the cookies—"

"She burned at least three batches," I say.

"And remade them," Steve says. "She's been drifting around the house aimlessly while you've been gone."

"I think Gabe," I say. "He makes that little forlorn face when no one's looking."

"Interesting," Abby says.

We're nearly there now. Two minutes away, maybe three.

"I'm sure all the kids have missed me," she says. "But I'm thinking the person who's going to be the most excited to see us is probably. . .David Park." Now Abby's grinning.

"What?" I roll my eyes. "You're funny. It's Christmas. I told him we'd get together sometime afterward."

"Don't you think even a fake boyfriend needs some kind of holiday photo?"

"He's Korean," I say.

"A lot of them are Christian," she counters. "He could be, too."

"Actually," I say, "Koreans aren't really like us, where you have to be all or nothing. They'll often be Buddhist, Christian, Catholic, and atheist at the same time."

"You can't be atheist and Christian," Abby says.

"Tell them that."

Abby has been unusually quiet and not nearly as feisty as usual over the past few weeks, as if her fear about the baby has drained away her usual verve. It's nice to be volleying verbally again, even if it is about David almighty Park.

Only, when we reach the house, a familiar, shiny SUV is parked outside. Abby must've texted him. I thought maybe he'd gone somewhere for the holidays, because I haven't heard from him in the past few days. I hate how weirdly excited seeing his car makes me. What kind of loser's happy that her sister's been messaging her fake boyfriend?

The second the car stops, the front door opens.

"Hey Steve," Izzy's shouts. "You said that if we wanted, now that the snow has been plowed, we could ride—" She freezes. "Mom?!" She drops the bag she was holding and runs down the porch steps, slipping on a patch of ice and nearly falling on her butt. She does right herself, luckily, and then she sprints until she reaches the car.

Izzy rips the car door open and practically falls on her mother.

In two million years, there's no way that either Abby or I would ever have done that to our own mother. Clearly Abby's doing something right.

After their sister left the door hanging open, it appears the other kids heard her screeching. Ethan, then Gabe, and finally Whitney all rush out the front door.

"Mom's home?" Gabe asks.

"Hey!" Ethan says.

"Yes!" Whitney practically rips Izzy away, trying to scramble in for a hug herself.

Maybe it's because their dad died. Maybe that's why they're so happy to see her when they've been to the hospital to visit, and it's not like she has anything terminal.

When Abigail finally stands up, even Ethan looks a little teary-eyed.

Gabe's smiling, but he sounds almost sad. "Now it can really be Christmas."

"It's Christmas whether Abigail stays at the hospital or not," I say. "Christmas is about Christ's birth and the celebration of it."

Izzy glares at me. "Yeah, yeah. But it's also about family. You're so clueless."

Maybe she's right. Maybe I am clueless about that. I never wanted to be around family any more or less because it was Christmas. Seems ridiculous to me.

But then David pokes his head around the door-frame. "Looks like a pretty exciting day."

"Why are you here?" I'm not sure why I'm so crabby. It's not like I care that a teenager just corrected me, or that I'm upset that no one cares whether I come home.

"Your sister invited me," he says. "Is that a problem?"

I roll my eyes. "May as well get a few photos out of it."

"Why do you need photos?" Gabe looks at me, and then he turns and looks at David with a studious expression. "Are you making him a photo album for Christmas?"

I laugh. "No, but we're doing—it's like a school project. We have to take photos and share them online."

Gabe nods. "Well, I hope you get an A. The last time I had to do a school project, Jacob Lyons sat on it and we all got a C."

That makes Ethan snort with laughter. "I hated group projects."

"Your whole life is a big group project with people who sit on things," Steve says. "You're working with cattle."

"And they poop on things, too," Gabe says.

The guys all laugh, because, poop. I find myself looking at David's face as he laughs. Which I should not be doing.

"Let's go inside," Steve says. "Your mom's not supposed to be standing for a long time or doing a lot of walking."

"I can make you breakfast in bed," Whitney says.

"It's two in the afternoon, dummy," Gabe says.

"Don't say dummy," Izzy says.

At the same time, Steve says, "You can make her lunch in bed." He waves his hands to get people moving. It's a good thing, too, because no one who just rushed out is dressed for the weather, and I think Whitney's lips are turning blue.

I'd been staying at the hospital for the past two days so Steve could deal with some horse stuff and work a shift. Even though they've sent me lots of photos, it's different to see it in person. The kids clearly spent every moment they've been off from school doing all the Christmas things they could.

"The gnome family looks really cute on the mantle," Abby says. "I like it better than the entry table."

"The entry table." Izzy sighs. "Why didn't I remember that?"

Her children follow her into her room like she's the Pied Piper playing a tune. Steve follows closely after, lugging her bags.

Which leaves me alone in the most festive family room in America with David almighty Park.

I sigh.

"Should I go?" He jabs his thumb over his shoulder. "Clearly Abby was wrong."

"What did she say?"

He shrugs. "No big deal. I have a few things to review for my new business plan."

"Oh? Let me take a look."

"I didn't bring it," he says. "Because it's Christmas Eve."

I sit on the sofa and pat the spot next to me. "Well, then you can tell me what you're doing. Did you decide to sell off the supplier with the contract we discussed?"

That buys us about forty minutes of stress-free conversation. But once we've covered everything he recalls, I'm back to not knowing what to say. Luckily, Izzy comes shooting out with a basket of laundry. "Hey! Mom wanted me to ask if you had any laundry you wanted done?" She looks pointedly at my bag that's still resting on the floor of the entry hall.

"Ah. I better get that put in my room." Abby hates things lying around, which makes sense. With nine hundred and forty-eight people living here, a few people leaving something out adds up fast. But I imagine pulling out my bras and whatnot and passing them to Izzy, and I physically shudder. "I'll do my laundry later."

"You alright?" David asks.

"I'm fine."

"I'm going to have to second his question," Izzy says. "In the entire time you've been here, and it's been a *long* time, you have never once done your own laundry."

"I pay you to do it," I hiss. The little brat's starting to tick me off.

"Actually, you probably overpay me." She grins. "Alright, well, whenever you're ready." She salutes. "At your service." And then she's gone again, and the awkwardness descends.

"Why is laundry a sensitive issue?"

"It's not," I say. "Not at all."

"Okay," he says. "Well." He stands up. "Looks like I should grab my stuff and go."

I don't want him to leave, which surprises me, but I have no idea what reason I'd give to ask him to stay.

"Alright." I stand up. "I better get my stuff put away."

"I'm glad your sister's home," he says.

"It only took an ultrasound machine in the game room, and a baby monitor right next to it." My laugh sounds forced.

"Wow, I wonder what that costs."

"It turns out, you can buy a crappy vet one they use in the field for under a few grand. Eddy could have loaned us that one, probably. Or you can get a refurbished one for humans that's only ten or twenty grand. But if you really want a good one, one capable of reading delicate things, like, say, the amount of amniotic fluid around your nephew, you're looking at eighty to a hundred grand."

"You're a good sister," David says. "That's a lot to spend to have her home for Christmas."

With the giggling and the laughter coming from her room, I don't even regret it. "I'm not sure that buying things really makes me a good sister."

"But you were there at the hospital with her, too."

"I wasn't when her husband was dying." The words just shoot out, like I've lost control of my mouth. Or maybe the guilt is just catching up to me.

David doesn't say anything, so I sneak a sideways glance. He looks thoughtful, which is totally useless to me. I have no idea what to say to someone unless I know *what* he's thinking.

"You should take some cookies with you," I say. "Here. I can grab you some." I hop up and head for the back of the house.

As if she heard me, the door pops open and Whitney emerges. Izzy's coming from the opposite direction, her arms now free of laundry. They almost run into each other. I need to go past them, into the laundry room Izzy just vacated. That's where the big chest freezer is.

The one that I don't have permission to use.

It's a little embarrassing, honestly. The first week I was here, I didn't push it hard enough or hold it long enough to close it, and since it was full of food, it all spoiled. Abigail was *not* pleased. My license to use it was revoked, and it hasn't been reinstated.

Which is stupid. I'm not ten years old.

I still use it whenever I want, just not when people are around who might rat me out. And the two girls in front of me are the two most likely people to rat me out in the entire house.

"Hey," I say. "Can one of you go grab a cookie plate for David?"

"They don't have the jam thumbprints yet," Izzy says. "Or the gingerbread men."

"I think he'll survive." The plates look so full already, I have no idea where more cookies would even go.

"But I love gingerbread." David's face looks entirely innocent, which is suspect in and of itself.

Whitney frowns. "Do you need to leave? Why can't you stay and wait until they're done?"

"Yeah, the gingerbread men are the best part," Izzy says. "Mom has a recipe where they actually taste good, because it uses less molasses. Only, they don't look quite as nice. They kind of spread out, like marshmallow men."

"Still, it's worth it," Whitney says. "We voted on them last year, and the marshmallow men won by a landslide."

"Only Mom picked the ones that looked better and tasted worse." Izzy laughs. "And she didn't really, she just wanted the plates to look pretty."

"I could stay," David says. "But I think your aunt—"

"Oh, never mind her," Izzy says. "She's always insisting on stuff, but we just ignore her."

"Sadly, that's true," I say.

David's laugh is larger than I've ever heard from him. "You know," he says when he's finally stopped. "If I could have gotten that on video, along with your beleaguered expression, we could have broken the financial part of Twitter."

"So will you stay?" Izzy asks. "It's annoying having to roll all the shortbread into balls. You could do that part."

"Here's a tip," David says. "When you want someone to do something you don't like, you'll have better luck if you don't tell them up front that it's annoying."

"Maybe," Izzy says. "But if I lied, you might get mad. If I tell you that I don't like that part and you stay, you'll feel helpful. Then you can flirt with my aunt and no one will be annoyed at *you* because you're doing something we don't like. It's a win for both of us." Izzy's shaping up to be just as big a brat as her mother.

"You're a little horrifying," David says.

"So will you do it?" Whitney asks. "I can go get the sesame seeds."

"And let's pull the cookie plates out too, so Mom can see them," Izzy says. "We'll deliver them later, but Mom has to stay in the car when we do."

They hop into action, and instead of hiding in my room like I usually do, I stay in the kitchen. At first they try to make me roll the balls David has made in sesame seeds, but after I mush three of four and wind up causing internal sesame seed intrusion, I'm fired.

"You're even worse than Aunt Amanda, so you have to sit over there and watch." Izzy points, looking so much like her mother I can barely stand it. A few minutes later, as they're starting the gingerbread men, Abigail comes out and sits on a stool to help.

Gabe, Steve, and Ethan come out too, and the room is pretty full, but no one seems to mind. They just drag more chairs over, and they're all laughing as they make some lovely and some impressively ugly gingerbread men. They're right that they do spread out as they bake.

"Mine looked pretty good, but now look." David's peering into the lit oven, and his shoulders sag. "It looks like it's been punched."

"All over its body." I'm laughing as I look over his shoulder.

"At least I got to make some." He turns and purses his lips.

"Hey, I made one."

"And then you ate too many red hots, and you got fired. Again." David's eyes are really cute when he's smiling.

"They should have bought more red hots. It's not my fault they didn't know that you buy one to eat and one to use."

"Red hots are gross," Gabe says. "You *only* use them for the gingerbread men."

"Their mom's been in the hospital," David says. "Cut them some slack. Geez."

"She does like red hots," Abby says. "I knew that."

"But I didn't," Ethan says, "so if you want to blame someone." He shrugs. "It's my fault that those guys all look like that." He points at the unbaked trays waiting for their turn. All the little doughmen have sprinkles for their eyes. After I ate all of the red hots, we had limited options.

"When these come out," I say, "you can finally get your cookies and go."

"But we're about to play games," Gabe says. "And

you promised to play with me." He looks up at David with painfully hopeful eyes.

"You did?" My eyes widen. "You're a chump. Gabe's the youngest, and he always overestimates what he can do. You're going to lose."

"He didn't say he'd be my partner," Gabe says. "He said he'd play with me. We're playing Candyland."

I slap my hand over my mouth. "Oh no, that's worse. Have you ever played that game?"

"Gabe's going to teach me," David says. "But how bad can it be? It's a game with candy."

"There's no actual candy," Whitney says. "Just a weird gameboard."

David's actually a pretty good sport about Candyland, which is heartwarming. Or it would be, if I ever wanted to have kids, which I don't.

Not that I'd want to have them with him even if I did.

I'm a mess. It must be the holidays messing with me.

A few moments later, David's phone rings. Instead of checking it and putting it back on the counter like he has every other time, this time he picks up. "I have to take this," he mouths.

Since he's speaking in Korean, I assume it's someone from his family. I've taken some basic conversational classes, but I don't understand most of what he's saying. It's even harder to understand anything when I have to pretend not to be listening.

"No," I snap when Izzy asks if I want to play Monopoly.

Her eyes are hurt, and I feel bad, but David just said no, and then he said something about not liking something.

Or someone?

Who's he talking to?

Finally, he hangs up.

"That was a long call," I say.

"Who was it?" Gabe asks.

He just earned himself a really nice gift. I wonder if they'll overnight something on Christmas Eve. Probably not.

"It was my mother," David says. "I can ignore most people at Christmas, but you should always answer if your mom calls."

"You guys hear that?" Abby nods. "He's right."

They laugh.

"Did you wish her a Merry Christmas?" Izzy asks. "Or do they not do that in Korea?"

"My mom's Christian," he says. "So we definitely did wish one another a happy holiday. It's already Christmas Day there, actually. They're ahead of us."

"Wow," Gabe says. "Did Santa bring her stuff?"

David laughs. "I'm sure he's already been by. It's a long day for him."

"Why did you talk so long?" Whitney asks. "Sounded like an important conversation. Are you in trouble?"

Bless her. I'll just have to get them all presents. Who knew that the answer to prying without prying was just having kids around to do it for you?

"Well, my ex-girlfriend's coming to the United States in two days, and Mom wants me to show her around and take her out."

"But you have a girlfriend," I blurt out.

David's head snaps my direction. "A fake one."

"Still, we don't want people to know that."

"Wait, you're his fake girlfriend?" Whitney asks. "Why? That sounds stupid."

Kids are always asking things and then answering

them before you have a chance. It's irritating. But she might also be right.

"Have you ever had a jerk say something and you just want to yell *wrong* in his face?" I ask.

Whitney frowns.

"No?"

"I'd just punch him," Whitney says.

Abby laughs, but then she sobers. "Whitney Brooks, we do not punch people."

Whitney sighs and rolls her eyes. "What I meant was that I would use my words to make him feel really dumb."

"What if you could use one fake photo to do the same thing?" I ask.

"Ooh, I totally would do that," Izzy says. Which is how the kids wind up finding out about David's and my fake-dating.

"So how long are you going to pretend for?" Ethan asks.

I take back all my nice thoughts about kids. Now they're asking things I don't want to answer, and it sucks. I do wonder whether David has a response.

But he just looks at me questioningly.

"Oh, I don't know."

"If we're breaking up soon, I can take her out," David says. "Mom said she'll be here for two or three weeks, so not a huge rush."

Soon. That word makes me want to hurl.

Why?

I shouldn't care.

I mean, I don't care. It's just annoying.

When his phone buzzes, I don't even try to hide the way I peer at the screen. It's a text from his mom.

"What's it say?" Of course it's in Korean, curse her.

I only know it's his mom because David saved the contact as *Mom*.

"She's just sending me information about when she's coming and her updated contact information."

I snatch his phone out of his hand before I can think about what I'm doing. My fingers fly over the keys as I type a response for David. I TOLD YOU. I HAVE A GIRLFRIEND. SHE'S THE JEALOUS TYPE, SO I CAN'T TAKE HER OUT. NOT EVEN IF SHE WAS HERE FOR A YEAR.

Then I hit send.

"What was that?" His tone's sharp, and now I'm nervous.

Abby, Steve, and all the kids are staring at us. What's wrong with me? Why did I do that? Even if I really was his girlfriend, snatching his phone and typing out texts would be way over the line.

"Sorry," I mumble.

"Helen."

Like a small company whose stocks are being bought in a hostile takeover, I turn slowly toward him, my hackles up, my glare set to full blast. It's totally my fault, but I always get defensive when I'm wrong. "What?"

Where his tone was sharp before, this time, it's not. It's calm and quiet. "Why did you just send that to my mother?"

I shrug.

Why is everyone just staring at us?

"Hey guys," Abby says. "Pull those cookies out before they burn, and come help me put my stuff away in my room while they cool."

"Right now?" Gabe asks. "But we have—"

Izzy slaps a hand around his mouth and drags him

with her into Abby's room. And then they're all gone. Like a puff of smoke.

The smell of gingerbread fills the room. We're basically standing in Santa's workshop, and I've just done something totally insane. Nothing about this moment feels normal or rational.

"I did it because I was upset."

"We're not really dating. It's fake." David's voice is still totally even. "So why are you upset?"

"What if we tried *not* being fake?" My voice is not even. It's not calm at all. In fact, I sound a little insane.

David reaches for me then, the fingers of his right hand brushing along my jaw. Fire claws its way up my belly and lights up my entire body. I suck in a quick breath. David grabs my face, curling toward me, and when our lips meet, it's like an explosion. I lean into him, and he practically consumes me.

I don't want him to stop. "Don't take out that stupid girl," I rasp.

He shakes his head, and then he's kissing me again. His arms wrap around my waist, tugging me closer, and I go. Happily.

A giggling sound from the hallway is probably the only thing that would have worked to stop us, so maybe it's good that Izzy and Whitney and Gabe got curious.

"I think your entire family's watching us," David whispers against my ear.

"Well, since you're my actual boyfriend now, and since I live here, you probably ought to get used to it."

His smile against my mouth is one of the best feelings I've ever had.

✾ 23 ✾

DONNA

My favorite author is this woman who, like Abigail, went to law school, and like Abigail used to, I think she lives in Houston. She has a ton of kids too. Four, five, six, maybe? Once you get up there, there's probably not much difference. She writes all over the place like a rabid squirrel. Fantasy. End of the world. Romance.

My favorite series of hers is called the Finding Home series. It's about all these people, real-life people, who have problems. They've had lousy parents, they've gone through bad breakups, or they're dealing with issues at work. The commonality is that they're broken, basically. But in the story, they fix themselves, and that's why they're able to find love.

I like the idea that it's not an unfathomable mystery why people are alone. It's something they can control, to an extent. It's something that, with enough patience, and time, and work, they can repair, and then they'll be capable of loving fully and deserving that same kind of love from someone else.

I referred the books to a friend of mine, and she

read the first book and liked it, so then she picked up the second one. That one's called *Finding Faith*, and it's about a lady who was engaged, but when her fiancé discovered she didn't want kids, he dumped her. The main story happens after all that, obviously. That guy's not the hero.

But my friend Eve said she didn't like it because of that backstory. She put the book down and walked away, because she "didn't like reading books where the main character has already loved someone else."

Because the character in that book had fallen in love and had her heart broken, my friend didn't think the love the heroine would find in the book was as pure.

My friend Eve's an idiot.

I thought I loved Charlie. That's why I married him. By her logic, I'm now impure, unworthy of love.

When we're kids, we think candy must be good for us. After all, how could something that tastes so good be bad!? We think that working out is a waste of time. Our heart health isn't even on the radar. Kids don't like doing anything that's hard, but in life, everything good requires effort.

At first, I just rolled my eyes and let it go, but it has circled back to bug me several times since. My first love crashed and burned. Does it mean my love for Will is worth less? Does it mean we're not special, because I'm dinged and dented and weathered?

As Abigail sits across from me, I can't help mulling it over again. If loving Charlie and losing him was bad, if it spoils the love I have with Will, how much worse would it be for her? She loved Nate and it was a perfect love, from what I can tell.

"That dress is perfect for you," Abigail says. "You're

lucky. There's no way I could wear Amanda's dress." She sighs and pats her enormous belly.

"I should hope not," I say. "You're pregnant! You've created another life."

"It's still a little depressing, seeing the toll it takes on me." She shakes her head. "I'm happy. But it's also a little hard."

"Does it really look nice?" I turn a little, trying to see my full profile in the cramped space of the dressing room.

"Oh, Donna." Abigail shakes her head. "With that gold overlay, the full skirts, and the fitted bodice? You look like a queen."

That makes me smile. "Can I ask you something?" I sit on the stool they provided, hoping it won't crush anything or cause wrinkles.

"Sure. Go right ahead."

"You really loved Nate, right?"

She blinks. "I did, yes."

"Your marriage was almost perfect?" That's what Amanda says.

Abby snorts. "No one's marriage is perfect, no matter how it looks."

"Yeah, okay, but you guys were happy most of the time? You still loved him after having four kids, right?"

"The kids were the best thing about our marriage," she says. "But Nate was pretty great, too. He made a lot of mistakes, and he always tried really hard to fix them and not make the same one twice."

"But after he died, did you think you couldn't love someone else?"

She sighs slowly. "It's not that I didn't think I could love someone. I knew a happy relationship was possible, and that always helps. I just didn't think I'd be lucky enough to find someone who would be as great a fit with me again. Does that make sense?"

I nod.

"Honestly, I probably overthought it."

Of course she did. That's kind of her thing. "Did you feel guilty about dating Steve? Like you didn't deserve to find love again?"

"For sure," she says. "Well, I felt guilty. It's not that I thought I didn't deserve it. I just felt like loving Steve was a little disloyal to Nate. Also, Nate had asked me not to have any more kids." She presses her hands on her belly and laughs. "Obviously that's not a promise I kept." She shrugs. "Ultimately, we have to make the best decisions we can make in the world we're living in."

The best decisions we can make.

"Are you feeling guilty?" she asks.

I tell her what my friend said.

"What an idiot."

"Right?" I feel a little dumb even mentioning it. "But for some reason it stuck with me."

"That lady's fundamental understanding of love is wrong. Maybe it's the media who failed her. They sell love as this thing that's pure and bright in every way. Remember all those stupid stories about unicorns coming only to virgins?" She rolls her eyes. "Love's not pure."

"What?" Now she's lost me. "Isn't love the purest emotion?"

"Love is greedy," Abigail says. "You look at someone and your heart says *mine*. You want them with you every second. You don't want to share. You want to have and be and possess everything about them." She shrugs. "And it's also selfless. When I see someone I love hurting, I would do anything, sacrifice anything, kill anyone, to keep them from pain."

"It's greedy *and* selfless?" Now I'm confused.

"It's also enduring. That person can hurt your feelings more than anyone else, and sometimes they will. If you don't really love them, you won't have the strength to move past it. They'll do things that are careless, and it takes energy and vulnerability to explain what they did. You need to have faith in them that they'll listen and care. It also takes energy to heal from their mistakes and from your own."

"Okay. It's greedy, selfless, and enduring." This is a lot more than I really expected.

"I'm talking too much," she says. "And it's almost time for you to go."

I laugh. "I did ask Abigail Archer something. I knew what I was doing."

She tilts her head. "Donna, love is complex. It's rich. And it's a living thing. It's not an emotion. It's not static. Love means that you keep trying when you want to quit. It means that you do things that are uncomfortable for you, to help the other person. It means that you want something that's hard and you stretch to get it. Above all things, it's active. Don't worry about love being pure or perfect, because at its heart, love is the messiest emotion of all."

Love is the messiest emotion of all.

That may be the truest thing she's ever said. That phrase keeps running through my head as I walk out of the dressing room. The bridal march is already playing, so we have to walk quickly to reach the entry.

"Are you sure this is fine?" I wanted Abby to walk me down the aisle since my dad's dead. And even if he wasn't, he was a jerk. I figured Abigail was about as anti-my-dad as it gets. She did know him though, and she advocated for him too, when neither he nor I deserved it.

Having her take his place is weird, but love is messy.

"I've been sitting down this whole time. I'm totally great," she says. "Steve checked me right before we left, and baby boy is doing fine."

Right before I duck through the open doorway, I pause. "The wedding's going to be fine, right?"

"Amanda planned it," Abby says. "She may not be perfect at everything, but she's flawless at things like this."

"We're inside, so no weather issues," I say. "And the flowers and everything else came right on time."

Abby nods. "No muss, no fuss."

As we walk up the aisle, which is lined on all sides by people I've known since forever, I catch a glimpse of Will. His dad's standing beside him, and his mom's on the other side. It's not normal to do that, but no one in the world is more excited than they are, so we decided to have them join us at the altar.

Aiden's right next to his mom.

"You look so pretty, Mom!" He probably shouldn't shout at a wedding, but you know. It's cute. The audience agrees. They all laugh. A few even clap.

I'm only three rows away when a little boy with a blue tie turns and leans out into the aisle. "Hey."

My head snaps toward him, and I stop. I scan him to see if anything is wrong. That's when he pukes all over me. The side of my dress is now bright orange. *What on earth was he eating?* And then the smell hits me.

Cheetos.

Oh, gross.

The audience begins to murmur. Steve leaps forward with a handkerchief.

I can't help laughing. "Oh, Steve. That's not going to make a dent."

Moments later, Amanda sprints down the aisle with a wet towel. "Do you want to have me try and wipe it up? Or should we go back and have you change, find a cleaner's and—"

I take the towel and lean over to wipe off the worst parts. The little boy's crying, and his mother sounds frantic. It's a woman I've known for thirty years. "Olivia."

She looks up.

I shake my head. "It's fine. Take him to the bathroom to get him cleaned up. I'm not upset."

"But your dress. I told Larry not to give him that whole bag of chips."

After wiping my gown off and making sure Olivia had her son calmed down, I straighten and gesture for the music to resume.

"Are you sure?" Abby asks.

"I am."

The audience is murmuring now more than ever before, but Will's smiling at me. His smile never faltered. It never wavered. He's just happy to be here.

The poor priest at the front looks a little flustered, but after both Will and I nod, he starts his service. When we get to the part about the vows, Will bites his lip.

"How about you go first?" I ask.

"This will be short," he says. "The first time I ever saw this woman, I knew I wanted to be by her side."

I roll my eyes. "Come on."

"You were rolling up your jeans so your socks would show, and you bumped your head when you stood up on the glass trophy case on the wall."

"Will." He must be kidding. There's no way he

could possibly remember the first time he saw me. We've been at the same school our whole lives.

"I may have seen you before that, but we didn't have the same teacher in kindergarten or first. I was in the headstart class." He shrugs. "Anyway, when you bumped your head, you said, 'razzle frazzit.'" He chuckles. "My mom was always getting after me for swearing, and I started using that phrase right away. When you use it around Aiden now, it still makes me smile." He looks around at the audience. "From that day until now, I've wanted you to look my way. I've wanted to be near you, and now I get to be near you forever. I can't think of anything better."

My mom's dead. She couldn't come today, but she's the reason I always said that. Hearing this story for the first time almost makes it feel like she's here.

So of course, I start to bawl.

"Oh, no," Will says. "What's wrong?"

"My mom used to say razzle frazzit when she got upset," I say. "She would have loved to be here. She wanted me to find someone just like you. I'm sorry it took me so long to notice you."

Will takes my hand and squeezes.

"You know, an hour ago, if my dear friend Abby hadn't been back there helping me prepare, I might not be standing here. I'd probably have run out and asked to have the dress cleaned." I look down at the Cheeto-puke stain. "But Abby told me something that has replaced some bad advice that was jammed in the back of my brain. She told me that love is messy."

I look her way, where she's sitting on a stool next to Steve. I swipe at my tears and smile. "Thank you for telling me that. Life is messy, and I know that as well as anyone. Families are complicated. You may have noticed that my brother's not here. He's currently boycotting the fact that his daughter is having a child. My father and mother's marriage was a mess, and now they're both gone. But I've found someone who is brave and strong and true about cleaning up messes and trudging forward through them whenever necessary." I sigh and angle my head toward Will.

He leans toward me too, and we meet in the middle, our foreheads touching. "William Earl, I promise that no matter how messy things get, I will love you. In the good times, and in the Cheeto-puke times. I'll try my best to stick to your side like glue, even when the razzle frazzit hits the fan."

Now everyone's laughing.

And if I'm crying a little bit when the priest says, "I now pronounce you man and wife," well. That's love.

After all that chaos during the ceremony, the rest of the wedding is practically boring. Sometimes boring's nice in its own way.

❧ 24 ❧

BETH

W hen I was little, people used to come up to me and touch my hair. It's curly, and it used to be really blonde, and I guess people feel entitled to do that when you're a child. I sort of liked the attention. If that had been my strongest memory of my hair, I'd probably have loved having curls.

But when my mom would comb the curls out, it hurt.

That started to color my feelings about my hair, and eventually I hated for people to touch it. Sometimes, if it was someone I didn't know at all, when they approached with their hand out like I was a dog they wanted to pet, I'd growl. If that didn't dissuade them, I bit them.

It horrified my mother.

She was always apologizing. "I'm so sorry. I have no idea why she did that." It was a lie, of course. She knew exactly why. I did it a lot. But Mom couldn't exactly say that her daughter was a feral child who took matters into her own hands and regularly bit people for violating her personal boundaries.

Luckily, as I got older, it stopped being an issue.

I have a bit of a resting scowl face, and that kind of helps keep people away. But mostly, people just don't feel entitled to walk up and touch adults in the same way they do with children.

Until you're pregnant, apparently,

I'm at the True Value with Ethan, who's apparently craving caprese salad. It's a problem, because Manila, Utah and caprese salad aren't exactly *simpatico*.

"I told you they wouldn't have fresh mozzarella," I say.

"We do have mozzarella sticks," the cashier says again.

Ethan sighs in disgust. "It's fine."

"Ooh." The woman who runs the car wash walks in the door. "You must be due soon, Beth. You look ready to pop." She walks toward me with her hand outstretched.

After I opened my mouth to bite a tourist at Brownings last week, Ethan's gotten better at running interference.

But it's not Ethan who stops her.

Dolores Jenkins practically sprints through the door and grabs Karla by the arm. "Did you see the buy one get one sale on peanut butter? It's limit two, and there are only four left. Better run grab it before it's gone."

"Really?" Karla heads for aisle three.

"Is there a sale on peanut butter?" I ask.

Dolores yanks a five-dollar bill out of her pocket and drops it on the counter. "There is now." She winks at the cashier.

"What's that for?" he asks. "There's no peanut butter sale."

"She's paying for the second jar," Ethan says. "Try to keep up."

"But why—"

Ethan shakes his head as he walks out.

Dolores follows us through the door. "You weren't buying anything?"

"Ethan thought they'd have fresh mozzarella," I say.

Dolores frowns. "Fresh mozzarella? Was it moldy?"

"Never mind," I say.

"How's the baby doing?" she asks. "Are you feeling alright?"

I feel bad. I haven't been by to see her much lately.

It wasn't on purpose, though. I happened to take a photo of a family in front of the crèche right before Christmas, and they used it for their holiday card. Then they asked if I'd do family photos for them. I agreed, of course, and now I have more work than I know what to do with. I actually had to drive into Green River last week for a shoot that someone referred me to handle.

"Baby's fine," I say. "She's right on track. I feel alright too, but my feet do ache when I'm on them all day."

"Typical pregnancy stuff, then," she says. "Are you still feeling good about giving her to Donna and Will?"

The entire town knows now, and people were surprisingly normal about it. They do try to rub my belly, but not a single person has said anything disparaging or even side-eyed me. It makes me think maybe the world has progressed more than I expected, even here in provincial Manila.

"They're really good parents," I say. "I get to see it every day with Aiden."

"I'm happy for you," Dolores says. "And I made a few new blankets last week, if you want to come by and pick one."

She's given me eight already, but I don't mention that. Anything she wants to give away is good for her. "I'd love to."

Ethan and I sit in her house long enough to have tea before I pick two new blankets for the baby I'm not keeping. "Baby's due in April, right?"

"On tax day," Ethan says.

"That'll be perfect," Dolores says. "You can come by a week or two later, when you're feeling better, and help me plant my tulips."

I'll be leaving after the baby comes. I've been super clear about that and Ethan knows, but it still makes him clench his jaw. Watching the muscles in his face work makes me a little sad.

But it's for the best.

I still can't even imagine living near Donna and Will after they're caring for my baby, and the idea of being there when she starts calling them Mom and Dad? I feel physically ill. Even if no one's given me a scarlet letter in town, I'm still not about to just stick around here while my aunt raises my baby right in front of me.

"Isn't your mom about to have her baby?" Dolores asks Ethan. "That's what I heard."

Dolores doesn't have any friends. She barely even talks to anyone other than me, as far as I can tell. "Who told you that?"

"Well, I saw her at the store with her husband." Dolores' face flushes a bit. "She looked like she was almost ready." She swallows. "I thought Ethan might want to take a blanket or two as well. You know, some boy colors."

I glance sideways at the monstrously large stack of blue, green, and yellow baby blankets, and it makes sense. "I'm sure he'd love some."

Ethan nods. "Yes, for sure."

When we finally leave, we're both carrying several baby blankets. "You'll have to show me a photo after he's born," she says. "You know, of him with the blanket."

She would never admit it, but poor Dolores is lonely. "How about you come by and visit?" Ethan asks. "Then my mom can thank you herself."

"Oh, no, I couldn't do that."

"If you made a little matching hat or mittens," Ethan says, "you could bring that by, right?" Ethan's so smart. He's definitely his mother's son.

"I mean, maybe."

"Great. I'll let you know when he's born." Maybe, if we can pry her out of her house, she might make another friend.

"Awesome," Ethan says. "Beth has said so many great things about you that I think Amanda Saddler's actually a little jealous."

"I doubt that very much," Dolores says. "She didn't even know who I was."

Ethan pulls a face, meeting my eyes. He's clearly wondering what I know, but it's the same as what he knows. I'll have to ask her about it another time. "I'm sorry I haven't been by much. I've been working, actually."

I tell her about all the jobs I've gotten.

"That's wonderful," she says. "Actually." She looks down at her hands.

"What?"

"It might be nice to get a photo or two of us."

Us? Does she mean. . .her plants? Or, like, her blankets? Aw, geez, this is going to be so strange. "Sure," I say. "You just tell me what you want, and I'll be happy to do it."

"Well, I might need some notice so I can do my hair." She pats her head. Her hair's long, and it's pulled back into a very thin ponytail. "When I blow dry it, I can pin it up into a twist and it looks better. Less like I'm a skeleton that's above ground."

Ethan laughs. "You look nothing like a skeleton."

Dolores blinks. "Are you saying I'm too fat?"

He coughs.

"Of course he is," I say.

Dolores has a strange sense of humor. When she starts laughing, Ethan's eyes finally stop bugging out.

"He's cute, your young man," Dolores says. "But listen, you're the one working a lot. I'm not picky, either. Just any day you feel like you look nice, if you call and let me know, I'll get ready. Anything your friend here can take will be great."

What? "You want *Ethan* to take your photo?"

Dolores frowns. "Unless you have some tripod or something. . ."

It finally hits me. When she said 'us,' she meant she and I. My heart swells. She wants a photo of the two of us, probably because I'm her only friend in town. "Ethan can do it for sure."

"Oh, yeah, I can for sure," he says. "I'm Gen Z. I got you."

"Gen. . .what?"

"Never mind." I'm saying that a lot today. Dolores is sad when we leave, but then she usually is. We wave through the car windows until she disappears.

"Let's go by my place," Ethan says. "My mom said the salt got dropped off, and I need to move it all into the barn. I think Steve's home for another hour or two and I want to do it when he can help me."

"Sorry that I can't help." I drop my hands on my tiny belly.

"You're not sorry." Ethan arches one eyebrow.

"I'm not sorry." I shake my head.

He laughs.

We're nearly to his house when I decide that we need to address this.

"Ethan, I know you don't want to talk about it, but when this baby comes, I'm going to move."

His hands tighten on the wheel.

"I just want to make sure that you're not being an ostrich. Ignoring it won't change my mind."

He pulls down the driveway and parks. "The thing is, I know you're planning to move. I know you're not the kind of person who says things like that lightly. I know it's not a manipulation, but I can't just break up with you now because you're leaving later. I know that would be the smart thing to do, but I can't do it. So I'm just going to love you while I can, and if you don't stay, then we'll deal with that when it happens."

"It's not that I want to—"

Izzy taps on the window.

Ethan nearly jumps out of his skin, but then he inhales and exhales and opens the door. "What, Pennywise?"

"Who's Pennywise?" Izzy asks.

Ethan rolls his eyes. "You haven't seen *It*?"

"Huh?" Izzy frowns.

"It's a movie by Stephen King with this freaky clown who keeps showing up in the sewer. Just tell me what you want."

"Mom's grabbing her hospital bag. Dr. Peters told

her to come in now. Someone else canceled, and he was free today."

"He's still more than a month early."

Izzy shrugs. "Steve's not worried, so I'm not either."

That's Izzy for you. The cutest little yes-man ever. Even so, I can tell she's a little nervous. That's when she gets the bossiest.

"Okay, lemme take Beth home and—"

"I'll come," I say. "Being there when Abby has her baby might help calm me down about mine."

Ethan and Izzy stare for a moment, and then Ethan nods. "Alright. Let's go."

At first, when we get to the hospital, my heart's racing. Maybe I'm a little more than a bit nervous. But after the first hour of sitting around while they fill out forms, and then waiting as they hook Abby up to the pitocin drip, and then another hour as they slowly increase the pitocin, my nervousness turns to boredom.

"Why'd you bring Beth?" Abby asks. "Having a baby induced takes forever. You may as well go get some food."

Thank goodness. I'm starving.

The nice thing about her delivering in Vernal is that there are lots of restaurants to choose from. Since she sent us, we take our time. We eat some of the best Italian food I've ever had in this place called Antica Forma that's in a strip mall, and then we get what everyone else wanted to eat 'to go.'

I feel way more at ease on our way back down the hospital hallway when I hear the cry of a baby. It's tiny, but it's strong, like the wail of a toy ambulance.

Ethan meets my eyes, and we both start to jog, or in my case, it's more of a waddle. We've barely reached the room when Ethan grabs my arm and turns me around. "Nope, nope, nope. Stuff I never wanted to see is all on display."

I laugh. "Like what?"

He covers my eyes. "It's too late for me, but save yourself."

"Ethan." I bat his hands away.

"Beth, I'm serious. Let's give them a minute."

A few moments later, the baby's being wheeled out of the room in a tiny cart. What's going on? I heard this hospital kept the baby in the room.

Moments later, Abigail's walking out the door in a gown, and when I look behind her, there's blood dripping on the floor.

Abigail's voice is clear and strong. "Go with them."

Steve comes shooting out the door and rounds the corner, catching up to the cart.

"Ma'am," someone in the room is saying, "you cannot be standing. Please lie back down."

"I feel fine." She bats at the nurse. "I want to follow him."

"Your son is just fine, but he needs some oxygen and heat. Now you will sit down, or I will bodycheck you." The nurse has followed Ethan's mom out, and she's big. She's also not afraid of Abigail.

I'm worried for her.

Abigail looks like she's about to plow right through that woman. But then her nostrils both flare, and she nods. "Fine. But I want to see him soon."

"Sit." The nurse points.

Abigail complies.

Ethan and I sneak around the corner and hover at the edge of the room.

"You had an epidural. You cannot just hop up and start running down the hall, you crazy lady."

"I'm pretty sure you're not supposed to call me crazy." Abigail arches her eyebrow.

I've seen that eyebrow cow very scary men. I've seen it make my dad pretty nervous, actually.

The nurse just sniffs. Abigail may have met her match. "Now lie back, and let me check your stomach."

Abigail's glaring at the ceiling while the nurse presses all over her midsection. She doesn't look very comfortable, but she doesn't make a peep either. "The epidural wore off before he was even born. They inverted me, remember?"

"Be that as it may, we have protocols. Before you can leave this room, you have to pass—"

"Alright." Ethan grabs my arm and wheels me out the door again. "Let's go see where Izzy and Whitney and Gabe are. Since they're not in there, they might not have seen anything. They may be able to eat food again sometime in their lives."

I swat his arm. "Stop being so melodramatic."

He shakes his head. "Oh, this is me being calm."

I'm still rolling my eyes when we find the kids. Izzy wants to see the baby right away, but the others are starving.

"I think we have to wait until we have permission," Ethan says. "But I'll go check again in a minute." He mutters, "Once I'm sure Mom will be fully dressed and upright."

Half an hour later, Steve comes to check on us. "The baby's doing great." He smiles. "He's on oxygen, but his saturation levels are alright, and he looks good. We're just going to have to be patient for a bit, until they can get him strong enough to breathe on his own."

At least helping the kids, and then walking in groups of two with Steve to see the baby, gives me something to do. I can't stop thinking about what will happen if my baby comes early. Will she be able to breathe? To eat? Will she be fine?

"You're young," Steve whispers.

"What?"

"You look nervous, and you keep touching your stomach." His half smile's a little sad. "Pregnancies are harder when the mother's over forty. Don't worry, alright? I bet yours is much smoother than this."

I sure hope he's right.

I really don't want to give Donna a defective baby. Something about my heart contracts when I think about that. I don't want to *have* a defective baby. What would that mean for the rest of her life?

An hour later, Ethan and I take the kiddos home. It's clear that the baby won't be released to his room any time soon, and it feels like the other children are stressing Steve and Abby out.

A few days later, Ethan tells me he's off the oxygen. "They just need him to eat on his own."

A week later, I get a job down by Vernal, and when I call Ethan, I find out the poor little guy's still not eating well. After my photoshoot, I decide to check in on them.

Abby's holding a sleeping baby in her arms when I walk in, but he's covered in something strange. It's like a little coat or something, but there's light seeping out of all the cracks and he's wearing some kind of weird glasses over his eyes.

Or maybe they're not glasses. Is it a mask?

"He has jaundice," Abby says. "Come on in, Beth. You can meet Nathan Archer."

Wasn't her first husband named Nate?

Abby laughs. "Yes, we named him after my kids' dad."

"Why?" I wish I hadn't asked, but she doesn't seem to be angry.

"Nate didn't want me to have more kids," she says. "He was a very smart guy, but I think he was wrong. I think more children means more love, and I think our family will be stronger for remembering all the good times we had before, and making more good times in the future." She shrugs. "Steve liked the idea, too."

It seems really weird to me, but she seems happy. I guess that's the important part.

"Well, I just wanted to drop this off." It's a plate of cookies Donna and I made. "They're probably not as good as yours, but I bet they're better than the hospital ones."

"Thank you." Abby tosses her head at the table. "Can you set them there?"

"What's jaundice?" I set the cookies down and then sit next to the bed.

"When babies poop and pee, they clear out things their body doesn't need. But when they don't eat enough, their body can't clear it all out. When they have too much bilirubin in their system, they start to look orange, kind of like an oompa loompa."

"Like a what?"

"You've never seen *Charlie and the Chocolate Factory?*"

I shake my head.

"Forget it, then." She smiles. "Beth, why did you really come?"

"I had a photoshoot," I say. "It was over here, so."

"So you came to see your boyfriend's mother in the hospital?"

I nod.

"If that was it, you'd have dropped those cookies and bolted like a rabbit." She tilts her head. "Why'd you stick around? What did you want to ask me?"

I don't want to ask her anything, so I shrug.

"You're planning to leave after you have the baby." She's not asking, so Ethan must have told her. "Did you come to see what I thought about it?"

"I'm sure you think it's stupid."

"I don't." She looks totally calm—much more like the Abigail I know. It was disconcerting, seeing her frazzled and upset after Nathan was born.

"You don't?"

She sits up a little more and sets the baby on the top of his table cart. "I know a lot about the law. I know a little about babies. I know a lot about Ethan. I know very little about your life, your goals, and your dreams." Her voice drops. "I'm not sure you know what you really want right now."

How does she always say stuff like that?

"I think you came by to see whether I'll try and convince you, like I'm sure my son will, to stay."

"I can't stick around," I say. "It'll be way too hard. I can't watch Donna raise my baby."

"Are you sure you want to give her up?" She looks like she can't even imagine the concept.

"I want what's best for her."

"Why isn't that you?"

I look down at my stomach. "Maybe it is."

"Is it?" She's not baiting me. She seems to really want to know.

"I know nothing."

"No new mother knows how to parent. We all learn as we go."

"I don't want a baby yet."

"I don't want another snowstorm to show up, but the weather says I'm out of luck." She looks pointedly at my belly.

"But giving this baby to Donna is a good option," I

320

say. "And she really wants her. Then this little girl would have competent parents who know what they're doing, and who are ready to have a baby."

"Is that what she needs most?"

"It's what *I* need," I say.

Abigail smiles. "Good."

"What?"

"You can't be a mother if you can't take care of yourself," she says. "And you need to put yourself first. Once you can manage your life, you can take on another one."

"So you think I should give her to Donna?"

She shrugs. "Only if *you* think you should give her to Donna."

Ethan's mom is making my head hurt.

And my heart hurt.

"Beth, I can't tell you what to do, because I don't know what you need, but I can tell you this." She leans a little closer. "All the things you think you know might look different after you're holding that little baby in your arms."

"Okay."

"Babies change us." She turns and looks at her new son. "They change *everything*."

⚜ 25 ⚜

HELEN

I should buy a hospital.

I bought that ultrasound machine, and that made the last few weeks way better. And now that we're here, and people keep coming in and poking and prodding Abby and little Nathan, I just want to scream. Why can't they all come in during the same hour? Why do they have to come in the second mom or baby fall asleep?

"Helen," Abby says.

"What?"

"Everything's fine."

"Huh?" I turn to face her. "What are you saying?"

"You're wearing your slay-a-dragon face, but there aren't any dragons. It's fine." She spins the bottle she's holding. "Now if this little guy would just eat another few ccs, I'd be delighted."

"Why does he fall asleep so much?"

"He's a preemie," Abby says. "They all sleep a lot. He'd normally still be in my belly."

Steve walks in right then.

"You're off shift?" Abby asks.

He nods.

"Why did you drive out here? I told you Helen would be coming by."

He pats Nathan's head, and practically collapses on the chair-bed thing that sits on the window wall. "I wanna see him when I get up."

"But now we have to be quiet," I complain. "Why can't he—"

He's already snoring.

Not a loud snore, but still.

"That's annoying," I say.

Abby smiles. "He only snores like that when he has a stuffy nose. I think it's kinda cute."

"Being in love makes you dumb."

"What about you?" Abby asks. "You're the one with a new boyfriend. You should be disgusting me, not the other way around."

"You're not disgusting me." I scowl at Steve. "He is."

Abby rolls her eyes. "How's it going with him?"

"I should never have said we should date for real." I fold my arms.

"Why not?"

I huff. "He wants to see me every single day."

"Some people would like that," Abby says. "They're called *everyone* who's dating."

I laugh. "Well, not me. It feels like he's trying to stick me in a box and tape it shut."

Someone clears their throat from the hall.

We both swivel our heads to look.

"I didn't bring any tape." David Park's standing there holding the biggest floral arrangement I have ever seen. "I swear."

Abby bursts out laughing.

I want to crawl into a box and disappear. "I didn't mean it like that."

David turns to glare at me. "Well, as it happens, I didn't even come by to see you. I came to see my girl-friend's *sister* and her new baby, and I waited several weeks to do it."

This man is infuriating.

"Also, for the record, it's not that I have to see you every single day. It's that I have to try to see you every day if I want to successfully see you a few times a week." He sets the floral arrangement made for a giant on the floor in the corner, and then he circles around to look at little Nathan. "He's so small."

"Yes, that's how babies come," I say. "I was shocked, too. If I ever did want one, I'd ask to get a larger size."

"He was born almost five weeks early," Abby says. "But we found out this morning that he can probably go home tomorrow."

"That's great," he says.

"Not for him." Abby leans forward. "It means he's getting circumcised today."

David winces, and then leans closer to Nate. "Sorry, my man. But trust me. Better now than later."

"If you're done talking about genitalia," I say.

"Actually, we are done with that," David says. "So maybe it's time for me to do what I came to do."

What does that mean?

He crouches down over the floral arrangement and pulls out a blue box.

A Tiffany's box.

What is *that* for?

He drops down on one knee. He's staring right at me. "The last few weeks have been some of the best of my life." He's smiling like an idiot.

"What are you doing?" I ask. "Get up."

"Helen, if you told me a year ago that I'd be dating the scariest woman in the business world, I'd have laughed in your face. But now that I know you, you aren't scary at all. Your threats and your posturing are all very endearing."

"David, stop right now."

"You and I started out fake, but now?" His eyes are intent on mine. "Now I wake up every day and look for a box that I can tape you into."

I am going to slap him.

"So, please, please do me the honor of—"

"No." I stand up. "No, I won't marry you. Don't even ask."

David opens up the box.

There's a gold pacifier inside. "I was hoping you'd hand this to your sister for me." He stands up. "But I guess I can do it myself."

My sister's trying really hard to keep from laughing. I'll give her that. "Wow, that's a fancy pacifier. I'm not sure what outfit it would match."

David shrugs. "You can melt it down and sell it and add it to his college fund. Whatever."

"Why in the world would you buy something that stupid?" I ask, getting angrier by the minute. "And you got down on one knee."

David takes my chair. "You see, just last week, I saw Steve working with a horse on a trailering issue."

"What are you talking about?" I ball up my hand, because no matter how hot he is, punching him feels like a good option right now. "You stole my seat." I kick the chair leg.

"No, you vacated this seat, and I claimed the empty spot."

"What were you saying about the trailer?" I saw it too. "Is that horse still struggling?"

"Denver," David says. "I think that was his name. He's a big chestnut with a blaze."

"Yeah, that's right."

"I asked Steve to help me find some good trail horses," David says. "You know, for the Ellingson's ranch that we're going to be opening up as an attraction soon." He leans a little closer. "You know, the one I didn't sell you?"

The ranch he stole from me. Like the chair.

"Anyhow, Steve told me that Denver would be a good option, but he can't sell him to me until he's gotten over his trailering fears. See, he got injured in the trailer once."

"David." I'm losing my patience. "Get out of my chair."

He stretches out, crossing his legs at the ankle. "Now he's spooked around them and doesn't ever want to get in. Trailers are scary for horses. They're prey animals, and the idea of getting into a tiny metal box that moves and makes noise?" He shakes his head. "It's a non-starter."

"And did he get in?" Abby asks. "My kids really like Denver."

"He didn't get in yet," David says, "but Steve has faith. See, horses need conditioning. If they're scared of something, like a big metal trailer, you expose them to it a lot."

Is he kidding? "Is that what you were doing with the ring?"

"What ring?" He stands up. "Here's your chair, milady."

I sit down. "The pacifier, I mean."

"Oh, that was just a gift for Abby's new baby." He smiles.

"He's a smart one," Abby says. "I wonder how many

times you'll have to fake propose to Helen before she stops spooking."

"Not funny," I say. "I'm not scared of being married."

"So you want kids now?" Abby asks.

"No way," I say. "And I don't want to get married, but it's not because I'm scared."

"Denver didn't get in the trailer yet," David says. "But he did put one hoof up there. He did it over and over. Steve thinks that, given enough time, he'll eventually get in."

"Maybe Steve should find you another horse," Abby says. "Denver sounds like he's a real pain."

David smiles so big that his dimples show up. "Oh, I'm a patient man. I don't mind waiting, if the horse is good enough."

"What if he turns out to be a janky old mess and Steve can never fix his idiocy?" Abby asks. "Then you'll have wasted all that time."

"I have faith in Denver," David says. "I think he'll pull through."

"I'm going to buy that horse and sell him to the glue factory," I say.

But later on that week, I notice Steve out by the trailer. Denver's still not on the trailer, but he's got both front feet on it, and he's standing still. It's not very fast progress, but he's getting closer.

I hate that David's using that stupid horse as an allegory for me. The more I think about it, the more angry I get. Angry enough that I call him.

"Hey, Killer," he says.

"No, that's your name."

"I've been thinking about it. You can call me Sunshine, and I'll call you Killer. They fit better."

I huff. "Sunshine and Killer are two names that would never go together."

"Opposites attract, or hadn't you heard?"

"But they never work out in the long run."

"How's Denver doing?"

"That's why I'm calling," I say. "You're pissing me off with all this horse stuff."

"I am?" David asks. "I mean, I told you about him that day at the hospital, but I don't recall bringing him up since."

"Maybe not, but Steve's working with him here at Abby's."

"Isn't the ranch Steve's place now, too?"

"I mean, yes. But they're moving to Steve's place once the renovations are done."

"So what's the problem?"

"I have to watch him try to get that stupid beast into the metal box every day, now. I hate watching it."

"Why? I think he's a pretty good-looking horse."

"He's an idiot," I say. "Clearly the trailer's fine, and he's just being stubborn."

"Why do you care?"

"Because you're saying I'm like him. I'm not. I'm not running from you. I just don't ever want to get married or have kids. It's not the same thing."

"Okay."

"What?"

"I said okay," David says. "Is our connection bad?"

"But you're clearly likening me to that horse, and I'm angry about it."

"I'm not," he says.

"You are."

"Okay, so let's say I am."

"I knew it."

"I didn't say you needed to get married or have kids."

"Then what's my trailer?" I ask. "Just tell me."

"It's me," David says. "You're happy to invite me back to a hotel. You're even willing to say I'm your boyfriend, but everything else spooks you."

"Everything else?"

"I love you, Helen Fisher. I think I've liked you for a long time, but when you bought your sister an ultrasound machine? And then when I found out you were banned from using the freezer, that sealed the deal."

"Who told you that?" I ask. "That was a misunderstanding. Plus, Abby's kidding about it. I'm not really banned."

"You love your family," David says. "And I love you for that. I just want you to love me as much as you love them. That's the trailer, and I'm willing to wait until you're ready to climb into it."

✿ 26 ✿

AMANDA

Donna's wedding was lovely. She walked down the aisle, got puked on—I was a little thankful in that moment that it wasn't me— and then she and Will got married in front of the entire town.

Eddy's parents might have loved that.

I would have hated it. Not because of some misplaced dislike of small towns. Manila has actually really grown on me. It's a little awkward to buy tampons from someone who knows my first and last name. Last month, Venetia actually said, "I thought I'd see you a week ago." And winked.

I did *not* explain that I'd run out after my period ended and I was stocking up for the next one. It's none of her business.

But even so, I don't really know everyone, and it would have felt like a spectacle to me, like Eddy and I were performing, just like it felt when I married Paul.

My mom's betrayal was terrible.

But in some ways, maybe I owe her a thank you. I mean, she was the last push that made me delete my social media account, and other than a few moments of panic in the first two weeks, it has been the best thing I've ever done.

I have a women's wellness center that's coming along right on schedule, and I have two backers who are both intelligent and financially solvent. They're paying me a salary with the intention that I'll run it once it's up. Mandy and I are still, albeit slowly, remodeling the properties she's been renting out for decades, and then selling them off at huge profits. I don't have the need for financial support that I used to have, so letting go of the uncertainty of public approval has been the most healing thing I've done since Paul died, I think.

My unpaid therapist—Abby—agrees.

But she has also been pretty busy, what with being stuck on a baby monitor, and then with a newborn in the NICU, and now having a baby at home who's hardly eating.

And that doesn't even include Maren's cheer competitions or Emery's play she just performed in. She got the role of Annie, which was perfect for her. Once all that shook out, it was already the beginning of March.

All I'd done was pick a new dress.

This one is everything I wanted, because I went shopping like a normal person and bought the one I liked. It's also off the rack.

The horror.

But I don't have to worry about what the glitterati might say, because they won't be privy to the details of my wedding. In another month or two, no one will even remember who I am. Actually, I'm probably flattering myself to think they might still remember or care now. Social media moves fast. You continuously feed content into the shredder, or you disappear.

When I asked Emery and Maren, they had one weekend that was clear for the next two months. This one. So I called Donna. She said she and Will could come. Eddy called his parents. They're never doing anything, so that was really more of a courtesy than anything else. His sister had a date, but she rescheduled. Mandy's always free, unless she has plans with me, Donna, or Abby. Or, you know, if she's planning to fake her own death.

Whatever.

I call Abby, hoping against hope that she and her multitude of children will be free.

"Hello?"

"Hey, so I know it's short notice, but what's going on for you tomorrow?"

Abby hmmms into the phone for a moment, and then she says, "Hair appointment. It's been like six months. People are asking me if I've gotten an ombré."

"But those are in right now," I say. "Save some money and cancel it."

"What? Have you seen my hair? It's not an ombré. It looks horrible."

"Well, Eddy and I were thinking of driving out to the Gorge tomorrow."

"Amanda. I have a newborn. I think I'll pass."

"But I *really* want you to come," I say.

"It's March."

"The snow melted."

"Take a photo for me," she says, clearly getting annoyed.

"I thought maybe you could take some photos of me," I say. "Since I'll be wearing my new wedding dress."

332

"What?" Her spluttering is very satisfying. That was fun.

"Can you and Steve make it? The weather is *perfect* this weekend, the nicest weather we've had, and I'm actually hoping Beth can take some decent shots."

"Steve's working the overnight tonight. What time were you thinking?" She snorts. "And can he wear scrubs?"

"If he throws a jacket on over them for photos, sure."

"I'm kidding," she says. "He can change."

"Let's do sunset. That'll give him time to sleep."

"Oh, Amanda. That's so exciting." She wails. "But oh, no. My hair will look terrible. Maybe I can move that appointment to like, eight a.m."

She must get it moved, because when she shows up for the ceremony, her hair looks perfect. Actually, when Eddy and I pull up to the gorgeous overlook my sweet fiancé found, most everyone's already there.

Abby brought flowers. A lot of flowers. There are buckets and boxes and vases everywhere. Steve's holding Nathan, and Abigail's unloading them.

"You're early," she says. "Helen should be here any minute with the frame."

"The frame?" I ask. "What are you talking about?"

"We got an arbor," Abby says. "You can't just get married on a rock with rocks behind you. It's nice as a backdrop, but this is a *wedding*."

Helen pulls up in a really nice Mercedes SUV, which I have never seen her drive. That woman buys luxury cars more often than most women buy handbags.

But the driver isn't Helen.

It's David Park.

I still struggle to see how he might actually be

dating her. I mean, sure. She's slim. She's pretty, in an obvious, Kate Beckinsale kind of way. But who wants to date someone who bullies people with her intellect and bulldozes them with her billions?

Pass.

But somehow, they've been dating now for *months*. At first I thought it was fake, but then I stumbled around the corner from the barn and saw them standing on Abby's front porch when they thought no one was watching. They were whispering like teenagers and David kept kissing her on the side of her face, her ear, and her neck. I almost couldn't sleep that night, I was so disturbed by Helen acting affectionate and *cute* while David, just, *ugh*. I can't think about it.

But the arbor she apparently helped Abby plan is breathtaking.

"It's a good thing you didn't want to ride in on a horse," Steve says, peering over the edge of the overlook. "Because one little scare, and. . ." He waves at the edge, like he's waving goodbye to someone falling over.

"No horses for me, thanks," I say.

"I know," Steve says. "Eddy told me how disappointed he was."

I roll my eyes. "But he *is* disappointed I vetoed bringing all the dogs." I can't even imagine. "They just hit twelve weeks, and we can finally send them to homes, and now he's finding reasons to delay."

"Wait, you can send them to homes?" Steve turns toward Abby. "Where's ours?"

"We have to go pick one," she says. "I told you that last week."

"It's hard to remember anything with a new baby." Steve yawns.

"I bet." Eddy wraps an arm around my shoulder.

"Well, there are two puppies that are my favorites. You should take one of those."

"I want the other one," Ethan says, popping up over his mom's shoulder. "Here. I'll take Nathan. I've got a bottle for him."

Steve passes him off without thinking.

"Excuse me?" Abby asks. "You have no objection to Ethan also wanting a dog? One puppy is more than enough, thank you very much. We don't need two."

"First," Ethan says, "they'll play. So two will be easier than one."

"Spoken like someone who has never had either a puppy *or* a child," Abby says.

"And second," Ethan says, acting like he didn't even hear her, "in another few months, you guys are all packing up and heading to Steve's. Who will keep me company then?" He turns toward me. "I want one."

"They're two thousand dollars," I say.

"What?" Abby blinks.

I laugh. "I'm kidding. I'd pay you to take one. Have you ever seen a border collie puppy?"

"They're adorable," Eddy says. "Cuter than you can imagine."

"And they chew on everything." Maren scowls. "I've lost *three* pairs of shoes. Mom's not kidding. You have to buy them, because I need to recoup my losses."

Finally Mandy pulls up. She was the only person who hadn't yet arrived. I wave at Donna and Will, who are on kid-watch, making sure none of the younger boys goes very close to the edge. Small boys are the dumbest members of the entire human population, I'm absolutely convinced.

Mandy has all the food in the back of her truck in coolers, but we won't need that until afterward. She's late, because she brought the pastor.

"What a lovely arbor," Mandy says as she climbs out. "It looks just as good as you said it would."

"Wait, you knew she was bringing flowers?"

Mandy tilts her head. "Girl, it was my idea."

Abby shakes her head behind her.

"Or, at least, it was my idea to use those big red and blue hydrangeas. They'll bring out the color in the Gorge, mark my words."

When the pastor gets out on the passenger side, my jaw drops. "Who's that?"

"Pastor Wesley was sick," Mandy says. "He called a friend."

"I'm Pastor Paul." The man who just hopped out of the car waves.

"His name's Paul?" Eddy looks irritated.

That makes me laugh. "His name could be Paul Brooks and I wouldn't care," I say.

"Isn't it kind of weird, though?" Eddy's brow is furrowed. "I mean, I don't really want you thinking about your first wedding right now."

I lean forward and kiss him right on his delicious mouth. "Honey, no one could think about anyone but you when you're right in front of them. Trust me."

Steve clears his throat.

Abby laughs. "He definitely looks better in a suit than Paul did."

"That's for sure," I say. "And Paul would never have worn this cowboy suit." I love what Eddy picked—a black suit with pale pinstripes, and gorgeous Lucchese boots he had to buy after Steve got a pair. But for his tie, he has a bolo tie, with two leather strings. Then holding them together, there's a big hunk of sky-blue turquoise.

"You're wearing Pa's tie slide," Eddy's dad says. He sighs. "It sure looks nice."

"You look really handsome," his mother says.

Eddy tilts his head toward me, his eyes wide. "Did they just agree on something?" he hisses.

It's a wedding day miracle.

"Any moment now, a bird's going to fly over and poop on someone," Donna says.

"Or someone's tire is going to go flat," Abby says.

"Or it'll start snowing," Will says.

But none of their predictions come to pass. Even though it started raining at Abby and Steve's, and there was Cheeto puke at Donna's, nothing bad happens at my tiny wedding at all.

Unless you think the pastor being named Paul is bad, but that doesn't even rate in my book. He does a pretty nice job, too. He talks and talks about the importance of always putting God first—*okay, dude. Save it for Sunday*—and then he spends quite a bit of time talking about the blessing that marriage is in our lives. But other than the pontificating, the wedding's just exactly what I wanted.

The pastor turns toward us and says, "You can share your vows now."

We agreed to keep our vows as short as our invite list. "I'll go first," I say. "I promise that I'll always give you the benefit of the doubt."

That makes Abby and Eddy laugh. They both know exactly how bad I've been at that in the past.

"And I promise that even if I don't always agree with you, I'll just let things go whenever I can." His worst fear is that we'll turn into his parents, fighting about every little thing.

"I promise you that I'll do my very best to never disagree with you," Eddy says.

"She's always right," Steve says. "Remember that, and you'll be fine."

Everyone chuckles.

"But in all seriousness, I have spent most of my life thinking that one mistake sort of ruined my future. It wasn't until you came along and your sister-in-law did some snooping, that I realized that my mistake didn't ruin my future as much as I just stopped trying. You helped me learn to dream again. You helped me want things, and yearn for success that I had given up on. I know we're not kids anymore, but when I'm with you, I feel like a colt that's out for a run. I made another big mistake, this one much worse than the first, and that was losing my focus. I should always have been looking at you. You forgave me, and I promise that I'll spend the rest of my life chasing you around, wherever that leads."

"I now pronounce you—"

"Wait." Emery waves. I can see it out of the corner of my eye.

"We have vows, too," Maren says.

"You're not marrying anyone," I say. "Hush."

"But he's joining our family," Emery says, "and that means we're involved."

"Let them," Eddy says.

I brace myself. This could be really bad.

"Dad wasn't really the best husband," Maren says. "And from what I remember, he wasn't always the best dad, either. When Mom dated guys, she usually only made it a few dates before kicking them to the curb. I was fine with that, because, like, the last thing I needed was another guy who would ignore us." She kicks at the dirt, and the end of her cute little yellow high heel gets dusty. "Only, when we moved out here, you met Eddy. He wasn't like the other guys." She flashes a smile. "He was way better looking."

Everyone laughs.

338

Except for David Park. "Rude," he mutters.

Which gets another round of laughs. Maren's slaying it, surprisingly.

"But for reals, me and Emery liked him. And more than that, he showed up."

"Showed up to what?" Eddy whispers.

"I mean that you did what you said you'd do," Maren says. "You made my mom happy, and you aren't too bad with us either."

"Although," Emery says, "Steve bought Abby's girls horses."

Everyone laughs again.

"I'm just saying," Emery says.

"I have two horses," Eddy says. "You can have one."

"I call Otis." Emery's not usually that quick off the draw. "Maren, you can have Noodle."

"Pass. He's the crappiest pony ever."

"He's not a pony," Eddy says.

"He's barely a horse." Steve sounds like they've discussed this before. "I told you he was too small. Buy a horse for the girls. Don't try to force them to take that twenty-year-old rescue who keeps trying to lie down whenever you saddle him."

"So this is just a shake down." Eddy's grumbling, but he's clearly not uphappy.

"At least they did it honestly," I say. "They didn't just call the press and bolt."

"Mom hasn't had the easiest life." Emery's eyes are as kind as ever. "I didn't think she'd ever find someone who would really value her. But more than that, you also help bring out the best in her, just like MSG!" Her eyes light up and she smiles.

"Great, I cause migraines," Eddy says.

"Some people like MSG." Steve's eyes sparkle.

"Not you, though." Eddy chuckles.

"I mean it, though." Emery doggedly presses on. "You make Mom better than she is without you, and she's happier than she ever was alone. So please don't ever leave her side again, okay?"

"Yes, because I doubt she'd believe I was really dead a second time," Mandy says.

"Everyone's a comedian," Eddy says.

It kind of feels that way, actually. Like we're here, promising our love, while surrounded by the people who really do love us.

"I love you, Eddy." Emery's lip trembles. "I'd like to call you Dad, if that's okay. That's my vow."

"Me, too," Maren says.

I don't have the heart to tell them that it's not really a vow.

"I'd love that." Eddy doesn't correct them either.

And when Pastor Paul finally pronounces us married, instead of Eddy being able to kiss me, Emery and Maren leap toward us, pushing us into some kind of strange, four-person group hug.

"I now pronounce us Mom, Dad, and daughters," Maren says.

It may not be as romantic as I might have wanted, but it's perfect anyway. There's just enough sunlight left for us to set up a table and cover it with some of our favorite foods from Brownings.

"I brought cookies," Abby says. "And a cake."

"I bought that," Helen says. "From the cake place Abby was obsessed with while she was stuck over there."

"Their frosting." Abby closes her eyes.

It's not fancy. It's not even organized. And it's just what we wanted. As the sun finally sets over the gorge, Eddy pulls me close, wraps his arms around my waist and presses a kiss to my forehead. "I'm so glad you're wearing the dress without the huge puffy skirt. Because I can do this." He tugs me closer, puts one finger under my chin and tilts it upward. Then he kisses me like he really means it.

Even though people are standing all around, my heart lurches and I kiss him back with my whole heart.

"Oh my gosh," Maren says.

"You're on your phone?" Emery asks.

"How do you even have reception up here?" Beth asks.

"Put the phone down," I say. "Beth's still trying to take a few more photos."

"But." Maren looks up at me, her eyes as wide as I've ever seen them. Her mouth's still dangling open.

"I hope a bug flies in there," Emery says.

"Whoa," Whitney says. "Look at you. I didn't realize you *could* be snarky."

I can barely make out Emery's blush in the fading light.

"Hey, Mom." Maren swallows. "How many views would you say it takes for something to be considered viral?"

I shrug. "I don't know. A million?" I glance at Eddy. "Two?"

"Sure," he says. "Why?"

Maren turns her phone around. "Because a song I wrote and recorded just hit ten million views. And I have a lot of messages from people saying they want to talk to me about a record deal."

Maren *recorded a song?*

"When?" I ask. "When did you do that?" The only place she sings is in the bathroom.

She shrugs. "I figured if Eddy could do it, maybe all it takes is a pretty face. I have one of those, too."

There it is. The Cheeto puke rainstorm I've been expecting.

"Oh, boy. Lemme call my manager," Eddy says. "Looks like we're in for a weird week."

"Weird?" Gabe asks. "That's *awesome!*"

"Why do you care, weirdo?" Izzy asks.

"I held the camera for her," Gabe says. "She said if it did well, she'd buy me Lego Rivendell."

Maren tousles his hair. "And I'll do it too, buddy. Just wait until I get my first album deal."

We are in so much trouble.

❧ 27 ❧

HELEN

I've been dominating the business world for decades now, and in all that time, my board has never once called for a vote of no confidence.

Until now.

If they think I'm just going to march in and apologize, they've lost their minds. The moment my jet lands, a car picks me up. I'm armed the best way I know how, in my favorite tailored suit from Alexander McQueen and my five-inch Louboutins.

When I walk into the boardroom, I'm expecting there to be a ring leader. I just haven't been able to parse out who it will be. I do *not* expect to see Kyle Saunders sitting on my right-hand side, just as he was before I fired him.

"What are you doing here?" I arch one eyebrow. "Get out."

"I'm a board member now," he says. "Or didn't you hear that I bought Jackson out last month?"

They must have structured the ever-loving stink out of that, because none of the paperwork had Kyle's stamp anywhere on it. "It's always *lovely* to see you," I say. "I'm assuming I have you to thank for this summons?"

"It seems like, without us calling a vote on something major, you can't be bothered to do any work these days." Kyle's wearing his 'I'm-so-smart' smile, and I hate it.

I really shouldn't strangle him right here. Even my lawyers would have trouble getting me off from that. "My sister—"

"Was in the hospital and just had a baby," Kyle says. "That's exactly the kind of thing no one here cares about. In fact, we all wish we didn't know about that at all." Kyle gestures at the other board members, all of which are male, now that Ilena Jackson sold her shares to him.

The hazards of needing rich investors.

"Why don't you tell me why you think I should be ousted?" I arch one eyebrow.

"Actually, the fact that you're here means that at least fifteen percent of the ownership is concerned about your fitness to run this company," Kyle says. "Maybe you should be the one doing the talking." He leans back in his seat and stretches, his boots bumping my feet.

"If you bought Ilena's shares, then you own roughly three percent of the company." I nod. "That must have cost nearly everything you've got."

Kyle scowls.

"And yet, you failed to do your research, Kyle. It's a common problem with you, in my experience. You may have even been able to rally your fifteen percent, but I own sixty-four and a half percent of the company, and you need a supermajority to oust me. So what in the world did you think you were doing—"

"We just wanted to see you here," he says. "We're

unhappy with how the acquisition of Hagemann has been delayed. It's been nearly six months now, and you're still not even coming into the office. If that deal falls through, we won't have done anything of note this year."

I sit in the seat at the head of the table. "We've turned an eleven percent profit in a period of economic freefall."

"We didn't invest all our funds with you for eleven percent, Helen," Abe Udon says. "You know that."

"The fact that I've always delivered more than triple that, sometimes ten or even twenty times as much, should buy me some latitude, don't you think?"

"When are you going to be done playing house in that tiny hick town?" Kyle leans forward. "And when will you be done fake-dating that irritating loser?"

"Kyle did some research too," Abe says. "We can't oust you since you own the majority of the company, but with a twenty-five percent share, we can force you to buy out our shares so we can move on." He stands up, dropping a stack of papers on the table. "And if you're not done taking your little hiatus, I want my money back."

I lean back in my chair. "Is that so?"

Abe nods. He's not the only one nodding.

"I'm ready for you," I say.

Abigail walks through the back door, holding the files we prepared. "Given the market trends, the high rate of exposure on the current acquisition, and the closely held nature of your interests, I'm prepared to make you the following offers for your shares."

Abigail drops paperwork in front of each of them.

"You can't buy us all out," Kyle says.

I lean toward him. "You have no idea what I can do."

"But this offer is only for a third of what my shares are worth," Abe says.

"Is it?" I arch an eyebrow. "It's eight times what you initially invested, and you've been getting dividends every single year." I tilt my head. "Would you like to keep sitting here, waiting on the whims of a fickle woman who's having a wonderful time dating some guy out West? Or would you like to be set free?"

Abe's face turns red. "I want a valuation done—"

Abby points at the bottom of the offer. "You can see here that the controlling documents provide that in the wake of a failed vote of no confidence, the majority shareholder has a right to call for the sale of all shares according to the valuation method listed, as long as the total profit is more than 200% of the initial investment over a ten-year term."

"What does any of that even mean?" Abe's fuming.

"It means I can force you to sell to me, and now that you've shown how little faith you have in me, I think I'm gonna exercise that right."

"But even paying a fraction of what our shares are worth, you don't have that kind of liquid capital." Kyle crosses his arms.

"How do you know?" I ask. "You know nothing about my finances or what I've done with the dividends I received each year."

"So what are you saying?"

"Abby, get the list of the parties who called for the vote of no confidence."

My sister hands it to me. "All but three of you," I say. "Well, that *is a pity* for you guys." I hold out my hand. "Since no one's offering to sell, we'll have to force it."

"What?" Kyle stands up. "You can't."

"Oh, I'm not at all sorry to say that I *can*."

"Are you ready for me?" David knocks on the open door.

"What's he doing here?" Kyle asks.

"Oh, you see, I only had the capital to buy, say, half of your interests at the extremely discounted rate. But my boyfriend always wants to support me, so he's loaning me the funds to buy the rest. Then I'll sell him those shares, to repay his generous loan, so you see, it's a win-win. I'll have a board I can trust, and I'll be utilizing a steep discount you opened up to do it."

I stand.

"Oh, and for the record? With the delay on the acquisition, as you would know if you understood anything about international finance, we'll now make almost twice as much as if we'd moved ahead six months ago. The legislation I've been waiting on is about to pass. And the euro has come up, up, up against the dollar, or didn't you know that?" I shake my head. "Do you really think I'd have delayed the acquisition because my sister was in the hospital? I could have managed it from Bora Bora using only my feet, if the timing was right."

"I can't wait to be a part of this," David says. "It's just a dream to finally work together."

"And this is probably a decent time to announce that we have a new member joining our legal team. Her name's Abigail Archer. She and I will be working remotely from Manila, Utah for the foreseeable future."

Forcing Kyle out was definitely fun, but it was David's idea to help so I didn't have to liquidate a bunch of assets. That would have tipped my hand.

As I walk out with Abby on one side and David on the other, I realize that this was the single most satisfying moment of my career. Yes, I stand to make an absolute killing on this next acquisition, thanks to Abby finding that strange loophole, and David fronting me some capital, but that's not why. At my stage, amassing more money has almost become meaningless.

No, it's because I had people, competent people who are brilliant and trustworthy, by my side.

"I wish you could come back with us," Abby says, when I drop her and David off at the airport.

"I'm sending you back in my jet," I say. "You're so demanding."

"How long do you think you'll be working on the acquisition?" David's holding his bag and Abby's, and his hand is on the railing of the walkway.

"Depends on how big of a pain your friend decides to be."

"Well, try and see if you can get back home in two weeks." He drops the bags and steps toward me. "I may be an irritating loser, but I'm *your* irritating loser."

"You're irritating alright." I grab the lapels of his suit and kiss him.

"Eww," Abby says. "You two are so gross."

"Says the woman who put up a curtain and *pumped* twice on the way here." David curls his lip.

"Look, I just had a baby, but here I am," Abby says. "Finding loopholes and showing up to scare the stupid board members with double Fisher power."

"Double Fisher power?" I scrunch my nose.

"I just heard it," Abby says. "Won't say that again."

"Two weeks," David says. "Or I'll show up on your doorstep and drag you back."

"You could move out here," I say. "New York's not that bad."

"Did you *see* all the human poop on the streets?" David shakes his head and steps away. "No thanks."

"Hey, they have a group called the Poop Patrol now. They're working on it."

David shudders. "The fact that New York City has a *Poop Patrol* should tell you why I don't want to move there."

"LA's not much better," Abby says.

"That's why I run things remotely now, whenever I can."

"Stop whining," I say. "You know you're going to California the second you drop Abby off."

He shrugs. "My people are almost as whiny as yours. They just keep complaining and whining and complaining more about how I'm never there."

"No moves to kick you out, yet, though."

"We structure our companies differently," he says. "We rely far less on boards, and our wealthy families usually don't welcome many outside investors."

"Smart," I say. "Only, I didn't get my money from my family."

"Yes, you've mentioned that." He shakes his head. "Not everyone is Helen Fisher."

"Can we go already?" Abby asks. "I really need to pump again."

David groans.

I can't help laughing.

David adores my sister, but they interact now almost just like she does with her kids. It's strange, really. I never thought I'd have a boyfriend, much less one that Abby might like. And the fact that our fake-turned-real relationship has lasted more than three months is the most baffling thing of all. I'm pretty sure a lot of our friends have lost some money over it, too. Well, David's friends.

I don't really have any friends.

Two weeks quickly turns into three, and it's starting

349

to close in on a fourth when someone knocks on my door. . .and I didn't order any food. Could it be David? Is he making good on his threat?

I whip the door open, but it's not him. It's a man in a red uniform, singing "I Will Always Love You," holding an enormous bouquet. It's even bigger than the ludicrous arrangement David brought to Abby in the hospital.

I suppose if he can't be here, this is a pretty good reminder that he's waiting on me. Roses on top of lilies on top of birds of paradise, and it reaches from the ground almost to my shoulders. When the man finally stops singing, I wave him in and point at the far corner of the room.

After the singing messenger—where on earth did David find that guy?—leaves, I realize there's a card. I whip it out with a smile on my face.

I wanted you to see this no matter where you're standing in the room. If you're not back by the time these flowers die. . .

It's not signed.

It's typical David. What an empty threat. How will he even know when they die? And if I'm not back, he'll do what? Yell at me? Stop texting and calling? I toss the card on the coffee table and get back to reviewing the final file. I was hoping to surprise him tomorrow, if I can get through all this tonight.

Abby will still need to make a final pass, but at least my numbers overview should be done, unless I find something big. When my eyes start to cross, I order food from Atomix.

They don't do to-go, but dating the owner's cousin who bankrolled the whole thing has some perks. My stomach's growling as I close in on the last two pages. So far, no hidden grenades. Everything looks pretty decent.

When there's a knock at the door, I practically sprint to answer it.

It's Korean alright, but it's not my food. It's David almighty Park, in a very hot, very beautifully tailored tan suit. The smile practically takes over my face. "You are the best thing I've seen."

"The best?" He tilts his head. "You know, they say absence makes the heart grow fonder."

"Do they?" I furrow my brow. "Because I'm not sure that's true."

"You haven't missed me?" He takes a step back into the hall. "Well, then I better—"

I grab his hand and pull him inside. "No way. I've missed you. But if I'd known you were coming, I'd have ordered more food."

"Oh, don't worry. Junghyun called when you placed an order. I told him to double it and make it quick. I thought if you were really hungry, you might mistake me for food."

"That's why I love you," I say.

And then I freeze.

So does he.

We've been dating for a while, but that's the first time I've said that.

"I knew it," David says. "I knew that if I waited, you'd eventually realize you couldn't live without me and beg me never to leave you."

"I hardly think that's—"

He presses a finger to my mouth, and pushes me inside far enough to close the door. "You love me."

I roll my eyes.

"Say it, Helen."

"It."

He laughs, but he doesn't move his finger, and his eyes don't shift either. "You love me."

Now that he's staring at me, I can't quite bring myself to say it. It feels like an admission of weakness. My voice is low when I say, "You know I like you, David."

He shakes his head. "Not like. No. Something more." He steps toward me, and I stumble back a step. "Say it."

"David."

He steps again, and I fall back. He presses, and I bump into the wall, right next to his gargantuan floral tower.

Before I have time to change the subject, he reaches down into the floral arrangement and pulls out a blue box, just like he did at the hospital. "Helen Fisher." He holds the box up, close enough that I can see the word Tiffany's written on it.

My heart stops.

With all his talk of working on the trailer, he hasn't even made any jokes since that day in the hospital. "I've been waiting to hear you say something for a very long time, Helen."

I can't look away from the box.

"Say it," he whispers.

Do I want this? I'd have said no yesterday. This morning. An hour ago. But staring at that blue box, I don't know anymore. Maybe I do want to spend all my time with this one guy.

He's kind to animals and children. Even the annoying ones.

He helps little old ladies with their groceries.

He's patient with me, and he never presses, unless I need it, of course. He comes up with solutions to things in my personal life and my business affairs. I can count on him.

I mean, that's not hot.

I'd have told you a year ago that 'counting on some-one' was not something I even wanted. But now that I have it, I realize I would have said that because I didn't think it was possible. Every man I'd met counted on *me* to help them out over and over.

Not David. He's never asked me to help him.

"Helen Fisher, say it again. Now." He's looking at me as intensely as he ever has. And without thinking about it, without giving it a moment's extra thought. . .

"I love you, David."

He beams, then, he presses the box into my hand, and he kisses me.

I nearly drop it. But then I wonder what it is I'm holding. "This better be a huge diamond."

I open the box, and the ring doesn't have a diamond on it at all.

"What in the world is this?"

It's a gold hook thing, in the shape of a letter 'u.' Then there are silver bolt-shaped joiners on either end, with a pin holding it all together.

"It's a shackle," he says.

"A. . .shackle?" I start laughing then, and I can't stop. "You bought me a shackle for my finger?"

David shrugs. "I looked at diamonds first, but the thing is, no matter how big I went, it would be way smaller than you could buy yourself. So I thought, what would better symbolize our relationship? I made them make this for me custom, you know. There's not another ring like this on earth."

"A silver and gold shackle."

"It's platinum," he says. "Silver tarnishes. You'll never get out of this one."

His mom calls then.

He hits the decline button.

"You ignored your mom?"

"She's been bugging me to lock you down for months," he says. "And now that I'm actually trying, I'm not doing it for her or the family." He huffs.

It's the cutest thing I've ever seen. "You should answer her call."

"No." He's sulking. He's honest-to-goodness sulking. It's so unlike him. "I don't want to talk to her. I don't want to give her the satisfaction."

I pull the phone out of his hand and dial his mother back.

She answers in Korean, and I've been practicing, but I don't even bother trying to use it. Not over a phone, and not with this woman who runs their entire family like a well-oiled machine.

"Mother?" In Korea, daughters-in-law call their parents-in-law Mother and Father.

His mother gasps.

"This is Helen Fisher. I understand that you speak wonderful English."

"I do," she says.

"Your son and I are getting married, but of course that's a separate thing from my company acquiring his."

"Excuse me?"

"We're not close enough in size for it to be a merger, of course," I say. "But I'd love to talk details over a meal. Would next week work for you?"

She coughs, but she recovers quickly. "Of course. I think you'll find that our American base of operations is quite diversified and would complement your firm's strengths well."

"I'm happy to hear that you've been looking into it."

His mother makes a strange noise.

"What is that?" I whisper.

"She's crying," he whispers back. "It's a good thing."

354

"See you soon," I say. "Thanks for raising such a wonderful son." It's a weird thing for me to be saying, but I mean it. After I hang up, I slide the shackle onto my ring finger. "This has been a weird courtship."

"The word 'courtship' is pretty weird." David smirks. "It's not eighteen-fifty-three."

"You know what I mean."

"Nothing normal could have shackled Helen Fisher."

"Speaking of that," I say. "I'm not changing my name."

"I never expected you to." David kisses me then, at least until the Atomix arrives.

Nothing comes between me and my delicious Korean.

28

BETH

April Fool's Day always kind of snuck up on me.

Sometimes my friends did goofy things to one another, to their parents, or even more often, to teachers. Not me. I usually forgot about it until it was too late to think of anything to do.

Teachers are notoriously hard to fool in any case. They've heard it all. Terminal illnesses, impending moves, you name it, they've heard it. If it happens on April 1, they're automatically suspicious.

Once, a girl named Tabitha wound up puking in the middle of class because no matter how many times she insisted she was sick, the teacher would not let her go to see the nurse. I actually felt a little bad for Miss Sims when Tabitha's parents bawled her out. She *had* been told by more than ten kids that they were sick. I couldn't really blame her for not believing the eleventh.

Two years ago, I had just gotten a phone in March, so when April rolled around, it was still a bit of a novelty. My best friend Hannah convinced me that we should each call our mothers and pretend that we'd

356

been involved in a car accident. Hannah had just gotten a car, and she was sure that her parents would flip. I didn't have a car yet, but I knew my mom would be easy to fool. I could tell her I was with Hannah, or I could tell her I'd borrowed her car without permission.

That certainly wouldn't be a strange occurrence in Manila.

Only, I wasn't at all sure that Mom would find it funny—she was a bit of a wild card on a good day. But Hannah was so sure, and when she called her parents, pretended for a few moments, and then said, "I'm kidding! April Fool's," they had laughed.

So after enough pushing, I dialed.

"Hello?" Mom had answered.

"Hey, Mom," I said.

"Is everything alright?"

"Not really." It was lunch tine. It was just occurring to me that it would be strange for me to be out driving around at lunch. So on top of wrecking a car, I was suddenly confessing to cutting class. "So, Mom, I have some bad news."

"What's wrong?"

"I've been in a car accident," I said.

"You've—what?" Mom murmured something I couldn't quite pick up.

"Hannah was driving, and I think she's okay, but her car's totaled. We've called for an ambulance, but we're in the middle of nowhere. I'm glad we even have cell reception."

"What on earth are you doing in a car, nowhere near school?" Mom sounded *ticked*.

I decided I had kept it going long enough. "April Fool's!"

"Excuse me?"

"I'm kidding, Mom. I'm at lunch. Everything's fine. No car accident. Got ya!"

She swore under her breath and hung up. I found out that night that she had her parents there, visiting, and she was absolutely furious with me for my stupid joke. Apparently she'd been telling them everything I said as I said it.

That pretty much cured me of wanting to fool anyone on April first. Which is why, when the contractions start at six in the morning and I realize the date, I cringe a little bit.

Maybe they'll stop.

They say that happens with new mothers, and I'm still two weeks early. But an hour later, they hurt more than before, and they feel quicker, too. I text Ethan.

I THINK THE BABY MAY BE COMING.

And then I tiptoe into the hall and pick up my hand to knock on Aunt Donna's door.

Only, she never gets to sleep in, and it's a Saturday. I should wait until I'm absolutely positive. Right?

"Beth?" Aiden's rubbing his eyes in the hallway. "Why are you just standing there with your hand up?"

A moment later, I hear noises coming from Uncle Will and Aunt Donna's room. Ten seconds later, Aunt Donna shoots out, a bathrobe wrapped tightly around her, her crossed arms holding it in place.

"Are you feeling alright?" She scans me from head to toe, and then her eyes widen. "Are you contracting?" She reaches for my stomach and then stops short. She's heard me rant about people touching my belly.

"I think maybe it's time to go to the hospital," I say. "It's been going on for a while."

Aunt Donna's eyes widen. "You should've told me sooner. Let's go! Will. *Will!*"

Poor Uncle Will's still buttoning the top of his pants when she shoves the door open. "It's go time."

He hefts two bags into the air while Aunt Donna's dialing. "Yes. That's right. It's time." Aunt Donna hangs up and nods. "She'll be here in less than five minutes. Do you think you can wait that long?"

"It's not like Aiden won't survive until Mom gets here," Uncle Will says.

"Even so," Aunt Donna says. "I'd rather make sure she makes it. You never know with stuff like that."

"You never know what exactly?" Uncle Will asks. "Whether my mom will die on the way here?" His easygoing mockery is the perfect match for Aunt Donna's high-strung, worry-wart tendencies.

"No, I'm not saying that."

"We're sure this isn't an April Fool's prank, right?" Uncle Will glances my way.

"I would never do that to you guys," I say.

Aunt Donna drops a hand on my shoulder. "I know you wouldn't. Believe me." Then her face drains of all color, and she inhales sharply. Then she inhales again. Her hand drops from my arm, and she leans forward and vomits all over the floor.

Partially digested noodles do *not* smell good, and a contraction is just starting, so I end up puking right on top of hers.

"Oh, Will." Aunt Donna wipes her mouth with the back of her hand. "Why did we try that new Thai food place last night? What were we thinking?"

"We were thinking it was date night, and new restaurants are rare in Green River." He shudders and points at the living room. "You two go sit in there, and I'll get this cleaned up." He mutters under his breath, though. "Thank goodness I had the fried rice."

"Are you alright?" Now I'm the one trying to make her feel better.

"Oh, my stomach," Aunt Donna says. "I'll be fine, but what a lousy time to have food poisoning."

"It could be a stomach bug," I say. "Or." I glance at Uncle Will. "You did just get married. Could you be. . ." I drop my voice to a whisper so Aiden, who's munching on a massive bowlful of Lucky Charms, won't hear me. "*Pregnant?*"

Aunt Donna laughs. "Uh, no. And besides. When I was pregnant with Aiden, I didn't have a single moment of nausea or sickness. Believe me, that's not what this is." She sighs. "Wouldn't that be nice?"

"Well, I'm about to have a baby," I say. "So maybe it's good that you're not."

"Should you stay home from the hospital?" Uncle Will's eyes are nervous.

His mother pulls up outside, her huge silver truck rumbling as she parallel parks on the road out front so she won't block us in.

"I'm sure it's those noodles. They didn't sit right last night, and I'm not shocked they came back up. I just wish I'd gone ahead and gotten sick last night instead of going right to sleep." She groans. "But truly, I'm sure I'll be fine. I insist on coming."

"Maybe we take two cars," Uncle Will says.

"Either way, we should go," Aunt Donna says. "She said the contractions are worsening, and Vernal's ninety minutes away."

Ethan's old truck pulls into the driveway, idling loudly like it always does. He doesn't cut the engine— he hops out and runs up the driveway, right up until he nearly plows into Mrs. Earl. "Ah, so sorry. I almost didn't see you." He looks pained as he slows his pace to cover the last four steps that separate him from the door, and once it's open, he searches the room for me.

"I'll ride with Ethan," I say. "Why don't you and Uncle Will meet us there. Then if you feel lousy, you'll have your own car to come back home in."

"Good plan," Uncle Will says. "Let's go."

I've been to Vernal for several appointments now, and the ninety-minute drive never felt too bad. Living in Manila, you get used to the fact that everything's an hour or two away. But this time, it's different.

"Breathe," Ethan says. "Remember? We watched this video. We can do this."

"Ethan."

"Alright, I'll keep quiet."

"I love you."

"Oh." He glances at me, and he smiles. "I love you, too."

The closer it gets, the sadder I get about the idea of moving. But when I try to consider sticking around, it still hurts too much. So no matter what I do, in a few days, I'm going to be miserable.

Why did this baby have to cut my time short? Ethan and I were supposed to have half a dozen more date nights.

He reaches around until his hand finds mine. "I'm excited." He smiles. "This is really neat. You're about to change Will and Donna's lives forever. And we get to meet that beautiful little girl. Your little girl."

"Aunt Donna's," I say.

"But still. It's because of you that she gets this little girl she wants so much. That's amazing."

It feels tragic.

This little baby didn't do anything wrong, and I'm about to abandon her. Aunt Donna and Uncle Will are happy, but I hope that years down the road, she understands that it's not because of anything she did. It's not because she's not wonderful.

"Are you alright?"

"Fine." I'm just breathing, or rather panting, my way through yet another miserable contraction. "They shouldn't call them contractions," I say. "They should call them pain waves. Or belly slaps. Or maybe abdominal misery spikes."

"I'm so sorry."

"It's not your fault."

Ethan snorts, and I realize, in this case, it really *isn't* his fault. This poor guy has been so amazing, so solid, and so present for all of this, and he had nothing to do with it. "I really do love you."

"I'm glad." He grins again. "I wish I could do something about the contractions, but I don't think babies really come out without them. Unless you get a c-section, I guess. But they say those are miserable too."

"I wonder what they'll name her."

Aunt Donna and Uncle Will keep insisting that they need to see her first. They keep saying that they can't give her a name until they've seen her face, but I've looked up images of newborns. They all look about the same. Pink, squishy, and a lot of them are kind of bumpy, too.

What kind of name are they thinking her newborn face will inspire? Potato? Turnip?

I'm in the middle of a horrible contraction when we finally pull into the parking lot of the hospital. I'm embarrassed about it, but I'm actually screaming. Once it ends, I reach for the door, but Ethan's already there. "Nice try, but no. I'm carrying you."

"Ethan, stop." I try to slap his hand, but he's not kidding.

He sweeps his arms under my back and knees and

swings me up like I weigh nothing. "There's a reason that pregnant women get wheelchairs," he says. "I can't have you screaming and contracting while you walk through the hospital, and we aren't waiting for them to bring a chair over."

As it happens, I'm screaming again as Ethan goes through the sliding doors into the ER. They move double quick to get me up to Labor and Delivery and into a room, and thankfully Uncle Will must have driven like a maniac, because they're already waiting for us.

"Right through here," Aunt Donna says. She's smiling.

After I change into the hospital gown, in between waves of misery, it all starts to feel very, very real. Aunt Donna helps me onto the bed and fluffs my pillow. She doesn't look pale anymore, thankfully.

"You must feel better," I say.

"Much," she says. "I'm telling you. It was the noodles."

"Thank goodness," I say. "I hate to be a brat, but I may need most of the attention for the next hour or two."

A doc shows up then, one I've never met. "I'm the OB on call, Dr. Isaacson." She smiles. "Looks like we're having a baby today."

Aunt Donna nods.

"Wait, who are you?"

"I'm the mother-to-be," Aunt Donna says. "And this is my niece, the actual mother."

Dr. Isaacson nods slowly. "Ah, gotcha. Well, that's great. I'm glad you have it all worked out." She walks toward me and flips the stirrups up. "I hear you've been contracting for a while, but first-time moms usually take a while before they're ready. I don't want you to be disappointed if you're not close to delivering yet, alright?"

"Sure," I say. And then a contraction starts, so I close my eyes and grit my teeth.

Ethan takes my hand.

I pant and stifle a shout. "Can we order an epidural, too?"

"For sure." Dr. Isaacson puts gloves on. "I'm just going to check to see how far we've come, alright?"

Ethan and Uncle Will step toward the front of the room, as we discussed they would, and Dr. Isaacson's cold hand checks my dilation. They've been doing this at my weekly checkups, and I brace for it. It's not fun.

Except, the horrible pressure doesn't happen. Instead, I just hear, "Oh."

"Oh?" Another contraction hits then.

"I need a cart in here, and a nursing team!" Dr. Isaacson turns to me and smiles. "How do you feel? Do you feel up to pushing?"

"Up to. . .what?"

"You're ten centimeters already," she says. "You're contracting, right?"

I nod.

"You could push, if you're willing."

"I could—"

Aunt Donna squeals.

When I glance her way, I notice that behind her, Uncle Will's face is entirely pale.

"Maybe you and Ethan should step out." Ethan's forced smile is all kinds of creepy.

"Yes, that's a good idea." Uncle Will grabs Ethan's wrist and practically drags him toward the door.

They collide with the nurses who were rushing in with a rolling cart full of stuff. They're all wearing weird blue apron things that cover them practically from neck to knees. It looks like they think I'm carrying the bubonic plague.

"Alright, we're ready," the nurse in front says.

"Pushing often takes quite some time," Dr. Isaacson says. "Don't worry if you push through several contractions and nothing happens. Alright?"

But after just three contractions-worth of pushing, there's a kind of burst and then a sliding feeling.

Aunt Donna says, "She's here!"

"Yes, she certainly is," Dr. Isaacson says. "Now just one more push for me."

Everything moves really quickly after that. I was prepared that they might take her away, whisking her off to the NICU. I was ready for her to have breathing problems, or not cry enough, or possibly need to be warmed.

But none of that happens.

"Would you like to hold her?" The nurse with the dark hair who seems to be in charge has cleaned her up after shouting numbers out loud. Now she's wrapped in a blanket. "Or should I hand her to this lady?" She tosses her head at Aunt Donna.

"I'd like to hold her. Is that alright?"

Aunt Donna's crying, but she nods. "Of course."

The nurse hands the tiny little baby to me. "She's very healthy. She has an APGAR of nine. Nice job, Mom."

The second she reaches my arms, I feel an overwhelming sense of relief. I can't help crying myself. She looks nothing like a turnip or a potato. She is tiny, and beautiful, and perfect. "Oh, she's so pretty."

Aunt Donna hasn't moved.

"Did you see her?"

She makes a sound that I can't quite comprehend.

"Look at her tiny nose," I say. "And her dark eyelashes."

Aunt Donna still hasn't moved closer.

"Aunt Donna?"

She shakes her head. "You want to keep her."

"What?" I stop staring at the baby girl and snap my head toward Aunt Donna. "Why would you think that?"

Now she's really bawling. "Who wouldn't want to keep her? She's just perfect. I knew you'd want to keep her when you saw her."

"Have you been worried about that this whole time?"

Aunt Donna shrugs, and I realize that she has been. "Come here. Now."

My sweet, kind, generous aunt finally takes two steps closer. "I'm not sure I can hold her and hug her if you are keeping her." She sniffs.

"Aunt Donna, this little girl is *your* baby. I just wanted to hold her for a moment, to make sure I got things right." After the big mistake I made that resulted in her creation, I've been worried for months and months that she might not be quite right.

But she's just perfect.

I'm giving Aunt Donna a perfect daughter, just like she deserves. I hold her up, my arms shaking a bit. All those contractions were exhausting.

Aunt Donna takes her from me, trembling every bit as much as I am. "Oh, Beth. Thank you." And now she's sobbing again, but this time, her eyes are firmly fixed on our darling little girl.

A moment later, the doctor starts tugging and pulling on things.

"What's going on?" I ask.

"Cleaning you up again." The doc's voice is flat, but her hands are steady.

The cleanup isn't wonderful, but eventually they get things put back together, and I'm allowed to take my legs out of the stirrups.

"Your recovery will be much quicker because you didn't get an epidural," Dr. Isaacson says. "You should be able to walk around and go to the bathroom, or whatever else you'd like to do at any point."

My body's not as excited about going to the bathroom as Dr. Isaacson seems to think it should be, but eventually, with the help of the dark-haired nurse, I do it. A few moments later, I make it back into the main room, cleaner, calmer, and finally cleared to eat. Aunt Donna's feeding the baby with a dreamy look on her face.

"Uncle Will can come in," I say. "I'm decent."

The nurses bring him in moments later, and he looks even dopier than Aunt Donna.

"Can I hold her?" he asks.

"You'll have to wait your turn." Donna makes no move to pass her over. "She's eating anyway."

Ethan laughs, and my eyes dart his direction. His smiling face feels like the nicest thing I've ever seen. It's like a balm on my raw heart. While Uncle Will and Aunt Donna wrap themselves around the new baby, Ethan slips over to my shoulder and wraps his arms around me. "You are amazing. That is a miracle."

"It kind of is," I say. "The best kind of miracle." I shift a little. "Or, you know, maybe close to a miracle. A real miracle wouldn't have left me feeling so lousy."

Ethan chuckles. "Even miracles have a cost."

"What do you think?" Aunt Donna asks softly. "Any of the names we've discussed feel like a good fit?"

"What about Althea?" Uncle Will says. "It's always

been my favorite and it means 'blessed with healing abilities.'" He glances around the room, his eyes meeting mine. "I feel like she's already healing this family."

I realize in that moment that carrying this beautiful child was a constant memory for me of my mistake. Of my poor judgment. Of how much my family was willing to pressure me for their own ends without any regard to my health or well-being.

Without meeting her, this baby was like a scarlet letter in my life.

But now that she's here, it feels *nothing* like the stupid story I had to read in school. This baby isn't like Pearl. She's not a constant reminder of my sin. She's far too beautiful and far too loved for that.

No, she's the promise that even when we make mistakes, beautiful things can come from them. She's the healing gift that has brought me a new family, one that I know will love me no matter what.

"I didn't even call my mom," I realize. "We just came straight here."

Even now, I don't feel like calling my parents.

"They're actually in Aruba right now." Aunt Donna looks a little sick as she says it. "Your dad told me that if you need them, we should email."

"Oh." For some reason, that makes me laugh. Not an uncomfortable or disappointed or manic laugh. No, it makes me laugh because it's *so* classic Patrick and Amelia. Their daughter's having a baby they didn't want her to have? Why not go on vacation. Maybe it will just go away.

But that's not the life my little girl is going to have. She's going to have amazing parents who put her first. She's going to be loved, to be cherished, and to be a priority for them.

Aunt Donna's been patting the baby's back, but then she passes the baby off to Uncle Will, finally. "I think Althea is perfect." She presses a kiss to her forehead. "Maybe we can call her Thea for short." She turns toward me. "What do you think?"

"I think you're both right. Althea sounds great."

"Thank you," Aunt Donna says. This time, she's not crying.

"Thank you so much," Uncle Will says.

"You're welcome," I say. "But can I ask you something?"

"Anything," Aunt Donna says. "Always."

"Did you mean it when you said you wouldn't mind if I stuck around?"

Uncle Will blinks.

Aunt Donna beams. "Will's house is almost done. In a few weeks, we can move out, and you can have my place to yourself."

"Wait," Ethan says. "Does that mean you're thinking about it?"

I didn't think that there'd be a place for me in this new, strange family I'm gifting them. I thought I'd feel strange, being Althea's mom and also her cousin. But it doesn't feel strange at all.

It feels right.

Maybe, sometimes, God answers prayers in weird ways. Maybe, sometimes, mistakes can still bring joy to everyone around them. And maybe this is one of those times.

At least, I really hope it is.

29

DONNA

I spent the first few months of my pregnancy with Aiden worried that I would miscarry. By the time the doctor told me that things looked good, I was so relieved that I never cared much about whether I felt lousy. What was a little discomfort if my baby was alright? What were a few headaches or a little heartburn, as long as he was growing as he should?

After he was born, everything was a bit of a blur. My mom came to help out, which was good, because I had no idea what I was doing.

Diapers, burping, colic, swaddling, and nursing were all new.

It was overwhelming. It was scary. It was also beautiful. His first real smile came at twelve weeks. His first word—dada—happened with no prompting from me. The day he learned to sit up was a Sunday, and that night he would not lie down in his crib at all. At least, not until he passed out. The day he learned to scoot— he never really crawled very well—was a huge shock. I had child-proofed nothing. All of those memories were the things that kept me going in an increasingly miserable marriage.

My husband was always busy at work, and it felt like he got busier whenever something difficult happened at home. If Aiden or I got sick, he had a huge project and would be gone around the clock. If Aiden was teething, he had to pull all-nighters. When I started baby food and Aiden spit out every single new food I tried, Charlie started holding morning meetings. Being alone for most of the memorable moments might have been a little disappointing, but Aiden made up for it.

This time around, I spent most of baby Thea's pregnancy hovering and nervous. Would Beth change her mind? Would my little niece really leave after the baby was born? It felt like the price I would pay for this miracle was the loss of something that had grown to be very dear to me.

But now Thea's here, and she's perfect even though she came two weeks early, and Beth has agreed to stay, at least for now. Unlike the last time, my husband's around as often as possible and that's a good thing. April isn't the best time for a rancher to have a baby, but he's still spending every second he can at the hospital with us.

"Today's the day you can both come home," I say. "How does that feel?"

"Pretty good," Beth says. "I bet it'll be nice for you too, since you haven't left the hospital in three days."

"Actually, I feel great," I say. "I didn't have to push this little angel out. That makes a big difference."

The nurse removes the blood pressure cuff. "Yeah, the happiest mothers I see in here are the adoptive ones. I've always felt like it was pretty hard that new mothers have to make the baby, endure childbirth, and then dive into newborn care and feeding right off the bat." She shakes her head. "It's like running a set of sprints before starting a marathon."

"Well, I'm happy that I'm done with the sprints," Beth says. "And I've passed the beautiful little baton to you for the marathon."

"You three are adorable," the nurse says. "We'll miss you around here."

There's a tap at the door, and a lanky man wearing green scrubs comes inside, carrying a tray. "Meal service."

Yesterday, breakfast was pancakes and eggs, but today's is something else. The smell is *not* good. "What is that?" I cover my mouth.

Beth pulls the tray off the top of the plate, and the smell doubles. "Chicken and waffles?"

The nurse nods enthusiastically. "It's new to the menu, and everyone loves it."

Everyone but me, I guess. I bend over and puke the protein shake I just drank into the trash can. An arm on my shoulder startles me.

"I really don't want to be annoying, but have you thought about getting a pregnancy test?" The nurse looks concerned.

I shake my head. "No way. Listen, the reason we're adopting is that I can't have kids. Trust me."

"But you have a son, right?" The nurse frowns.

I hate having to go over this and over this. Each time it reminds me that I can't do what I wanted to do most.

"Right, but trust me. I'm not pregnant."

"Before I switched to OB, I was an ER nurse for a while. If you knew how many people told me they couldn't possibly be pregnant, and then were. . ." She shrugs. "It's fine if you don't want to test for it, but you're at a hospital. I could do a simple blood draw and then you'd know for sure."

"You should do it." Beth's voice is quiet, but her eyes are full of worry.

She hasn't really asked for anything. No special favors. No fancy food. No high-strung demands like I read about on the social media adoption threads. Not that I'm surprised. Beth's always been sensible and calm.

"You think so?"

Beth shrugs. "What would it hurt?"

I'll feel like a failure all over again when it comes back negative, like I know it will. That doesn't feel like a compelling enough reason. Apparently if you throw up twice in three days and you're a woman, everyone assumes it means you're pregnant. "Fine," I say. "I'll do it."

I don't mention it to Will when he shows up to pick us up.

"The bassinet's all set up," he says. "The changing table's assembled, and the wipe warmer's hooked up, even though you said you don't need one."

His mother's so funny. She keeps insisting that I'll want it in the middle of the night. She also bought a boppy, although I won't be nursing, and a changing table, even though I always just changed Aiden on the floor.

"I also went by and checked on my place. They're right on schedule, which means in two weeks, we should be able to move in."

"How do the floors look?"

"They're not in yet," he says. "But they're there, acclimating to the humidity. They're supposed to start tomorrow morning. The new furnace is installed. It feels great, at least."

Running his ranch, checking on me and Beth and the baby, and monitoring the new build all on his own wouldn't have been possible without his parents. I still feel a little bad for the way I jumped to conclusions with them before. They're amazing people, just like their son.

I insist on sitting in the back of my car, next to the carseat. Like the day I brought Aiden home, my gaze stays focused on Althea the entire ride.

"She's fine?" Will's even worse than I am, checking the rearview mirror every ten seconds to make sure we're alright.

"Rear-facing carseats are horrible," I say. "If they weren't safer, no one would ever use then. She's just fine. Actually, she's better than fine. Her hand is right by her face like she's posing for a glamour shot."

"Oh man," Beth says. "I should have sat in the back, too."

Beth has been pretty interested in Althea, acting like a doting big sister. After I stopped worrying she'd change her mind, it's been wonderful to have her nearby. I might be the saddest one when we leave Beth to live in Will's renovated farmhouse.

"Ethan wants to know if he can come over when we get back." Beth looks a little nervous. "Or will it be too many people?"

"He's always welcome," I say. "Just like before."

The rest of the ride goes smoothly. Babies sleep so much in the first few days that it makes trips a snap. When we get home, Will's parents are there, standing in the front yard with Aiden, holding a banner.

Welcome Home Althea! Welcome Home Beth!

Clearly an adult did the lettering, but Aiden drew flowers and hearts and butterflies with colorful markers, and it makes me smile. My sweet little man finally has a sibling.

After snapping a flurry of photos of Althea in her carseat, and plenty of oohs and aahs at her little outfit, which is covered with embroidered strawberries, we finally take her inside. Will makes carrying a carseat easy. When I have to carry one, it always feels like my arm's going to pop off like a defective Barbie doll.

As we carry her into our bedroom, I notice a new quilt draped over the back of the glider. "Whoa." I cross the room.

"My quilting club has been working on it," Will's mom says. "I hope you like it. We had to wait until you'd picked a name to finish it off."

It perfectly matches the theme I chose, with alternating white and blue stripes, offset with blocks of pink cherry blossoms. "I love it so much." I run my fingers across the soft fabric. "Once we move and I have a separate room for her nursery, I'll have to decide whether to hang it on the wall or use it."

"Please use it," she says. "It'll make me happy to see her holding it."

On the bottom edge, on one of the white blocks, her name, Althea Grace Earl, is embroidered with little hearts on either side.

"Thank you, Grace." I hug my mother-in-law tightly, happy that my little daughter will have such a wonderful grandmother and namesake.

"Thank *you*." His mom's crying, but I know it's from joy. She's not perfect, and neither am I, but I'm so happy that I've learned to understand her better.

My phone starts buzzing between us, and she backs up. "What's that?"

"Just a phone call," I say. "Hang on."

I pull out my phone, but it's an unknown number. I

usually screen those, but I'm in such a good mood, I just answer. It's probably someone who wants to ask about my car's warranty, but today, I don't mind.

"Hello?"

"Mrs. Earl?"

"Yes, that's me." Though it still feels weird answering to that.

"This is Bonnie from Ashley Regional."

"Oh, no. Did we forget something?" It's such a long drive. I hope it wasn't anything important. "When I don't get enough sleep, I have to tie my head on or I'll leave it somewhere."

"No, it's not that," she says.

"Is that the hospital?" Will asks. "Is anything wrong?"

"What is it?" Now I'm worried. They do a lot of testing when your baby's first born, and I thought we had results on all of it, but maybe I got confused. My brain starts running through things one by one. Is it her hearing? Was her last bilirubin too high? She doesn't look too yellow, but sometimes that changes fast.

"I'm actually calling about you," she says. "You had a pregnancy test this morning."

"Oh, right," I say. "Okay."

"It was positive."

"Excuse me?"

"Your test came back positive. You're pregnant. You'd need to schedule an ultrasound for us to estimate your due date, but it looks like you're going to be having a baby."

"Okay, thanks for calling." The words shoot out, but it feels like I'm in a daze.

"Please do call back if you want to set up the preliminary appointment."

"Will do." I hang up.

Could it really be true?

"What's wrong?" Will passes Althea to his mom and crosses to where I'm standing. "You look nervous."

"I—the hospital." I close my mouth. "The nurse this morning made me take a pregnancy test."

Will frowns. "What?"

"I threw up when Beth went into labor, remember?" I don't wait for him to say anything. "I vomited again this morning, and I guess that means everyone thinks. . ." Except no one thinks that anymore. The nurse says I *am* pregnant.

When I turn my head up toward Will's, I see Beth standing in the doorway. "Did you say you're pregnant?" She swallows, her eyes wide.

I nod slowly.

"I thought you couldn't get pregnant."

"So did I," I say. "Until we've had an ultrasound to confirm and we know how far along I am, I'm not holding my breath." It sounds terrible to say, but it's not the first time I've thought I was pregnant.

Beth nods, and a few moments later, I hear that Ethan has arrived.

"Wouldn't that be amazing if you were," Mrs. Earl says.

"It would be hard," I say. "But yes. A complete miracle."

Will and his mother both want to rush me off to an emergency room right away for testing. "It's not urgent," I say. "Let's schedule something and get it checked out by someone who does this for their job."

I call Abby for a referral—if I am pregnant, I'm much older than I was last time, and that means that I'm high risk. She loved her doc, apparently, so I make an appointment to see him.

Of course, he can't see me until the day we're supposed to be moving. The days fly by, but the nights drag on, which is always true with a baby. I'm packing a box in the family room after a two a.m. feeding when Beth taps on my door.

"Hey. I hope we didn't wake you up."

She shakes her head. "I got up to get a drink, but I saw the light." She coos as she holds out a finger to Thea. "She's gotten so much bigger in just two weeks."

"Her cheeks are filling out for sure," I say.

"And she cries way louder, too."

"I'm sure you won't miss that."

"I've been wanting to ask you something. I know you have a doctor's appointment tomorrow."

I nod. "I'm pretty nervous, to be honest. These have often not gone well for me."

"If you are pregnant, and if everything looks good. . ." She swallows. "Will you still want to keep Althea?"

My heart stops for a moment. I'm glad I'm not holding the baby. I sit down on the edge of the sofa. "Beth, have you changed your mind?" She's already signed the paperwork, but we're still waiting on a signature from the father, so it's not really a done deal in my mind.

"Me?" Her eyes widen. "No."

I close my eyes and breathe. Then I force them back open. "You're just worried about us?"

She nods.

I grab her hands with mine. "Althea is my daughter," I say. "To me, there's nothing that could change that. Not a force on earth."

A tear rolls down Beth's cheek.

It's hard to force out the next sentence, but I love Beth too much not to say it. "Unless *you* told me you changed your mind." I force myself to look caring and calm.

Beth shakes her head. "No, that's not it."

My sigh of relief is a little larger than I intended. "Whether I'm pregnant or not, Althea's my daughter. We'll always keep her safe. We'll always be her parents."

Beth starts to cry. "Okay. Good. That's good."

How worried has she been all this time? "Listen, if I am pregnant, poor Mrs. Earl will have her hands full at the hotel alone again, and I may need some of her help with the babies here. But some women have twins. Others get pregnant right after delivering. We'll figure the rest of it out if it is true, okay?"

She wipes her face. "Okay."

"And if this little baby is alright too?" I place a hand on my stomach. "Then maybe I'll have the big family I always wanted."

Her words are very, very soft when she says, "Sometimes it feels like I'm your daughter, just a little bit."

I hug her then, tightly, and now I'm the one who's bawling. "So do I, Beth." It's a long time before I let her go. "I'm glad you're staying here. I don't know what I'd have done if you tried to move to Seattle."

"I didn't think, if you were taking care of my baby, that you would want me hanging around and acting like I was your kid, too."

"The thing about love that's different than everything else in the world, really, is that the more you do it, the more there is. And even if it's messy, that's okay." Abby's words come back to me again, and I marvel that the advice she gave me the day of my wedding is still so true. "Real love is messy, Beth, and that's okay."

The next morning, when I'm about to leave for my appointment, Will's mom is already waiting, ready to babysit.

"I could watch her while you all go, if you want," Beth says. "I mean, it's fine if you don't want me to, but if Mrs. Earl wanted to be there for the appointment."

"I would love that," I say. "I think Thea would love to have you here, too."

Beth has hovered around the edges of the room while we cared for Althea, mostly, unsure how involved she could be. But the few times we've helped her burp and change the baby, it's been really special to watch. Like a startled colt, she picks her up with wide eyes. "Hey, little one."

I watch for just one moment, even though it'll probably make us late, as my little niece spends some time with the daughter she gave up. She thought it would hurt too much to stay. I worried it might make her waver in her decision. But the words I spoke in the middle of the night feel more true than ever before. Love is messy, but that doesn't mean it's not beautiful.

There's no one way to do things if you're doing them with love. I think this little girl's going to be very, very lucky to have so many people in her life who care about her.

I hold that thought, that moment, in my head as I sit and wait in the waiting room.

"It's going to be alright," Will says. "Either way."

Only, now that I have this hope dangling in front of me, it doesn't feel that way. In my life, nothing ever goes quite right. When I got into Stanford, I had to agree to forgo my inheritance. When I met the perfect guy, he turned out to be a monumental jerk. When he started a company, I had to sacrifice my tuition to bankroll it. I finally had a child, but it was only after multiple heartbreaks. And after doing all I could for my marriage, it broke down anyway. Things weren't smooth when I moved back home, either. Nothing with my family ever has been.

But it's been all good news lately, and that makes me even more wary. Will proposed. We lucked into an already planned wedding. And then my niece gave up her daughter, *and* she stayed with us.

I'm nervous about getting the signature from the birth father. Each day that passes, I wonder why he hasn't signed. I worry that he might not ever send us the paperwork. But other than that niggling fear, things have been mostly perfect.

Which means I'm overdue for bad news.

When the doc starts asking me questions, like confirming the date of my last period, my heart rate really goes nuts. "Yes, I thought I'd had two in the last four months," I say. "But it's always been erratic. As you can see—"

He holds up his hand. "It's fine. Don't stress out."

As if I can just choose not to be stressed.

Will takes my hand, and I'm pretty sure he's regretting it. I'm worried I'll cut off his circulation with how hard I'm squeezing, but I can't seem to stop.

"We're going to start with a transvaginal ultrasound. Have you had one of those before?"

That makes me laugh, but it sounds strange. Strangled, kind of.

"Donna," Will says. "Do you want us to stay or step out?"

He and his mom both look nervous, like they're not quite sure what to say or do.

"Stay," I say. "Please stay." That stops me from laughing, at least.

A few moments later, when the ultrasound machine's finally ready, I want to close my eyes. I want to look away and have someone tell me later, like the way Bonnie called and let me know hours after the test. I can't do that, though. I have to face what's right in front of me.

"You are definitely pregnant," Dr. Peters says. "And judging from the measurements and size, I'd guess you're about twelve weeks along." He clicks some buttons and takes a few photographs. "That means that while you aren't entirely safe, you're mostly out of the woods." His smile isn't forced. "I hear that you just adopted a baby."

I nod.

"Well, I hope you're ready for this. It looks like you're going to have another one quite soon."

"I'm ready," I say. "More than ready."

It feels unreal as we drive home, and I can't stop staring at my new photograph.

"Guesses?" Will's mom asks. "A sister or a brother for Thea and Aiden?"

"I'd be happy with either," Will says.

"Same." I still can't stop looking at the image. I've only had one other twelve-week photo. Beth didn't get an ultrasound until she was twenty weeks, and my others didn't make it this far.

"You should have added two bedrooms," Mrs. Earl says, "instead of just that one."

"Kids learn a lot from sharing," I say. "I think it'll be fine."

"I hope you still think that when someone is pulling someone else's hair." But she's smiling.

We're nearly home when Patrick calls me. We've invited both Patrick and Amelia out several times to meet Thea, but so far they haven't made it. Calls from him are never good, so I brace myself before saying, "Hello?"

"Donna."

"Patrick."

"I have something for you." That sounds even worse than I expected.

"What is it?"

"I think you want it pretty badly." He clears his throat. "I'm looking at this and thinking, wow, I wonder what Donna would do for this piece of paper."

"Patrick, cut the crap. What do you want?"

"Nothing," he says. "If you give me your current address—Beth says you're moving—I'll drop this in the mail."

Normally, I'd already have hung up, but today has been such a good day that I'm a little more patient than usual. "What is it? Or are you just not telling me?" I'm sure he wants something, and I wish he'd just get around to it. "If you're suing me, just tell me why."

"Suing you?" He wheezes, like I'm being nuts. "It's a paper with a very particular kid's signature on it. He didn't want to sign, because he felt that it could be used against him later, to prove that he had fathered a child."

Now I can barely breathe. "You said it's *signed*?"

"It is," Patrick says. "I told him that if we had to do a DNA test first, I'd be sure to hold a copy on file forever, and that I would use it to make his life miserable until he died. I can't believe this little jerk had the ausperity to ruin Beth's life, and then insist he hadn't done it."

I'm pretty sure he meant audacity, and it didn't ruin Beth's life. I think she's learned a lot. It also blessed my life in ways I can't even express. But trying to correct Patrick is a total waste of time. Always has been. I've finally stopped banging my head against that brick wall.

"You really have his signature on the form?" I hate how desperate I sound.

383

"I do," Patrick says. "And I really am going to mail it to you."

I wait for the catch.

"I'm sorry that we haven't really helped with anything," Patrick says.

I can't believe what I'm hearing.

"You have been there for Beth, even when we weren't. I'm glad that you're going to take care of her baby."

I have no idea what prompted this bizarre and unexpected growth moment for my brother, but it's almost unbelievable, like a stunning rainbow after a heinous storm. "Thea is one of the most beautiful babies I've ever seen, just like Beth was. You're both welcome to come and meet her any time."

I'm sure on the day they finally do, I'll be cursing them for saying fifty rude, obtuse things. But roses almost always have thorns, and I'm prepared to deal with them.

"I'll text you my new address."

"Thanks." I think about telling him about the pregnancy, but there's no telling how Patrick will react to anything. I decide to keep my mouth shut until the paper he's holding is in my hands and the future for my family is secure.

It takes almost a week for the mail carrier in Manila to finally bring the paper to our new place. We've unpacked almost everything, and Althea's asleep on her cherry blossom blanket when the paper arrives, signed and notarized just as Patrick said.

Will was helping me put wallpaper up on the side wall of the nursery when the mail came—a large cherry tree that's blooming—but we stop to stare at the paper we've been waiting and praying we'd get. "It's here."

"I won't lie and say I wasn't nervous." Will's beaming.

In that moment of stillness, I feel it. Our new baby's first kick. I put Will's hand on my stomach, but it's too faint for him to feel yet. "I think that this is the best moment of my life so far."

"The best is yet to come, I promise," my handsome husband says.

Will has kept every promise he's ever made to me, so I can't wait to see how much more beautiful our lives can really be. And how messy.

EPILOGUE: MANDY

Since 1896, the US Postal service has provided rural mail delivery. It was pretty revolutionary at the time. Previously, people had to travel into town to pick up their mail.

In spite of that huge step forward, the mail wasn't always reliable in Manila, Utah.

For a while, it only came twice a week. By the 1970s, it was coming every day, but things would often get lost and not show up for several weeks after they were due. Now, with Amazon deliveries and UPS and FedEx, it's easier than ever to have a package delivered to my door.

I still get excited when things show up.

When they were living here, Roscoe would always bark so I never forgot and left anything sitting outside. Jed's useless. Now that Amanda and her girls have moved to Eddy's place, I often fail to notice when someone drops off a delivery. After a package of popping pearls for the drinks the girls love froze and burst in February, I started sitting in the front room so I would be more likely to notice things arriving.

Today, I'm trying to finish reading Amanda's proposal on furniture purchase orders and Helen's update on the overall financials so that I'll be ready for our call in an hour, so I don't hop up to grab the package that arrives right away.

Right as our call ends, I remember it. I hop up and yank the door open. I don't expect to see a startled but familiar face.

Emery's holding the package, standing on my front porch.

"Goodness child, what are you doing here?"

"I have to interview someone who lived through a war for my history class. Mom said she'd tell you I was going to take the bus here today."

Amanda must've forgotten, but I'm always happy to see the girls. "Come on in."

"What's this?"

The package is large, and it must be heavy, judging by the way she's holding it.

"It's not from Amazon," she says. "And instead of listing the company it came from, it says T. Collins."

"That's common for old people like me." I reach for the box. "Using our first initial instead of our name."

"Is T. Collins a friend?"

"Emery, didn't your mother ever teach you that asking a lot of questions is rude?"

She blinks. "It's heavy. Just tell me where to put it."

I grumble, but I let her follow me inside.

"I'm sorry if I'm being rude, but not telling me who it's from just makes me more curious." Emery's smile is like the sunrise over the Gorge. Bright, brilliant, beautiful. "Come on. Who's T. Collins?"

"Thomas Collins was my best friend, ever since I was a kid."

"It's a boy?"

I laugh. "It's a boy, yes." I point at the corner of my family room, and she puts it down.

"Do you know what he sent you?" Her eyes light up. "Or is it a surprise?"

"Emery Brooks, you stop asking me questions right now, or I'll tan your hide."

"You always say that, but I don't even know what it means. Tanning is bad for your skin, and you'd never do something bad."

That makes me laugh. "Tanning a hide means taking a skin and turning it into leather."

She recoils in horror. "Ew."

"You don't want me to do that."

"No one wants *anyone* to do that."

"Taxidermists make a decent living out of it."

"Why are you being so weird about a box?" Emery taps it with her foot. "What's in there?"

"I have no idea what's in there, but he's the person I stayed with when I let you guys think I'd died, so it's probably something I forgot there." I'm ready for it—her scolding. Every time anything about this comes up, Amanda flips out. I know what I did was probably ill-advised, but at the time it seemed like a good idea.

Actually, it felt like the only thing I could do to drive home the importance of forgiving Eddy instead of holding her grudge. I understand that I'm still paying for it, and that I should have handled it better, but at the time. . .

I still don't think I was too extreme. She was messing things up.

"Wait, you stayed with someone?" Emery doesn't look upset. She looks even more curious. "Someone I've never even heard of?"

"He moved to Montana," I say. "He's got a business there."

"What kind of business?"

I roll my eyes. "Why do you care?"

"Can we open it?" She jogs toward the kitchen and starts rummaging in drawers. "Here. I'll grab the scissors."

"Of all the ridiculous—"

But she's already slicing it open.

"It's letters and photos," she says. "Cool." Then she squints. "Wait, these are letters from you."

I feel heat rising in my cheeks. I have no idea what stupid things I said in those letters. "Give me those."

But Emery's too busy staring at one photo, and she's stopped asking questions, too.

"What is that?" I crane my neck to look over her shoulder.

"This is Jed, right?" Emery's eyes are intent.

"Well, the guy on the right is Jed," I say.

"And who's this guy?" She points at the man to my left.

"That's Tommy."

"*Tommy?*" Emery bites her lip. "They're both looking at you. Like, you're smiling at the camera, but they're both focused on you."

"Don't read anything into that," I say. "That photo's more than sixty-five years old."

"But the guy in this photo's still sending you packages. You're *living* with him when you need someone you trust."

"You're blowing this out of proportion," I say.

"Is he married?" Emery looks genuinely interested, as if Tommy's marital status matters.

"He was," I say.

She beams. "Okay, I need to know more."

"More about what?" I ask.

Emery waves the photo in front of me. "This photo tells me there's a story, but you know what else does?"

I roll my eyes.

"Your reaction. Because ever since I picked up this box from T. Collins, you've been acting all weird and bubbly."

"Bubbly?" I huff. "I'm not a soda."

"I want to know how you met *Tommy*."

"You're supposed to be interviewing me about a war."

She waves her hand through the air dismissively. "Who cares about that? It's boring. I want to know about this." She's back to staring at the photo. "Jed was okay looking, I guess, but this Tommy guy, he's pretty cute too."

"Did you miss what I said? We're friends. He's my oldest friend in the world."

"Now we're getting somewhere." Emery bites her lip. "Tell me more about your dreamy friend Thomas."

"No one's dreamy," I say. "Like I said. We're just friends."

My phone rings where it's sitting on the table then, and we both look at it immediately.

The caller ID says *Tommy*.

I lunge for it, but Emery gets there faster. "Hello?"

I'm really going to tan her cute little interfering hide now. I wonder what I could make with an Emery-skin pelt.

"Why, no, this isn't *Mandy*," Emery says. "In fact, I thought we were the only ones who called her that."

She's quiet.

"Yes, this *is* Emery, Mr. Collins. You're so smart."

Another pause.

"I do know who you are, but I'm beginning to think I don't know nearly enough about you."

Her eyes widen and she nods. "Yes, that's a remark-able coincidence. I'd also love to meet you! When can you come visit? We used to be living with *Mandy*, but now we've moved out and she has *loads* of space."

"Emery, give me the phone. Now."

"Next week would be perfect. I'm in a school play, and I can definitely get you tickets." She pauses again. "Alright. I better hand you to Mandy so you can work out the details. Can't *wait* to meet you, Mr. Collins."

I hang up. I'll call him back later. Right now, I've got a little girl to murder.

"I hope you don't mind that I invited him to visit, Grandma, but I have a lot of questions for him, since you won't answer them," Emery says. "I figured it was about time I started calling you Grandma. Hope that's alright."

My heart lurches.

"And don't you think a granddaughter should know everything about her grandma?"

"I don't think—"

Emery plops down on the sofa and whips out a notebook. "Let's start with how you met your oldest friend." She's smiling, her pen poised over the notepad.

A vibrant memory surfaces.

I was twelve. I'd just been thrown off a horse I was trying to help break. The horse was running toward the open gate in the corner of the arena.

A tall, lanky kid stepped out in front of the horse like a maniac, lifted his hand, and the horse just stopped dead. Then he grabbed the reins, righted them, and swung on in a simple movement, bringing the horse forward at a smooth, easy trot. He stopped right in front of me. His dark brown eyes were intense. His hair fell forward across his face.

"You were shutting the front door," he said. "If you

392

tell a new horse to go, but you keep your hands too tight, he'll get upset. You need really soft hands with green horses."

As if I didn't know that. I hated him immediately.

He slid off and offered me the reins. "I'm Tom. What's your name?"

Half of me wanted to slap him, and the other half of me was in awe of him. If I'm being honest, I've felt that same way about Tommy Collins ever since.

۞

If you're keen on hearing more about Amanda Saddler and Tom Collins, don't worry. You can read their story, as well as a little bit more about your favorite Birch Creek characters in the final Birch Creek Ranch book, *The Lookback*. (I've said this before, but this time, I really mean it!)

Here's the blurb:

Amanda Saddler has lived a long and happy life. She's not ready to die or anything melodramatic, but she's long since given up on finding her fairytale ending.

But when her adoptive granddaughter Emery picks up a box that was delivered to her doorstep, some new stories from the past come to light. Amanda Saddler may have spent her life pining for her neighbor, Jed Brooks, but he's not the only man she ever knew.

Emery doggedly asks after a man from an old photo, who turns out to be the man Amanda Saddler stayed with when she left town for a few months. When that same man calls Amanda's phone, of course Emery answers and invites him to come for a visit.

Can Amanda Saddler reconcile the wrongs in her past to set her story right in the present, or is it too late for her to find her happy ending alongside a man who has always wanted a place in her heart?

ACKNOWLEDGMENTS

Thanks to my kids for their patience, to my hubby for his unfailing support, and to my parents for cheerleading.

Thank you to my readers. I adore you all.

Thanks to Elana for listening to me whinge and complain.

And thanks to my editor Carrie. You are always throwing down miracles for me, and I appreciate you.

ABOUT THE AUTHOR

I have animals coming out of my ears. Seven horses. Three dogs, three cats, thirty-ish chickens. I'm always doctoring or playing with an animal... and I wouldn't want it any other way. But Leo (my palomino) is still my very favorite.

When I'm not with animals, or even if I am, I'm likely to have at least one of my five kids in tow, two of which I'm currently homeschooling.

My hubby is the reason all this glorious madness is possible. He's the best parts of all the amazing men I write (although he's bald and his six pack sometimes goes into hiding because of cookies.)

I also love to bake, like to cook, and feel amazing when I find time to kickbox, lift weights, or rollerblade. Oh yeah, and I'm a lawyer, but I try to forget that whenever I can.

I adore my husband, and I love my God.

The rest is just details.

PS— I'm active on social media and have a facebook group I comment in often. (My husband even gets on there sometimes, but his sense of humor is strange. You've been warned.) Please feel free to join me here: https://www.facebook.com/groups/750807222376182

ALSO BY B. E./BRIDGET E. BAKER

The Scarsdale Fosters Series:

Seed Money

Nouveau Riche

The Finding Home Series:

Finding Grace (1)

Finding Faith (2)

Finding Cupid (3)

Finding Spring (4)

Finding Liberty (5)

Finding Holly (6)

Finding Home (7)

Finding Balance (8)

Finding Peace (9)

The Finding Home Series Boxset Books 1-3

The Finding Home Series Boxset Books 4-6

The Birch Creek Ranch Series:

The Bequest

The Vow

The Ranch

The Retreat

The Reboot

The Surprise

The Setback

The Lookback

Children's Picture Book

Yuck! What's for Dinner?

I also write contemporary fantasy and end of the world books under Bridget E. Baker.

The Russian Witch's Curse:

My Queendom for a Horse

My Dark Horse Prince

My High Horse Czar

The Magical Misfits Series:

Mates: Minerva (1)

Mates: Xander (2)

The Birthright Series:

Displaced (1)

unForgiven (2)

Disillusioned (3)

misUnderstood (4)

Disavowed (5)

unRepentant (6)

Destroyed (7)

The Birthright Series Collection, Books 1-3

The Anchored Series:

Anchored (1)

Adrift (2)

Awoken (3)

Capsized (4)

The Sins of Our Ancestors Series:

Marked (1)

Suppressed (2)

Redeemed (3)

Renounced (4)

Reclaimed (5) a novella!

A stand alone YA romantic suspense:

Already Gone

.

Made in United States
Troutdale, OR
01/02/2024

16596035R00249